PR
DAVID GEMMELL

"Gemmell not only knows how to tell a story, he knows how to tell a story you want to hear. He does high adventure as it ought to be done."
—GREG KEYES
Author of *The Briar King*

White Wolf
"Clean, swift action and a rich undercurrent of human understanding support Gemmell's characters at each turn of the tide."
—*Kirkus Reviews*

"Engrossing."
—*Publishers Weekly*

Stormrider
"Excellent . . . The heroes are heroic, the women are strong and beautiful, and the plot carefully planned and neatly constructed. Gemmell is a fine writer."
—*West County Times* (CA)

"Superb . . . *Stormrider* explores the power of a noble idea to inspire and transform even the basest of men."
—*Starburst*

THE SWORDS OF NIGHT AND DAY

A NOVEL OF SKILGANNON THE DAMNED

DAVID GEMMELL

DEL REY

BALLANTINE BOOKS • NEW YORK

A Del Rey® Book
Published by The Random House Publishing Group

Copyright © 2004 by David Gemmell
Excerpt from *Lord of the Silver Bow* by David Gemmell copyright © 2005 by David Gemmell

Published in the United States by Del Rey Books, an imprint of The Random House Publishing Group, a division of Random House, Inc., New York.

Del Rey is a registered trademark and the Del Rey colophon is a trademark of Random House, Inc.

www.delreybooks.com

ISBN 0-345-45834-6

Map by Dale Riipke

Manufactured in the United States of America

First Edition: April 2004
First Mass Market Edition: March 2005

OPM 9 8 7 6 5 4

The Swords of Night and Day *is dedicated with love to Don and Edith Graham, to the magical Cloe Reeves, and to all the residents of Old Mill Park, Bexhill, U.K., who have made the last seven years a joy.*

Acknowledgments

My thanks, as ever, to my regular test readers, Jan Dunlop, Tony Evans, and Stella Graham. Also to my old friend—and editor—Ross Lempriere, and to Lawrence and Sally Berman for their help in guiding the story. I am also grateful to my two editors, Selina Walker (U.K.) and Steve Saffel (U.S.) for their invaluable input, and to my copy editor, Laura Jorstad. Lastly, my thanks to two friends, Alan Fisher and Steve Hutt, who listen to my ramblings about plots and character threads and never complain. (And, yes, Steve, you did come up with the cathedral doors scene in *Ravenheart*, and no, you still can't share the royalties!)

Prologue

The sun was warm in a blue sky as the Priestess Ustarte stood at the graveside, watching her aides disguising the tomb. Carefully they placed rocks upon the small, island site and transferred plants to cover the recently turned soil. Ustarte pushed back the hood of her scarlet-and-gold gown, revealing a hairless head and a face of startling, ageless beauty.

A great sadness settled upon her. Ustarte had witnessed many deaths in the hundreds of years of her life, but few had touched her as strongly as the passing of this hero. She gazed down at the dry riverbed. In spring the water would rush down from the mountains and flow around the island on both sides before becoming a single waterway to the south. Now, in the height of summer, the island was merely a small hill, dusty and unmemorable. Not a good resting place for a great man.

An elderly priest in yellow robes approached her, his back bent, his gaunt, malformed features and huge brown eyes showing clearly to the initiated his status as a Joining, a meld of man and beast. Happily there were few in this benighted world of swords and spears who would recognize his origins. To most he would merely be an ugly little man, with friendly eyes.

"He deserved better than this, Holy One," said the priest.

"Aye, he did, Weldi, my friend."

Ustarte turned away from the graveside and, leaning on her staff, moved down the hillside into the shadows. Weldi hobbled after her.

"Why have we done this? The people would have built a great tomb for him, and erected statues. He saved them, after all. Now none will know where he lies."

She sighed. "He will be found, Weldi. I have seen it. It may be fifty years from now, or a hundred. But he will be found."

"And what then, Holy One?"

"I wish I could say. You remember the Resurrection priest who visited us several years ago?"

"A tall man. He wanted your help with an artifact."

"Yes," she said, reaching into a deep pocket in her gown. From it she drew a section of shining metal, indented and set with polished gems. Weldi gazed at it.

"It is very pretty. What is it?"

"It is part of a larger artifact used to produce creatures like us, my dear. To meld and to change matter. To extract the essence of life and cause it to be reproduced, or reshaped. Beasts to walk like men, or men to act like beasts."

"Magical then?"

"In a way, Weldi. This is an old world we find ourselves in. It has been through many births and rebirths. Once there were cities, where buildings were so tall that clouds gathered around their summits. In that time magic was common-place—though it was not called magic. I have seen it in the Mirror. It was a time of evil so colossal, so all-consuming, that men no longer recognized their own evil. They built weapons so horrifying that they could devour whole cities and turn entire continents to ash. They poisoned the air, and poisoned the seas, and tore down the trees that kept the earth alive."

Weldi shivered. "What happened to them?"

"Mercifully they destroyed themselves before they could kill the whole planet."

"And what has this to do with our friend, and his death?"

Ustarte glanced back at the work party. The hilltop was bare once more. Within a few weeks there would be no sign of the tomb. The wind would blow dust over the site, grass would grow, and *he* would lie beneath the earth, silently waiting. She shivered.

"These ancients left many artifacts, Weldi. In the Resurrection Temple there are objects like these, used for manipulating life itself. In other places there are more sites, dedicated not to life but to death and destruction. The more the priests delve into the secrets of these artifacts, the closer they will come to re-creating the horror of those ancient days."

"Can we stop them, Holy One?"

She shook her head, an angry glint in her blue eyes. "I cannot. I do not have the power, and my time is running out. I have looked in the Mirror and seen many desolate futures. It tore my heart to watch them. Armies of Joinings rampaging across the nations, corrupted priests wielding arcane powers, the skies dark with deadly rain. Fear, desolation, and evil rampant. I saw the end of the world, Weldi." She shuddered. "But in one future I did see our friend, born again to fulfill a prophecy that might end the terror."

"A prophecy? Whose prophecy?"

"Mine."

"Yours? What is this prophecy?"

Ustarte smiled. "I do not know yet, Weldi."

"How can that be, Holy One? It is your prophecy."

"Indeed it will be. But such are the frustrations of seeing time fragments out of place. All that I truly know *now* is that our friend will live again. I know the Swords of Night and Day will aid him. I know that the dead will walk beside him. More than that I cannot say."

"And he will save the world?"

Ustarte stared back at the hilltop. "I do not know, Weldi. But if I were looking for a man to achieve the impossible, that man would be Skilgannon the Damned."

One

First there was darkness, complete and absolute. No sounds to disconcert him, no conscious thoughts to concern him. Then came *awareness* of darkness and everything changed. He felt a pressure against his back and legs, and a gentle thudding in his chest. Fear touched him.

Why am I in the dark? In that instant a bright, powerful image filled his mind.

A man snarling with hatred, leaping at him, spear raised. The face disappeared in a spray of crimson as a sword blade half severed the skull. More warriors attacked him. There was no escape.

His body jerked spasmodically, his eyes flaring open. There were no painted warriors, no screaming enemies yearning for his death. Instead he found himself lying in a soft bed and staring up at an ornate ceiling, high and domed. He blinked and took a deep breath, his lungs filling with air. The sensation was exquisite—and somehow unnatural.

Confused, the man sat up and rubbed at his eyes. Sunshine was streaming through a high, arched opening to his right. It was so bright and painful that he raised his arm to shield his eyes from the brilliance. Then he saw the dark blue tattoo upon his left forearm. It was of a spider, and both ugly and threatening. His eyes adjusting to the brightness, he stood and padded naked across the room. A cool breeze rippled against his skin, causing him to shiver. This, too, in its own way, was confusing. The feeling of cold was almost alien.

The opening led to a semicircular balcony high above a walled garden. Beyond the garden lay a town, nestling in a mountain valley, the buildings white with red tiled roofs. His eyes now accustomed to the light, he gazed at the snow-capped peaks beyond the town and the brilliant blue sky above them. Slowly he scanned the rugged landscape. There was nothing here that tugged at his memory. It was all new.

He shivered again and walked back into the domed room. There were rugs upon the floor, some embroidered with flowers, others with angular emblems he did not recognize. The room itself was also unfamiliar. On a table nearby he saw a water jug and a long-stemmed crystal goblet. He reached for the jug. As he did so he caught sight of his re-flection in a curved mirror on the wall behind the table. Cold, sapphire-blue eyes stared back at him, from a face both stern and forbidding. There was something about the reflected man that was unrelentingly savage. His gaze traveled down to the tattoo of a snarling panther upon the chest.

He knew then that a third tattoo was upon his back, an ea-gle with flaring wings. Though why these violent images were etched upon his body he had no idea at all.

Becoming aware of a gnawing emptiness in his stomach, he recognized—as if from ancient memory—the symptoms of hunger. Filling the crystal goblet with water, he drank deeply, then looked around the room. On another narrow table, along-side the door, he saw a shallow bowl filled with dried fruit, slices of honey-dipped apricot, and figs. Carrying the bowl back to the bed, he sat down and slowly ate the fruit, expecting at any moment that memories would come flooding back.

But they did not.

Fear flared in him, but he quelled it savagely. "You are not a man given to panic," he said, aloud.

How would you know? The thought was unsettling.

"Stay calm and think," he said.

The snarling faces came again. Hostile warriors all around him, hacking and slashing. He fought them with two deadly, razor-sharp blades. The enemy fell back. He did not seek to escape then, but hurled himself at them, seeking to reach . . . to reach . . .

The memory faded. Anger swelled, but he let it flow over him and away. Holding to the memory of the scene, he analyzed what he did remember. He had been bone weary, his swords unnaturally heavy. No, he realized, not just weary.

I was old!

The shock of the memory made him rise again and return to the mirror. The face he saw was young, the skin unlined, the close-cropped hair dark and shining with health.

The image returned with sickening intensity.

A broad-bladed spear plunged into his side. He winced at the memory of it, the hot, agonizing rush of blood over ripped flesh. The spear all but disemboweled him. A mortal wound. He killed the wielder with a reverse cut and staggered on. The Zharn king screamed at his guards to protect him. Four of them charged—huge men bearing bronze axes. They died bravely. The last managed to bury an ax blade into his right shoulder, almost severing the arm. The Zharn king shouted a war cry and leapt to attack him. Mortally wounded, he swayed from the king's plunging spear, the sword in his left hand cleaving through the king's side, slicing through his backbone. With an awful cry of pain and despair the Zharn king fell.

The man looked down at the skin of his shoulder. It was unmarked. As was his side. There was not a scar upon his flesh. Was he seeing visions of the future, then? Was this how he was to die?

A cold breeze blew in from the balcony. He rose and searched the room. By the far wall was a tall chest of drawers. The top drawer contained carefully folded clothing.

Removing the first item, he saw that it was a thigh-length tunic of fine blue wool. He pulled it on, then opened the second drawer. Here he found several pairs of leggings, some in wool, others in soft leather. Choosing a pair in dark, polished leather, he donned them. They fitted perfectly.

Hearing footsteps outside his door, he stepped away from the chest and waited, his mind tense, his body relaxed.

An elderly man entered, bearing a tray on which was set a plate of cured meats and smoked cheeses. The man glanced at him nervously but said nothing. He moved to the table, set down the tray, and backed away toward the door.

"Wait!"

The elderly man stopped, eyes downcast.

"Who are you?"

Mumbling something under his breath, the old man rushed from the room. Only after he had departed did the man manage to piece together the answer he had given. The words were familiar, but somehow mangled. He had said: "Just a servant, sir." The man had heard: "Jezzesarvanser."

Moments later a second figure appeared in the doorway, a tall man with iron-gray hair receding at the temples. He was lean and slightly round shouldered, his eyes deep and piercingly green. His clothes were somber, a tunic shirt of gray satin and leggings of black wool. He smiled nervously. "Mataianter?" he asked.

Might I enter. The man in the bedroom gestured for him to step inside.

The newcomer began to speak swiftly. The man held up his hand and spoke. "I am having difficulty understanding your dialect. Speak slowly."

"Of course. Language shifts, changes, and grows. Can you understand me now?" he asked, speaking clearly and enunciating his words. The man nodded. "I know you will have many questions," said the newcomer, pulling shut the door behind him, "and they will all be answered in time." He glanced down at the man's bare feet. "There are several pairs of shoes and two pairs of boots in the closet yonder," he said, pointing to a panel against the far wall. "You will find all the clothes fit you well."

"What am I doing here?"

"An interesting first question. I hope you will not think me rude if I respond with one of my own. Do you know yet who you are?"

"No."

The gray-haired man nodded. "That is understandable. It will come back to you. I assure you of that. As to what you are doing here"—he smiled again—"you will understand better once you have remembered your name. So let us begin with *my* name. I am Landis Khan, and this is my home. The town you see beyond is Petar. It is, you might say, a part of my domain. I want you to think of me as a friend, someone who seeks to help you."

"Why have I no memory?"

"You have been—shall we say—asleep for a long time. A very long time. That you are here at all is a miracle. We must take things slowly. Trust me on this."

"Was I injured in some way?"

"Why would you think that?"

"I recall . . . a battle. Painted Zharn tribesmen. I was stabbed. Yet I have no scars."

"Excellent," said Landis Khan. "The Zharn! That is excellent." He seemed massively relieved.

"What is excellent?"

"That you recall the Zharn. It tells me we have succeeded. That you are . . . the man we sought."

"How so?"

"The Zharn faded from history long ago. Only shreds of legend remain. One such legend tells of a great warrior who stood against them. He and his men led a desperate charge against the center of a huge Zharn army. It was said to have been magnificent. They charged to their deaths in order to slay the Zharn king."

"How would I recall an event that happened long ago?"

Landis Khan rose. "Find yourself some footwear and let me show you the palace and its grounds."

"I would appreciate some answers," said the man, an edge appearing in his voice.

"And I would like nothing more than to sit down now and supply them all. It would not be wise, however. You need to arrive at your own answers. Believe me, they will come. It is important for you that we do this in a careful manner. Will you trust me?"

"I am not a trusting man. When I asked you why I had no memory you said I had been asleep for a long time. More accurately, you said *shall we say you have been asleep.* Answer this one question and I will consider trusting you: How long have I been asleep?"

"A thousand years," said Landis Khan.

At first the man laughed, but then he realized there was no trace of amusement to be found on Landis Khan's face. "I may have lost my memory, but not my intelligence. No one *sleeps* for a thousand years."

"I used the word *sleep* because that is the closest to the actuality. Your . . . soul . . . if you like, has been wandering the Void for the past ten centuries. Your first body was slain in that battle with the Zharn. This is your *new* body—fashioned from the bones we discovered in your hidden tomb." Landis Khan reached into a small pouch hanging from his belt. From it he took a small, golden locket and a long slender chain. "What does this mean to you?" he asked. The man took the locket, his fingers closing gently around it.

"It is mine," he said, softly. "I cannot say how I know this to be true."

"Say a name—if you can."

The man hesitated and closed his eyes. "Dayan," he said, at last.

"Can you describe him?"

"Him?"

"The man, Dayan."

"It is no man. Dayan was a woman . . ." A brief flash of memory flowed through his mind, causing him to wince, as if in pain. "She was my wife. She died."

"And you carried a lock of her hair?"

The man looked closely at Landis Khan. "You seem surprised. What were you expecting?"

"It is not important. An error occurred somewhere. You are quite right. Our earliest tales of . . . of you . . . have you wed to a princess named Dunaya. It is said she was slain by a demon and carried away into the underworld. You went after her. For years you were lost to the world of men, as you journeyed through the deepest places of the earth seeking to bring her back." Landis Khan chuckled. "A fine tale, and there is probably a grain of truth in there somewhere. Now come with me, my friend. I have much to show you."

Landis struggled to contain his excitement. Through what seemed endless years of fruitless toil he had held to the vision that one day he would find a way to redeem himself. For the last twenty-three years he had waited so patiently, hoping against all reason that this latest experiment would prove to be decisive.

The first three failures had been galling, and had dented his confidence. Now, however, in one glorious moment, it was restored.

Two names had rekindled the fires of his hope. *The Zharn* and *Dayan*.

He glanced at the tall man with the brilliant sapphire eyes and forced a smile.

"Where are we going?" asked the man.

"To my library and workplace. There is something I am anxious for you to see."

Landis led the man along a narrow corridor and down a set of stairs. The lower levels were cold, despite the lanterns hanging on cast-iron brackets. Landis shivered, but the man beside him seemed untroubled.

At last they came to a set of double doors. Beyond them was a long room, with five soft chairs and three couches, festooned with embroidered cushions. A tall arched window showed a view of the distant mountains. The curtains billowed with the afternoon breeze. To the left was a second arch, leading through to a library, the scores of shelves bent under the weight of the books upon them.

Landis walked on to another door at the rear of the room. This he opened with a key taken from his pouch.

Inside, it was windowless and dark. Landis lit a lantern, hanging it from a bracket. Golden light flickered in the room, shadows dancing upon the plain walls. "What has been removed?" asked the man.

Landis smiled, noticing the rectangular dust patterns that showed where objects had been taken down from the walls. "Just some paintings," he answered, swiftly. "You are very observant." Moving to a desk, Landis reached down and lifted what at first appeared to be a short, curved ornamental staff. At each end were sections of beautifully carved white ivory, though the center was smooth, polished ebony. Turning, he offered the object to his guest.

The man's face darkened, and he stepped back. "I do not want to touch them," he said.

"Them?"

"There is evil in them."

"But they are yours. They were buried with you in the tomb. They were laid upon your chest, your hands clasped over them."

"Even so, I do not want them."

Landis took a deep breath. "But you know what they are?"

"Yes, I know," answered the man, a wealth of sadness in his voice. "They are the Swords of Night and Day. And I am Skilgannon the Damned."

Landis curled his hand around one of the hilts. "Do not draw that blade," said Skilgannon. "I have no wish to see it." With that he swung on his heel and walked back through the library. Landis placed the Swords of Night and Day on the desktop and ran after the warrior.

"Wait!" he called. "Please wait."

Skilgannon paused, sighed, then turned. "Why did you bring me back, Landis?"

"You will understand why when you see the world outside

my domain. There is great evil here, Skilgannon. We need you."

Skilgannon shook his head. "I do not remember much as yet, Landis, but I know I never was a god. In every generation there are war leaders, heroes, men of valor. I may—just may—have been special in my day. But you must have men of equal skill in this time."

"Would that we had enough of them," said Landis Khan, with feeling. "There is a great war being fought, but not—in the main—by men. We have a few doughty fighters, but we have survived this long here for two reasons. Firstly, my domain is largely inaccessible and offers no mineral wealth. Secondly, the passes are guarded by our own Jiamads." Landis hesitated, seeing the look of noncomprehension on Skilgannon's face. "Ah, but I see that I am getting ahead of the tale. You have no knowledge of the Jiamads. In some ancient lands they were known as werebeasts, I believe, though in your time the word was *Joinings*. Men and beasts melded together."

Skilgannon's face hardened, his eyes glittering in the lantern light.

"You remember them?" asked Landis.

"A glimpse only. But yes, I fought them."

"And you won!"

"There is nothing that bleeds that I cannot kill, Landis."

"Exactly my point! You will not find more than a handful of men in this land who would dream of saying that about Jiamads. We are on the verge of becoming a defeated species, Skilgannon."

"And you think I can change this unhappy situation? Where is my army?"

"There is no army, but I still believe you are the one man who can save us."

"Why?"

Landis shrugged and spread his hands. "There was a prophecy concerning you, Skilgannon. It was originally inscribed on tablets of gold. And signed by the Blessed Priestess herself. But these were lost. Copies were made from memory, but many of these contained contradictions. However, there was a map that showed the place where the Priestess hid your body. It was a cunning map. Delightfully conceived. And all who followed it found only an empty sarcophagus in a cave. Beside it was a shattered lid. So they went away, disconsolate."

"But you didn't?"

"Oh, yes I did. Many times. I wish I could say that I deciphered the riddle of the map through the enormous power of my intellect alone. But I did not. I had a vision—a dream, perhaps. I had been searching the cave again—my fifteenth journey there, I believe. I was tired and I fell asleep. I dreamed of the Blessed Priestess. She took me by the hand and led me from the cave, and down onto the arid wasteland at the foot of the mountains to a dry riverbed. Then she spoke. 'The answer is here, if you have the eye to see it.' This was similar to what was written at the base of the map: *The hero lies here, if you have the eye to see it.*

"I awoke with the dawn and walked out to the cave entrance, staring out over the land below. There was the dry riverbed. Once the water had flowed, and the river had been bisected by an island. Now there were only two dry channels etching the ground on both sides of a high, circular mound of rocky earth. From the high point of the cave it looked as if someone had carved a giant eye in the land. I cannot tell you how excited I was as I led the digging party across to the mound. At the center of it we dug. Some seven feet down we struck the stone lid of your coffin."

"I can appreciate your delight," said Skilgannon, "but I am finding this talk of my coffin unsettling. Move on to the prophecy."

"Of course, of course! Forgive me. The prophecy promised that you would be the man to . . . to restore our freedoms."

"You hesitated."

Landis gave a nervous smile. "You are very sharp, my friend. I was trying to avoid unnecessary explanation. It actually says that you are the man who will steal the power of the silver eagle and restore peace and harmony to the world."

"So you have based all your hopes on an old prophecy?"

"Yes, I have. But I am heartened by the fact that the Resurrectionists also believe it. Both sides have been searching for your remains for hundreds of years. There was—still is—a huge reward for whoever finds your tomb. They fear you, Skilgannon. It is my earnest hope that they are right to do so."

Skilgannon said nothing for a moment. "Who was this Blessed Priestess?" he asked, at last.

"Some believe her to have been a goddess, who surrendered immortality for her love of humanity. Others say she was the human child of the Wolf God, Phaarl. For myself, I believe her to have been a brilliant arcanist and philosopher and prophet. A gifted woman, and holy, who was allowed to see the future, and to have a part in saving humanity from the Dawn of the Beasts."

"Did she have a name, this paragon?"

"Of course. She was Ustarte. It was said that you knew her."

All color drained from Skilgannon's face. "I knew her. She came to me in the last days."

He stood on the hillside outside his home and watched as the rider galloped back toward the city. A great heaviness settled on his heart. Slowly he strolled up the hillside, moving out onto the cliff path above the bay. Skilgannon had grown to love this place during the last eight years. A stone seat had been set on a jutting ledge of rock. He did not know who had set it here, but something in his heart had warmed to the man who had. The ledge was perilously overbalanced and looked as if it might drop at any moment, falling the hundreds of feet to the rocky beach below. Yet someone had decided to set a seat here, as if to hurl a challenge at the gods.

Kill me if you will, but I will choose to sit here, in this place, and defy your power.

Skilgannon walked out onto the ledge and stretched himself out on the seat. The air was warm, the sunshine bright. Far out on the Jian Sea he saw the fishing boats, and the gulls swooping and soaring around them. Pain flared in his neck, and he winced. The fingertips of his right hand grew numb. He stretched his neck, then looked down at his hand. The fingers were trembling. Making a fist, he tried to quell the tremor. Slowly the pain in his neck dulled, merging with the other aches in his tired body. His lower back troubled him at night; the old scar on his hip would grind if he rode a horse for more than an hour. His left knee had never recovered from the arrow wound. Angry now, he pulled the parchment from his belt and opened it once more. Bakila has refused our offer, *he read,* though he has accepted the gifts and tributes.

Gifts and tributes.

For years Skilgannon had tried to tell them that Bakila could not be bought off forever. The Zharn king had a hunger that would not be satisfied by tributes. He also had an army that needed to be fed with plunder. The young Angostin king had not understood this. He did now.

Now that it was too late.

"Ho, General!" came the call. Skilgannon swung on his seat. The pain flared in his neck once more. The young captain, Vakasul, came striding up the cliff path. He halted just before the ledge and stood there, grinning and shaking his head. "That will fall, you know," he said.

Skilgannon smiled affectionately at the dark-eyed young warrior. "Come sit with me—and dare it to fall," he answered.

"I think not."

"You know the Zharn are coming?"

"Of course."

"And you will ride with me to fight them?"

"You know that I will. We will scatter them, General."

Skilgannon rose and walked back to where the officer

waited. Vakasul was in battle dress, black breastplate and helm of hardened leather, thigh-length riding boots, reinforced at the knee with bronze. His long dark hair had been braided in the Angostin fashion, lengths of silver wire placed within the braids to offer added protection to the head. "You will fight a massive enemy army," said Skilgannon, "and yet you will not walk onto a stone ledge."

"The ledge is not under my control," said Vakasul. "On the battlefield my sword and my bow will protect me."

Skilgannon looked into the young man's eyes. Both men knew that nothing could possibly protect them in the coming battle. Bakila would have twenty thousand foot soldiers and eight thousand horsemen. The Angostin force would number around four thousand trained infantry and two thousand cavalry. Eight years before, Skilgannon had led a coalition army against Bakila and turned back his horde on the southern border of Angostin. Forces from Kydor and Chiatze, and the Varnii nomads, had fought a ferocious battle. More than thirty thousand Zharn had perished, and some twelve thousand of the allies. Bakila had managed to withdraw his surviving forces during the night. Skilgannon had urged the Angostin king to allow him to pursue Bakila. The request had been denied. The king had been horrified by the losses and believed that Bakila would have learned a harsh lesson.

Indeed he had. The following year he had taken a new army southwest and crushed the Varnii. The next summer he had swept into Kydor, sacking the cities and pillaging the capital. Two years later he had made an alliance with the Sechuin people on the eastern coast and attacked Chiatze, smashing their armies in two great battles. The Chiatze had surrendered and offered Bakila a huge yearly tribute. To prevent a new invasion the Angostin king sued for peace, and also offered to send a yearly tribute to Bakila. Seven hundred pounds of gold was the agreed sum in the first year. Then it rose to a thousand. Then two thousand. Now the Angostin treasury was virtually bankrupt.

And the Zharn were coming.

"How long do we have, General?" asked Vakasul.

"Perhaps ten days."

"And you will contrive a splendid battle plan to destroy them. I look forward to hearing it."

"There is only one hope of success, Vaki. You know it as well as I."

"It will be a miracle if we get to within two hundred feet of him."

"Then we'll have to make a miracle."

Vakasul swore softly, then edged past Skilgannon and onto the ledge. He sat down and stared out to sea. "By the way, General," he said, "there are some odd-looking people waiting at your house."

"Odd? What do you mean?"

Vakasul grinned. "There is a bald woman in a gown of satin. Quite attractive, if you like bald women. The two men with her are astonishingly grotesque. As my father used to say: 'They look as if they fell out of the ugly tree and landed on their faces.'"

The memory faded.

Back in his apartments Skilgannon began to exercise his body, moving through a series of dancelike steps, leaping and twirling. Several times he stumbled upon landing, and once he fell heavily. His brain knew how to execute the moves, but his body seemed sluggish. Keeping the moves simple, he continued the exercise, seeking to free his thoughts. The images in his mind were sharp, and yet fractured. There was no real flow to his memories. Scenes appeared, and then were cut off or overlaid by some other image. Names flashed into his consciousness: *Dayan, Jianna, Druss, Vakasul, Bakila, Greavas* . . . Occasionally a face would merge with the name, and then disappear.

He exercised for an hour and then sat on a rug, a blanket around his shoulders. Bowing his head, he sought inner calm, focusing only on one word.

Ustarte.

The stars were bright, and the rain clouds had moved

away toward the west. This was a blessing. The ground tomorrow would be dry and hard, the speed of the charge increased. With luck it would carry them deep into the Zharn ranks. How deep? he wondered. And would Bakila position himself on the left, as he had five years before? Skilgannon strode to the top of the rise and gazed down at the battlefield. It was wide and flat. A stand of trees covered the hillsides to the west. To the east was the river. He pictured the likely formation the Zharn would adopt. The Angostin infantry had no choice but to stake out a position on the high ground north of the valley. The slopes were steep. The enemy charge would be slowed. More heavily armored and wielding short, stabbing swords, the Angostins would be able to hold for some time. Skilgannon scanned the valley. The eight thousand Zharn horsemen would sweep out to the east and west in an encircling move. The two thousand Angostin cavalry would be expected to split into two groups and seek to hold them on the wings. It was not possible. The cavalry would be either broken and scattered, or pushed back against the flanks of their own infantry.

It was galling in the extreme. The Zharn, for all their savagery, were well-disciplined fighters who did not fear death. No sudden charge would break their spirit. No clever strategy would see them thwarted. There was only one hope for the Angostins. Bakila was the head and heart of the Zharn. Strike him down and the enemy would break.

Skilgannon walked back to his horse and stepped into the saddle. Then he rode across the moonlit valley, heading up into the stand of trees. From the high ground he could see the distant campfires of the Zharn some five miles to the southwest. Dismounting, he trailed the reins of the chestnut and walked up to the tree line. The air was fresh and cool. Tomorrow he would hide three hundred of the finest of his Silver Hawk cavalry here. As the battle lines drew together he would lead them in a suicidal charge down the hillside.

His shoulder and neck ached, and he could feel the weight of his fifty-four years. Sitting down with his back to a tree, he closed his eyes, remembering the days of his youth. He had such dreams then, such vaunting ambitions. He wanted to be like his father, a great warrior and hero, adored by women and admired by men. He smiled. Such were the dreams of the young. Jianna's face appeared in his mind—not as the dread and beautiful Witch Queen of Naashan, but as the young princess he had first known. Those had been the great days of his life. The days of first love. He had believed then that his future would be with Jianna. What force on heaven or earth could prevent it? In that moment Skilgannon heard a soft rustling. He pushed himself to his feet and turned to see Ustarte moving toward him, her long satin gown shimmering in the moonlight. "It saddens me to feel your sorrow," *she said.*

"Sorrow is the constant companion of the old," *he told her, forcing a smile.* "When you came to my house you said you would be asking a favor of me. Ask it—and if it is in my power I will grant it."

Ustarte sighed and looked away. "What I am to ask might cost you dear."

Skilgannon laughed then. "Did you not tell me that I would die tomorrow? How much more dear can it be?"

Ustarte ignored the question. "Tell the Angostin king that if you fall tomorrow your body and your weapons are to be given over to me for burial."

"That is all you require?"

"No, Olek. To win you will need to wield the swords once more."

"I can win without them! I do not want their evil in my hands."

"You will not reach Bakila without them, and the Zharn will plunder and burn and slaughter their way across Angostin—and beyond. These are the two favors I would ask of you. Carry the swords into battle, and allow me to conduct your burial."

"And you can tell me no more?"

She shook her head, and he saw a tear fall. "No more," *she said.*

*   *   *

On the fifth day of the resurrection Landis Khan climbed the winding staircase and entered the high turret room in the east wing of the palace. The old blind man, Gamal, was sitting on the balcony, a warm blanket around his thin shoulders. Landis shivered as he gazed upon Gamal. He was very frail now, his skin so thin as to be almost translucent.

Gamal laughed, the sound rich and musical. "Ah, Landis, my friend, your thoughts fly around like startled pigeons."

"There was a time when you had the good manners *not* to read the thoughts of friends," Landis pointed out, stepping forward and kissing the old man's cheek.

"Sadly, that is not true," said Gamal. "What I had was the ability to *pretend* not to read them."

Landis feigned surprise. "You lied to us all these years?"

"Of course I lied. Would you have wanted to spend time in the company of someone you believed knew *all* your thoughts?"

"No. And I am not sure I want to now."

Gamal laughed again. "Ah Landis! As well you know, I cannot read *all* of a man's thoughts. Never could. I can tell when people are lying. I can tell when they are being deceptive. I can *feel* their sorrows and their joys. When you walked in you were concerned about Skilgannon. His face was in your mind. Then you saw me—and thoughts of death and loneliness overwhelmed you. So put your mind at ease, and tell me why you are concerned about our guest."

"He is not what I was expecting."

"How could he be?" asked Gamal. "You thought he would be godlike. You expected fire to blaze from his eyes."

"Of course not. I knew he was a man."

"A man who once flew a winged horse?"

"You are doing it again!" complained Landis. "I do not *believe* he flew a winged horse. But that is one of the first stories I remember learning about him. I was a child, for goodness' sake! These stories fasten themselves to the mind. That is why I *see* the winged horse."

"Forgive me, my friend," said Gamal. "No more winged horses. Go on."

"It has been five days and he remains in his room most of the time, doing nothing. He asks no questions when we speak. He listens as I tell him of events, but I know nothing of his opinions. Could the old stories have been so wrong? He does not seem like a warrior at all. He is not chilling like the Shadowmen, nor overtly terrifying like Decado."

"I can see why you are worried," said Gamal. "However, there are a lot of misconceptions in what you say. Firstly, you say he sits in his rooms doing nothing. This is not true."

"Yes, yes," interrupted Landis. "I know he exercises. I know the servant girls are besotted with him. My guess is he has already bedded one of them."

"Two of them," corrected Gamal. "And a third is with him as we speak. As to what you call his *exercises,* they are very ancient and require high levels of suppleness, strength, and balance. Once his body would have flowed through these rituals smoothly. His new body, however, is neither as supple nor as strong as the one he recalls. Before he can truly become *himself* he must bring his new body into harmony with his memories. As to him not *seeming* like a warrior—" The old man spread his hands. "—what can I tell you? Yes, the Shadows are chilling. They were intended to be. They are bred for murder. The same, I think, can be said of Decado. He is not entirely sane. Of course Skilgannon is not frightening to you. You have done nothing to cause him to see you as an enemy. Let us hope you never do." For a moment the old man fell silent. Then he drew in a deep breath. "Skilgannon was once a priest," he said.

Landis Khan gasped. "There is no mention of this in any history."

"Yes, there is," said Gamal. "If one knows where to look. I found the references in Cethelin's *Book of the Empty.* A fascinating piece."

"I have read it many times," said Landis. "Skilgannon is not mentioned, not even as a reference."

"Of course he is—but by the name he adopted as a priest, Brother Lantern. Cethelin called him the Damned."

Landis Khan sat openmouthed. Goose bumps appeared on his arms, and he shivered. "Lantern was Skilgannon? Sweet heaven! The madman who slew all those people outside Cethelin's church?"

"For a man of science, Landis," said Gamal, "you spend rather too much time leaping to conclusions. Yes, Cethelin wrote of him as a madman and a killer. But was he? One fact is clear: The mob had arrived at the church intent on killing the priests. Lantern stopped them."

"With murder," pointed out Landis.

"Only after one of the mob had stabbed Cethelin." Gamal chuckled suddenly. "You chide me for mentioning the winged horse, my friend, but you are still trapped in memories of childhood. Skilgannon was a hero. Of this there is no doubt. He was also a killer, Landis. Those who stood against him died."

"He was a warrior. I know that!" snapped Landis.

"He was *more* than a warrior. However, for now you should not be concerned about how *frightening* he is, or how *chilling* he appears. Give him time, Landis. Then we will see if Ustarte was gifted or demented."

"We have had this conversation before," said Landis with a wry smile. "Always you find a way to cast doubt on the prophecy."

"As I recall the Blessed Priestess left a book of *many* prophecies."

"Ah, but that is unfair, Gamal. You know that they were not *prophecies* in the real sense. She said that there were many futures, and gave examples of how those futures might be shaped. Her prophecy concerning Skilgannon was altogether different."

"The principle remains the same, Landis. The Priestess saw many futures. She was unable to distinguish between what *would* be and what *could* be. I have no doubt that in her visions she saw the rise of the Eternal. Equally I have no doubt that she saw the return of Skilgannon as a means of combatting the Eternal. But don't you see, Landis, that it still remains one of *many* futures. Nothing in life is certain."

Landis sighed. "I *need* to believe in the prophecy, Gamal. And you know why." Rising from his chair, he walked to the edge of the balcony, staring out over the mountains. "All the while it was a dream it burned bright in my heart and my mind. I did not doubt it for a second. Now that the reality is here it seems . . . lessened. I thought to bring back a mighty hero, a man of unconquerable spirit. Now I am beginning to feel like a fool."

"Well, don't! Do not judge him yet, Landis. I saw him in the Void. I felt his power and the *unconquerable spirit* you speak of. There are beasts there more terrifying than any that walk this earth. Skilgannon faced them with courage. I think you will discover that the myths did not exaggerate his skills. And do not take too much notice of my cynicism. Like so many cynics I am a romantic at heart. I, too, would like to believe in the Blessed Priestess and her prophecy. I, too, would like to see the Eternal humbled, and the rebel armies disbanded. So let us concentrate on all that is positive. Skilgannon is reborn. That is the first miracle. We must now help him to restore his memory. Memories are what make us who we are, Landis. They are the building blocks of our souls."

Landis relaxed a little. "So much rests upon him. It frightens me."

"It no longer frightens me," said Gamal. "Perhaps that is a gift of mortality."

"Why will you not let me revive you? I could give you another thirty years of perfect health. You know this. I still do not understand this yearning for death."

Gamal chuckled. "I am content, Landis. I have lived many full lives. Too many. Now I find myself content with increasing frailty. Even my blindness is, in some ways, a blessing. I think my death will be, too."

"But we need you, Gamal. Humanity needs you."

"You put too great a store in my talents. Now, tell me how Harad is faring."

Landis leaned back in his chair. "He is strong—stronger than any man I have ever known. He seems to be enjoying his work. But he is short tempered and still prone to sudden violence. People avoid him, and he has no friends." He glanced at the old blind man. "You think it is time for Skilgannon to meet him?"

"No. Not yet. But very soon." Gamal fell silent, and Landis believed him to have fallen asleep. As quietly as he could, Landis levered himself upright. Gamal sighed. "It is not too late, Landis," he said. "There is still time for you to change your mind."

"Skilgannon is here now. I cannot put his bones back in the casket."

"That is not what I meant. I am talking of the *other* Reborn. What you are doing is more than foolish, Landis. It will bring ruin upon all you have built here."

Landis sank back in his chair. "How long have you known?"

"Almost from the moment I arrived here in the summer. I saw her face in your thoughts. I could scarce believe that any man who knew the Eternal could be so foolhardy. She has Memnon. His skills are far greater than mine. If I discovered your secret, so will he."

"Perhaps. Perhaps not." Landis rose and moved to stand alongside the old man. Leaning down, he patted Gamal's hand. *"You* already knew my weakness. Memnon does not. And I, too, know how to cast ward spells."

"Ward spells will not turn aside a Shadow blade, Landis."

"No one knows but you and I," said Landis.

"Long may that prove true," replied Gamal, with feeling.

Two

Skilgannon stood naked on the wide balcony. His breathing deepened. Drawing in a long breath, he began to work through a series of stretching exercises. His body was more supple now, the young muscles lengthening easily. Balancing on his left foot, he bent his knee and stretched out his right leg behind him. Raising his arms, he placed his palms together and slowly—his breathing controlled and synchronized to the movement—arched his spine backward until the curve of his body formed the shape of a perfect crescent moon. Then the muscles of his right thigh began to ache and tremble, and he felt a slight pain flare under his left shoulder blade.

Once he could have accomplished these exercises with ease. Fragments of memory, jagged and transient, came to him. Slowly he straightened and stood, leaning on the balcony, allowing the images to form.

In his mind he saw a tall building, lit by moonlight. There was a high parapet above sharp rocks far below. He saw himself standing on the parapet, then leaping and spinning to land in perfect balance. One wrong step, one tiny misjudgment and he would have plunged to his death.

The image faded. Skilgannon continued to exercise, not pushing his body too hard, seeking instead to stretch the muscles rather than work them at this stage. Even so it was tiring, and after an hour he stopped.

Donning a shirt of cream-colored linen and dark leather trousers, he pulled on a pair of soft leather ankle boots and walked out of the room, making his way toward the library Landis Khan had shown him on his first day. He saw several male servants in tunics of blue cloth. They moved past him with downcast eyes. It did not bother him. He had no wish to speak to anyone.

In the library he continued his search through the oldest of the records. Stories of his own life had not proved as helpful to his memory as he had hoped. Apparently he had fought dragons at some point, and had owned a winged horse that flew above the mountains. He had also been gifted with a cloak that made him invisible to his enemies. Incredibly he was supposed to have been born in six different lands, to four different fathers and three separate mothers. He had been golden haired, black haired, bearded, and beardless. He had been tall, and short, immensely muscled, and yet slim and lithe.

The agreements were few. He had owned two fighting swords that sat in a single scabbard. They were called the Swords of Night and Day. He had died in a battle to save a nation. He had been a general whose wife had died. He had also loved a goddess, mysterious and enigmatic. All agreed on this, though none could agree on her name. In some tales she was the goddess of death, in others the goddess of love, or wisdom, or war.

Today he chose stories not of his own legends, but of the ancient lands. He was searching for details that would offer him links to a past he could not summon. Skilgannon carried a bundle of ancient scrolls to a window seat and slowly began to read them.

The first of them brought no fresh insights. It told of a war among races he had no memory of, but the second, far older, talked of a people called the Drenai. Skilgannon felt his heartbeat quicken. A name came to him.

Druss.

He saw a powerful figure, in clothes of black and silver. Holding to the memory, he closed his eyes. Scenes flowed up from his subconscious. Druss the Axman, storming the stairs at the citadel, seeking . . . seeking . . . the child Elanin. Another face appeared, the features disfigured. Another name surfaced. *Boranius.* Ironmask. Skilgannon saw himself fighting this man, blades flashing and blocking, lunging and parrying. The image began to shimmer. Skilgannon struggled to retain it, but it flowed away from him like a dream upon wakening.

Returning to his room, he found a cloak of dark brown wool edged with black leather. Swirling it around his shoulders, he walked out of the palace. For the first time since he had returned to life he felt relaxed and free. He walked through the town of Petar, bypassing the crowded marketplace, coming at last to an old stone bridge spanning a fast-flowing river. He saw a young lad sitting on the parapet of the bridge, a fishing rod in his hands. Beyond the bridge, the area leading to the hills had been fenced off. This was puzzling to Skilgannon, for he could see no cattle or sheep. He walked on to a locked gate.

"Hey there, Outlander!"

Skilgannon turned. The blond-haired boy put aside his fishing rod. "Best not to walk the hills," he said. Swinging his legs back over the parapet, the boy jumped onto the bridge and walked over to Skilgannon. "Dangerous up there."

"Why is that?"

"Jems. That's where they train. They don't like people."

Skilgannon smiled. "I don't like people, either." With that he vaulted the gate and set off toward the hills. After a while he broke into an easy lope, then a run. Higher and higher he went, pushing his body hard. At last, breathless and weary, he halted beside a stream. Kneeling, he drank deeply. The water was cold and wonderfully refreshing. Sitting beside the water, he saw that the streambed contained hundreds of rounded pebbles. Most were pure white, but here and there he could see darker stones, some green, some jet black. Plunging his hand into the water, he ran his fingers over the pebbles, scooping up several. Once his life would have been as full of memories as this stream was full of stones. Now all he had were a few scattered remnants. Tipping his hand, he dropped the pebbles back into the water and rose.

The sky was bright and clear, and a cool breeze was blowing across the mountain foothills. Skilgannon gazed out over the land and the white town far below. *I do not belong here,* he thought as his eyes drank in the alien landscape.

A sound came to him. Then another. A series of dry cracks and thuds. Intrigued, he followed the sounds, climbing over the crest of the hill and making his way down into the trees beyond. In a clearing far below he saw what at first seemed to be a group of bearded warriors practicing with quarter staffs. They were wearing body armor of black leather and leggings of leather and fur. Skilgannon stood and watched them. His eyes narrowed, and something cold touched his heart.

They were not men at all. Their faces were twisted and misshapen, jaws elongated.

Jems, the boy had called them. *Joinings* was how Skilgannon remembered them. A brief memory flared, of women and children huddling together in a circle while Skilgannon and a group of fighters prepared to face an attack. The beasts had been large, some close to eight feet tall. Much larger, in fact, than the Jiamads training below. And more bestial in appearance. These seemed to Skilgannon to be more human. Perhaps it was that they were clothed in breastplates of black leather, and leather kilts.

The wind shifted, carrying his scent down into the clearing. Almost immediately the Jiamads ceased their training and turned, staring up toward where Skilgannon stood, hidden in the shadows of the trees. Though tempted to turn and walk away, he did not. Instead he strolled out into the open and down toward them. As he approached he noted that each of them wore a blue jewel upon its temple. It seemed incongruous that such beasts would wear adornments.

The largest of the creatures, almost seven feet tall, its fur jet black, stepped toward him. "Skins stay away," it said, the

voice guttural. Skilgannon, who was a tall man, found himself staring up into a pair of golden eyes, which glittered
with cold malice.

"And why is that?" he countered. The other Joinings shuffled forward, surrounding him.

"Our place. Danger for Skins." The elongated mouth
gaped, showing sharp fangs. A snorting sound rasped from
it. The sound was echoed by the others. Skilgannon took it to
be laughter.

"I am new to this land," said Skilgannon. "I am unaware of
the customs here. Why would it be dangerous?"

"Skins brittle. Break easy." It stared hard at Skilgannon,
and the warrior sensed its hatred. "You go now."

The other beasts gathered around even closer. One, its face
flatter than the rest, the mouth more widely flared, like a cat
began to sniff the air. "No other Skins," it said. "It is alone."

"Leave him," said the first.

"Kill it," said another.

The first beast snarled suddenly, the sound harsh and chilling. Then it spoke. "No!" The golden eyes stared at Skilgannon. "Go now, Skin."

Skilgannon turned. The cat creature's quarter staff suddenly jabbed out toward his legs. Instantly, and without conscious thought, Skilgannon spun on his heel and leapt high,
his foot hammering into the beast's face, hurling it from its
feet. Skilgannon landed lightly and stepped in, hefting the
quarter staff dropped by the creature. With an angry growl
the Jiamad sprang to its feet and lunged at the man. Skilgannon twirled the staff, cracking it hard against its temple. The
Jiamad slumped to the ground, dazed. Stepping back, Skilgannon raised the weapon against any new attack. For a moment there was no movement, then the leader stepped
forward.

"Not good," he said. "Go!"

Skilgannon smiled coldly—then tossed the staff to the
ground. "I am sorry to have disturbed your training," he said.
"What is your name?"

"Longbear."

"I shall remember it."

With that Skilgannon walked away.

As he topped the rise he heard a terrible cry, full of pain and despair. It was a death cry. He did not look back.

As Skilgannon made the long descent back toward the town he saw a horseman riding across the bridge and through the gate. It was Landis Khan. Skilgannon waited. Landis was not a natural rider, his body out of balance. He jerked around in the saddle, unable to harmonize himself with the rhythm of the sturdy chestnut he rode. A memory came to Skilgannon, of a chubby priest with a frightened face. It was as if a window had opened in his soul, and he saw himself back at the temple of Cobalsin, working the land, studying in the library, beneath the benevolent gaze of Abbot Cethelin.

Skilgannon took a deep breath. The air was fresh and cold, and he felt suddenly at peace. More memories flowed then. The chubby priest had been called Braygan. Skilgannon had left him in the war-torn city of Mellicane, before he and Druss the Legend and a group of fighters had set off to rescue the child, Elanin, held in a citadel by Nadir warriors.

A savage exultation coursed through Skilgannon, drowning the frustration of these last few days. He could not remember everything, but he knew he had fought no dragons. There was no winged horse. Nine-tenths of the stories of his life were legends, and the rest were stretched and twisted beyond recognition.

Landis Khan came alongside him and gratefully stepped down from the saddle. "You had us worried," he said.

"I met some of your Joinings. They are less fearsome than those I recall."

Landis looked at him closely. "You are recovering your memories?"

"Not all. There are large gaps. But I know a great deal more now."

"That is good, my friend. Then you should meet Gamal."

"Who is he?"

"An old man—the wisest of us. I invited him to live in my home when he finally lost his sight last spring. It was he who found your soul in the Void and brought you back to us."

Skilgannon shivered suddenly. A sharp image came to him, of a slate-gray sky and a landscape devoid of trees or plants. Then it was gone.

They walked together, Landis leading the chestnut. A line of women came into sight, moving up the hillside toward the timberline. All conversation ceased as they came close to Landis Khan and his "guest." The women passed by with eyes downcast. Skilgannon saw they were carrying baskets of food. Landis noticed his interest. "They are bringing food to the loggers working beyond the timberline," he said.

"A wagon and a single driver would be more effective, surely," observed Skilgannon. "Or do the women bring more than just food?"

Landis smiled. "Some of them are wed to loggers, and perhaps they creep off into the undergrowth for a while. In the main, however, they just bring food. You speak of effectiveness. Yes, a wagon would bring more supplies, more swiftly, with considerably better economy of effort. It would not, though, encourage a sense of community, of mutual caring."

"That is a good principle," said Skilgannon. "How does it equate with the fact that when they passed here none of them spoke, and not one of them looked up at us?"

"A good question," observed Landis, "and I am sure you already know the answer. It is important to encourage a sense of community. People need to feel valued. It would be exceedingly foolish, however, for a leader to join in. He needs to set himself apart from his followers. If he were to sit among them, and chat to them, and share with them, eventually someone would ask him *why* he was the leader. By what *right* did he rule? No leader wishes to engage in *that* conversation. No, I am like the shepherd, Skilgannon. I muster the sheep and lead them to good grazing land. I do not, however, feel the need to squat down and munch grass with them. Was it so different in your day?"

"For many years I served a warrior queen," replied Skilgannon. "She would tolerate no defiance to her will. Those who spoke against her—those she even *thought* were speaking against her—died. In many ways the society prospered. The Drenai, on the other hand, had no kings. All their leaders were elected by the votes of the people. Yet they also prospered for many centuries."

"Yet in the end both fell," said Landis.

"All empires fall. The good, the bad, the cruel, and the inspired. For every dawn there is a sunset, Landis."

Back at the palace a groom led away the chestnut and Landis and Skilgannon climbed to the uppermost level, entering a high circular tower. "Gamal is very old," Landis told Skilgannon. "He is blind now, and frail. He is, however, an Empath and versed in the ancient shamanic skills."

Landis pushed open a door and the two men stepped into a circular chamber, the floor scattered with rugs. Gamal was sitting in an old leather chair, a blanket around his thin shoulders. His head came up, and Skilgannon saw that his eyes were the color of pale opals. "Welcome, warrior, to the new world," he said. "Pull up a chair and sit with me for a while."

Skilgannon settled himself in another armchair. Landis was about to do the same when the old man spoke again. "No, Landis, my dear, you must leave Skilgannon and I alone for a little while. Come back in an hour and we will all talk."

Landis looked surprised, and a little concerned, but he forced a smile. "Of course," he said.

After Landis had gone the old man leaned forward. "Do you know yet who you are?"

"I know."

"I will be honest with you, Skilgannon. I am not a man who places great faith in prophecies. Landis—dear though he is to me—is a man obsessed. I brought your soul back because he asked me to. However, like so much in our modern world, it is against nature to do such a thing. Worse than that, it was morally wrong of me. I should have resisted it."

"Why did you not?"

The old man gave a rueful smile. "A question that deserves a better answer than I can give. Landis asked it of me, and I could not refuse." Gamal sighed. "You must understand, Skilgannon, Landis is trying to protect this land and its people. He is right to fear for the future. The Rebel Armies are currently fighting among themselves. But that war is nearing its conclusion. When it is won the Eternal could turn her eyes toward these mountains. Landis would do anything to prevent his people being enslaved. Can you blame him?"

"No. It is the nature of strong men to fight invaders. Tell me of the Eternal."

Gamal smiled. "I could tell you all I know, and that would be but a fraction of all there is to know. Suffice to say she is the queen of all the lands between here and the southern seas and the far western mountains. Her armies are now fighting battles on two continents. We live in a world that has been at war for more than five hundred years. For most of that time the Eternal has ruled. She is, like you and I, Skilgannon, a Reborn. I would imagine she has lost count of the number of bodies she has worn and discarded."

Gamal fell silent, lost in thought. Skilgannon waited for the old man to continue. After a while Gamal drew in a deep, shuddering breath. He shivered. "I served her for five lifetimes. In those three hundred and thirty years I almost lost my humanity. Just as she has. We are not created to be immortal, Skilgannon. I do not fully understand it even now, but I know that death is necessary. Perhaps it is merely that we need the contrast. Without the darkness of night how can we fully appreciate the glory of the sunrise?"

Skilgannon ignored the philosophical question. "If she has ruled all this time, why is it that Landis Khan has not been troubled before?"

"He served her faithfully. These lands were his reward."

"No," said Skilgannon. "I think there is more to it. That is why you did not want Landis here when we spoke."

The old man hesitated. "Yes, there is," he said, finally. "You are very astute. Landis and I developed a talent for discovering artifacts of the ancient world—the world long, long before you fought your battles, Skilgannon. The elder races had powers beyond imagination. Despite all our discoveries we still know very little. Like finding part of a rotted leaf, and trying to extrapolate from it what the tree might have been like. What we do know is that the ancients destroyed themselves. How or why remains a mystery."

"All this is fascinating," said Skilgannon, "but can we hold to the path?"

"Of course, my boy. Forgive me. The mind wanders. You want to know why Landis has been so favored." Gamal paused, then drew in a long breath. "He discovered her bones. He fought for her right to a new life, and when he succeeded, he and I went on to refine and improve the power of the artifacts, giving her immortality. We created the Eternal."

"I can see why she would reward you," said Skilgannon. "Why do you now fear her?"

"One answer to that would be you, my boy. The Blessed Priestess and her prophecy. You know of whom I speak?"

"Ustarte," said Skilgannon. "She came to me before the last battle. She told me I was to die, and she asked me to grant her a wish."

"She wanted the right to conduct your burial," said Gamal.

"Yes."

"Was she as wise as the legends tell us?"

"I have not read all your legends. Those concerning me are ridiculous and far-fetched. But, yes, Ustarte was wise. She told me she had seen many futures, and some of them were bleak beyond despair."

"Did she tell you why she wanted your body?"

"No. Nor did I ask. My concerns were for the battle against the Zharn. She assured me that I would win it."

"And you did."

"Yes."

"You had put aside the Swords of Night and Day for more than ten years. Why did you wield them again?"

"I had no choice. I was fifty-four years old and long past my prime. They aided me."

"They also cursed you, Skilgannon."

"I know."

"It is why you were wandering in the Void for all those centuries. You could not pass on to the green fields."

"That is *not* why. None of the legends of my life you have here tell of the evils I committed."

"You are speaking of the massacre at Perapolis."

Skilgannon was surprised. "How is it that you know of it?"

"I know many things I have not yet shared with Landis. You and I spoke in the Void. You were reluctant to return at first. There was a great part of your soul that desired the punishment the Void offered. Yet when the demons attacked, you fought them. You would not willingly let your soul be extinguished."

"I have no memories of this."

"Some will come back. You are now a creature of the flesh once more. Memories of the flesh return far more swiftly than the recollections of the spirit."

"Why am I here, Gamal? What does Landis think I can do?"

The old man shrugged. "He does not truly know. I do not know. Perhaps you can do nothing. It seems to me that even were you to take up the swords again, you would not be able to turn back Jiamad armies. It is a mystery, Skilgannon. Life is full of mysteries." Holding tightly to the blanket around his shoulders, the old man rose to his feet and tottered out to the balcony. Skilgannon followed him. Gamal settled himself into a wicker chair, a thick cushion against his lower back. "Beautiful, is it not?" he said, waving a thin hand toward the distant mountains.

"Yes," Skilgannon agreed.

"I can still see them in my mind, though if I need to I can float my spirit free. I did so earlier, and observed your meeting with some of our Jiamads. You are not a man who scares easily."

"Whom did they kill?"

"I think you know the answer to that. Longbear killed the one you downed. Tore out his throat." Gamal sighed. "Once—a long time ago—Longbear was a friend of mine. A good man."

"Yet you turned him into a beast."

"Yes, we did. Needs must when the wolves gather." Gamal gave a weak laugh. "I gave him the name *Longbear*. He was a man who admired bears. The admiration he felt for them was what killed him. He used to observe them. Full of confidence, he would walk the high country, learning all he could about their habits. He wrote many of them down. One day he was watching a female leading her cubs to one of the upper waterfalls. She suddenly turned on him. Have you ever seen a bear attack?"

"Yes. For creatures so large their speed is terrifying."

"As he discovered. He was mauled by it. A group of hunters found him. They brought him back, but there was nothing we could do. Not only were the wounds hideous, but they became infected. When he was dying he offered himself for the joining. We melded him with a young bear."

"Does he remember who he was?" asked Skilgannon.

Gamal shook his head. "Some Jiamads do. They do not last long. They are driven mad. Mostly a new personality emerges. Some things remain, though we do not understand why. A loyal man will become a loyal beast. A sly man will remain untrustworthy. Yet another mystery."

"Are all your Joinings volunteers?"

"No. Most are criminals—outlaws, thieves, rapists, killers. They are condemned to die by the judges, and, upon their deaths, they are melded."

"It does not seem wise," said Skilgannon, "to make a killer even more powerful."

"No, it does not," agreed Gamal, "and that is where the

jewels come in. You saw that they had stones embedded into their skulls?"

"Yes."

"Through them we control the Jiamads. We can administer pleasure or pain, keep them alive or kill them. They know this. It keeps them subservient. The Eternal's Jiamads have no such stones. But then she cares nothing if they go on a rampage and slay peasants."

A light breeze whispered over the balcony wall. Gamal shivered and returned to his room. There was a fire lit. The old man went to it and knelt before the dying flames. Holding out his hand he gauged the heat, then fumbled for a log, which he added to the blaze. "Being blind is such a bore," he said.

"It seems to me that if you have the magic to meld man and beast, you should be able to heal your eyes," observed Skilgannon.

"And we can. But I will use it no more," said Gamal. Returning to his chair, he sat down and sighed. "I have lived for many lifetimes. I was arrogant, and believed in the greater good. It was a deceit. Reborns deceive themselves so easily. We are immortal and therefore, somehow, important. Such nonsense. But let us talk of you. What do you desire now?"

"I don't know yet. Not another war. That is certain."

"And understandable. You have been fighting in the Void for a thousand years. Enough, I feel, for any man."

"What was I fighting?"

"Demons, and the dark souls of the cursed. The Void is a terrible place for those condemned to walk there. Most pass through it swiftly; some wander for a while. Few accomplish what you did. But then you had help. You recall?"

"No."

"When I was with you, a shining figure came. He helped you in a fight against several demons that had cornered you in a ravine."

"As I said I have no knowledge of the Void. Nor—I

think—do I wish to recall it. You ask what I desire here. What if I were to tell you that I desire to leave? To journey back to lands I remember?"

"Then I would wish you well, Skilgannon, and furnish you with coin, and weapons, and a sound horse. I fear, however, you would not get far. This war is being waged across two continents. Death and desolation are everywhere. There are roving bands of renegade Jiamads; there are men who have given themselves over to the darkest beasts of their own natures. Some areas are now desolate of life, others suffer famine and disease. War is dreadful at any time, but *this* war is particularly vile. If you leave here alone it will be much as the Void was to you—save there will be no shining figure to help you."

"Even so I think I will risk it," said Skilgannon. "I have been studying maps in Landis's library. Petar is not on them. Where are we now, in relation to Naashan?"

"In your time this would have been Drenai land, bordering the Sathuli realm. Naashan is across the sea. You can sail from Draspartha . . . I believe it was called Dros Purdol in the past. However, might I ask a favor before you go?"

"You can ask."

"Give it one month before you decide. You are a young man again. A month is not a long time."

"I will think on it," Skilgannon told him.

"Good. In the meantime there is a mystery you can help us solve. Tomorrow Landis will take you up into the hills. There is a man there I would dearly like you to meet."

"What is the mystery?"

"Bear with me, Skilgannon. Meet the man, and then we will talk again."

"You still have not told me why you now fear the Eternal," said Skilgannon. "Nor why you did not wish Landis to be here when we spoke."

"Forgive me, my boy. I am very tired now. I will tell you all when next we speak. I promise you."

* * *

When the fight started Harad walked away. It was none of
his concern. The loggers from the upper valleys were arrogant men, and argumentative. Harad usually ignored them,
and they, in turn, wanted no trouble with him. Truth was, *no
one* wanted any trouble with the man now known as Harad
Bone Breaker. It was not a title the huge, black-bearded
young logger had sought, nor was it one that he liked. It had
proved effective, however, and life was generally more calm.
He had not been provoked into breaking anyone's bones for
more than five months now. People avoided him—which was
exactly how he preferred it.

Moving back from the fight, Harad sat down on a felled
tree and took up his meal pack. Fresh bread and strong
cheese. The bread was just as he liked it, slightly overbaked,
the crust dark and crisp, the center soft and full of flavor.
Tearing off a chunk, he chewed slowly, trying to ignore the
sounds of fists on flesh and the shouting of the watchers. The
cheese was disappointing. There was no tang to the flavor.
Good cheese would cause the tongue to cleave to the roof of
the mouth, and the eyes to water.

A slim, golden-haired young woman approached him.
"You have bread crumbs in your beard," she said. Harad
brushed them away. He could feel his tension rising. Charis
had not walked across the clearing to talk about crumbs.
"Someone should stop this fight," she said.

"Then go and stop it," snapped Harad. Charis ignored the
tone and sat down on the log beside him. He tried not to look
at her, and struggled to avoid reacting to the fact that her leg
was touching his. It was impossible. With a heavy sigh he
put down his bread.

"What do you want from me?" he asked, trying to sound
angry.

"They are going to hurt him," she said. "It is not right."

Harad glanced across to the fight. The young logger, Arin,
was battling gamely, but the High Valley man he was fight-

ing was taller and heavier. There was blood on Arin's cheek, and his lower lip had been split. A crowd had gathered. They were shouting encouragement to the fighters.

"What is the fight about?" he asked.

"The High Valley man made a comment about Kerena." Harad switched his gaze to Arin's young wife, a plump girl with dark blond hair. She was standing some distance from the fighters, her hand over her mouth, her eyes wide and frightened.

"So are you going to stop it?" asked Charis.

"Why should I? It is not my fight. Anyway, the man is defending his wife's honor. That's as it should be."

"You *know* what will happen if Arin wins," said Charis.

Harad said nothing, returning his attention to the fight. The High Valley man was called Lathar. He and his two brothers were known troublemakers. Tough men and brutal, they were constantly involved in scuffles and fights. Harad knew what Charis meant. If Arin was to beat Lathar, then his brothers would pitch in. No one would stop them. And Arin would take a severe beating.

"It is not my problem," said Harad. "Why do you seek to make it so?"

"Why do you set yourself apart?" she countered.

Harad felt his anger rising. "You are an irritating woman."

"I'm glad you've noticed I'm a woman."

"What does that mean? Of course I know you're a woman." Harad was growing increasingly uncomfortable. A great cheer went up as Arin landed a powerful right cross into Lathar's chin. The High Valley man stumbled back. Arin surged in after him. One of Lathar's brothers, a stocky bearded man named Garik, thrust out a foot. Arin tripped over it and tumbled to the ground. It gave Lathar a few more moments to recover.

"See!" said Charis. "It is beginning."

Harad turned toward her, looking into her deep blue eyes. He felt the breath catch in his throat. Hastily he looked away. "Why do you care?" he asked. "Arin is not your husband."

"Why do you not?"

"Can you never answer a damned question? Always you have one of your own. Why *should* I care? Arin is not my friend. None of them is."

"Of course," she said. "Harad the Loner. Harad the Bone Breaker. Harad the Bitter."

"I am not bitter. I just . . . prefer my own company."

"Why is that?"

Harad surged to his feet. "When will you stop these questions?" he thundered. At that moment Lathar was knocked from his feet. He struggled to rise as Arin stood over him. Another brother, a tall pockmarked lout named Vaska, ran in from behind, punching Arin in the neck. The burly Garik joined in, kicking Arin in the hip. The young logger, surprised by the sudden assault, fell heavily.

Harad stalked across the clearing. "Back off!" he roared.

Vaska and Garik turned away from the fallen Arin. Lathar himself was back on his feet. Harad moved in close, pushing past them. Arin was sitting on the ground, looking groggy. Just as Harad reached out to lift Arin to his feet, he heard movement from behind. Harad turned. Garik rushed at him, his fist drawn back. Harad stood still. He could have avoided the blow. Instead he merely thrust out his chin. The High Valley man's fist hammered against Harad's face. Harad stared hard at the man who had struck him, noting with some satisfaction the sudden fear in Garik's eyes. "Not the best idea you've ever had, pig-face," he said. His right hand flashed out, grabbing the attacker's tunic. With one swift tug he pulled him into a head butt that smashed the man's nose. Holding him upright, Harad tapped him with a straight left. Garik hurtled back into the crowd, then slumped unconscious to the ground. Vaska charged in. Harad stopped him in his tracks with a straight left, then delivered a right cross that spun Vaska from his feet. He tried to pull his punches, but even so Vaska lay on the ground unmoving. Harad transferred his gaze to Lathar. The big logger was already bloody from his fight with Arin. His right eye was swollen and closed. Harad ignored him and turned to the fallen logger Arin, who was now sitting up. The man was still groggy. Reaching out, Harad hauled Arin to his feet. "Go and drink some water," he advised. "It will help clear your head." Arin's wife, the blond Kerena, ran in, taking her husband's arm and leading him away. As Harad turned he saw Lathar stumble forward, fists raised. Stepping in, he blocked a weak blow and grabbed Lathar's arms.

"Wait until you feel better," he advised. "Then I'll be glad to break your bones for you."

Leaving the surprised logger standing there, Harad walked away, returning to the log and his food. Charis joined him. Closing his eyes briefly, he sighed. "What do you want now?" he said.

"Don't you feel better for helping Arin?"

"No. I just want to eat in peace."

"Are you coming to the Feast?"

"No."

"Why not? There'll be food, and dancing, and music. You might enjoy yourself."

"I don't like noise. I don't like people."

She smiled. "Come anyway. I might dance with you."

"I don't dance."

"I'll teach you."

Taking a deep breath, he closed his eyes again. When he opened them he saw her walking away down the hillside with the other women who had brought the midday food. Some of the men had already begun taking up ax and saw, ready to begin work. Lathar's brothers, still unconscious, had been pulled away from the work area. Lathar was kneeling alongside them. The work overseer, a tall thin man named Balish, was talking to Lathar.

Harad finished his meal. As he rose to take up his ax he saw young Arin walking toward him. The boy's right eye was swollen almost shut, and his face was heavily bruised.

"My thanks to you, Harad," he said.

Harad wanted to tell him that he had fought well. He

wanted to say something in a friendly fashion. But he didn't know how. He merely nodded and moved away.

Balish the Overseer approached him. "You best watch your back, Harad," he said. "They are vengeful men."

"They'll do nothing," said Harad. "Now let me work."

Raising his ax, Harad swung it smoothly, the blade slicing deeply into the tree trunk.

Three

As the seventeen village women made their way down the hillside, the plump Kerena moved alongside Charis. "Thank you for getting the brute involved," she said. "They would have hurt my Arin."

Charis felt a stab of annoyance. She liked Kerena, but the girl was like so many of the others, judgmental. "Why do you have to call him that?" she asked, struggling unsuccessfully to keep the irritation from her voice.

"What? What did I say?"

"You called Harad *the brute.*"

"Oh, it was just a manner of speaking," answered Kerena, brightly. "It's what everyone calls him. That and *Bone Breaker.*"

"I *know* that. What I don't know is why."

Kerena was surprised. "How can you not know? Last summer he broke a man's back in the high country."

"His jaw," corrected Charis.

"No, I definitely heard it was someone's back. Arin's sister's husband told me. Anyway, even if it was a jaw that's not the point. Harad is always getting into fights."

"Like today?" countered Charis. "I expect it will only increase his reputation as a brute. I wish I had not asked him to get involved."

Kerena reddened, her expression hardening. "Oh, you really are *too* argumentative today, Charis. I was only trying to be pleasant, and to thank you for your help." With that she moved away and began chatting brightly to one of the other women. As Charis walked on she saw both women glance back at her. She guessed what they were talking about.

Charis and the brute.

It seemed to Charis to be manifestly unfair. Anyone who took the time to study Harad would know that he was not the monster they feared. But they could not see. When they looked into his blue-gray eyes they saw them as cold and forbidding. Charis recognized the loneliness there. They observed his immense strength and feared he would break their bones. She saw a man uncomfortable with that strength, and too shy to express his fears to them.

At the foot of the hill the wives moved off to their various homes and Charis wandered back to the palace with the other servants. They would return to the woods at dusk with more food for the itinerant workers. The timbermen would be working here until the day of the Feast in ten days' time, and they needed feeding. They would receive wages, and many of them would carry their coin into town and spend it on a night of revelry. Then, broke and happy, they would wander off seeking other work to keep them fed during the coming winter. Harad would not spend his money in such a way. He would hoard it, then buy supplies and carry them up to his mountain cabin. He would stay away from the settlements for as long as possible.

Charis sighed.

For the rest of the afternoon she worked with four other women in the palace kitchens, preparing the food for the evening meal. At one point she heard the rumble of a wagon outside and moved to the rear window. It was the wolf catcher, Rabil. In his caged wagon four timber wolves prowled behind the bars. Charis watched the wagon draw up at the gated entrance to the lower levels. She shuddered and touched her brow in the sign of the Blessed Priestess, Ustarte.

"Charis!"

She turned to see the elderly head servant, Ensinar. Charis smiled. Ensinar was a sweet-natured old man, kind and accommodating. He had one vanity, which made the other servants smile. Though utterly bald on the crown of his head he had grown his gray hair long above the ears. The strands were then swept up and over the crown. Ensinar obviously thought this gave him the appearance of a man whose hair was merely thinning. The effect, however, was comical. Especially if he was outside and a sudden gust of wind caused his hair to flap wildly. The old man approached Charis and gave a shy smile. "Have you served the lord's guest yet?"

"No, sir."

"Take him some food and a fresh jug of water. There is a side of honey-cured ham in the pantry. It is very fine. Cut some thick slices from that. Some fresh bread, too. Today's loaves are a little underbaked, I feel. Still . . . it should suffice." With a second shy smile Ensinar moved away.

Charis was nervous. All the servants knew about the stranger with the sapphire-blue eyes. Mira and Calasia had both been seduced by him, and Charis had scolded them both for boasting of their exploits. "It is unseemly to speak of such things in public," she said. The girls both laughed at her.

"You won't be laughing if Ensinar finds out. You'll be dismissed."

"Nonsense," snapped Mira, a slim, dark-haired girl. "We were told to make him happy. And he certainly made me happy," she concluded, with a laugh. The other girls gathered around, begging for more detail. Charis had walked away disgusted.

She had only seen the stranger from a distance, a handsome man, dark haired, with a spider drawing upon his arm. One of the other female servants said she had gone to his room and found him standing naked on the balcony, his limbs contorted, one leg around the other, his arms raised above his head and similarly twisted. She said there was a painting on the man's back, a large eagle with wings outspread.

"Why would anyone have a painting on their back?" the girl had asked Charis. "They could never see it, could they?"

Charis had no definitive answer. All she said was: "My

brother tells me there are many strange customs Outside. He says there are people who paint their hair different colors, and others have ink marks stained into the skins of their faces, some blue, some red. Outsiders are not like us."

"Then I hope they don't come here," said the girl. Charis agreed. Everything her brother told her about the Outside left her feeling uneasy. People lived in stockaded towns, and there were battles everywhere between Jiamad armies. The latest Temple Wars had been raging now for eighteen years. They had begun the year before she was born. Charis had no understanding of the reasons for the fighting—nor did she wish to acquire such knowledge.

Putting such thoughts from her mind, she prepared a tray of food as Ensinar had instructed, with ham and bread, adding a dish of sugar-dried fruit. Placing a flagon of fresh water on the tray, she carried it out of the kitchens and up the two flights of stairs to the upper quarters. She hoped the mysterious stranger would be standing on the balcony as the girl had described. She was curious to see the painting on his back. In this she was disappointed. He was indeed on the balcony, but dressed in a loose-fitting shirt of pale blue satin and leggings of tanned beige leather. He turned as she entered, and she saw the brilliant blue of his eyes. A deeper shade than Harad's, and even less welcoming. His expression warmed as he looked at her. This annoyed Charis. Always men reacted in the same fashion. It was as if they were admiring a fine horse or a cow. The good-looking ones were the worst. They seemed to think that merely being handsome was enough to woo a girl. Charis found them all insubstantial—especially when set against Harad.

This stranger was by far the most handsome man she had ever seen, and this only fueled her irritation. She curtseyed and placed the tray on a nearby table.

"What is your name?" he asked. His accent was strange, the words carefully enunciated.

"I am just a servant," she replied. If he tried to seduce her, he would find that not all the women in the palace were of easy virtue.

"Does that mean you have no name?"

She stared at him, looking for signs of sarcasm. There were none. "My name is Charis, Lord."

"I am not a lord. Thank you, Charis." He smiled, then turned away from her. This was unexpected, and her interest was piqued.

"It is said you have a painting on your back," she said.

He gave a soft laugh and swung back to face her. "It is a tattoo."

"Is that a kind of bird?"

"No. It is . . . a description of the method used to make the stain on the skin permanent."

"Why is it done?"

He shrugged. "A custom among my people. Ornamentation. Fashion. I do not know how it began."

"There are many strange customs Outside," she told him.

"I notice that the people here wear no jewelry of any kind, no earrings or bracelets or pendants."

"What is an earring?"

"A small circle of gold or silver that is pushed through a pierced hole in the earlobe."

"A hole? You mean they make a hole in the ear for this . . . this ring?"

"Yes."

She laughed. "Are you making fun of me?"

"No."

"Why would anyone want a hole in their ear?"

"To hang an earring from," he answered.

"What purpose does it serve?"

"It looks attractive, I suppose. I have never really considered it before. It is also an indication of wealth. The more expensive the jewelry, the richer the wearer. The rich always have more status than the poor. So a woman who wears sapphires in her ears will command more respect than one who does not." Suddenly he laughed aloud, the sound rich and almost musical. "How odd and stupid it all sounds now. Have you worked in the palace for long?"

"A little more than a full year. They offered me a serving role after my father died. He was one of the town's bakers. He made wonderful bread. They can't make it now. He did not write down his recipes. That's a shame, isn't it, when something good just goes away?"

"Are you speaking of your father or the bread?"

"The bread," she admitted. "Does that make me seem shallow?"

"I do not know. Perhaps your father was an unpleasant man."

"No, he wasn't. He was kind and gentle. But his illness went on for so long that it was a blessing when he passed away. I still find tears in my eyes when I pass a bakery and smell fresh-baked bread. It reminds me of him."

"I do not think you are shallow, Charis," he said, his voice gentle. Her eyes narrowed and she stared hard at him. He saw the change in her. "Did I say something to offend you?" he asked. "I thought it to be a compliment."

"I know why you compliment women," she said, stiffly. "You seek to take them to your bed."

"There is some truth in that observation," he replied. "Though it is not always the case. Sometimes a compliment is merely a compliment. However, I am keeping you from your work."

With that he returned to the balcony. Charis stood for a moment, feeling foolish. Then she left the room, angry with herself.

He was not what she had been expecting. He did not leer, or make suggestive comments. He had not tried to seduce her. *How different am I from Kerena and the others?* she thought. *I judged the man on what others had said, just as they judged Harad on hearsay.*

And now he thought her witless and foolish.

It doesn't matter what he thinks, she told herself, sternly. *Why should I care about the opinion of a man with a painted back?*

* * *

Most of the itinerant loggers had brought tents in which they slept at night. Others sat outside under the starlight alongside cook fires, and some merely found a dry spot beneath the trees and slept rough, under thin blankets. Harad always found a place away from the main groups, settling himself down alone. He liked the night, and the awesome quiet. It calmed him.

Harad had always preferred to be alone.

Well, not always, he admitted to himself, as he sat with his back resting against the trunk of a huge oak. He could remember, as a child, wanting to play with the other children of the mountain village. The problem was always his strength. In play fights and scraps he would try not to hurt them. Yet always some child would run away crying and in pain. "I only patted him," Harad would say. One day, when he grabbed another boy, the child had screamed. His arm was broken. After that no one wanted to play with Harad.

His mother, Alanis, a shy, reserved woman, had tried to comfort him. His father, Borak, a brooding logger, had said nothing. But then Borak rarely spoke to Harad, unless to scold. Harad never understood why his father disliked him, nor indeed why Borak would always leave when Landis Khan visited. The lord would sit with the boy, asking him questions—mostly about whether he dreamed. No one else seemed interested in his dreams. He would always ask the same question. "Do you dream of long-ago days, Harad?"

It was an odd question, and Harad didn't know what it meant. He would tell the lord that he dreamed of mountains, of woods. Landis Khan was disappointed.

Borak was killed in a freak accident when Harad was nine. A felled tree crashed to the ground, and a dead branch snapped upon impact. A shard of sharp wood flew through the air, piercing Borak's eye, embedding itself in his brain. He did not die swiftly. Paralyzed, he was carried down to the palace, where Landis Khan himself fought to save him. Harad still remembered when the lord rode up to the cabin with the news that Borak had died. Strangely his mother shed no tears.

Alanis herself had died three years ago when Harad was seventeen. There was no drama. She said good night and went to her bed. In the morning Harad tried to wake her. He brought her a tisane of sweet mint and placed it by her bedside. Then he had touched her shoulder. As he looked into her face he knew she had gone. There was no movement, no flicker of life.

That was the first moment Harad felt truly alone.

He had run his hand through his mother's dark, graying hair, wanting to say something by way of farewell. There were no words. Their relationship had never been tactile, but each night she would kiss his brow, and say: "May the Blessed Priestess watch over you as you sleep, my son." Harad cherished these moments. Once she had stroked his cheek as he lay abed, his body battling a fever. This was the single greatest moment of his childhood.

So on that last day, he stroked his mother's cheek. "May the Blessed Priestess watch over you as you sleep, Mother," he said.

Then he walked down to the village and reported her death.

After that he lived alone. His strength, and an awesome stamina, made him a highly valuable asset as a logger. Yet that same strength still caused him problems. Other men would feel compelled to test that strength against their own. Like young bulls vying for supremacy. Harad traveled throughout the timberlands. Everywhere it was the same. At some point someone would engineer a disagreement, no matter how hard he tried to avoid confrontation.

He thought this bleak period in his life had ended last year, when he broke Masselian's jaw. Masselian was a fist-fighting legend in the high country. After that Harad had been left alone. In some strange way he had transcended the other "bulls," reaching a plateau that made him untouchable.

Now, however, he had earned the enmity of Lathar and his

brothers. He had told the overseer, Balish, that the brothers would do nothing. He had said it to end the conversation with Balish, a man he didn't like. As he sat in the dark he knew it wasn't true.

They would come seeking revenge.

If only Charis hadn't been there that morning. He could have enjoyed his meal, finished his work, and even now be sleeping dreamlessly.

Harad swore softly. Thoughts of Charis filled his mind. He tried to think of other things, but it was no use. If Harad found the company of men difficult, he found women impossible. He never knew what to say. Words would catch in his throat, and he would grunt some inanity.

Worse, he found much of the conversation of women incomprehensible. "Isn't it a beautiful day? It makes one feel good to be alive." What did that mean? It was *always* good to be alive. Naturally it was more comfortable when the sun shone, but did that make it beautiful? Charis had once asked him: "Do you ever wonder about the stars?" That question had haunted him all last winter. What was there to wonder about? Stars were stars. Bright little points in the sky. Night after night he had left his cabin and sat on the porch staring malevolently up at the heavens. He found no answers. But then Charis was like that. She would say things that seeded themselves in his brain, causing him endless discomfort.

Last week she had brought him some food and sat down beside him. She had picked up an acorn. "Isn't it wonderful to think that an oak tree can grow from this little thing?"

"Yes," he said, simply to say something that might end this conversation before it wormed its way into his brain.

"The acorn, though, comes from the oak tree."

"Of course it comes from the oak tree," he said.

"So how did the first oak tree grow?"

"What?"

"Well, if the oak tree makes the acorn, and the acorn makes the oak tree, what made the first oak tree? There couldn't have been any acorns, could there?"

And there it was. Yet another seed, whose growing roots would torment his mind through the long cold winter ahead.

The night breeze rustled the leaves above him, and he sighed. Perhaps when Charis married she would lose interest in tormenting him. This was a new thought for Harad. It made him uneasy, though he couldn't understand why. His mood darkened. Uncomfortable now, he rose to his feet and walked to the stream. Squatting down, he cupped his hands in the water and drank. In that moment he heard stealthy sounds in the undergrowth. Harad sighed. Rising silently, he walked to a nearby tree and leaned against it, waiting.

The first of the brothers, the bearded Garik, crept out of the darkness. He was holding a three-foot length of stout wood, which Harad saw was an ax handle. Behind him came Lathar and Vaska. Moonlight suddenly bathed the area as the clouds parted above. The men stood stock still, then Garik pointed the ax handle at Harad's blanket by the tree. In that moment Harad realized he did not want to break any bones tonight. He stepped forward.

"Isn't it a beautiful night," said Harad. "Makes one feel good to be alive." All three men swung around in shock. "Have you ever wondered about acorns?" continued Harad, moving away from the tree and toward the waiting men. "If an oak grows from an acorn, and acorns grow from the oak, then how did the first oak tree grow?"

He crossed the small clearing until he was standing directly before them. "Acorns?" said Lathar, mystified. "What did you say about acorns?"

"Did you want to see me?" asked Harad, ignoring the question.

"We were just . . . out walking," said Vaska, suddenly frightened.

"Ah," said Harad, stepping forward and laying his huge hand on the man's shoulder. "Good night for it. Lots of stars. Have you ever wondered about the stars?"

"Gods, what is he talking about?" Garik asked Lathar. Lathar shrugged and backed away.

"Forget it, Garik. Let's go." Garik stood there confused, the ax handle hanging to the ground.

"I thought—"

"I said forget it!"

The three men ambled away into the darkness. Harad chuckled and returned to his blankets.

Then he slept, deeply and without dreams.

Though there were many gaps in his memory, Skilgannon was beginning now to feel more complete. He recalled his childhood back in Naashan, the death of his father, Decado Firefist, his upbringing with the gentle actor, Greavas, and the middle-aged couple, Sperian and Molaire. He remembered their deaths at the hands of Boranius, and his subsequent flight with Jianna, the princess, and the long battles to restore her throne.

He recalled also the death of his wife, Dayan, and his search for the Temple of the Resurrection, a place steeped in mystery and myth. It had been his quest to bring Dayan back to life. Memories of those years of searching were vague, misty. Disconnected recollections flashed before his eyes, so swiftly his mind could not make sense of them. An old man in crimson robes. A tall room with walls of white marble and metal, lights glittering on gems set in the walls.

So many other memories spilled across his mind like scattered pearls. Many were of wars and battles, or long journeys by land and sea. He remembered a warlord he had fought alongside, a powerful man . . . he struggled for a name . . . Ulric. The Khan of Wolves.

Moving to the balcony, Skilgannon drew in a deep breath and began to work through a series of stretching exercises. His body was more supple now, the young muscles stretching easily into the Eagle pose, the left foot hooked behind the right ankle, the right arm raised, the left arm wrapped around it, the backs of the hands pressed together. Motionless he stood, in perfect balance. A long time ago this exercise would have brought with it a sense of peace. He could not find it now.

I should not be here, he thought.

I lived and I died. My journey was complete.

A beast leapt at him from behind a jumble of boulders. It was scaled like a snake, but the face was human. A sword lashed toward his neck. Swaying back, he drew the Swords of Night and Day and slew the demon. Others were gathering.

The memory was sudden and jarring.

His journey had *not* been complete. He had wandered the Void for what Gamal told him was a thousand years. He shuddered as more memories of that cold, gray soulless place filled his mind. Then he smiled grimly. Soulless? It was exactly the opposite. It was full of souls—souls like his own. Skilgannon the Damned, in a world of the Damned.

The sun was shining brightly in a clear blue sky. Skilgannon moved to the balcony wall and drew in a deep breath. He could almost taste the sweetness of life upon the breeze as his lungs filled with cold, crisp air.

Why am I here? he thought. If the Void had been a punishment, was this some kind of reward? If so for what? It made no sense.

He heard a knocking at his door and went back into the apartment. It was Landis Khan. He smiled as he entered, but Skilgannon sensed nervousness in him. "How are you feeling, my friend?"

"I am well, Landis. And do not use the word *friend* so lightly. Friendship is either bestowed or earned."

"Yes, of course. My apologies."

"There is nothing to apologize for. Gamal says there is someone I should meet. Something about a mystery."

"Indeed so. I have horses being prepared."

"Is it far?"

"About an hour's ride."

"Would you prefer to walk?"

Landis grinned. It made him look younger. "You noticed my lack of skill? Yes, I would prefer to walk, but I have many duties today. So I must bounce upon the saddle and endure more bruises."

Half an hour later they were riding over the hills toward the upper timberland. "Who is this mysterious person?" asked Skilgannon as they reached a long level stretch and the horses slowed.

"Forgive me, Skilgannon, but I would prefer it if you waited until we get there. Then I will answer all questions. Might I ask a favor of you?"

"There is no harm in asking, Landis."

"We have visitors coming in tomorrow from Outside. I would like you to be with me when I meet them. It will be vital, however, for your name not to be mentioned. I will, by your leave, introduce you as my nephew, Callan."

"Who are they, these people?"

Landis sighed. "They serve the Eternal. May we walk for a while?" he said, suddenly. "I feel as if my spine is a foot shorter than when we began." Drawing rein, he climbed clumsily from the saddle. Skilgannon joined him, and they walked on, leading their mounts.

"This world is suffering, Skilgannon, in a way that is unnatural and perverse. We had the chance, I think, to make it a garden, a place of infinite beauty, without threat of famine or disease. Even death could be held back. Instead we have the grotesque violence of a terrible war, fought by unnatural beast against unnatural beast, and by men against men. The suffering Outside is prodigious. Disease, pestilence, and starvation, murder and horror abound. How one man was supposed to put an end to this I do not know. As I said, I was swept up in the prophecy. I truly believed—*believe*," he added, hastily, "that the Blessed Priestess *did* know the role you would play."

"And this prophecy promised I would overthrow the Eternal?"

"Yes."

"What *exactly* did it say?"

"It was written in an archaic tongue, and in a form of verse. There have been several translations, all subtly different, in that they sought to create rhyme in the modern tongue. The one I prefer begins: *Hero Reborn, torn from the gray, re-*

united with blades, of Night and of Day. The rest of it is deliberately obscure and allegorical. Almost whimsical. The Hero Reborn will steal or destroy the magical egg of a vain silver eagle, battle a mountain giant bearing the golden shield of the gods, and bring about the death of an Immortal, restoring the world to balance and harmony."

"A vain eagle?" asked Skilgannon.

"In love with its own reflection," said Landis. "As I said, some of the ancient texts were expanded, or exaggerated. In full, however, the story indicates that Ustarte knew the nature of the evil we now face. In some of the ancient texts she talks of an undead queen and armies of Joinings. By her reckoning the world of men would face ruin. The Blessed Priestess predicted that only you, and the Swords of Night and Day, could defeat them. I believe she had truly seen the future, Skilgannon."

"I knew her, Landis. She spoke of many futures. Every decision we make, or refuse to make, creates a different future. None of them is carved in stone. She knew this."

"I accept that. Gamal has made similar points. But she predicted the Eternal, and the monsters that now serve her. So perhaps she was also right in naming you as the savior."

Skilgannon saw the hope flicker in the man's face and said nothing. He walked on. Landis hurried alongside. "What was she like? Was she beautiful, as the legends say?"

"Aye, she was beautiful. She was also—to use your own description—a Jiamad."

Landis stopped abruptly. "No! How was that possible?"

"I can give you no answers. When we went to her we had a Joining with us. He had once been a friend of one of our company. We were hoping that Ustarte could separate him from the beast he had become. She said it was not possible. If it were she would have done it for herself. She showed me then her arm, which was covered in fur. She was part tiger, part wolf, as I recall."

Skilgannon saw that Landis Khan had grown pale. The older man walked on in silence for a while. Then he turned to

Skilgannon. "Do not mention this to anyone else, I beseech you. The Priestess is venerated now. People pray to her, worship her."

"Why should it make a difference? She was who she was. Nothing is changed except her form."

"Nothing and everything," said Landis, sadly. "Let us ride on. We are almost there."

Skilgannon had little experience with lumber camps, but it seemed to him that this one was well organized, teams of men felling trees, others stripping away branches. He saw one long trunk being dragged by two shaggy ponies toward an area where wagons were waiting. Here there were loggers wielding two-man bow saws. The trunks were shortened before being lifted by pulleys to the backs of wagons. The work was swift and efficient, and there was a sweet smell in the air, the perfume of pine.

Landis Khan drew rein a little way back from the workmen and waited. A tall, round-shouldered man made his way through the workers and bowed to him. "Welcome, Lord. The work, as you see, is going well."

"I am sure that it is, Balish. This is my nephew, Callan. He is visiting for a while."

Balish bowed to Skilgannon. "Where will we find Harad?" asked Landis Khan.

The man looked suddenly frightened. "There was little I could do to stop the fight, Lord," he said. "It happened so swiftly. No one was seriously hurt. I have spoken to Harad and warned him about his behavior."

"Yes, yes, but where is he?"

Balish pointed toward the west. "Shall I have him brought here?"

"Yes. We will be a little way down the slope there. Where the stream forks."

So saying, Landis Khan swung his horse and rode away from the camp. Skilgannon followed him, and the two men dismounted by the stream. "Balish is a good organizer," said

Landis Khan, "but weak and mean spirited. He does not like Harad."

Skilgannon said nothing. He stared at the mountains and watched two eagles soaring on the thermals. For some reason the sight of the birds filled him with a sense of emptiness, and a longing to be free of this place. Much as he respected Ustarte, she was long dead now, and he felt no obligation to be the savior of a world that was not his. Soon he would leave and see if he could find a way back to what was once Naashan. His studies in the library during the past few days had taught him that Naashan was across the sea to the east. To get there he would have to journey to the port now called Draspartha, though in Skilgannon's time it had been Dros Purdol.

Landis Khan was still talking, and Skilgannon wrenched his mind from thoughts of travel. "I am going to ask Harad to show you the high country," said Landis Khan. "He is a dour man and does not talk much. Gamal feels a little time away from—" He chuckled. "—away from civilization will help you to readjust to this new life."

"Why Harad?"

Landis Khan looked away. "He knows the high country as well as anyone."

Skilgannon knew this was—at least in part—a lie, but he let it pass. "Ah, here he comes," said Landis Khan. Skilgannon swung to meet the newcomer—and his breath caught in his throat. He felt his heart beating hard and struggled for calm. He glanced at Landis Khan, anger in his gaze. "Say nothing for the moment!" insisted Landis.

The black-bearded logger strode down to where the two men waited. "It is good to see you, my friend," said Landis. "This is my nephew, Callan." The logger merely nodded and turned his pale eyes on Skilgannon. Landis Khan spoke again, "I would like you to act as his guide, up into the mountains."

"I am working here," said Harad.

"You will receive the same wages, my boy. I would take it as a personal favor if you would agree."

Harad stared hard at Skilgannon. "No horses," he said. "It will be a long walk."

"I can walk," said Skilgannon. "However, if you would prefer not to guide me, I will understand."

Harad swung to Landis Khan. "How long do you want me to guide him?"

"Three . . . four days."

"When?"

"The day after tomorrow."

"Meet me here at sunup," said Harad to Skilgannon. With that he nodded to Landis Khan and strode back toward the logging camp.

After he had gone Landis stood silently alongside Skilgannon, who sensed the man's unease. "Are you angry?" Landis asked, at last.

"Oh, yes, Landis. I am angry." Landis took an involuntary backward step, his face showing his fear. Skilgannon gave a cold smile. "But I will not harm you."

"That is a relief," said Landis. "What can you tell me of Harad's . . . ancestor?"

Skilgannon shook his head. "I see why you wanted me to meet him, but I will tell you nothing. I need to think on this. Alone." With that he stepped smoothly into the saddle and rode away.

Harad was uneasy as he returned to work—not that anyone would have noticed. He still swung his ax with unfailing power, his strength seemingly limitless. He worked throughout the morning, silently as always, his face grim, his expression set. At one point he saw Balish staring at him, but ignored him. Lathar and his brothers were close by, and twice he found himself working alongside them. They did not speak, but during one short break Lathar offered Harad a drink from a water canteen. Harad accepted it.

Lathar sighed. "I couldn't sleep," he said. "So where did the first oak tree come from?"

Harad relaxed and suddenly chuckled. "I don't know. A woman said it to me. Now I can't get it out of my head."

"Me, too," said Lathar. "Women, eh?"

Harad nodded. No more was said, but the enmity between them melted away.

The day was warm, the work exhausting. By the midday break Harad had been toiling for six hours. He found himself looking forward to seeing Charis, to sitting quietly on a log with her beside him. When the women came he walked away to sit alone, and waited for her. She was wearing a cream-colored smock and a green skirt, and her feet were bare. Her long, golden hair was tied back with a green ribbon. Harad felt his heartbeat quicken. Charis was carrying a basket of food. She moved among the men, offering them bread. Harad waited, his impatience growing. Finally she turned toward him and smiled. He reddened.

"Good day to you, Harad," she said.

"And you," he replied, struggling for something intelligent to say. Charis handed him a small loaf and a block of firm cheese. Then she swung away. Harad was astonished. Always she stopped and spoke to him. It was bizarre. On all the occasions when he wished to be alone she would hover close by. Now that he actually *wanted* to talk to her she was moving away.

"Wait!" he called, before he could stop himself. Charis looked around, obviously surprised. "I . . . I wanted to speak with you."

Charis wandered back to where he sat. "What about?" she asked, though she did not sit.

"I am going away for a few days."

"Why would you need to share that with me?"

"No, not that. I wanted to ask about the lord's nephew. I am to take him into the high country."

"The painted man?"

"Painted?"

"He has tattoos on his chest and his back. A great cat, and

a hawk or eagle. A hunting bird anyway. Oh yes, and a spider on his forearm."

"You have seen these things?"

"No. One of the other girls told me. He stands naked in his room."

"Naked? In front of women?"

"He is from Outside. They act differently there, I suppose," said Charis. "He is very good looking, don't you think?"

Harad felt anger swelling inside him. "You think so?"

"Of course. I spoke to him. He is very polite. He complimented me. Why does he want to go to the high country?"

"I didn't ask him," growled Harad, wondering what the compliment might have been.

"Well, you can ask him while you travel." With that she walked away. Harad's mood darkened, and his appetite disappeared. He pictured the tall, dark-haired young man. His eyes were very blue. Maybe that was what she meant. *In a heartbeat I could lift him and snap him in two,* he thought. Then he recalled those eyes. As a fighter Harad had an instinct about the strengths and weaknesses of other men. He did not doubt he could crush the man—but it would not be done in a heartbeat.

Leaving the food untouched, he strode back to work ahead of the others, easing out his frustration with every swing of the long-handled ax.

Toward dusk Balish approached him. Harad did not like the man. There was something sly and mean about him. Yet it was Balish who controlled the work gangs and distributed the wages. Harad sighed and tried to avoid showing his contempt.

"What did the lord want?" asked Balish.

Harad told him about the trip to the high country with the nephew, the foreigner. "Hard country up there," offered Balish. "It is said there are renegade Jiamads roaming the upper passes."

"I have seen one or two," Harad told him. "They are like the bears and the big cats. They mostly avoid men."

"What is it that he wants to see?"

"Maybe the ruins," said Harad.

"I have never heard of this nephew before," said Balish. "Why is he here, do you think?"

Harad shrugged. How would he know? Balish stood around for a few more moments, making increasingly idle conversation. Then he wandered away. Harad sat down, annoyed now that he had not eaten his meal. Hungry, he walked back to where he had left his loaf and cheese. It was gone. It would be a long wait to breakfast.

He thought about the ruins. Every autumn Harad would travel to them, clambering over the old stones. There was something about the place that eased his spirit. He felt at peace there, in a way he could find peace nowhere else. Perhaps it was the solitude. Harad did not know. What he did know was that he did not relish the thought of taking a stranger there.

Four

Thirty miles to the south a small group of cavalry and infantry made their way up the steep slopes toward the pass of Cithesis. Two scouts rode ahead of the main party. One of them carried a long lance, from which fluttered an unadorned flag of simple yellow. The rider glanced nervously about him. Too many of his comrades had been killed while carrying a flag of truce for him to feel at ease.

Some distance behind him rode the herald, Unwallis. Alongside him was the swordsman, Decado, and fifteen riders of the Eternal Guard, in their armor of black and silver. Bringing up the rear were twenty Jiamads.

Unwallis was not a young man, and he loathed these missions to outlying lands and settlements. Of late he had grown ever more fond of his palace back in Diranan. There was a time when he had reveled in intrigue and politics, but he had been younger then. This latest war had sapped both his ambition and his energy. He glanced at the dark-haired young man riding beside him on a white gelding. He was everything Unwallis had once been: ambitious, ruthless, and driven by a desire to excel. Unwallis hated him for his youth and his strength. He kept that hatred well masked. Decado was not a man to endure enemies, and, more, he was the latest favorite of the Eternal. Mostly, however, Decado was at least an interesting companion. He had wit, and a sharp, dry sense of humor. Unless of course, as now, he was suffering. Unwallis glanced at the young man. His face was unnaturally pale, his dark eyes narrowed in pain. Unwallis himself had suffered severe headaches in his long life—but nothing compared to what the young swordsman went through. Last month he had collapsed in the palace, and his ears had bled. Unwallis shivered. Memnon had administered a heavy narcotic, but even this had not quelled the pain, and Decado had spent three days in a darkened room, crying out in agony.

"How much farther?" asked the young swordsman.

"We should make contact with their scouts within an hour," answered Unwallis. "Landis Khan will make us welcome."

"I do not see why we did not merely bring a regiment and take the damned place," said Decado.

"Landis Khan served the Eternal well for many lifetimes. She wishes to give him the opportunity to declare his loyalty anew."

"He is creating Jiamads. That makes him a traitor."

Unwallis sighed. "His *role* was to create Jiamads. His *expertise* is in creating Jiamads. The Eternal knows this. It was unlikely he would retire here and spend his days growing vegetables."

"So you are to ask him to renew his vow of loyalty?"

"That is one of our missions."

"Ah yes, the hunt for the long-dead hero," said Decado, with a laugh. "The One. It is a nonsense."

Unwallis gazed at the young killer. *How curious,* he thought. *You are jealous of a man who has been dead for a thousand years.* "He was an interesting figure," said Unwallis, innocently, knowing that talk of Skilgannon would irritate the swordsman. "It is said that no one could stand against him, blade to blade. Even in middle age he was deadly."

"All legends say that about heroes," snapped Decado, rubbing at his eyes.

"True. However, the Eternal herself says there was no man like him."

"As far as I can tell he killed a few primitive Jiamads and won a few battles. It doesn't make him a god, Unwallis. I don't doubt he was a good swordsman. But I could have taken him. Have you ever seen anyone as skilled as me?"

"No," admitted Unwallis. "You are exceptional, Decado. As indeed are the blades you carry," he added, glancing at the single scabbard hanging on the man's back, twin swords sheathed in it. "I would imagine there is no one in the world today who could stand against you."

"There never will be anyone to stand against me."

"Indeed, let us hope you are correct," said Unwallis. *The young,* he thought, *have such arrogance. They assume they will never suffer the ravages of age.* He glanced at Decado. *Will you still have such a belief in twenty years' time?* he wondered. *Or thirty, when your muscles are stretched and your joints rheumatic? But then again,* he thought, *the Eternal* might *not tire of you, and might offer you longer life.* She had done this with Unwallis for a few decades. Extended youth had been a wondrous gift. Sadly, it had mostly been enjoyed in retrospect. Only when that youth began to fade had he truly appreciated its wonder.

By then the Eternal had tired of him as a lover, and he became . . . what had he become? A friend? No. The Eternal had no friends. What then? Sadly he had to accept he had become merely another follower, a servant, a slave to her whims. In truth, however, there was no cause for complaint. In a world savaged by war, pestilence, and disease Unwallis had a palace and servants, and riches enough to last any man for several lifetimes. Not that he had several lifetimes. He was a ninety-year-old man in a fifty-year-old body. He looked again at Decado. *What will you do when she abandons you?* he wondered.

They rode on for some time. Then there came a shout from the lead rider.

Two Jiamads stepped from the shadows of the trees and stood waiting. Unwallis rode up to them. Both were quite primitive melds, obviously wolves. Landis Khan had clearly not acquired enough artifacts to hone the process. "I am Unwallis," he told the pair. "The Lord Landis Khan is expecting me."

"No soldiers," said the first Jiamad, the words slurring in his misshapen mouth. "You ride on. They stay."

Unwallis had expected this, but the young Decado was furious. Edging his horse forward, he reached up to one of the swords that hung between his shoulder blades. In that moment other Jiamads appeared from behind the trees. They outnumbered Unwallis's force by more than two to one. The situation was tense. Unwallis heeled his horse forward. "The soldiers will await us here," he said. "Myself and my companion will ride up to meet the Lord Landis Khan."

"This is intolerable," said Decado.

"No, my friend, it is merely inconvenient," said Unwallis. Swinging in the saddle, he called back to the captain of the Eternal Guard: "We will return tomorrow. I shall have food sent down to you."

With that he heeled his horse past the Jiamads. Decado rode silently beside him. He knew what the young man was thinking. Their own force, though outnumbered, could have defeated these primitive melds. The Jiamads of the Eternal were bigger, stronger, and more delicately honed than those of Landis Khan. Decado was a warrior. He had fought in a score of battles. He had, Unwallis believed, the simplistic nature of the fighting man. Enemies were to be slain wherever they were found. There was little understanding of intrigue, or the necessity to nurture one's enemies, either making them friends or lulling them into complacence for later annihilation. As far as Decado was concerned Landis Khan represented a small threat, and one easily crushed. This, of course, was to miss the point. The war was finely balanced. The Eternal had the advantage on this side of the ocean and, barring unforeseen disasters, would gain the final victory sometime this year. This would allow a seaborne invasion of the east next year, and a final victory perhaps the year after. An eastern invasion now, however, would leave forces on this side of the ocean thinly spread. Which was why Landis Khan had become an important factor. If the Eternal needed to use her regiments to destroy Landis and his Jiamads, it would strengthen her chances of a swift victory on this side of the ocean, but delay her invasion of the east. Such a delay might allow the enemy to regroup. The balance of power could then shift.

Landis Khan needed to be neutralized without the need of a costly invasion.

Unwallis rode on, coming at last to a stretch of open ground between two high crags. A new wall had been built here, some twelve feet high, a bronze-reinforced gate set at the center.

As the riders approached, the gate was drawn open and a horseman rode out to meet them.

"Unwallis, my dear old friend," said Landis Khan. "You are most welcome."

Skilgannon watched from his balcony window as Landis Khan rode from the palace, heading south to meet the messengers. Then, his expression grim, he left his rooms and walked down to the long library. He did not pause by the bookshelves, nor seek out any tomes. Moving through the archway into the rear of the library, he approached the locked door to Landis Khan's private study. The door was solid oak. Skilgannon paused before it, closing his eyes and gathering his strength and concentration. Leaning to his left, he hammered his right foot against the lock. Three times more he repeated the maneuver. Then he waited, drawing in deep, calming breaths. His boot crashed against the frame twice more—and the door sprang open.

Striding inside, he began to search the room. There were papers scattered upon the desk. Skilgannon scanned them, seeing references to his own history. He searched the drawer of the desk, but found nothing of importance. At the rear of the room was another door. This, too, was locked, but the timber was thinner and Skilgannon splintered the wood around the lock with a single kick.

It was dark inside, the small window shuttered. Skilgannon opened it and turned. The first thing he saw chilled his blood. It was a large picture frame, though there was no picture inside. Instead a section of human skin had been stretched over the inner frame. The skin bore a tattoo of an eagle with outspread wings. Beside it was another frame, this one facedown. Skilgannon turned it over. As he expected this also contained tattooed human skin. The identical snarling panther that even now adorned his chest. On a small desk he saw a sheaf of papers, bound with ribbon. Sitting down, he untied the ribbon and spread out the papers it held. Then he began to read, his mood darkening with each sentence.

Landis Khan was a meticulous note taker. Much of what he had written was lost on Skilgannon, but even more was easily digestible. As the light began to fade he gathered up the papers and rose from the desk. He had promised Gamal he would stay for a while. He would keep that promise. Then he would leave and make the long journey to what had once been his home. Skilgannon had no interest in silver eagles, or the Eternal, or the war that was being fought here.

He had once been a general, issuing orders, preparing strategies. He had fought for an empire. Now he was being used like the lowliest foot soldier. It galled him.

The blond-haired servant girl, Charis, brought him some food as he sat on the balcony reading Landis Khan's notes. She hovered close by even after he had thanked her. He glanced up, his expression stern. "You want something, child?" he asked.

"You are going into the mountains tomorrow," she said.

He sighed and shook his head. "Is that a question or a statement?"

"A statement."

"Why would you make it? I *know* where I am going tomorrow."

"Are you always so argumentative?" she asked.

He laughed aloud, feeling some of the tension leave him. "What kind of training have you received as a servant?" he countered.

She smiled and walked past him to stand in the sunshine bathing the balcony. "How much training does one need to bring a tray to a guest's room? It is a pretty view. I can see my father's bakery from here."

"Shall we return to your interest in my journeyings?"

"Oh, I am not interested in where you go. It is just that you will be traveling with Harad. He is not as fierce as he appears. Best to remember that. He is, in fact, quite shy."

"Not the first adjective that would spring to mind," he said. *"Surly,* perhaps. *Discourteous. Cool.* But, yes, *shy* would account for them. Why does it concern you?"

"Harad is my . . . friend. I wouldn't want him to get into trouble with the lord. Is it true you are his nephew?"

"Is that so surprising?"

"No," she said, moving back past him. "There are many rumors about you. Some say you are a new form of Jiamad."

"And what animal do they say I am melded with?"

"Perhaps it is a panther," she suggested. "You have a certain catlike grace."

"You should go now," he said. "I have much to do, and, fascinating as this conversation is, it does not seem to be going anywhere."

"Be a little gentle with Harad," she said. "He is a fine man."

"I shall bear it in mind. However, I know Harad better than you think. Be at ease, Charis. We will walk the mountains and then return."

When she had gone Skilgannon picked up the papers and began reading once more. Toward dusk Landis Khan entered the room. He did not knock, and his face was flushed and angry.

"Is this how you repay me?" he thundered. "Breaking open my study and stealing my papers?"

Skilgannon rose smoothly. "Do not bluster," he said softly. "You are not a man of violence. Do not pretend to be one. And I have nothing to repay you for. Did I ask for you to hunt my bones and collect my skin? Did I request you to copy my tattoos? We will begin anew, Landis Khan. No more evasions. No more games. Why did you take the bones from my locket?"

Landis Khan's shoulders sagged. "You mind if I sit down?" he asked.

"Not at all."

The lord slumped into a chair. "Back in Diranan I had access to a great many of the artifacts of the elders. I had learned how to use them, to create exceptional Jiamads, and to . . . to ensure the success of any rebirth. Here I have few. You were too important to risk. So before I attempted to bring you back I took the bones from your locket, and Harad was the eventual result. Was he your brother, your father . . . something else?"

"He was my friend, Landis. He was a great man."

Landis Khan brightened. "Another hero from the past? Who? Who was he?"

"To use your own words, Landis, let us take matters carefully. Trust me. When the time is right I might tell you. Why is it that his memories never returned?"

"There was no way we could bring his soul back from the Void. We did not know who he was. If you tell us, perhaps we can restore him to the man you knew."

"No. My friend does not wander the Void. He passed beyond it. His deeds would have ensured him a place in the Hall of Heroes, or paradise . . . or whatever exists beyond the gateway." He smiled ruefully. "And even if you could find his spirit he would not return. He would ask: *What will become of Harad?* No, Landis, he will not return, though it would lift my heart immeasurably were it to happen. I liked him better than any man I ever met."

"You are sure? Gamal could search for him."

"I am sure. Why do you want me to travel the mountains with him?"

"It was Gamal's idea. He felt you needed time away, to consider your actions. He thought also—as do I—that the company of someone familiar to you would help you link more strongly to the memories of your previous existence."

"He was right about one thing," said Skilgannon coldly. "It will be good to be away from here for a while. Did your guests arrive?"

"Aye, you will see them at dinner this evening. There are two, Unwallis and Decado. The first is an adviser to the Eternal. He is sharp and observant, with a brain that is cunning and subtle. Not an easy man to read, and a difficult one to fool. I did have a nephew called Callan. He ran a farm near Usa, in the lands you would have known as Ventria. He died last year. His ship was lost in a storm. Should he ask you about this you can say you survived by clinging to a piece of driftwood. Whatever you choose. Best, though, to say little."

"And Decado?"

Landis took a deep breath. "No more evasion, you said. So be it. Decado is a failed Reborn, like Harad. The Eternal had his bones brought back from a tomb on an old battle site. The original Decado was the leader of a group of warrior priests called the Temple of the Thirty. He was known, in his day, as the Ice Killer, a ferocious and deadly swordsman—possibly the greatest of his time."

"I sense there is more," said Skilgannon.

"Indeed there is." He sighed. "I had a long conversation with Gamal this morning. He knows far more about you than I realized. For reasons best known to himself he did not share this knowledge with me until now." He glanced up at Skilgannon. "According to Gamal the original Decado was your direct descendant."

"More myths, Landis. I had no children."

"Gamal told me that a woman called Garianne bore you a son. He was born in the temple of the Blessed Priestess eight months after your battle with a villain. I don't recall his name."

"It was Boranius."

"Yes, I remember now. Anyway, your bloodline was strong and true—a line of warriors. On the instruction of the Priestess, Garianne continued the tradition of your House, Skilgannon. The first male child was called Decado, and his

first son was Olek, then Decado, and so on. Gamal knew only
the outline of the story. History tells us nothing of Garianne
and her life, her thoughts or her dreams. However, back to
the present. The Reborn Decado is also a swordsman, and
one of great repute. He carries two blades in a single scabbard—like your Swords of Night and Day. He has killed
twenty men in single combat, or duels. Like his namesake he
is deadly. He is also—according to Gamal—existing on the
borders of insanity."

The shock was intense, but Skilgannon disguised it and
forced his mind to focus. "Why is he here?"

"To study our defenses, I should imagine. He is a skilled
strategist."

"And Unwallis? What does he require?"

"He will seek to persuade me to renew my oath of allegiance to the Eternal. This will be a difficult request to deal
with. To the north of us is one of two armies of the Rebellion; to the south, the forces of the Eternal. If I swear allegiance to her, then the rebels will seek to kill me or conquer
my lands. If I refuse then the Eternal will send an army to re-
occupy Petar."

"The choices you face are not enviable," said Skilgannon.
"What will you do?"

"I shall play it like a maiden being wooed. I will hedge and
I will prevaricate, and do my best to keep both suitors at
arm's length. And now it is time to prepare for dinner. Do
you wish to sit beside the politician or the madman?"

"The madman. I do not like politicians."

The rooms assigned to Unwallis were in the southern wing
of the palace, but there was a balcony terrace that overlooked
the western mountains. An hour before the meal he stood
upon it, watching the sun set behind the snowcapped peaks.
It was his favorite time of the day, and he liked to spend it
alone.

He found himself missing his garden back in Diranan.
During the last few years Unwallis had discovered great joy

in tending his flower beds. The cycle of life, death, and re-birth in his garden fascinated him. Below, upon the western wall of the palace gardens he saw a climbing plant, with huge blooms of lilac and gold, clinging to a trellis. It was called Ustarte's Star, and Unwallis had never had any success with it in his own garden. He would plant it in good earth. It would grow voraciously for half a season, then inexplicably die back. The topmost leaves would turn black, and then nothing would save it. Unwallis found it most galling, and decided he would ask Landis Khan for advice over dinner.

Unwallis sighed. *What a strange world we live in,* he thought. *I am to dine with a man I shall—in all likelihood—order to be murdered. Before that, however, I will ask his help with a gardening problem.*

The thought weighed heavily upon him. He had always—despite his best efforts—liked Landis Khan. The man was a legend in Diranan when Unwallis was a student, an enduring part of modern history. He had served the Eternal for centuries. Indeed, no one knew how old he was, nor how many lives the Eternal had granted him. His powers were enormous, and yet, despite them, he was easygoing and cordial with the young men who came to serve. He had been most helpful to Unwallis in those early years. Seeing him with gray hair and the lines of age upon his face had seemed almost unnatural. Unwallis sighed and found himself hoping that Landis would agree to the Eternal's demands.

Will it matter if he does?

The thought was immediately chilling, and Unwallis tried to push it from his mind. The Eternal had told him to convey her wishes to Landis, but had then told him he would be accompanied by Decado. This had surprised him. Why send a deranged killer on a mission of diplomacy?

The sun was going down. Unwallis heard the door of the apartment open and turned to see a young woman bearing a lantern and a taper. She curtseyed to him and moved around the apartment, lighting lanterns.

Unwallis poured himself a goblet of wine, adding water to it. He did not want his senses impaired during the coming meal. There would be only four people present, he and Decado, plus Landis Khan and his nephew, Callan. Unwallis wondered why Gamal would not be joining them. His understanding was that the old man was now living with Landis.

The girl curtseyed again and left the room.

It would be an uncomfortable meal. Decado, when in pain, was not an easy man to spend time with. His manner became harsh and confrontational, his conversation limited to weapons and warfare. Unwallis found himself wondering what the Eternal saw in him as a lover. He recalled his time with her, and found once more the ache of regret filling him. It was not merely the joining of bodies, the passion and the extremes of pleasure, that haunted him. More it was the quiet times afterward as they lay upon the satin sheets and talked. Those moments lay in his memory like hidden treasures. He had been in love. Massively, completely, irrevocably in love. Then she had discarded him. He had felt like a man deprived of food and water, his soul starved. She had sent him across the sea, to serve her in the eastern empire. He had labored long and diligently there, hoping that one day she would call him back again to that satin-covered bed. She never had.

Unwallis imagined the Eternal lying in the moonlight and talking and laughing with Decado. Free of pain he was a witty man, and he was young and handsome. The Eternal's lovers were always young and handsome. It always surprised Unwallis when he thought of her laughing. The sound was rich and almost musical. It was a sound of joy that lifted the spirits of all who heard it. He found it hard to equate this wondrous woman with the ruthless queen who could casually order the deaths of thousands. Unwallis was forced to admit that he did not understand the Eternal at all. She could be harsh beyond reason, and cruel beyond measure. She could also display great affection and loyalty.

A sense of melancholy settled on him, so great that his spirits were raised when Decado appeared in the doorway.

The young swordsman's long dark hair was pulled back from his head into a ponytail, and he was wearing a tight-fitting black shirt and leggings with calf-length riding boots of black leather. The only adornment he sported was a wide belt edged with silver.

"Let's get this over with," said Decado.

"How is your headache?"

"Bearable."

Unwallis looked into his eyes. The pupils were distended, and the statesman knew he had imbibed more of Memnon's narcotic to relieve his pain. Donning a cloak of cream-colored wool edged with silver, Unwallis walked out of the room.

A servant was waiting at the far end of the corridor. She led them up a flight of stairs and into a long room, lit by glowing lanterns. A table had been set near a huge window overlooking the mountains. Landis Khan was standing by the window, talking to a tall young man. Both men turned as the guests arrived.

"Welcome once again, dear Unwallis. And to you also, Decado. It is good to have guests from Outside. I fear we are so cut off here that I long for news from the city." Unwallis looked at the young man with Landis. His eyes were an astonishing blue. "My nephew, Callan," said Landis. "He is visiting from Usa."

"A troubled land," said Unwallis, shaking the man's hand. "You are a soldier?"

"A farmer," said Landis, swiftly.

"You have the look of a soldier," said Unwallis.

"Looks can be deceiving," put in Decado. "He looks to me like a farmer."

Callan laughed aloud, the sound full of genuine good humor, which was a relief to Unwallis, but seemed to irritate Decado further. "What is so amusing?" asked the young swordsman.

"The choice of words. If *looks* can be deceiving and yet I *look* like a farmer, does this suggest I am—or am not—a farmer?" Before Decado could consider a response the young man pointed to the black scabbard hanging from Decado's back. "Is it the custom here to come armed for dinner?" he asked.

"They are always with me," said Decado, staring hard at the man.

"Well, put your fears to rest. There are no enemies here."

"Fears? I have no fears."

"Might I see one of the swords?" inquired the man. Unwallis saw Decado hesitate. There was sweat on his face, and the statesman guessed the exchange was increasing the intensity of his head pain. Unwallis thought he would refuse the request. Instead he pressed a jeweled stud on the hilt of the lower sword and drew it, passing it to Callan. Landis Khan's nephew hefted the blade, then stepped back and swung it expertly several times. Then he flicked his wrist and released his grip on the hilt. As the weapon rose from his hand he slapped the hilt. The sword spun viciously, the razor-sharp blade slicing through the air. Unwallis flinched. Callan's left hand snapped forward, smoothly grasping the ivory hilt. Unwallis could scarcely believe what he had seen. One tiny mistake and the blade would have slashed through his fingers, or his wrist, or ricocheted across the room, spearing through one of the watching men. "Beautiful balance," said Callan, reversing the blade and offering it to Decado.

"Where did you learn that?" asked Unwallis. "It was incredible."

"We farmers learn a lot of things," said Callan. He glanced at Decado. "You do not look well, boy."

Decado tensed. "Call me *boy* one more time, you whoreson, and I'll show you how a sword *should* be used."

"This has gone quite far enough," said Unwallis, trying to sound stern. "We are guests here, Decado. And you, sir," he said, addressing Callan, "should not seek to provoke a soldier of the Eternal."

"I accept your rebuke, sir," said Callan, with an easy smile. "I, too, am a guest in this house and should have known better." He bowed gracefully, then turned to Landis Khan. "Perhaps we should eat, Uncle."

The meal was conducted in near silence. Unwallis was relieved once it was over and Decado rose, offered cursory thanks to Landis Khan, and stalked from the room.

"Believe me, sir, that was very unwise of you," Unwallis told Callan. "Decado is a deadly swordsman, and not a man to forgive an insult. I suggest you return across the sea as soon as is convenient to you."

"I intend to. It is my hope to explore the old kingdom of Naashan."

"You are a historian?"

"Of a kind."

"Naashan, eh? One of your favorite places of excavation, Landis, was it not?"

"Yes indeed," said Landis Khan. "A great many artifacts were discovered there. And now, I think, it is time for you and I to sit down and talk." Turning to Callan, he said: "I fear our conversation would bore you, nephew."

"Then I shall leave you," said Callan, rising from the table. Bowing once more to Unwallis, he left the room.

"By the Blessed!" whispered Unwallis. "Does the man have a death wish? Or has Decado's reputation not reached the east?"

"He knows his reputation, my friend. Callan is not a man who scares easily."

"He has an odd accent. I have traveled in Naashan and never heard one quite like it."

"East coast," said Landis with a smile. "I had immense trouble understanding any of them."

Unwallis sighed. "I shall try to keep Decado from killing him. Though I cannot guarantee it. The man is somewhat inhuman when he is sick. If his head pain clears he may be in a more forgiving mood."

"Why is he with you?" asked Landis as he filled two goblets with wine.

"I have asked myself the same question. Perhaps the Eternal is tiring of him and wanted him away from Diranan. I really don't know. But let us talk of you, Landis. You know the peril you are in."

"I know. Old habits die hard, my friend. I found some artifacts and could not resist experimenting with them. As you could see my Jiamads are not of the highest quality."

"You told the Eternal you wanted a quiet life away from the turmoil of the empire. She granted you these lands."

"Does she now want them back?"

"Of course not. The Eternal merely wants right of passage through them, so that our armies can clear the north of traitors."

"Come now," said Landis, "you know that the fastest way to the north is across the plain and through the ruins. You already have an army camped below the southern pass. To send a force this way would take an extra month, and for what? So speak plainly, Unwallis. What does the Eternal really want from me?"

"You do not need me to scribble it on a tablet of clay. You were the most senior of her advisers, and the longest serving. Even I do not know how long you were in her service. But longer than Agrias. And whom are we fighting? The same Agrias who swore to serve her for life. Agrias who has caused us untold harm. More than a hundred thousand dead in battle, and five times that starved or fallen to disease."

"You are saying she fears I will become another Agrias?" Landis laughed. "Nothing could be farther from the truth. I want no power, other than that which I wield here."

"Do you still love her, Landis?"

"*You* of all people should not have to ask this. Of course I love her. She was my life, and my dream. She was everything to me, from the moment I first saw her statue." Landis sighed. "I shared her bed for many years." He shrugged. "Aye, and I was also forced to share her with whatever lover she took a liking to. None of that mattered. I would give a hundred years of life merely to share that bed one more night."

"As would I—though I do not have a hundred years to spare," said Unwallis. "You did warn her about Agrias. I remember that."

"You remember what else I told you?"

"I remember. I am still not convinced. But that is in the past and not relevant. The Eternal wishes to be sure of your loyalty. She wants a small force in your lands to protect the borders. Would that be so terrible, Landis? A few soldiers, a few Jiamads?"

Landis filled a goblet with wine and sipped it before answering. "Yes, it would. Agrias has several armies in the north. If the Eternal's forces come here, Agrias will hear of it. Then the war will spread to my lands, which, at present, are mercifully free of terror."

Unwallis took a deep breath. "Then let us move on to another point, and one of great delicacy. The tomb of Skilgannon."

"What about it? It was empty."

"Not the cave, Landis, but the site half a mile distant on the dry island."

"It wasn't him. I dug there and found some old bones, but the artifacts in the grave were of the wrong age."

"One of your diggers reported that you found two swords in a single scabbard."

"Not so. We found a massive ax, double headed, which had not rusted, and a few pots containing gold coins. The coins were of the late Drenai period, stamped with the image of King Skanda. I still have some of them, should you wish to see them."

"Why do you have ward spells over your domain, Landis?" The question was asked softly, and Unwallis watched his old friend closely. Landis did not look him in the eye.

"I do not like being watched. I am a private man and it irked me to have Memnon spying on me. I never liked the man. I live in the hope that the Eternal will realize he is a snake and place his head upon a spike."

"Yes, yes," said Unwallis. "No one likes Memnon. But let

us run over the facts. Like Agrias you are creating Jiamads. You refuse the Eternal the right to cross your lands. You have cast ward spells to prevent the Eternal from seeing what you are doing here. Does this accurately cover what we have discussed?"

"It does not sound good, does it?" said Landis, forcing a smile.

"No, Landis. It does not sound good at all. I am your friend. I would like to help you. If I leave here, however, with no agreement, I fear for you."

"She knows I would never . . . harm her." Landis was frightened now. Unwallis could hear it in his voice.

"I cannot say what the Eternal *knows,* Landis. I only know what she *does* to those she believes are a threat. You think your long relationship with her will keep you alive? You are deluding yourself. Memnon has sent Shadows to the southern pass you spoke of. It could be they are heading north to eliminate some rebel general. Equally they could be coming over the mountains to find you."

"She would not kill me, my friend. I gave her life. You wondered how long I served her. I was here before the Eternal, Unwallis. She was the first Reborn. I brought her back. She will not kill me. Go back and tell her that I am not her enemy. Tell her you are convinced of this. She will believe you. Tell her I need a little more time to consider her offer."

Unwallis felt his heart sink. "Do you not know her at all, Landis? Have you not seen how many men she has killed? Many of those loved her in their own way. I am telling you that your life is in danger."

"A little more time, Unwallis. Just ask that from me. You will see. She will grant it. Now, would you like to see those Skandian coins? They are remarkable."

It was late but Skilgannon was not sleeping. Standing on the balcony, he breathed in the sweet night air and gazed at the distant mountains, bathed in moonlight. Garianne had been pregnant, and he had never known. This was hard to bear. He had never loved the tormented warrior woman, but he had come to care for her. Why had she not told him? Why had Ustarte not told him? Did a man not have the right to know that he had a son?

My son died a thousand years ago.

The thought was painful.

Decado's face flickered into his mind. *Did my son look like you?* he wondered. He had hoped to like Decado, to find something in the man that reminded him of himself. There was nothing, and within moments he had found himself detesting the arrogant young swordsman. In turn the man had obviously detested him. *Ah well,* he thought with a smile, *perhaps we are not so different then.*

He heard the apartment door open and turned. The elderly head servant, Ensinar, entered the room. Seeing Skilgannon, he bowed. The swept-over hair on his bald head flapped as he did so. "The lord asked me to see if you were awake, sir," said Ensinar. "He hopes you will join him in the library."

Skilgannon nodded and followed the man through the night-deserted palace down to Landis Khan's study. In the lantern light Landis Khan seemed drawn and pale. As Ensinar departed, Landis bade Skilgannon to sit down. "It did not go well," he said with a sigh.

"I am sorry that I baited your guest," said Skilgannon. "It was discourteous."

Landis Khan waved his hand. "That is not what I meant. I have been very foolish. Unwallis is a sharp and intelligent man. In my arrogance I thought to deceive him, and the Eternal. I have not succeeded. I think there is still time. Yes, yes I am sure there is."

"You wanted to see me," pressed Skilgannon.

"Yes. Forgive me. Too many thoughts buzzing in my brain like hungry bees." Landis rose and moved to the far wall, easing back a panel there. From within it he hauled out a black-handled, double-headed ax. It was heavy, and he struggled to lift it. "You know this weapon?"

"Yes," said Skilgannon, rising and taking it from Landis's hands. "It is Snaga, the ax of Druss the Legend."

"The Blades of No Return," said Landis. "That is what the runes say, that are engraved upon the handle. It would take a mighty man to wield this in battle."

"He was a mighty man. I take it this was in my tomb."

"Yes. How did you come by it?"

"It was a gift from a great warlord. His men had slain Druss at the Battle of Dros Delnoch. I went to him and asked for the ax."

"And some bones, which you placed in the locket around your neck."

"Indeed so. Does Harad know he is a Reborn?"

"No. But now that we know who he was I could ask Gamal to seek his soul in the Void."

"As I have already told you, he would not find him," said Skilgannon. "Druss was a fine man. A hero. He would not be wandering that accursed place. He would have passed beyond it. You have meddled enough, Landis. Let it be."

Landis slumped back to his chair. "There is more truth in that than you know. When you go to Harad tomorrow, will you take him the ax as a gift from me?"

Skilgannon smiled. "Since it was in *my* tomb I would say it should be a gift from *me*. But yes, I will give it to Harad. I think Druss would like that. I will walk the mountains with Harad, Landis. Then I will leave this land. I have no interest in your struggles with the Eternal."

"I understand. Truly, I do. For all my age and wisdom I have been such a fool, Skilgannon. Ustarte was not a goddess, nor even blessed by the Source. She was a talented Jiamad, created by someone probably just like me." He gave a grim laugh and shook his head. "I thought bringing you back would balance the scales in my favor. I thought that if I fulfilled Ustarte's prophecy the Source would forgive me."

"What is there to forgive?" asked Skilgannon.

"The world's torment, my boy." Landis Khan sighed. *"I brought the Eternal to life. I discovered how to manipulate* the machines that create the Jiamads. All the unnatural horror on the face of this blessed earth is down to *me.* "

"There were Joinings on this world before you were born, Landis. Nadir shamans could create them. You take too much upon yourself."

"A few, perhaps. Enough to give rise to legends of monsters. Not armies of them, Skilgannon. Gamal told me of Perapolis, and the few thousand whose souls weigh heavily upon your own. I have hundreds of thousands upon mine. For your sins you walked the Void for a millennium. What of me? I will never pass the gateway you spoke of. And I will not be able to fight the demons there."

"Probably not," agreed the warrior. "What will you do now?"

Landis sighed once more. "I shall run. I shall seek a place to live out my days. Will you grant me one last request?"

"I don't know. Ask and you will find out."

"Take the Swords of Night and Day with you. Bury them if you like. Cast them into the sea. I care not. I would not want them to fall into the wrong hands if . . . if matters go awry. Will you do this one deed for me?"

Skilgannon sat silently for a moment. "Wrap them in cloth, and have them brought to my rooms tomorrow before I leave."

They had walked for more than four hours. There was little conversation, which pleased Harad. The man, Callan, was strong and uncomplaining. By midafternoon it had begun to rain. At first Harad ignored it, but it grew steadily worse, the ground underfoot becoming slick and treacherous. He glanced up. Thunderclouds were gathering, and a bolt of lightning flared to the west. Harad angled their path toward a cliff face close by. It was pitted with shallow caves, and the powerful logger chose one and moved inside, dumping his pack to the ground. Callan also shrugged off his pack and removed his ankle-length, dark leather topcoat. He stood for a moment, lifting his arms and easing the muscles of his shoulders. Below it he wore a sleeveless doeskin jerkin. Though he was slim, his arms and shoulders were powerful. Harad saw the dark tattoo of a spider upon one forearm. Harad glanced at the man's pack. Strapped to it were two items wrapped in dark cloth. One was around five feet long and slightly curved. The other piqued his interest more. Wide at one end and narrow at the other, its shape reminded Harad of the stringed instruments musicians played on feast days. Yet it was too flat.

They sat in silence for a while, then Callan donned his topcoat and walked out once more into the rain, returning with a bundle of deadwood. He repeated this maneuver several times until there was at least enough fuel to last the night. Then, removing his coat and draping it over a rock, he quietly prepared a fire. With the wood damp it took some time to get a blaze going, but Callan showed no irritation. Finally, with the flames catching, he leaned back against the cave wall. Harad opened his own pack and produced some dried meat, which he offered to Callan. Still nothing was said.

Lightning flashed, immediately followed by a rolling burst of thunder. The rain outside became torrential, lashing down against the cliff face. Harad, who had been hoping the man was not a chatterer, now found himself uncomfortable with the continued silence. "Might as well wait out the storm," he said. He felt like slapping himself in the head. Of course they would wait out the storm. Why else were they inside the cave with a fire lit?

"It is a good idea," said Callan. "I am more tired than I expected."

"Aye, it is a long climb for those unused to it," agreed Harad. Callan rolled smoothly to his feet and untied the thongs holding the oddly shaped item. Squatting down again, he removed the cloth. Harad watched with undisguised interest. As the cloth fell clear, the firelight gleamed on a double-bladed ax with a black, silver-engraved haft. Harad had never seen a more beautiful weapon. The blades were shaped like the wings of a butterfly. He shivered suddenly, and felt gooseflesh on his arms.

Callan hefted the weapon and passed it to Harad. It was heavy, and yet the balance was perfect. Harad let out a long breath as he grasped the ax.

"It is a gift from Landis Khan," said Callan.

"He must value you highly to give you such a gift."

Callan smiled. "The gift is for *you,* Harad."

The Outsider returned to the fire, adding two thick chunks of wood.

"Why would he give me such a gift?"

Callan shrugged. "Ask him when we get back. The ax has a name. It is called Snaga. The runes upon it say: *The Blades of No Return.* It is an ancient weapon. Once it was carried by a great hero."

Harad stood and moved back into the cave. Hefting the ax, he swung it lightly a few times. "He must have been a powerful man to wield this in battle," said Harad. "It is not light."

Callan did not reply. He sat quietly in the firelight eating the dried meat.

Outside, the rain pounded on. Thunder rolled and lightning flashed. A shape loomed at the cave entrance. It was a black bear. It stood for a few moments, then caught a whiff of the smoke and padded away.

"Lots of bears up here," said Harad. "A few big cats, too. Where are you from?" he asked. "I have not heard that accent before." Returning to the fire and sitting down, he laid the ax beside him but could not resist continuing to touch it.

"A long way from here," said Callan. Harad thought he detected a note of bitterness in the answer, and did not press him. After a while it became obvious that the storm was locked in for the night. Both men unrolled their blankets. Callan fell asleep almost instantly, but Harad sat up, holding the ax and staring at his reflection in the butterfly blades. Just for a moment he felt as if he were looking at someone else, and he shivered and put the ax down. A feeling of disquiet touched him. He looked over at the sleeping Outsider. He had to admit the man was easy company. Callan did not question Harad or seek to impress him. Perhaps these few days in the mountain would not be so arduous.

Harad stood and, ax in hand, wandered to the mouth of the cave.

Snaga.

It was a good name. The Blades of No Return. He found himself wondering about the hero who had carried it. Where was he from? Where had he fought?

In that moment the bear returned, ambling through the rain. Harad stood very still. The bear came closer, staring at the powerful figure in the cave mouth. Suddenly he reared up on his hind legs, towering above the man.

"Let's not do this," said Harad softly. "We are not enemies, you and I."

For a moment more the bear continued to loom above him. Then he dropped back to all fours and moved off into the trees.

"You have a way with bears," said Callan. Harad glanced around. The tall, blue-eyed Outsider was standing behind him, a hunting knife in his hand. Harad had not heard him approach.

"I have seen him before. He once got into my cabin and ate three months' of supplies. My own fault for leaving the door open." Harad glanced down at the knife and grinned. "Good blade, but you'd need a lot of luck to kill him with that."

"I am a lucky man," answered Callan, sheathing the knife and walking back to his blankets.

The storm lasted for most of the night, but the dawn was bright and clear, the sky cloudless

They walked without ~~conversation~~ for most of the morning, though this time ~~distance~~ Harad caught sight of several and pleasant ~~and~~ a small herd of deer. They were grazing gray, ~~the~~ ruins in an area of flatland. "Who used to live ~~here?~~" asked Callan. "In the old days."

Harad shrugged. "I don't know much history. They were

called Sathular—or something like it. They were wiped out way, way back."

"Sathuli," said Callan. "I have heard of them. Fierce tribal warriors. They were constantly at war with the Drenai."

"Whatever," muttered Harad, embarrassed by his lack of knowledge. "Good land. Few people. There's a small settlement to the north. No others. A man can walk here for weeks and never see anyone. I like that."

They moved on, crossing a small valley before climbing again. "Still tired?" asked Harad as dusk approached.

Callan smiled. "Less so since I gave you that ax. A heavy piece."

Harad hefted it. "It is a beauty. I feel as if I have carried it all my life."

They camped that night in a small hollow. The wind had picked up. It was cold with snow from the mountain peaks. Callan lit a fire against a boulder, seeking to gain some added warmth from reflected heat. But the wind whipped through the hollow, scattering sparks. Eventually the fire went out, and both men sat wrapped in their cloaks.

"Do you know anything about the hero who carried Snaga?" asked Harad.

"Yes. His name was Druss. He was known as Druss the Legend. A Drenai hero."

"What was he like?"

Callan's bright blue eyes suddenly met his own pale gaze. Harad sensed a moment of tension. Then it passed. "He was mighty. He lived by a code of honor."

"What does that mean?"

Callan shrugged. "A set of standards, rules, if you like. You want to hear it?"

"Yes."

Callan took a deep breath. "Never vio... harm a child. Do not lie, cheat, or steal. These woman, nor lesser men. Protect the weak against the evil stro.. e for never allow thoughts of gain to lead you into the pursui.. evil. That was the iron code of Druss the Legend."

"I like that," said Harad. "Say it again." Callan did so. Harad sat silently, thinking it through. Then he spoke the code himself. "Did I get it right?" he asked.

"Aye, you did. You mean to follow it?"

Harad nodded. "If I carry his ax, I think I should carry also the code that went with it."

"He would have liked that," said Callan. "Where are we heading tomorrow?"

"The ruins. I go there sometimes. I thought perhaps you would like to see them."

Five

They left the cave soon after dawn and climbed a series of steep, rock-strewn rises for more than two hours. Topping a crest, Harad paused. Skilgannon moved alongside him. His breath caught in his throat. From this high point he could see the land stretching out over the steppes to the north, and the wide plains to the south. Far below was a huge and derelict fortress, with six walls and a once mighty keep, now shattered and partly collapsed. The walls stretched across the pass, blocking the way north. Skilgannon shivered. For the first time since he had awoken in this new body he knew *exactly* where he was. The weight of a thousand years bore down on him. When he had last seen this fortress it had been mighty, and impregnable, towering and majestic. Yet now it was broken, ruined by time and the power of nature. It was a vivid reminder of how greatly the world had changed, and made him even more like a man out of his time.

He glanced at Harad. This man was the image of a younger Druss, and yet he knew nothing of the struggle for survival that once took place on these now shattered ramparts.

"Magnificent, isn't it?" said Harad. "It's called the Ghost Fortress."

"Once it had another name," said Skilgannon softly. Shrugging off his pack, he sat down and stared at the ruin. Sometime in the last hundred years there had been an earthquake here. The first wall was fractured and half covered by an avalanche. The keep had split and crumbled.

"What name?" asked Harad, sitting alongside him.

"Dros Delnoch. It was said it would never fall while men with courage stood upon its walls."

"It did fall, though," said Harad. "I don't know much history, but I do know it was conquered by a warrior chief named Tenaka Khan. The Nadir swarmed over it. Conquered the old lands."

"I never heard of him," said Skilgannon. "The last battle I know of was fought by Druss the Legend and the earl of Bronze. Druss died here. And the fortress held. Ten thousand men against an army fifty times greater."

Skilgannon drew in a deep breath, remembering the day he had ridden into the Nadir camp.

Two hundred thousand warriors were besieging the Dros. But on this night there was no assault. A great funeral pyre had been prepared, and the body upon it was that of Druss the Legend. He had fallen that day, battling impossible odds. The Nadir, who knew him as Deathwalker, both feared and revered him. They had carried his corpse from the battleground and were preparing to honor him.

Skilgannon had dismounted close to the tent of Ulric, Lord of Wolves. The royal guards had recognized him and led him into the presence of the khan. "Why are you here, my friend?" asked the violet-eyed man. "I know it is not to fight in my cause."

"I came for the reward you promised me, Great Khan."

"This is a battlefield, Skilgannon. My riches are not here."

"I do not require riches."

"I owe you my life. You may ask of me anything I have and I will grant it."

"Druss was dear to me, Ulric. We were friends. I require only a keepsake, a lock of his hair, and a small sliver of bone. I would ask also for his ax."

The Great Khan stood silently for a moment. "He was dear to me also. What will you do with the hair and bone?"

"I will place them in a locket, my lord, and carry it around my neck."

"Then it shall be done," said Ulric.

"You are lost in thought," said Harad, "and you are looking sad."

"It is a sad sight," said Skilgannon.

The earthquake and the subsequent avalanche meant that it was now possible to access the fortress from the mountains, rather than through the high keep above the Sentran Plain to the south. The descent was still perilous, but Harad and Skilgannon slowly made their way down until they were standing on the ramparts of Wall One. Two of the towers that were set every fifty paces had been smashed by the avalanche. The others still stood. Skilgannon walked to the crenellated rampart wall and stared down. Sixty feet high, and four hundred paces wide, it had been the first line of defense. Harad strolled along it, ax in hand. Skilgannon watched him. Druss would have been sixty years old when he last stood on this wall. Now—in a way—he was here again. Once more Skilgannon shivered.

"You want to go farther up?" asked Harad. Skilgannon nodded. The two men walked down the rampart steps and crossed the open ground between the first two walls. The second wall had ruptured during the earthquake, and they climbed the crack that had opened between them.

Beyond Wall Two the gate tunnels had been cleared, and Harad and Skilgannon made their way up to the ruined keep. Here Harad prepared a fire close to an old well, and the two men sat quietly. Harad produced a pot from his pack and walked to the well. Lowering a bucket to the water below, he hauled it back, drank deeply, then half filled the pot. "Brought the bucket and rope here last year," he said. "The water is cold and sweet to the taste. Makes for a good stew."

He glanced at Skilgannon. "I thought you would enjoy seeing this," he said, "but I think I was wrong."

"You were not wrong. I am glad we came. How often do you come here?"

"As often as I can," said Harad. "I feel—" He gave an embarrassed smile. "—I feel at peace here."

"A sense of belonging, perhaps."

"Yes. That's it exactly."

"Do you have a favorite place here?"

"Yes."

"Is it at the gate of Wall Four?"

Harad gave a start, and instinctively made the sign of the Protective Horn. "Are you a wizard or some such?"

"No," said Skilgannon. "I saw the ashes of old campfires at the gate as we passed."

"Ah!" Harad seemed satisfied and relaxed.

"Can you read the inscriptions above each gate?" asked Skilgannon.

"No. I have often wondered what they meant. Just names, I suppose."

"More than that, Harad. Wall One was called *Eldibar*. It was from an ancient tongue. It means 'Exultation.' It is where the enemy is first fought and turned back. The defenders are exultant. They believe they can win. Wall Two was called *Musif*. This means 'Despair.' For the defenders of Wall Two have seen Eldibar fall, and that is the widest, strongest wall. If that can fall, then perhaps they are doomed. Wall Three was *Kania*. 'Renewed Hope.' Two walls have fallen, but the men on Wall Three are still alive, and there are still walls to retreat to. Wall Four is *Sumitos*. 'Desperation.' The three strongest walls have fallen, and it is now a desperate struggle for survival. Wall Five is 'Serenity.' The defenders have fought hard and well. The best of them have survived this far. They know death is coming, but they are brave and determined. They will not run. They will face the end with courage." He fell silent.

"And Wall Six?" asked Harad.

"Geddon. Wall Six is *Geddon.* 'Death.'"

"Where did Druss the Legend fall?"

"At the gate of Wall Four."

"How is it you know all this, but you don't know about when the fortress fell?"

"My memory is not what it was."

They fell silent, and Harad prepared a broth of barley and dried meat. After they had eaten Harad wandered off into the ruins, and Skilgannon sat alone, lost in thought and ancient memory.

The stars were bright above the ancient fortress, the night calm and windless. Harad had built the fire from a small stock of wood piled against the keep wall. It was gone now, and the flames were slowly dying away. Skilgannon stood and wandered around the area, seeking any source of fuel. There was nothing, just stony ground, scattered rocks, and a few tiny bushes. He felt a sense of unease, though he could find no reason for it.

Moving away from their camp, he walked up to the ramparts of Wall Six. From here he could just see a twinkling campfire. Harad had other stores of wood down at Wall Four, yet he obviously wanted to be alone. Skilgannon decided to return to his own blankets. Just then a sudden breeze whispered across him.

Where are you, laddie?

Skilgannon froze—then spun around. There was no one close. His heart began to beat wildly. "Druss, is that you?"

Come down to my fire, whispered a voice in his mind.

Skilgannon knew that voice, and it was as if a cool, welcome breeze had arrived on a hot summer's day. Swiftly he set off through the darkened tunnel and down to the gate of Wall Four. As he emerged on the open ground before it, he paused. The campfire was burning brightly. Close by, Harad was swinging the ax in a series of overhand sweeps and sideways cuts. But it was not Harad. Skilgannon had watched the young logger earlier practicing with the weapon. His movements had been clumsy and untrained. This man was a master.

Skilgannon did not move. Moonlight glistened on the flashing ax blade. Memories flowed through the swordsman's mind: the attack on the citadel, the rescue of the child, Elanin, the last farewell on the high ramparts. He stared at the giant figure, his emotions roiling.

The axman plunged Snaga into the ground and turned toward him. "Good to see you, laddie," said Druss the Legend.

Skilgannon took a deep, shuddering breath. "Sweet heaven, it is *better* than good to see you, Druss."

Druss stepped in and patted Skilgannon's shoulder. "Don't get used to it," he said. "I shall not be here long." He swung around, his pale eyes scanning the ancient ramparts. "Egel's Folly they used to call it," he said. "But it proved its worth." Druss wandered back to the fire and sat. Skilgannon joined him.

"Why can you not stay?"

"You know why. This is not my life, boy. It belongs to Harad. Ah, but it is good to breathe mountain air again, and to see the stars. But let us talk of you. How are you faring?"

Skilgannon did not answer at first. The shock at seeing Druss had been replaced by a huge sense of relief. He was no longer alone in an alien world. That relief had now been dashed. The loneliness was merely waiting in the shadows. "I should not be here, Druss. It is that simple. I lived my life."

"No, you shouldn't, laddie. What are your plans?"

"To go back to Naashan. Apart from that I have none."

Druss remained silent for a moment. "Perhaps that is your destiny," he said, doubtfully. "I don't think so, though. You came back. There will be a reason for it—a purpose. This I know."

"I was brought back because an arrogant man believed in an ancient prophecy. He thought I rode a horse with wings of fire. He thought I could change the horrors of this new world."

"Maybe you can."

Skilgannon laughed. "I am one man, with no army."

"Ah, laddie! If you need an army you'll find one." He looked around at the ruined fortress. "This was what I was born for, all those centuries ago. To come to this place and help save a nation. One old man with an ax. That was my destiny. This is yours. Here and now."

"More like punishment than destiny," said Skilgannon, without rancor. "A thousand years in the Void. Now this. At least I knew why I was in the Void."

"No, you did not," said Druss, quietly. Before Skilgannon

could reply the axman glanced up at the high peaks. "There is evil here, walking these mountains. I can feel it. Innocent blood will be shed."

"What evil?"

"Do you have your swords?"

"I will not use them, Druss. I cannot."

"Trust me, you are stronger than the evil they carry. You will need them, boy. And Harad will need you." Druss sighed. "Time I was leaving."

"No! Stay just a little while longer." Skilgannon heard the sound of desperation in his voice, and struggled for calm.

"I can only guess at how lonely you must feel, laddie," said Druss. "But I cannot stay. There is someone I must protect. The Void is no place to be alone for long."

"I don't understand. *You* are trapped in the Void? It makes no sense."

"I am not trapped. It is my choice to be there now. When I choose to leave, I can. You don't remember much of it, do you?"

"No."

"Probably just as well." He sighed. "Take care now."

Skilgannon felt a sense of desolation, but he forced a smile. "You, too, Druss. I don't remember much, but there are beasts in the Void that could kill even you."

Druss laughed, the sound rich and full of life. "In your dreams, laddie!" he said.

Returning to the blankets by the fire, the axman lay down. His huge body relaxed—then jerked suddenly.

Harad rolled to his feet, eyes staring, fists clenched. He saw Skilgannon and suddenly looked embarrassed. "I had a nightmare," he said. He was breathing heavily. Rising, he walked to the ax and hefted it. His breathing calmed. "I don't usually dream much," he said. "When I do it is always here."

"What did you dream of?" asked Skilgannon, heavy of heart.

"It is fading now. Gray skies, demons." Harad shuddered.

"This time I had the ax. That is all I remember. What are you doing here?"

"I came down to take some of your wood," said Skilgannon. "My fire went out."

They sat in silence for a while. Then Harad spoke. "You know a great deal about this Druss. Do you know what he wore?"

"A black jerkin, edged with silver plates at the shoulder. And a helm."

"Were there skulls upon it? In silver?"

"Yes, alongside an ax blade."

Harad rubbed at his face. "Ah, I am being stupid. Someone must have told me the story. Maybe my mother. Yes, that's it."

"You dreamed of Druss?"

"I don't remember now," said Harad. He glanced at the sky. "Dawn is close. We should be heading back."

Landis Khan bade his guests farewell and watched as they mounted their horses. He was shaken by the look Decado gave him. There was a glittering hatred in his eyes, and something else. A look of anticipation that unnerved Landis. He turned back into his palace, heavy of heart, and walked to his library study. *How could you have been so arrogant?* he asked himself. *To believe that you could deceive the Eternal; to think that you could re-create the one great moment of your life?*

He sat down on the wide leather chair by the window, his head in his hands.

Life had changed that day, so many centuries ago, when he had excavated the ruined palace in Naashan. One of his workers had called out to him. The man was on his knees in the mud at the bottom of a newly dug pit. Beside him, protruding from the earth, was a face, sculpted in white marble. As Landis stared at the face it seemed that the universe suddenly shifted, and all that was broken and disharmonious suddenly became perfect. The face was that of a woman—a woman more beautiful than any he had ever known in life. Scrambling down into the muddy hole, he had dropped to his knees and wiped the wet dirt away from the stone face. The man beside him let out a low whistle of appreciation. "Must be a goddess," he said.

Landis Khan called more men to the pit, and slowly they unearthed the full statue. It was of a woman sitting on a throne, her arm raised to the heavens. A snake was entwined around the arm. For the next few days Landis had teams working both day and night to clear away the earth. They discovered the edges of a curved marble wall. Landis estimated it would have a diameter, if fully excavated, of around two hundred paces. As more of the wall was unearthed Landis realized it must once have edged a man-made lake. He cared nothing for the lake, nor for the ruined city. His entire focus was now on the statue. Days were spent examining it, sketching it, staring at it. Landis Khan, the young priest of the Resurrection, forgot all his teachings and found himself dreaming of the woman who had inspired this exquisite sculpture. There were engravings on the base of the statue. Landis sent for an expert in the hieroglyphic writings of Naashan. An old man arrived. Landis remembered him well. He had a crookback and a twisted neck. He had crouched by the base of the statue in the moonlight, and scribbled his findings on a tablet of wet clay. Then, awkwardly, he had climbed from the pit.

"It says she was Jianna, Queen of Naashan. It speaks of her victories and the glories of her reign, which lasted thirty-one years. Her bones are probably interred at the base of the statue. That was the custom then."

"Her bones are *here*?" Landis could barely control his excitement. His hands began to shake.

The crookback had been correct. A secret compartment had been located in the base, just beneath the carved throne. There had also been the rotted remains of a box, and two rusted hinges. From the ruined debris Landis guessed the box had contained parchment scrolls. But water had seeped in at some point and destroyed them. He had the bones packed away, and he returned to the mountain temple, hidden within the desert. The journey took three long months, across the Carpos Mountains, then northwest to the city port of Pastabal, which had once been named Virinis. From here they sailed west, then north, moving through the straits of Pelucid and finally reaching the western shore at the mouth of the Rostrias River. Few of the priests there were concerned, as he was, with the more recent history of the world. His finds in Naashan were greeted with mild interest, for they had dedicated their lives to rediscovering the greater secrets of the ancient, long-lost peoples who, it was said, had mastered the magic of the universe and then destroyed themselves.

Landis had never had any abiding interest in the origin of the artifacts, only in how their use could benefit him. It was well known that the priests enjoyed preternaturally long lives. This appealed to Landis. It was also believed—and Landis now knew this to be true—that it was possible to return from death itself. These secrets, however, were known to very few. Landis had befriended one of them and become an assiduous student. His mentor, a Reborn named Vestava, loved to talk of the ancient days when the temple was first founded.

It had followed the archaeological research of Abbot Goralian more than fifteen centuries ago, and had led to the creation of the first Temple of the Elders on the present site in the desert. Below the rock of a lonely mountain here Goralian had discovered a series of buried chambers, containing arcane machines constructed of a metal that did not rust or decay, and white wood that did not rot. Goralian spent much of his life studying the machines, but it was only after his death that a second abbot, the mystic Absyll, had reactivated them. Landis Khan would have liked to have witnessed that moment. According to Vestava the abbot had entered a dream trance and had pierced the mists of time, floating back through the ages. He had watched the ancients at work on the machines. When he awoke he led the priests to a high, secret chamber on the mountainside. Here he pressed a series of switches and levers. Within moments a groaning sound had been heard, and the mountain chamber began to tremble. Some of the priests ran, fearing an earthquake. Others stood rooted to the spot. Absyll led the still-frightened priests to a stairway, and slowly they climbed higher into the mountain, emerging at last onto a metal platform hundreds of feet above the desert. Once into the open he pointed up the mountain. On the high peak above them something was moving. At first it appeared to be a thick column of gold, rising from the mountain. Then the tip of the column began to swell, and then to open, like a giant flower. Vestava stated there were originally twenty-one petals, but they shimmered and merged together, creating a perfectly round metal mirror resting on the mountaintop. Absyll had called it the Mirror of Heaven.

If the priests on the platform had been amazed at the sight of the golden shield, then the others inside the mountain were equally astonished. Lights blazed from chamber walls throughout the ancient structure. Machines began to hum. Men scrambled from the buildings, running out onto open ground.

Many of the priests had written their memories of that day, and Landis had studied them all. Excitement had been high, and a sense of destiny had touched all of them. In the years that followed many more discoveries were made, but only one matched the opening of the golden shield. Abbess Hewla, before her fall into evil, had become fascinated by a shimmering mirror in one of the higher antechambers. Strange markings flickered on its surface, changing and flowing. Hewla copied many of the markings and became convinced they represented the lost writing of the elder races. After eighteen years of patient study Hewla finally deciphered them. It brought her to a knowledge of the use of the machines. Landis had read and studied Hewla's writings. Her work had led to a renaming of the temple, and a new direction for the priests who labored there. It became the Temple of the Resurrection, and use of the machines initially gave the priests extended life and energy. More than this, however, it eventually allowed the priests to conquer death itself; to be reborn.

By the time Landis came to serve the temple Hewla was long gone, though stories of her, and the dark deeds of her life, had become legend. Landis had taken the bones of the long-dead queen to Vestava and suggested—humbly—that it would "enhance our understanding of the past if we were to restore her life."

Vestava had smiled. "There would be little advantage in such a process, Landis. Her soul would long ago have left the Void. One day you will understand it. When you are ready I will teach you myself."

That *one day* had been twenty-six years, four months, and six days away. During that time he returned to Naashan and had the head of the statue removed, and brought back to his rooms at the temple. At nights he would sit and stare at it, and even at times talk to it. His passion for the long-dead queen did not fade. In fact it grew stronger. He began to dream of her.

When Vestava at last chose to share the Mysteries with his student, Landis learned that the key to successful resurrection lay in an ancient ritual Hewla had called the migration of souls. In order to accomplish the transfer it usually had to be made within a day of death. On rare occasions it could be longer, if there was a mystic with power who could enter the Void and guide a soul back to the haven of his new body. But the longest time recorded was eight days. The queen of Naashan had been dead for five hundred years.

The disappointment felt by Landis Khan was intense. That first night he lay in his chamber and wept.

Three years passed, and then came the most glorious moment of his life so far. He showed the statue head to a young priest training in the mystic arts. The man's skill lay in touching objects and seeing visions of their past. He and Landis had been joking about the young man's gift. "Tell me of the statue," said Landis. The young man had placed his hands on the cold, white stone, then taken a long, deep breath. "It was crafted by a one-eyed man. It took him five years of his life." The young priest had smiled. "He was helped by his son, who was, perhaps, even more gifted than the father. The queen came to their workshop and sat with them. They sketched and drew her, and laughed and joked with her. Her name was Jianna."

"You would know that from my reports," said Landis, trying not to be skeptical.

"I have not read them, Brother, I assure you. The statue was placed by a lake." He suddenly jerked. "Blood was shed there by assassins seeking to kill the queen. They failed. She did not seek to flee. She fought them. There was a man with her, his head shaved, though not on the top of his head. Odd. It looks like a horse's mane." Suddenly the young man screamed and threw himself backward, falling onto a couch.

"What is wrong?" asked Landis, shocked.

The young man shivered. "I don't know. I felt . . . Oh, Landis I feel ill."

"What did you feel?"

"She touched me. The queen touched me. She haunts this statue."

"Her soul is still connected to the world?"

"I believe so. I shall not touch the thing again."

Landis had taken the news to Vestava. "We can bring her back," said Landis. "Is that not so?"

"It is not that simple, student. And if she still haunts the world then that might be reason enough never to try. Don't you see? She has not passed the Void. What evils must she have committed to be damned for so long in that hellish place?"

"But she could answer so many of the mysteries of that bygone era. We have mere fragments. Are we not here to pursue the path of knowledge, Master? This is what you have taught me all these years. She would know of the growth of empires that are lost to us, and the fall of civilizations. She might even have knowledge of the ancients."

"I will think on it, Landis," said Vestava. "Give me time."

Landis knew better than to press the old man, who could be obdurate when he felt pressured. What followed was the longest year of Landis's life. As the following winter approached, Vestava summoned him to the upper council chamber. The Five were assembled there, the most senior priests of the Resurrection. Vestava spoke: "It has been decided that this is an opportunity too promising to let pass. We will begin the process of Rebirth. Bring the bones to the lower chambers tomorrow."

As Landis sat quietly, locked into memories of the past, a lantern guttered and went out. He shivered and forced his mind back to the present.

Leaving the library, he returned to his apartments in the western wing. It was growing dark; servants were in the corridors lighting lanterns. He found Gamal waiting for him in the main room.

"You did not deceive Unwallis, Landis," he said, sadly. "The Black Wagon will be coming. You should leave this place and journey across the sea. Find a new life somewhere beyond her power to reach you."

"You are wrong," said Landis, seeking not to convince his friend, but to bolster his own failing confidence.

Gamal sighed. "You know I am not. To bring Skilgannon back was perilous—but the girl? This was madness. Oh Landis, how could you be so foolish?"

Landis sank into a chair. "I love her. Thoughts of her are always with me. Ever since I found the statue. I just wanted to be with her, to touch her skin, to hear her voice. I thought I could . . . I thought I could do it right this time."

"She *knows* what you have done, Landis. She will never forgive you."

"I will leave tomorrow. I'll journey north. Perhaps Kydor."

"Do not take the Reborn with you. She will be the death of you. They are already hunting her, and they will find her."

Landis nodded. "Jianna was not always evil, you know. I

am not fooling myself with this. I knew her, Gamal. She was warm and loving, and witty and . . . and . . ."

"And beautiful," said Gamal. "I know. I do not think we were intended for immortality, Landis. I knew a man once who fashioned artificial flowers from silk. They were gorgeous to behold, but they had no scent. They lacked the ephemeral beauty of a real bloom. Jianna is like that. There is no humanity left in her. Do not wait for tomorrow, Landis. Leave now. Gather what you need and ride north."

Gamal made his way slowly to the door, his hand reaching out ahead of him to steer him around the furniture. "I shall take you back to your rooms," said Landis, stepping in to help the blind man.

"No. Do as I advised. Pack and leave. I can find my own way."

"Gamal!"

"What is it, my friend?"

"You have always been dear to me. I thank you for your friendship. I will never forget it."

"Nor I."

The blind man moved out into the corridor. Landis walked out to watch him making his slow way toward the far stairwell.

Then he returned to his apartment and closed the door.

Landis Khan sighed and moved out to the balcony. The sun was behind the mountains now, but still casting a golden glow in the sky above the peaks. He felt tired and drained. Gamal had urged him to ride out into the night, but Landis convinced himself his friend was merely panicking. Decado and Unwallis had left, and he had no wish to ride a horse in darkness, nor camp in some dreary cave, locked in thoughts of despair.

Dawn would be a good time. The sunlight would lift his spirits.

Landis returned to his rooms and filled a goblet with red wine. It tasted sour.

The lanterns flickered, as if a breeze were blowing through the room. Yet there was no breeze. One by one they went out. Landis stood very still, his mouth dry.

"I never thought you would ever betray me," whispered a voice.

Landis spun. A shimmering light began in the darkest corner of the room, swelling and growing, forming a human shape. The image sharpened, and Landis gazed once more upon the features of the woman who had haunted his dreams for five hundred years. Her long dark hair was held back from her face by a silver circlet upon her brow, her slender body clothed in white. Landis drank in the vision, his eyes drawn, as ever, to the tiny dark beauty spot just to the right of her mouth. Somehow this blemish only enhanced her.

"I love you," he said. "I always have."

"How sweet! How foolish. You fell in love with a statue, Landis. What does that tell you about yourself?"

"I gave you life," he said. "I brought you back."

The image shimmered closer to him, shifting and changing. The white gown disappeared, replaced by a shaped silver breastplate and leather leggings, reinforced by silver bands upon the thigh. At her side was a sword belt.

"You did not love me, Landis. You loved an image of me. You desired to possess that image, to have it for your own. That is not love. Now you have re-created that image. Without my permission. That is not love."

"Have you come here to kill me?"

"I am not going to kill you, Landis. Tell me the truth. Are there any more bones of my past bodies?"

"Do not harm her, Jianna. I beg you."

"Are there any more bones, Landis?"

"No. She is innocent. She knows nothing, and could never harm you."

The Eternal laughed. "She will serve me well, Landis. She is the right age."

Landis's heart sank. "Were you always evil?" he heard himself ask.

"This is hardly the time for philosophical debate, my dear. However, I will say this: When I was a child my father was murdered, my mother killed. People I thought loyal sought my death. They all had their reasons. When I came to power I killed them. Self-preservation is a paramount desire in all of us. Good and evil are interchangeable. When the wolves pull down a fawn I don't doubt the doe would consider it an evil act. For the wolves it is a necessity, and they would see the arrival of fresh meat as good. So let us not spend these moments in meaningless debate. I have one more question for you, Landis, and then we can say farewell. What did you find in Skilgannon's tomb?"

"I never found his tomb," he lied. "I found the ax and the bones of Druss the Legend."

"I remember him," said the Eternal. "I met him once. Describe the ax." Landis did so. The Eternal listened intently. "And you sought to bring him back?"

"Yes. We could not find his soul. All we have is a powerful young man who works as a logger."

"Druss would have been beyond you," said the Eternal. "He did not wander the Void. Very well, Landis, I believe you."

The door opened. Landis turned to see the young swordsman Decado enter the room. The dark-haired warrior smiled at him, then drew one of his swords. Fear engulfed Landis, and he backed away. He looked at the shimmering image of the Eternal. "You said you would not kill me," he said.

"And I shall not. He will." She floated toward Decado. "Not a trace of flesh or bone to be left," she said. "Burn him to ash. I do not want him reborn."

"As you order, so shall it be," said Decado.

"Do not make him suffer, Decado. Kill him swiftly, for he was once dear to me. Then find the blind man and kill him, too."

"The nephew, Beloved. He insulted me. I want him, too."

"Kill him, my dear," said the Eternal, "but no one else. Our troops will be here by morning. Try to remember that we will still need people to till the fields, and I would like servants to remain in the palace ready for my arrival. I do not want blind terror causing havoc here."

The vision swirled, appearing once more before the terrified Landis Khan. "You once told me you would die happy if my face was the last thing you were allowed to see. Be happy, Landis Khan."

Six

Harad was unnaturally silent as they began their return journey. He strode on ahead tirelessly, despite the weight of his pack and the double-bladed ax he carried. Skilgannon had no wish for conversation, either. The brief meeting with Druss had merely reinforced his feelings of loneliness in this new world. The two men made the long climb back into the mountains. At the top Skilgannon swung to gaze down once more on the old fortress. Then he turned away and followed Harad.

More memories came to him then. He remembered his journeys across the Desert of Namib, in search of the lost Temple of the Resurrection. Three years he had spent in that desolate land. In order to survive he had joined a band of mercenaries and fought in several actions near the old Gothir capital of Gulgothir. Roving bands of Nadir outlaws were harassing the farmlands. Skilgannon and thirty men had been hired to find them and kill them. In the end the situation had been reversed. The captain of mercenaries—an idiot whose name Skilgannon gratefully could not recall—had led them into a trap. The battle had been furious and short. Only three mercenaries escaped into the mountains. One had died of his wounds. The others had fled south. Skilgannon circled back and entered the Nadir camp at night, killing the leader and six of his men. The following day the rest of the outlaws had pulled out.

Lean times followed, working for a pittance as a soldier in New Gulgothir, scraping together enough coin to make more journeys in Namib. The dream had kept him going. His young wife, Dayan, a woman he had never truly loved, had died in his arms. He'd carried fragments of her bones and a lock of her hair in a locket around his neck. These bones, according to the legends, would be enough to see her live again.

And then one day he had discovered the temple. It was in an area he had traveled through many times. This time, however, he was in the company of a young priest he had rescued from bandits. *How strange are the ways of fate,* he thought. The priest had been chased by five Nadir riders. Skilgannon had watched from a nearby rise as they caught him. Then they had prepared a killing fire. It was a barbarous and ghastly ritual. The priest had been thrown to the ground, his full-length pale blue robes torn from him. Naked he had been staked out on the steppes while the Nadir piled kindling and firewood between his open legs. He would have died screaming in terrible pain as his genitals roasted.

The hideous pleasures of Nadir tribesmen were of no concern to Skilgannon. He was about to ride away when he thought of Druss the Legend, and his iron code. Old Druss would not have left this stranger to his fate. *Protect the weak against the evil strong.* Suddenly Skilgannon had chuckled. "Ah, Druss, I fear you have corrupted me with your simple philosophy," he said as he heeled his horse down the slope.

The Nadir, seeing him coming, rose from the bound prisoner and waited. Skilgannon rode up, lifted his leg over the saddle pommel, and jumped lightly to the ground. The warriors looked at him. "What do you want?" asked one, in the western tongue. Then he turned to the others and said in Nadir: "The horse will bring much silver."

"The horse will bring you nothing," Skilgannon had told the surprised man. "All that awaits you here is death. There are two outcomes, Nadir. You will ride from here and sire more goat-faced children, or you will die here and the crows will eat your eyes." They had spread out in a semicircle. The warrior on the far left suddenly drew a knife and rushed in.

The Sword of Day flashed in the sunshine and the man fell, blood gushing from a terrible wound in his neck. Instantly the other Nadir charged. Skilgannon leapt to meet them. Three died within moments, and the leader fell back, his right arm severed just below the elbow, blood gouting from the open arteries. His legs gave way and he fell to his knees, staring stupidly at the bleeding limb. Desperately he grabbed the stump with his left hand, seeking to stem the flow. Ignoring him, Skilgannon walked to the young priest and cut him free. Hauling him to his feet, he said: "Are you hurt?" The man shook his head and moved to the fallen Nadir.

"Let me bind that," he said. "Perhaps we can save your life."

The Nadir struck at him weakly. "Leave me be, *gajin*. May your soul rot in the Seven Hells."

"I just want to help you," the priest had said. "Why do you curse me?"

The Nadir stared malevolently up at Skilgannon. "For this worm you have destroyed me? There is no sense to it. Kill me now. Set my spirit free."

Ignoring the dying man, Skilgannon handed the priest his tattered robe and took him by the arm, leading him to his horse. Mounting, he drew the priest up behind him and rode away.

They had camped that night out in the open. Skilgannon lit no fire. The priest, dressed in his torn blue robe, sat shivering and staring up at the stars. "I do not want those men on my conscience," he said, at last.

"Why would they be on your conscience, boy?"

"They died because of me. Had you not come they would be alive still."

Skilgannon had laughed. "You are an irrelevance in this. All over this land people are dying, some because they are old and worn out, some because they are diseased, and some merely because they are in the wrong place at the wrong time. They are not your concern. No more were those torturers. You are a Source priest, yes?"

"Yes, I am."

"Then you must ask yourself why I was here at this time. It might be that the Source sent me, because He wanted you alive. It might be mere happenstance. But you *are* alive, priest, and the evil men are dead. Where were you heading?"

The young man had looked away. "I cannot tell you. It is forbidden."

"As you wish."

"What are you doing here, in this awful desert?" the priest asked.

"Trying to keep a promise."

"That is a good thing to do. Promises are sacred."

"I like to think so." Skilgannon unrolled his blankets and threw one to the young man. The priest gratefully wrapped it around his thin shoulders.

"What is the promise?"

Skilgannon had considered telling the young man that it was none of his business. Instead he found himself talking of his time in Naashan, and the death of Dayan. Lastly, he tapped the locket and said: "So, I search. It is all that is left to me."

The young man had said nothing then, and had stretched himself out on the ground and gone to sleep. But soon after dawn, as Skilgannon was saddling the gelding, the priest approached him.

"I have given much thought to your words about the Source," he said. "And I think it is true that He sent you to me. Not just for my own safety. I am apprenticed to the Temple of the Resurrection. I am journeying there now. I will take you with me."

Fate was a mysterious creature. It almost made one believe in the Source.

Almost.

The temple had been shielded by a powerful ward spell, and only when the young priest took Skilgannon to the hidden gateway did it fade. He'd looked up at what had been the blank rock of a massive mountain, and seen the many windows carved into the stone. More than that he'd seen a great shield of gold, gleaming on the high peak.

His heart had soared. Finally his dream would be realized, and Dayan would live again, to enjoy the life she should have known.

Thinking on it now, Skilgannon smiled ruefully.

The priests of the Resurrection had made him welcome. Yet he had languished inside the temple for almost a month before the chief abbot had summoned him. The man's name was Vestava. Round shouldered and slender, he had kindly eyes.

"We cannot do what you wish," he said. "We can take the bones you carry, and we can resurrect, if you will, a girl child, who, in time will look exactly like your wife. Indeed, she will be, in almost every way, identical to the woman you knew. But she will not be Dayan, Skilgannon. She cannot be."

The shock had been great, the disappointment intense. "I will find another temple," he said. "There will be someone who can do this."

"There will not," said Vestava. "We have searched the Void and her spirit has passed through the Golden Valley. She will be at peace there, having found joy. Believe me on this."

"I will not accept it," Skilgannon said, anger flaring.

"You need to question your motives here, my boy," the older man had replied.

"What does that mean?"

"You are an intelligent man. You also have great courage. However, this quest was not to resurrect Dayan, but to salve your own conscience. In short, it was not for her. It was for you. I know you, Skilgannon, and I know your deeds. You carry a terrible weight upon your soul. I cannot ease that. Let me ask you this: Did you love Dayan with all your heart?"

"This is none of your business, priest."

"You did not love her. So what would you do if I brought her back? Chain yourself to her out of duty? You think a woman would not realize that your heart was not hers? You would have me draw her back from a place of perfection so that she could spend unhappy years with an unhappy man in an unhappy world?"

Skilgannon quelled his anger and sighed. "What do I do now?"

"You have helped one of our brothers, and for this we are grateful. We will, if you wish it, give life to the bones you carry. In this way Dayan's flesh will once more walk the earth. She may grow to find love, and have children of her own. For most people this is the kind of immortality they understand. It is their gift to the future. They live on through their children."

Skilgannon rose from his seat and wandered to a window, staring out over the bleak desert landscape. "I need time to think on this," he said. "May I stay here for a while?"

"Of course, my son."

For several days Skilgannon had dwelled in the temple, observing the priests, wandering the halls and passageways. It was a place of great serenity. There were beautiful halls, and libraries where men studied without urgency. Every piece of furniture, every painting had been chosen to enhance the harmonious atmosphere. All the harshness and violence of the world outside seemed far away. Men from all nations studied here, without rancor. The tranquility of the temple allowed Skilgannon to open his mind to truths he had hidden deep.

Vestava's words haunted him. He could no longer deny the truth of them. Finally he returned to Vestava. "I have given over my life to this quest," he said. "I told myself it was for Dayan. But you are right, priest. It was for me. A poultice for the wound on my soul."

"What do you wish us to do?"

"Give life to the bones. She was pregnant when she died. At least this way a part of her will feel the sun once more upon her face."

"A wise decision, my son. You are disappointed. I understand that. It will be as you wish. I will watch over the child, and see her grow strong, if that is the will of the Source. She will be like any other child, and subject to the whims of fate, disease, or war. I will, however, do my best to see her happy. Come back to us in a few years and watch her grow for a while. It will ease your heart."

"I may do that," he had said. That afternoon he had ridden from the temple, and had not looked back.

Up ahead Harad took off his pack and dropped it to the ground. Then he wandered down to a rippling stream and drank deeply. Skilgannon joined him. They sat in silence for a while. Harad looked intently at Skilgannon, then shivered.

"What is wrong, Harad?"

"I can't get the dream from my mind," said the young logger. "Gray skies, dead trees, no water, and no life. Demons everywhere. It was so real. I have never dreamed anything like it before."

"You were in the Void," said Skilgannon. "It is a dark and dangerous place."

"How do you know of this?"

"I know many things, Harad. I know that you are a good, strong man, and that you will carry Druss's ax with pride and do his memory honor. I know that you are short tempered, but that you have a fine heart and an honest soul. I know that you have courage beyond reason, and would be a true friend and a terrible enemy. Ah yes," he said, with a smile, "I also know you prefer red wine to ale."

"Aye, that is true. So, I ask again, how do you know all this? Speak truly."

"You are a Reborn, Harad."

"I have heard the word. But what does it mean?"

"A good question. I do not have the best of answers. The priests of the Resurrection have great magic. They can take the bones of dead heroes and somehow cause them to be born again. Don't ask me how. I have no understanding of magic, nor do I wish to acquire any. What I do know is that you were created from a shard of bone."

"Pah!" said Harad. "I was born to my mother. I know this."

"A long time ago—" Skilgannon sighed. "—a very long

time ago, my wife died of the plague. For years I sought the Temple of the Resurrection, hoping that by some miracle they could restore her to life through a piece of her bone and a lock of her hair. When at last I found it I was told by the abbot there that my quest was impossible. What they *could* do was to allow her to be reborn. By some magical process they could take the bones and a willing woman, and the result would be a birth—a rebirth, I suppose. But they said that my Dayan would not return as I knew her. Her soul had already passed beyond the Void. What there would be was a child in every way identical to the wife I had lost."

"And she would be without a soul?" asked Harad.

"I understand souls less than I understand magic, Harad. All I know is that I agreed to let them use Dayan's bones in this way. Some years later I returned, and saw a little girl with golden hair. She was a happy child, full of laughter. When I saw her the last time she was sixteen, and had fallen in love."

Harad looked at him closely. "You are no older than me. Sixteen years? It is nonsense."

"I am infinitely older than you, my friend. I died a thousand years ago. I, too, am a Reborn. Only with me they *did* find my soul. I had not passed the Void. I could not pass it. The evil of my life prevented me from finding paradise. What I am telling you is the truth. Do you not yet understand why Landis Khan gave *you* that ax?"

Harad's face paled. "Are you telling me that I am Druss the Legend? I do not believe it."

"No, you are your own man, Harad. Every inch your own man. The reason you were in the Void last night was because Druss's spirit returned to speak with me. We were friends back then. Good friends. I loved the old man like a father."

"And now he wants his body back," said Harad, a hard edge in his voice.

"No, he does not. It is not *his* body. It is yours. He wants you to have a full life. Druss never had sons, Harad. You are like the son he never had. I think he might be watching over you with pride."

Harad sighed. "Why did Landis bring us back?" he asked. "What was his purpose?"

"Ask him when next you see him. My name, by the way, is Skilgannon. You may call me Olek, if you wish."

"Is that what Druss called you?"

Skilgannon relaxed and smiled. "No. He called me laddie. But then he called every man laddie. In truth I think he had trouble remembering names." Moving to his pack, Skilgannon untied the cloth binding around the Swords of Night and Day and lifted them clear. His mood darkened as his hands touched the black scabbard. Pressing the precious stones on the ivory hilts, he drew the weapons clear, two curved blades, one bright and gold, the other silver-gray as a winter moon.

"They are beautiful," said Harad. "Did Landis Khan give them to you?"

"Yes. But they were always mine."

"You sound regretful."

"Oh, *regret* does not begin to describe it. But Druss said I would need them, and I trust him."

Stavut the Merchant topped the last rise before the settlement and halted his wagon, allowing his exhausted two-horse team to rest. The climb had been long and hard. Applying the brake and locking it into place with a leather strap, he stepped down to the road and walked alongside the lead horse, stroking his gleaming chestnut neck. The trace leathers were covered in white lather, the horses themselves breathing heavily.

"Almost time to replace you, Longshanks," said the young merchant. "I think you are getting a little too long in the tooth for this." As if it had understood him the chestnut shook his head and whinnied. Stavut laughed and moved to the gray gelding on the other side. "As for you, Brightstar, you have no excuse. You're five years younger and grain fed. A little climb like that should be nothing to you." The gray stared at him balefully. Stavut patted his neck, then walked closer—

though not too close—to the cliff edge and stood staring down at the valley below. From here the settlement looked tiny, and the river running alongside it seemed no more than a shimmering thread of silk. Stavut sighed. He loved coming to this place, even though the profits were meager. There was something about these mountains that lifted the soul. They made thoughts of war drift away like wood smoke on the breeze. His eyes drank in the scene, from the majesty of the snowcapped peaks, through the mysterious deep green forests, and over the apparently tranquil fields dotted with cattle, sheep, and goats. Stavut felt himself relax, all tension easing from his tired frame.

The last week had been particularly stressful. He had been warned about deserters from the rebel army. Some Jiamads had attacked outlying farms. There was talk of mutilations and murder, and the devouring of human flesh. These were not subjects Stavut liked to dwell upon. The journey south with his laden wagon had been long, but had seemed longer because every waking moment Stavut had scanned the land, expecting at any instant to see ferocious Jiamads moving toward him. His nerves were in tatters by the time he finally saw them.

The wagon had been rounding a bend between high cliffs when several beasts emerged from behind the rocks. Stavut found it curious to recall that all his fears had suddenly vanished. The terrors he had felt had all come with the anticipation of danger. With the danger now real he drew rein, took a deep breath, and waited. Stavut carried no sword, but at his side was a curved dagger so sharp he could shave with it. He did not know whether he would have the strength, or the speed, to drive that blade through the fur-covered flesh of a Jiamad.

There were four of them, still sporting the baldrics and leather kilts of an infantry section. Only three of them still carried swords; the fourth was holding a rough-made club.

The scent of them caused the horses to rear. Stavut applied the brake and spoke soothingly to them. "Steady now, Longshanks! Stay calm, Brightstar. All is well." Transferring his gaze to the Jiamads, he forced a cheerful tone and said: "You are a long way from camp."

They did not reply, but moved past him, lifting the cover from the back of his wagon and peering at the contents.

"I am carrying no food," he said.

The closest Jiamad suddenly lunged at Stavut, grabbing his crimson jerkin and hauling him from the wagon. He landed heavily. "Oh, but you are, Skin," said the Jiamad. "You are scrawny and small, but your blood is still sweet. And your flesh will be tender."

Stavut rolled to his feet and drew his dagger.

"Look!" snorted the Jiamad. "It wants to fight for its life."

"Rip its arm off," said another.

A great calm had settled on Stavut then. He found he had only one regret. He would not see Askari again. He had promised her a new bow, and had searched long to find the perfect weapon, a beautiful recurve bow; a composite of horn and yew, the grip covered in the finest leather. He wished he had it in his hands now.

And then the miracle happened. With death only heartbeats away there had come the sound of galloping hooves. The Jiamads had turned and run toward the hills. Cavalrymen came hurtling past Stavut.

"I think you can sheathe your dagger now," said a familiar voice. Stavut looked up to see the young mercenary captain, Alahir. The man was grinning at him. "I did warn you about the Jiamads, Tinker," he said, removing his bronze helm and pushing a hand through his long blond hair.

"I am a merchant, as well you know," said Stavut.

"Nonsense! You mend kettles. That makes you a tinker."

"One kettle does not make me a tinker."

Alahir laughed. Replacing his helm, he heeled his horse forward. "We will talk again when I have finished my task."

With that he rode away. Stavut started to walk toward his wagon, but his legs began to tremble, and he had to reach out to grab the rear of the wagon to steady himself. He tried to sheathe the dagger, but the trembling now reached his hands and he could not insert the blade into the scabbard. Laying it on the wagon cover, he took several deep breaths. He felt suddenly nauseous and slumped down with his back to the wagon wheel. "No more trips north," he promised himself. "After the settlement I shall go down and winter with Landis Khan, and then head south to Diranan."

He sat there quietly waiting for the nausea to pass. Eventually the riders came back. Alahir dismounted. "Are you hurt?" he asked.

"No," answered Stavut. "Just enjoying the afternoon sunshine." Pushing himself to his feet, he was relieved to find the trembling had passed. "Did you catch them?"

"Yes."

"Tell me they are all dead."

"They are all dead."

Stavut looked up at Alahir. There was blood on his arm. Glancing around at the cavalrymen, he saw three riderless horses. "You lost men," he said. "I am sorry."

"It is what we are paid for. You don't fight Jiamads without losses."

"Are there more of them in the mountains?"

Alahir shrugged. "I do not know everything, Stavut, my friend. We were told there were four in this area. Will you be coming back in the spring?"

"Maybe."

"Bring a cask of Southern Red. The wine in this land tastes like vinegar."

Alahir swung his mount and raised his hand: "Hala!" he shouted. And the troop rode off.

Standing now close to the cliff edge, Stavut felt a great warmth toward the young cavalryman. If he did ever journey north again, he would make sure he had a cask of Lentrian Red for him and his men.

Stavut sighed. Edging forward to the lip of the cliff, he stared down at the awesome drop. Immediately he felt the familiar sense of giddiness, and a growing desire to jump. It was so beguiling. Then fear struck him and he staggered back from the cliff edge. "You are an idiot!" he told himself. "Why do you always do that?"

He saw Longshanks staring at him. Stavut patted the chestnut. "I wasn't going to jump," he said. The horse snorted. Stavut imagined the sound to be derisory. "You're not as clever as you think you are," he told Longshanks. "And I won't be criticized by a horse."

Climbing back to the driver's seat, he settled himself down and took up the reins. Releasing the brake, he flipped the reins and began the long descent toward the valley.

Stavut always enjoyed his visits to the small settlement—and not just for the opportunity to seek out Askari's company. Though the dark-haired huntress was dazzlingly attractive and fired his blood as no woman ever had, there was a spirit of calm and joy that radiated throughout this mountain village. The people were friendly, the hospitality warm, and the food at Kinyon's kitchen extraordinary. Kinyon was a stout and powerful man whose house also doubled as the village inn. The first time Stavut had visited the settlement—two years ago now—he had found the arrangement faintly comical. Looking for somewhere to dine, he had received directions from a woman outside the bakery and had drawn up his wagon outside Kinyon's small house. It was an old building with tiny windows and a thatched roof. Stavut had wondered if he had misunderstood the directions, though that was unlikely in a village as small as this one. Climbing down from his wagon, he had approached the front door. It was coming toward dusk, and he could see a man beyond the open door, lighting lanterns and hanging them from the walls.

"Good day," called Stavut.

"And to you, stranger. Are you hungry? Come in. Set yourself down."

Stavut had walked into the room, which was no more than twenty feet long and around fifteen wide. A fire was burning in a stone hearth, and there were only two armchairs, set to the left and right of the blaze. It was an ordinary living room, with the exception that it contained three rough-hewn tables with bench seats. "I have a venison pie, with fresh onions, and a raisin cake, if you have a taste for sweet delicacies," said the tall, sandy-haired man.

Stavut looked around. He could not understand how any profit could be made from a dining hall in a village as small as this. "Sounds fine," he said. "Where shall I sit?"

"Anywhere you please. My name is Kinyon," said the man, thrusting out his hand. Stavut shook it, then walked to the farthest table, set alongside a narrow window overlooking a vegetable garden.

"I also have some ale. Dark ale, but tasty if you have the stomach for it."

The ale had been extraordinary, almost black, but with a head that was white as lamb's fleece, and the food was the best Stavut had enjoyed in a long time. Later that evening other villagers had turned up and sat in Kinyon's house, chatting, laughing, and drinking.

Askari had entered the small room late in the evening, resting her longbow against the wall by the door and laying her quiver of arrows alongside it. Stavut had been transfixed. She was tall and slim, and wearing a sleeveless buckskin jerkin, leather leggings, and calf-length moccasins. Her long dark hair was held back from her face by a black leather headband. Stavut had sat very still. He had seen some beautiful women in his twenty-six years—had even had the extreme joy of sharing their beds—but never had he seen anyone as beautiful as this girl. She laughed and joked with Kinyon, and then sat down at a table close by. He waited until she looked at him, then gave his best smile. All the women he had known always complimented his smile. He had come to think of it as his strongest weapon of seduction. The girl had nodded to him, then looked away, apparently unimpressed.

Undeterred, he leaned forward. "I am Stavut," he said.

"Of course you are," she responded. Then she ignored him. She had eaten a meal and then left.

Later that evening, after the villagers had gone, Stavut paid Kinyon for his meal and made to leave.

"Are you intending to sleep by your wagon?" Kinyon asked him.

"That was my plan."

"I have another bed. Use that. I think it will rain tonight."

Stavut had accepted gratefully, and after seeing to his horses he had sat with Kinyon by the fire, chatting about life, his travels, and entertaining the tanner with amusing stories from Outside. "Who was the girl who came in with the bow?" he asked, at last.

Kinyon laughed. "I saw you looking at her. I think your tongue almost flopped to the tabletop."

"That obvious?"

Kinyon nodded. "She is Askari. Extraordinary girl. You should see her shoot. She can bring down a running quail with a head shot. Can you believe that? I've seen her do it. More like magic than skill. And that bow has a sixty-pound pull. You'd think a slim young child like that would never be able to draw it."

"Is she a relative of yours?" asked Stavut, anxious not to say anything that might offend the man.

"No. She was brought here as a child with her mother. Nice woman. Looked nothing like Askari. Sweet and diffident. Weak lungs, though. Always coughing. Died when Askari was around ten. After that she lived with Shan and his wife . . . the baker who was here earlier." Stavut recalled the man, small and round shouldered, but with powerful forearms and large hands. When the girl had left she had walked to him and kissed his brow.

"Is she betrothed?"

"No," said Kinyon. "And unlikely to be to anyone here."

"Why is that?"

Kinyon suddenly looked wary. "The Lord Landis sometimes visits, and often rides out to speak with Askari. I think he entertains a certain fondness for her. Still, best we don't speak about the ways of the mighty, eh? I'll show you your room."

It had taken Stavut three visits to the settlement before he managed to engage Askari's interest. Stavut had given the matter a great deal of thought on his travels. She was obviously not interested in his smile, and therefore he would need to plan his campaign with care. There would be no point in bringing her jewelry. People in Landis Khan's realm wore none. Perfume would be equally useless. No, the girl was an archer. So Stavut sought out bowmen in other towns and asked about the craft. He learned there were many different arrowheads, some heavily barbed, some smooth, some cast in iron, some in bronze. He knew from Kinyon that Askari fashioned her own from flint. He had purchased twenty arrowheads, said to be perfect for the hunting of deer. Askari had looked at them with interest, but with no enthusiasm. Stavut had finally taken the problem to the Legend rider Alahir. His warriors all carried bows and were highly skilled with them.

"Her biggest problem is probably with the fletching of the arrows," said Alahir. "The thread that binds the feathers also separates them. This affects the accuracy. The thread needs to be strong, but very thin. Were I you, I would take some high-quality fletching thread."

"I'll try that," Stavut told him.

Alahir grinned. "You want a little more advice?"

"As long as it's free."

"Don't give her the thread."

"What then would be the point of taking it?"

"*Sell* her the thread. A gift will make her nervous, and she is likely to refuse it. If you sell her the thread you'll have opportunities to talk to her about how effective it is."

"And then I can use my charm to win her over."

"You have charm? You have kept it well hidden."

"Ha! This from a man who has to pay for female company?"

Alahir laughed. "I *choose* to pay. I am cursed with a staff a stallion would be proud of. It takes an experienced woman to accept it. There are even some whores who hide when they see me coming."

"Yes, you keep telling yourself that's why they hide," said Stavut. "Why am I taking seduction advice from a man whose idea of foreplay is to slam coins on a table and shout: 'Who wants to ride the big horse?' "

Alahir leaned in and chuckled. "Because he knows best, Tinker."

Annoyingly enough, he *had* known best. When Stavut took the fletching thread to Askari, she had looked at it, then at him, and said: "All right, I will accept your gift."

"Gift? You misunderstand, huntress. I am a merchant. I am offering this for sale."

It was the first and only time he had seen her discomfited. She had reddened. "Of course," she told him. "How much?"

"A hundred gold Raq," he said, with a smile, "or one kiss to my cheek."

She had laughed then. "I have no kisses to spare at present."

"Then I will give you credit. I will claim the kiss on my next visit."

Askari had relaxed, and he had walked with her to the high hills. Here she had a camp and a rough-built lean-to covered with branches. Stretched deerskins had been tied to poles for cleaning and drying, and there was a bag of food hanging from a high branch.

"How did you learn to use a bow?" he asked her as they sat in the sunshine, eating raisin bread.

"How does anyone learn to use a bow?" she countered.

"No, I meant you were raised by the baker. Is he an archer?"

"No. There used to be an old hunter who traveled these mountains. He taught me. He made me my first bow. I liked him greatly."

"I take it he died."

"No, he married a nomad woman and now lives out on the steppes. Are you really letting me have the thread for one kiss?"

"Yes."

"No wonder you are not a rich merchant."

"A kiss from you and I would be richer than the Eternal."

She looked at him closely. "Kinyon says you would make me happy in bed and unhappy in life."

Stavut sighed. "Kinyon is a very wise man. My friend who gave me the fletching thread said that the longbow is not as accurate as the recurve bows he and his men carry. He claims that, although the recurve is shorter, it has greater power."

"I have heard that. Is your friend with the Legend riders?"

Stavut smiled. "Yes. Strange folk—but noble in their way. They call themselves the Last of the Drenai. No magic in their lands, no Jiamads. They hold to the old ways—or they did. Now they have to give tribute to Agrias and fight along-side his forces. It is the price they pay to keep the Jiamads from their lands."

"Who is your friend?"

"His name is Alahir. He is a fine man, and ridiculously brave."

"I would like to meet him."

"—and very ugly," added Stavut. "No manners at all. And he hears voices in his head. Did I mention that?"

"Voices?"

"He told me once—when drunk—that he hears voices whispering in his mind."

"Ghosts, you mean?"

"I don't know," Stavut told her. "Can we stop talking about Alahir? He really is very boring, you know."

"But he knows archery," she said.

"I may have overstated his skills."

"You are a funny man, Stavut. I like you."

And so had begun the friendship. Stavut had never claimed his kiss. Kinyon was right. Askari deserved a better man than he, though it would break his heart when she found him.

The huntress Askari had never felt comfortable for long around people. She preferred the solitude of the high country and the lonely mountains. It was not that she disliked any single individual in the settlement, nor indeed that she did not enjoy the occasional evening in Kinyon's kitchen, talking to villagers about the events of the day or the vagaries of the seasons. Sometimes, after several weeks in the wilderness, she found herself longing for the laughter and camaraderie of the little town. But these needs were short lived. Mostly she found peace and harmony in her own company, walking the forest paths or climbing to a high vantage point and sitting staring out toward the northern steppes under a magnificent sky.

Sometimes she would run over the hills, not for any purpose other than to feel the cool mountain air filling her lungs, and joy in the strength and stamina of her youth. Even in childhood she had been solitary—she had awaited eagerly the visits of the Lord Landis Khan. He would bring her small gifts, and sit and talk with her. He was like a favorite uncle whose arrival made the child clap her hands with glee. But since she had become a young woman the tone of the conversations with Landis had changed. She had seen him looking at her with an interest that disquieted her. One day recently he had reached out and stroked her long dark hair. Askari did not like to be touched and had drawn back.

"I meant no offense," said Landis, softly, a look of hurt on his face. He had run his hands over his close-cropped, iron-gray hair. "Once my own hair was the color of yours," he said, seeking to lighten the mood. Askari had forced a smile, and tried to relax. "Are you content here?" he asked her.

"Yes."

"But would you not like to travel? Too see a little more of the world? I am thinking of journeying across the ocean. There are beautiful places there to see."

"It is beautiful here," she told him.

"Yet dangerous. The war will come here one day. It would please me greatly if you were to accompany me."

And there was that look again, his gaze straying to her slim body. Askari suppressed a shudder. Even if young and handsome, she would not want this man too close to her. It was not that she disliked him. He had, after all, always been kind to her, and she felt great affection for him. But the thought of him lying beside her naked was repulsive. Askari was young and inexperienced, and yet she knew instinctively that he desired her.

He had come once more only ten days ago, but Askari had seen him from a distance and faded back into the forest, traveling up to one of her high camps.

Thoughts of Landis faded from her mind as she saw Stavut's wagon on the ridge road. She smiled and stood quietly, her longbow in her hand. Stavut had gotten down from the wagon and was inching toward the edge of the drop, then peering over. He always did that. She wondered what he was looking at. Thoughts of the red-garbed merchant lifted her spirits. He was a good companion, witty and sharp, and she loved his gift for storytelling. When he regaled her with tales of his travels, he would act out conversations, his voice mimicking the people he spoke about. His friend Alahir's voice was deep, with a slow drawl. Of course he spoke about Alahir less often now. Askari smiled. "He sounds wonderful," she had said once. She had watched Stavut's expression darken as jealousy flared. Askari knew he desired her. Unlike Landis that desire was open and honest. There was nothing sly about Stavut. And he had a beautiful smile, which was impish and infectious.

He had promised her a new bow, though she did not desire one. Her own longbow was powerful and accurate and had served her well. She was, however, anxious to see the recurve weapon he had spoken of. Koras the Hunter had told her of such weapons, maintaining they were perfect for mounted warfare. The Legend people could nock an arrow at full gallop and send it unerringly into any target.

For a while longer she watched Stavut negotiating his wagon down the steep slope, then returned to her main camp, just inside the tree line. Stavut would stop first at Kinyon's house and eat. Then he would tend to his horses. It would be late afternoon before he strolled up to her camp. She thought of going down to the settlement to greet him, but decided against it. She did not want to seem anxious to see him. Stavut was a man used to having women fawn over him, and Askari had no desire to boost his ego. Even so it was an effort to merely sit and wait.

The long afternoon wore on. Askari bathed in the stream, ate a meal of hard bread and broth, then gathered wood for the evening's fire. She kept glancing back down the slope to the settlement. It was an hour before dusk before she saw him walking up the hill. He was carrying a canvas rucksack, and she could see a bow hanging from it. But by now she was irritated. He had tarried in the settlement for too long, making her wait.

Before he could see her she moved back into the trees and squatted down behind a screen of bushes.

He strode up to the campsite, looked around, then called out her name. She ignored him. Stavut doffed his pack and sat down on a log. From her hiding place she watched him. She saw a swelling on his right cheekbone and a touch of blood upon his brow. Had he been in a fight? Askari sat quietly. Stavut began to whistle a cheerful tune, but as the darkness gathered she could sense his nervousness. Not a man who enjoyed wilderness nights. Askari hunkered down farther, then, cupping her hands over her mouth, let out a low wolf howl. Stavut leapt to his feet, eyes fearfully scanning the trees. She watched him grab the bow from the pack, then scout around for arrows. There were none. Dropping the bow, he pulled out a small knife, looked at it, swore, and sheathed it. Then he ran to the pile of wood Askari had gathered for the night's fire and hefted a large chunk, holding it two-handed like a club. Holding back laughter, she crept through the undergrowth then let out another fearsome howl—this time closer.

Stavut backed away from the trees and then stood very still, awaiting an attack.

Askari rose from her hiding place and strolled out into the camp. "What do you think you are doing?" she asked.

"Wolves," he said. "You must have heard them."

"They do not attack people unless there is no other source of food. You should know that."

"I know that," he said, wandering back to the camp and dropping the club. "But do the wolves know that?"

"What happened to your face?"

Stavut sighed. "I was attacked by Jiamads on the northern road."

"And all they did was bruise your face?"

"No," he said, an edge of irritation in his voice, "they were going to kill me. Happily for me a group of warriors were hunting them. They arrived before I could be eaten."

"Legend riders?"

"Yes."

"Your friend Alahir?"

"Er . . . No, just some other riders. Anyway . . . as you can see I have your bow."

"Did you try it out on the Jiamads?"

"No. It was in the wagon, under the cover."

She laughed then. "You will never be a warrior, Stavut. You are always so ill prepared. Let me see it." Strolling over to him, she took the weapon and hefted it. The grip was covered with the finest leather. Askari traced her fingers along the graceful lines of the weapon, all the way to the recurved tip. "It feels good." Extending her arm, she smoothly drew back the string until it nestled against her lips. "Let's see what it can do," she said, drawing an arrow from her quiver. "Pick up your club again and walk out onto the slope. I will tell you where to stop."

Stavut took the club and strolled away. After thirty paces she called out for him to halt.

"Where do you want me to put it?" he shouted.

"Hold it up in the air."

"Then what?"

"I shall shoot it."

"I think not!" he said, dropping the club as if it were on fire. He strode back to where she waited. "You think my mother raised stupid children?"

"You don't trust my skill?" she asked sweetly, her eyes narrowing.

"Ah," he said, "I know this scene. A man thinks he is on solid ground, and suddenly he is tiptoeing through quicksand."

"What does that mean?"

"Of course I trust your skill. It is your arrows I don't trust. You could hit the club, the arrow could glance off and kill me."

"I would wager that Alahir would not be afraid to hold the club."

He wagged his finger at her. "True, but Alahir, wonderful friend that he is, is still an idiot. And you can't goad me into a display of stupidity by mentioning Alahir."

"I always thought you to be a brave man," she said, shaking her head, as if in disappointment.

"No, that won't work either," he said brightly. "Now, would you like me to plunge that wood into the ground, so that you can shoot at something?"

"You do that," she said, nocking the arrow.

Stavut walked back to the club and lifted it. Just as he turned it to push it into the earth an arrow slammed into the wood. Stavut leapt back, tripping and hitting the ground hard. "It is a good bow," she called out. He pushed himself to his feet and marched toward her, his expression furious. Askari knew just how to deal with this. "And you lied to me," she said. "Friends do not lie to one another."

"What?" he asked her, confused now. Askari laughed inwardly. It was so easy. Like shooting a tethered goat. On the surface, however, she kept her face stern.

"You said Alahir did not rescue you. I could tell you were lying."

Walking past him, she recovered her shaft, replaced it in her quiver, and returned to the camp. "So tell me about your travels," she said.

"I'm not sure I want to talk to you," he said. She smiled at him, and he burst out laughing. "Yes, Alahir rescued me. It is what he's good at. Killing things."

"Is he married?"

"No. He doesn't like women."

"Another lie!"

"They teach you witchcraft in the mountains?"

"I know you, Stavut. You think you are a good liar, but you are really not. You give it away with your expression."

"There was no expression."

"That's what I mean. When you lie your face goes blank."

"Nonsense."

"And a little crease appears above the brow of your nose. Shall I prove it to you?"

"Yes."

"How many women have you slept with since last you visited?"

"None."

"Liar."

He laughed nervously. "Very well. Three."

"Liar!"

"Seven."

Askari's good humor faded. "You've only been gone two months! Kinyon was right about you!"

"Can we start again?" he said. "Let's go for None!"

"I don't want to talk to you anymore. Go back down to the settlement. Leave me in peace."

Stavut sighed, then rose to his feet. "You are in a strange mood today. You are right, though. I think I'll go back." Moving toward his pack, he stopped.

A dark plume of smoke was rising into the air. "There's a fire in the settlement," he said.

Seven

Throughout the morning Harad walked on, keeping a little distance between himself and the lean swordsman. In truth he did not want to talk for a while. He needed time to think through all that had been said. Harad was never comfortable with instant judgments—except in the case of brawling. When violence was in the air there was little time for reflective thought. Now, however, he needed to absorb all that Skilgannon had told him.

Like all the residents of the land he had heard of Reborns. He had never been interested enough to learn more about them. He was not even sure he wanted to learn more now. It did not concern him that the bully Borak was not his father. In some ways this was a relief. What concerned him was the question of souls. As a child he had attended the small school run by two Source priests. Here he had learned of the journey of souls, and the passage through the Void to the Golden Valley. Harad had always liked the idea of a journey beyond death. However, to make this journey one needed to have a soul. Since this body was not truly his, but created without the soul of Druss the Legend, where did this leave Harad?

He strode on, his mood darkening. Anger flickered to life, and he struggled to control it.

Toward dusk Skilgannon called out to him, and he turned. The swordsman was pointing to the north, where a plume of smoke was rising. "A forest fire?" he inquired.

Harad shook his head. "We've had too much rain for that."

He watched the smoke, then scanned the land, gauging distance. "It looks like it's coming from the settlement. Maybe one of the houses caught fire."

"It would have to be a big house," muttered Skilgannon.

Harad stared hard at the smoke. It seemed to him that there were several plumes, all merging.

"How many people in the settlement?" asked Skilgannon.

"Fifty . . . perhaps a few more."

"Should be enough to deal with a fire."

"I think there is more than one blaze," said Harad. "I can see at least three plumes at the base. Strange, for the houses are not close together, and only one of the roofs is thatched. There would be no reason for a fire to spread."

"Do you have friends there?"

"I have friends nowhere," snapped Harad. He sighed. "But I think I should go there and see if they need help. Can you find your way back to the caves?"

"Of course. However, I shall travel with you. I am in no hurry to see Landis Khan again. How long until we reach the settlement?"

"Close to four hours. It will be dark by the time we arrive." Without another word the two men set off. Skilgannon moved ahead of Harad and began to scout the ground as they walked.

"What are you looking for?" asked Harad.

"Something I hope I don't find," was the cryptic answer.

They walked on for another hour, at first descending into a lightly wooded valley, then climbing again toward a thicker forest. Skilgannon halted at the tree line, doffed his pack, and asked Harad to wait for him. Then he set off along the tree line, searching the ground. Harad sat down and watched the man until he vanished over a ridge.

Harad lifted Snaga and stared at his reflection in the blades. "Who am I looking at?" he said, aloud. "Are you Harad? Are you Druss?" Flipping the blade, he plunged it into the ground.

The sun was almost set. Harad opened his pack and pulled

clear his last loaf of black bread. Ripping it open, he began to eat. As he did so he remembered the times Landis Khan had come to his parents' cabin, squatting down to talk to the child Harad. "Do you dream of ancient days?" he had asked.

His father, Borak, had always left as soon as Landis Khan arrived. And after the lord had gone Borak's mood would turn sour. He would shout at Harad's mother, and sometimes cuff Harad himself.

At least now Harad had some understanding of what Borak had gone through. The child had not been his. Did Borak know of the arcane ritual involving dead bones? Or had he thought his wife had been seduced by Landis Khan? Either way it would have been hard for Borak, who was a proud man. Also, Alanis had not been young when she gave birth to Harad. She had been wed for sixteen years, and had no other children. This meant that Borak was unable to sire sons of his own. Another blow to his pride. No wonder he was so often angry, thought Harad.

Skilgannon came loping back to where Harad waited. "A party of Jiamads—around twenty, maybe a few more—passed this way yesterday. There were two men with them. It may be coincidence, but it is a possibility that the fires in the settlement were not accidental. I do not know the ways of the people of this time. But if I were in my own time I would say this was a raiding party."

"There is nothing of worth in the settlement," said Harad. "Jiamads would have had to have marched from south of the old fortress. What purpose would such a raid serve?"

"As I said, I do not know the ways of the people now, Harad. We should, however, move with care. If it was a raid, then it has been carried out, and we must assume the beasts will be coming back this way."

Harad rose to his feet. "If they have attacked my people then they will suffer for it," he said, raising the ax.

"I applaud the sentiments," said Skilgannon, wryly. "But let us take this one step at a time. I have been involved in wars and battles for most of my life, and I have fought Joinings. I tell you twenty is too many for us. Let's make for the settlement and see what we find."

"Would twenty have been too many for Druss?" asked the young logger.

Skilgannon looked into the man's pale blue eyes. "At your age, with your lack of experience, yes. And even in his prime twenty would have overpowered him. Druss was a man of immense courage. He was also a cunning fighter. He knew how to pick his ground, and mostly he chose where to make his stands. His greatest advantage, though, lay in the nature of ax combat. Any swordsman who wanted to kill him had to come within range of that awesome weapon. And when the fight started Druss would never back away. He just surged forward, unstoppable." Skilgannon patted the young man's shoulder. "Give yourself time to learn, Harad. You will get there."

"I don't have his soul," whispered Harad. "Maybe that is what made him great."

Skilgannon sighed. "When I was in the Void I recall one awful fact. My skin there was scaled, like a lizard. It was because my soul had been corrupted by the deeds of my life. You have a good soul, Harad. And it is yours. Now let us move on, with care."

The wind changed, blowing burning cinders across the gaunt infantry officer. Corvin cursed and moved away, brushing the embers from his new scarlet cloak. His irritation levels were already high, but now he felt the onset of rage. The buildings were burning fiercely—which, under normal circumstances he would have enjoyed. Not now. Everything had been going so well, despite the mundane nature of the mission. Move into the mountains and capture a young girl named Askari. Bring her to Captain Decado. What could have been simpler? No soldiers or Jiamads to fight, no opposition expected. It was merely another killing raid, and Corvin specialized in those.

More smoke billowed over him. He crossed the open

ground toward a low wall and sat down, removing his white-plumed brass helm and laying it on the stone. There was a body close by, a large man with his throat torn out. His right arm had been torn off. Corvin gazed around to look for it. Another touch of annoyance pricked him. One of the Jiamads had obviously taken it away for a forbidden meal. Gods, what did it matter? Dead flesh was dead flesh.

He glanced across at another body, a dead Jiamad. The creature was lying on its back, a black-feathered shaft jutting from its brow.

Decado might have warned him that the girl was a huntress. Damn, but that was a fine shot. Corvin had just killed the big, sandy-haired peasant who had refused to reveal the girl's whereabouts when she had appeared at the far end of the road. The Jiamads had picked up her scent first, and one of them called out to Corvin, pointing. He saw her, tall and slim, bearing a recurve bow of wood and horn. She pulled an arrow from her quiver and in one smooth motion drew and let fly. The shaft had buried itself in the head of the closest Jiamad—and he was more than two hundred feet from her. Then she had turned and sprinted away.

"Get after her!" yelled Corvin. Fifteen of his Jiamads had given chase. However, they were bred for power and not for speed. Still, they would find her by scent and bring her back before morning. Which meant he would have to spend the night in this squalid ruin.

The home of the big peasant was not ablaze, and Corvin crossed to it. It was an odd little place, the main room full of tables like a tiny inn. The officer rummaged around the untidy kitchen, finding a fresh-baked fruit pie. Breaking off a section, he tried it. Surprisingly good, he thought. The pastry was light, the filling sweet but not cloying. Some kind of berries had been used.

His young aide, Parnus, entered the room, saluting sharply. The boy was useless and would never make a soldier. He had rushed away to be sick almost as soon as the killing began. Even now his face was sallow, with a faint sheen to it.

"The pie is excellent, Parnus. I recommend it."

"No, thank you, sir." The young man's tone, though deferential, was cooler than before.

"What is wrong with you?"

"Might I speak freely?"

"Why not? Who is there to hear you, save me?"

The young man's eyes blazed, but he fought for control. "This was an act of evil," he said. "We were to capture a girl. Nothing was said about killing villagers."

"We *always* kill villagers in hostile territory. I think you are too weak for the role you have chosen. I shall recommend you be relieved of duty when we return. Then you can go back to your father's estates and learn how to raise sheep."

"Better to raise than to slaughter," snapped the young man. "This was not the work of warriors. This was cowardice."

"Are you calling me a coward, boy?"

"No, Corvin. What you did here today was heroism of the highest order. I think they will sing songs about you in future days. By the way, some of the Jiamads have gone off into the woods. They dragged off two of the bodies of the women. I expect they are feeding—which is contrary to the rules of engagement. Any officer who knowingly allows cannibalism is subject to death by strangulation. Rule One Hundred and Four, I think."

Corvin laughed. "Quite right, Parnus. Then you had better find them and tell them to desist—especially since you are the officer on watch, and the responsibility is yours. It would pain me to have to report you for such a flagrant breach of the rules."

The young officer grew more pale. Then he spun on his heel and stalked from the room. "What a puppy!" muttered Corvin, taking up a long knife and carving himself another section of pie.

Corvin had spent the last ten years in the western army of the Eternal. The soldier's life suited him far better than his days as a clerk in the Diranan treasury. What a waste that had been. Women he had wanted spurned him; men treated him with mild contempt. Not so now. As an officer of the Eternal he had merely to snap his fingers and women would obey his every whim. It was better this way. He liked the fear in their eyes, and enjoyed the fact that they loathed his touch. It merely increased his sense of power. Men no longer treated Corvin with disrespect. They bowed, they smiled, they paid him compliments. The richer of them offered him money, or goods. This was not merely because of his military status. As a soldier Corvin had discovered a skill he had not realized he possessed. His speed of hand was extraordinary, and he had a natural talent with the blade. As a swordsman men spoke of him in the same class as Decado, and Corvin had now fought eleven duels. He had enjoyed every one of them. There was something exquisite about watching the change of expression on the face of an opponent. When the swords were first touched the duelists always looked the same, full of arrogance and the belief that they were invulnerable. This look would remain for the first few exchanges. Then a tiny trace of doubt would insinuate itself. The eyes would grow more wary, and they would focus their concentration. Finally there would be fear, naked and obvious to all. Their movements would become more frenzied as the fear wormed its way deeper into their souls. At the last there would be a look of total surprise as Corvin's blade plunged into their hearts. Corvin would step in then, his face close to the dying victim. He would stare into their eyes, holding them up as he watched life evaporate.

Corvin trembled with pleasure at the thought of it.

He felt truly blessed by the Source.

Belching loudly, he pushed himself to his feet, took up his helm, and walked back out into the night. From the east he heard a high-pitched howl. They were closing in on the girl. He swore suddenly. Had he told them that she must be taken alive? He swore again. No, he had not. Decado would not be pleased, and that was something Corvin needed to avoid. People who displeased Decado did not survive.

A low groan came from his left. Glancing down, he saw

the big, sandy-haired man he had stabbed earlier roll over. Good humor returned briefly. Corvin strolled toward him.

"You make a fine pie," he told the man. Drawing his saber, Corvin tapped the man on the shoulder. "You could have been rich in Diranan."

The man groaned again, struggled to rise, then fell back. Blood was seeping through the apron he wore. "I could have sworn I pierced your heart. Lie still. I will end your misery."

The man looked up at him. He said nothing, made no attempt to defend himself. "Let me think," said Corvin. "If I cut your throat you will bleed to death more swiftly. It will be less painful. Or perhaps the large artery in the groin would be better. At least that way you will not choke to death. Which would you prefer? I am feeling generous toward you."

Corvin heard footsteps and turned. His young aide was running toward him. Parnus stumbled and half fell. Corvin squinted against the smoke. The boy's breastplate was smeared with blood.

Parnus reached him and collapsed sprawling to the ground. Corvin looked down at him. The side of his bronze breastplate was smashed, and Corvin saw a gaping wound in his side. Parnus tried to speak, but blood bubbled into his mouth and he sagged back. Corvin stared hard at the ruined breastplate. What on earth could have destroyed it in such a fashion? No sword could possibly have shattered the metal.

Ignoring the dying boy, Corvin moved out onto open ground. "Jiamads to me!" he bellowed. "At once!" Wherever they were feeding, they would hear him.

Returning to Parnus he knelt beside him. "What happened? Tell me."

"Two . . . men. Ax . . . am I . . . dying?"

"Yes, you are dying. Two men, you say. Where are the Jiamads?"

"Three . . . dead. Swordsman . . . killed two." More blood gouted from the boy's mouth, spattering Corvin's sallow cheek. A sound came from his right. Glancing up, he saw a hulking Jiamad moving through the smoke. Leaving the dying boy, he called out. "Over here!"

The beast lumbered toward him. "Which one are you?" demanded Corvin, who rarely bothered with the names of Jiamads.

"Kraygan," answered the creature. There was blood on its extended maw, and it had obviously been feeding.

"There are two men out there. Can you scent them?"

"Too much smoke." Then it snorted. "Need no scent," it said. "They are here." It pointed a taloned hand toward the south.

It was as Parnus had said. There were two men. One was tall and slim, wearing an ankle-length coat of dark leather, the other hulking, black bearded, and brutish. This one carried a glittering, double-headed ax. "Kill the axman," he told Kraygan. "I will deal with the swordsman."

The Jiamad drew a heavy longsword and lumbered toward the men.

The beast charged the axman. Corvin watched as it bore down on the peasant. Instead of trying to escape, he leapt to meet the creature. The sword swept down. The ax crashed against it, shattering the blade, then almost instantly reversed its sweep and clove through Kraygan's neck. The speed of the Jiamad's charge carried the dying beast forward, his body hammering into the axman and hurling him from his feet. Kraygan staggered on for several steps, then pitched to the ground. The axman rose and turned toward Corvin.

"Leave him to me, Harad!" called out the swordsman. The black-bearded peasant hesitated.

Corvin raised his saber in mock salute. "Ah, you intend to duel with me?" he asked the slim man.

"No, I shall merely kill you."

Corvin smiled. There was that familiar arrogance again. He glanced at the curved sword the man carried. It was similar in shape to Decado's treasured weapons. Indeed, the man

also wore a scabbard across his shoulders. Corvin could see
the ivory hilt of a second sword contained in it. *I will be the
envy of the regiment when I return with these,* he thought.

Stepping forward, he slashed the air to left and right, loosening the muscles of his shoulder. His opponent stepped in.
Corvin knew he should finish the duel swiftly and then kill
the clumsy axman, but such moments were too sweet to
rush. He looked into the sapphire eyes of his opponent and
wondered how they would look when the light faded from
them.

Their swords touched. Corvin stepped back.

"Show me what you have," said the swordsman.

Corvin launched a careful attack, testing the skills of his
opponent. The man had speed and good balance. He blocked
and parried with ease, and offered no counterattack that
would open him up to a riposte. Corvin increased the tempo,
his blade slashing, plunging, and cutting with bewildering
speed. Again all his attempts were blocked. Twice more he
attacked, using techniques that had won for him in the past.
The man merely parried them, or stepped smoothly aside.

Corvin leapt back and reached for his dagger. He stopped.
If he drew it then his opponent would bring his second sword
into play.

The man smiled. "Pull your blade," he said. "I would like
to see how well you use it."

Corvin drew the dagger. Far from increasing his confidence, the new weapon seemed to leach it away. The swordsman was waiting calmly. "I do not need it!" said Corvin,
hurling the dagger aside.

"You certainly need more than you have," replied the
swordsman.

Corvin swallowed hard. A sense of unreality gripped him.
This could not be happening. He was Corvin, the great du-
elist. He attacked again, taking more and more risks, coming
closer and closer to the death blow. One lunge missed the
man's throat by a hairbreadth. Just a few moments more and

victory would be his. Their blades clashed. A sharp pain erupted in his groin. Corvin sprang back. And staggered.

He had not realized he was so weary. All strength seemed to be fading from him. His right leg felt warm and wet. He looked down. His dark leggings were stained. Corvin's legs gave way and he fell to his knees. There was a deep cut in the cloth over his groin. Dropping his sword, he pulled open the cloth. Blood pumped over his fingers. The femoral artery had been severed.

Pushing his hand against the wound, he struggled vainly to stem the flow.

"Help me," he begged his killer. "Please help me."

The man gazed around the burning settlement. "Men like us are beyond help," he said. "We are the Damned. I fear you will not enjoy your time in the Void."

Running was not an activity Stavut enjoyed, but then enjoyment was the farthest thought from his mind as he sprinted after the long-legged huntress. He had followed her down to the edge of the settlement and had seen the Jiamads, the fires, and the bodies. That had been enough for Stavut.

"Let's get out of here!" he said, grabbing her arm.

Askari shook herself loose and stepped out into the open, nocking an arrow to her bow. Her face in the moonlight had looked hard as stone. Stavut watched in horror as the Jiamads saw her. He had followed the flight of her arrow, seeing it punch through a Jiamad skull.

Then she had turned and run back past him. For a moment only Stavut had remained where he was; then he, too, ran for his life. Stavut was slim and young, but years of riding wagons and avoiding physical labor had taken their toll on his stamina. Even so all it took to give him fresh strength was to glance back and see the bestial creatures following hard, their lupine jaws gaping, their golden eyes gleaming with feral hate.

Once into the woods he almost lost Askari as she leapt fallen trees and swerved through breaks in the undergrowth.

Stavut did not dare look back now. He had no idea if the creatures were farther behind or so close as to almost touch him. His lungs were burning, his calves on fire. He could no longer feel the toes of his right foot.

Up ahead he saw a massive wall of rock. Askari reached it and immediately began to climb the sheer face. There was no way Stavut was going to follow her. Then a blood-chilling howl came from somewhere close behind—and Stavut found a way. He ran to the rock face and scrabbled for a hold, heaving himself up. He climbed on, not looking down, his heart hammering in his chest. Above him Askari levered herself onto a ledge.

"Move faster!" she said, swinging around to look down past him.

Before he could stop himself Stavut glanced down. A Jiamad was climbing just below him—so close that he could almost reach out a taloned hand and drag Stavut from the rock face. But it was not the Jiamad that caused Stavut's hands to clench hard to the rock. It was the height he had reached, some ninety feet above the ground. He began to feel dizzy, and the cliff seemed to sway against him. Unreality gripped him and his mind began to swirl.

An arrow slashed past him, and he heard a grunt from below. Looking down again he saw a black-feathered shaft jutting from the Jiamad's neck. A second shaft thudded into its head and it fell, its body spinning to crash into the rocks below.

"What are you doing, idiot?" Askari asked him.

Anger roared through him. The dizziness was swamped by it. Stavut surged upward, clawing at the handholds until he heaved himself onto the ledge alongside the huntress.

"What am *I* doing? It wasn't me who shot one. It wasn't me who caused these creatures to come after us. We could have just slipped away. But no, you had to be the warrior woman."

Askari leaned out over the drop. There were no other Jiamads climbing. "We couldn't have slipped away," she said.

"The wind was changing. They would have picked up our scent."

"Well, they didn't need our scent, did they? Not after you showed yourself."

Askari sighed and sat back. "They have killed my friends and burned my home. You think I would let them walk away unscathed? I will hunt them and kill them all."

Stavut suddenly grunted in pain as a cramp struck his right calf. He swore loudly and tried to massage the twisted muscle. "Lie back," said Askari, laying aside her bow and kneeling beside him. Her fingers dug into his calf. It was agonizing for a moment, and then the cramp eased.

"You are not very fit," she said. "Your muscles are soft."

As she continued to rub his leg he realized, with a sudden rush of embarrassment, that at least one part of his anatomy was no longer soft. "That's fine! That's fine!" he said, easing himself back from her, hoping that the sudden erection would pass unnoticed.

She laughed. "The old hunter told me that danger and arousal always came together."

"Nothing to do with danger," he snapped. "I usually get excited when women rub my leg. Anyway, what are we going to do now that they've gone?"

"Oh, they haven't gone," she said, brightly. "I would imagine they are taking the long path up to the cliff top. Within the hour they will be both above and below us."

"And there is a reason you are reacting to this so cheerfully?"

"I don't want them gone," she said. "If they go it will be harder to kill them."

"Are you insane? These are Jiamads. They are bred to kill. There are twenty, maybe thirty of them."

"There are fourteen still following us," she said. "I have enough arrows left—and more close by. We will survive."

"You *are* insane."

"I have already killed two," she pointed out.

"True. One was shot before he realized you were there.

The second was hanging on a rock face. These creatures can tell where you are by scent alone. How will you hunt them down? How will you get close enough to pick them off? One mistake and they will be upon you."

"I do not make mistakes."

"So now we move from insanity to arrogance. *Everyone* makes mistakes. It is part of life. I watched Alahir and his men go after a few Jiamads. The Legend people are great warriors and fearless. Three were killed. All it would take for you to die would be one misplaced arrow."

"I do not miss."

"There you go again. It took *two* shafts to kill the beast climbing below me. If he had been on level ground, and charging you, then that first *miss* would have seen it reach you and rip your arms off."

"I missed because I was trying to shoot around *you.*" She sighed. "But there is truth in what you say. So tell me your plan."

"My plan? What plan would that be?"

Askari took a deep breath and stared at him hard. "You don't want me to fight them, so what do you think we should do? At the moment they are looking to surround us. I know a way through the rock face, but that will only bring us out onto open ground again. There they can come at us in a group. So what do you advise?"

Stavut sighed. "I'd go for prayer, but I don't think the Source likes me. Perhaps we could sit here and hope they go away."

She laughed then, the sound rich and infectious. "Oh Stavut, were there ever any warriors in your family?"

"I had an uncle who liked to get into arguments in taverns," he said. "Does that count?"

Askari leaned out over the ledge and scanned the ground below. Then she looked up. Clouds were gathering, but at that moment the moon was bright in the sky. "When the clouds cover the moon," she said, "I want you to follow me."

"And where would we be going?"

"Into the cliff. There is an entrance farther along the ledge. It leads to a series of caves and tunnels. I camp here sometimes."

"Will it be safe?" he asked.

"There are other entrances from above. However, the tunnels are narrow, and they can only come at us one at a time. I should be able to kill them as they seek us."

"Good. More killing. More terror."

She laughed again. "Do not be so downcast, Stavi. It is lucky you brought me this bow. It is shorter and easier to use than my longbow. Especially in the confines of the tunnels."

"Are you not frightened at all?" he asked.

"What difference does it make? Would an increase in my fear bring us closer to safety? I am Askari. These creatures do not scare me. Nothing that lives or breathes can escape death, Stavi."

"That is the second time you have called me Stavi. I prefer Stavut."

"Why? Stavi is more . . . friendly."

"My mother called me Stavi. I do not see you in a maternal role."

"I see. What does your friend Alahir call you?"

"He has taken to calling me Tinker. I don't like that either."

"And I shall call you Stavi—because I like the sound of it. I think it fits you well."

A sudden darkness fell upon the cliff face. Askari stood and, taking Stavut by the hand, moved along the ledge. It began to narrow. Within a short distance they were edging along a shelf of rock less than a foot wide. Stavut began to sweat. It dripped into his eyes. Askari squeezed his hand. "Not much farther," she said. Stavut's legs began to tremble, but he found the touch of her hand reassuring. They inched on. He saw Askari glance up at the clouds. The moon was almost clear. Then they came to a crack in the rock face no more than two feet wide. Askari edged into it. Stavut followed. Within it was pitch black.

"Keep hold of my hand," she said. "We will need to move

slowly." He could not see her. He could not see anything. Yet such was the relief at being away from the high ledge that he was relaxed as they made their slow way through the darkness. She stopped often, and subtly altered the line of their advance. Stavut did not ask why. He just followed her into the cold, gloomy depths of the cliff. After a while they halted. "We will wait for moonlight," she whispered.

"Moonlight?"

"Yes. We need to climb again. Be patient. It will come."

Stavut did not know how long they were standing together, but at last a faint light began to glow above them. He saw there was a crack in the rocks, and moonlight was seeping through it. He could just make out Askari's face. She was standing alongside another sheer rock wall. "Up there," she whispered, "is another cave. I have tools there, and a few items we might find useful. It is an easy climb. You go first. I will follow and guide your feet as you climb."

"Gods!" whispered Stavut. "Do we have to climb again?"

"If you want to live," she said.

Stavut climbed. The rock face here was heavily pitted, and, as she had promised, the climb was not difficult. Toward the top, however, the holds were smaller. Askari braced herself beneath him, supporting his feet. Finally Stavut dragged himself onto yet another wide ledge. Askari came alongside him, then moved on, crawling along a narrow tunnel into a wider cave. Here there was another jagged opening in the wall, some twelve feet high—a natural window through which moonlight shone. Weary now, Stavut stumbled into the cave. There was wood here for a fire, and an old lantern stood on a shelf of rock. A quiver of arrows was lying nearby, and a long spear with a leaf-shaped iron head. There were also three blankets and some clay pots.

"Very homey," said Stavut. Askari gestured for him to remain silent. Stepping in close she whispered in his ear.

"Sound travels far in these caves. Let us not speak."

"How many ways in?" he replied, his lips close to her ear.

"Just the way we came. The Jiamads are too large to crawl

through. You will be safe here. Get some rest. I shall scout."
She pointed up to a narrow shelf of rock just below and to
the left of the window in the cave wall. "Take a blanket and
climb up there. I doubt your scent will carry to them from
there."

This seemed sound advice to Stavut. Taking her bow,
Askari returned to the entrance, dropped to her stomach, and
eased her way into the low tunnel. Stavut wandered across
the cave to where the blankets lay. Then he glanced at the
spear. Hefting it, he practiced a few stabbing motions. It
would probably be useless against a Jiamad, but he felt more
comfortable with it in his hands. Taking blanket and spear,
he returned to the far wall. At this point he realized he could
not climb to his hiding place with the spear in his hands. He
tied the blanket tightly around his waist. Then he slid the
spear, haft-first, between his shoulder blades and under the
blanket. The spear was six feet long, which meant that the iron
point jutted above Stavut's head. Satisfied the blanket would
hold the spear in place, he began to climb.

Everything went well until he tried to lever himself over the
lip of the shelf. The jutting spear point scraped against the
rock. Stavut had to bend and twist in order to tumble onto
the shelf. The area he found himself in was no bigger than a
large bed. The roof was low, and there was certainly no
space to use a spear. It took an age to squirm around and un-
tie the blanket, pulling the spear loose. "Gods, you are an idiot!" he told himself.

Skilgannon moved past the dead officer and knelt beside
the wounded villager. Harad came alongside. "This is
Kinyon," he said. A flash of lightning illuminated the sky,
followed by a series of rolling thunderclaps. The skies
opened and rain began to pour down on the burning village.

"Help me get him inside," said Skilgannon. "Careful
now—that wound might open further."

With great care they lifted the burly villager, who groaned.

His head sagged against Skilgannon's shoulder, and he tried to speak. "Stay quiet, man. Conserve your strength."

Carrying him into his house, they laid him on a table in the dining area. Skilgannon untied the leather apron the man wore, pulling it clear. He had been stabbed just below the heart, and he was bleeding profusely. Skilgannon took a lantern from the wall and bade Harad to hold it over the wound. There was a long tear to the skin, indicating the dagger blade had slid against a rib. There was no way of knowing how deep the wound was, but it had missed the heart; otherwise the villager would have died some time ago. There was no blood on his lips, and no major swelling around the wound itself. With luck the blade might also have missed the lungs, or only nicked them.

"See if you can find some wine and honey," Skilgannon told Harad. The logger laid the lantern on the table, then moved off toward the kitchen. "Can you breathe deeply?" Skilgannon asked Kinyon. The man gave the merest nod. "I think you might be lucky, though it probably doesn't feel that way just at this moment. Do you possess needle and thread?"

"Back room," whispered Kinyon. Skilgannon moved away to the small bedroom at the rear of the house, searching through drawers and cupboards. Finally he found a length of white thread and several needles. He also uncovered a pair of scissors. Taking a sheet from the bed, he cut strips from it for bandages and returned to the dining room. Harad was beside Kinyon when he returned. Carefully Skilgannon stitched the long wound, then smeared honey over it. With Harad's help he sat Kinyon upright and bandaged his chest. Lastly, he poured wine over the area of the wound, watching as it seeped through the bandage. Kinyon's face was gray. Skilgannon fetched a goblet and filled it with water. "Drink," he said. The villager sipped at it, then sank back.

Touching his fingers to the man's throat, Skilgannon took his pulse. The heart was fluttering wildly, but this was as likely to be as a result of shock and terror as the wound itself.

He and Harad helped Kinyon to his bed. Outside the rain was lashing down in a torrent, thunder constantly rolling across the sky.

Once Kinyon was sleeping, Skilgannon walked out into the dining room. Harad was by the window, staring out into the darkness. Many of the house fires were beginning to fail, but there were still enough flames to illuminate the bodies on the ground outside.

"Why did they kill these people?" asked Harad. "What purpose did it serve?"

Skilgannon shrugged. "Fox in a henhouse."

"What?"

"A fox gets into a henhouse. It doesn't just kill to eat. It kills everything. An orgy of death. I don't know why. Some men just like to kill. That officer was such a man. We shouldn't stay here long. There are far more of those Joinings—Jiamads as you call them."

"We can't leave Kinyon to them."

"He is not my responsibility."

"Then leave," snapped Harad. "I will defend him."

Skilgannon laughed. "No, Harad, I will not leave. Kinyon may not be my responsibility, but you are."

Harad turned and stared at the swordsman, his pale blue eyes glittering. "I am no one's responsibility."

"Try to control your anger," advised Skilgannon. "I meant that you are my friend, and I do not desert my friends."

Harad relaxed. "Will he live, do you think?"

"I don't know. He is strong."

"There was a lot of blood."

"Not really. A little blood goes a long way. I have bled worse than that, and recovered within days. It depends on whether the dagger pierced any vital organs. We will not know for a while."

Harad rose from beside the window and walked back to the kitchen, returning with the remains of a pie. He sat quietly for a while eating. The storm continued into the night, and eventually all the fires went out. Skilgannon found the remains of a loaf and half a round of cheese. Then he, too, ate. There was no conversation for some time, but the silence was comfortable. Several times the swordsman moved back into the bedroom, checking on Kinyon, who was sleeping.

The rain eased away just before the dawn. Harad was dozing in a chair by the hearth. Skilgannon left the house and walked out into the open. The smell of smoke was still in the air. In the gathering light he walked down the main road, scanning the ground for tracks. He found the body of a Jiamad with a black-feathered shaft jutting from its skull. So someone had put up a fight. Moving farther on, he came to rising ground. Here there were other tracks. With great care he examined them. Someone had come down from the high country, stopped, then turned and run back into the hills. A group of Jiamads had followed. The Jiamad tracks were large. The person they were chasing had small feet, like a child, but the length of the running stride showed it was no child. More likely it was a woman. He followed the tracks for a while. It was not easy. The pursuing Jiamads had run over the same ground, mostly obliterating the trail of the quarry. Here and there, however, Skilgannon found traces of human feet. Two sets of tracks. Someone wearing boots, and the second person—the one with the small feet—wearing moccasins.

He did not want to venture too far and returned to Kinyon's house. When he got back he found several people there, a small man with frightened eyes and two weary women. They were sitting with Harad. They, and some of the other villagers, had escaped into the woods to the east. Skilgannon moved past the group and into Kinyon's bedroom. The sandy-haired man was awake, and his color was better.

"I thank you for your help," he said. "Have the beasts gone?"

"For now. Do you know why they came?"

"They were looking for Askari."

"Who is he?"

"She," corrected Kinyon. "A young huntress who lives here."

"Ah! That explains the dead Jiamad shot by an arrow. Why did they want her?"

"I don't know."

"Who was with her?"

"A merchant named Stavut. Nice young man. He is very fond of her, though I think his hopes will be dashed. The Lord Landis Khan takes a great personal interest in Askari. I think he wants her for himself."

"I take it she is beautiful."

"All women are, in my experience," said Kinyon with a smile. "Did she escape them?"

"She made it to the high woods. What happened then I do not know. The beasts were following her."

"She'll kill a lot of them," said Kinyon. "A year back we had a rogue bear in the high country. Butchered three travelers. Askari hunted and slew it. She is fearless and very, very good with a bow."

"I like the sound of her. I hope she made it."

"On her own she'd get away from them," said Kinyon. "I'm not sure, though, if Stavut is with her. He is a good lad, but not a woodsman. He'll slow her down, for sure. Added to that he always wears red clothes, so they'll not be able to hide very easily."

"You don't think she'll leave him behind?"

"I wouldn't think so. Not the kind of woman who would leave a friend to his fate, if you know what I mean."

"I know what you mean," said Skilgannon.

Leaving Kinyon, he returned to the main room. More villagers had arrived, and the room was crowded. They had lit a fire in the hearth and were sitting with the others. Harad was outside. Skilgannon joined him.

"What do we do now?" asked the young logger.

"Either we leave and forget about the beasts, or we follow them and kill as many as we can."

"I say follow them."

"I thought you would. This time I agree with you."

"You do?" said Harad, surprised. "Why the change of heart?"

"They came to capture a woman dear to Landis Khan. I want to know why she is important enough to send a raiding party."

Eight

Stavut lay in his blankets, unable to sleep. Images of Jiamads with slavering jaws filled his mind. He had fought hard to retain his composure while with Askari. No man liked to look feeble in front of a woman he desired. Alahir called it the "swan impersonation"—serene on the surface, little legs paddling furiously below. But the horror of the night's events were telling on Stavut now. His hands were trembling, and his fertile imagination produced more images of dismemberment and death.

"Imagination is a curse to a warrior," Alahir had said once. He was mildly drunk, and working hard to reach a comatose state. "I once saw a friend have his spine snapped. We were out riding—racing in fact—and his horse stumbled and threw him. When I got to him I thought he was just stunned. But he was awake and couldn't move. Took him a month to die." Alahir had shivered. "That haunted me for a while."

"How did you overcome it?" Stavut had asked.

"You know the Dragon's Horns?"

Stavut nodded. A tower of rock close to Alahir's home city of Siccus. Around two hundred feet high, the top was split, creating the impression of horns. "Well, I saw a holy man and told him that I couldn't get the thought of Egar's accident out of my mind. He told me to leap the Dragon's Horns, then mention my fears to the Source."

Stavut was horrified. "You didn't do it?"

"Of course I did. Holy men know what they're talking about."

"You jumped across a chasm."

"It wasn't a chasm, idiot. No more than ten feet wide at the narrowest point. Then I sat down and talked to the Source. After that all my fear went away."

"Did the Source answer you?"

"Of course He did. Didn't I just say my fears went away?"

"No, I mean did you hear His voice?"

"I don't hear voices anymore," replied Alahir, his expression hardening. "I wish I'd never mentioned them to you. Anyway, that's not the point of the story."

"What is?"

"I don't know," said Alahir, returning to his ninth jug of ale and draining it. "Can't remember why I even mentioned it. Oh yes!" he added, brightly, "fears and suchlike."

"The Source had nothing to do with it," insisted Stavut. "You became aware of mortality when your friend died, and then did something mindless, stupid, and dangerous in order to convince yourself that you are really immortal and nothing can hurt you."

"Sounds good to me," said Alahir amicably, his voice slurring. "I don't much care which it was. The fear went away. Maybe you should try it."

"I will. I'll put it high on my list of things to do. Just behind slapping the balls of a hungry lion."

Alahir smiled. "You are a strange man, Tinker. You talk yourself down all the time. But I know you—better than you know yourself. You are stronger than you think. And that's your problem, you know. You think too much." Then he belched loudly. "You think this ale is a little weak?" he asked. "It doesn't seem to be hitting the spot."

Stavut was about to answer, but Alahir rose to call for another jug. His legs gave way and he sank slowly to the floor.

"What do you think you are doing?" asked Stavut.

"I think I'll camp here for the night," said Alahir, lying down.

Thoughts of his friend helped ease Stavut's fears as he lay wedged on the narrow rock shelf.

A noise from below jerked him back to the present. Fear blossomed. Easing himself up, he glanced over the shelf. Moonlight was shining through the high opening in the roof of the cave. By its light he saw that Askari had returned. There was blood on her face. Then the moonlight was cut off. Stavut swung his head. A huge Jiamad was clambering through the window opening. Askari swept up her bow and loosed a shaft. It slammed against a wide bronze rivet on the creature's leather breastplate and ricocheted away. With a bloodcurdling roar the beast leapt into the cave.

Grabbing the spear Stavut levered himself over the ledge and jumped, screaming at the top of his voice. The Jiamad spun and looked up. Stavut slammed into the beast, the spear hammering into its neck, then plunging down through its chest. Stavut hit the ground hard. He rolled to his knees. Askari was shooting again. A second beast fell to the cave floor, an arrow through its eye. It was thrashing around in its death throes. Stavut glanced around at the Jiamad he had leapt upon. It was dead. The spear had hit it at the base of the neck and been driven through it, impaling the heart.

"We are in trouble," said Askari. "There is no way out."

Harad sat in the entrance of a shallow cave, overlooking a sheer cliff face. Moonlight bathed the rocks only intermittently, as gathering rain clouds filled the sky. They had followed the tracks to this spot, but lack of light led Skilgannon to call off the hunt until dawn.

The swordsman was sleeping lightly at the rear of the cave, his two swords lying beside him unsheathed.

Harad felt at peace. He knew this was strange. All his life he had struggled with a volatile temper, and an underlying anger that troubled him. Now, however, in the midst of a hostile forest, in pursuit of terrifying beasts, he felt calm and untroubled. Hefting the ax, he stared at the silver runes engraved on the black haft. The weapon was beautiful. There was not a single nick in the blades, not a speck of rust. With Snaga in his hands Harad felt almost immortal.

"You should get some rest," said Skilgannon, moving silently alongside him. Harad jerked.

"By heaven, must you always creep up on a man?"

Skilgannon smiled. "My apologies, Axman."

Harad shivered. "Don't call me that. It feels . . . wrong somehow. I can't explain it."

"You don't have to." The moon appeared again, shining down on the Jiamad body at the base of the cliff face, some thirty feet below them. "They climbed that cliff," said Skilgannon. "The Jiamads did not follow. They skirted it to the west. The girl and the merchant found either a way over, or a way in. Let us hope it was the latter."

"A way in to what?" asked Harad.

Skilgannon pointed to the cliff wall. It was pitted with cave entrances. "I'd say there were tunnels and crevices within the cliff. I think she knew where she was going. On the other hand she may have tried to outrun them. That would not have been wise. Joinings have immense stamina."

"How long do we wait?"

"Until dawn. We don't want to be stumbling around in the dark."

"They could kill her by then."

"Yes, they could. But once inside, in the dark, we could face two sets of perils. She is a huntress. As far as she knows there are only enemies close by. I would rather not be shot by someone I am trying to help."

"Good point," agreed Harad. They sat in comfortable silence for a while. Then Harad spoke again. "How skilled was that officer you killed?"

"He had talent and speed of hand."

"You beat him easily."

"He lacked heart, Harad."

"Courage, you mean?"

"Not exactly. A warrior with heart can reach inside himself and find the impossible. Druss was like that. He was an older man when I met him—around fifty. He was ill. Yet when we were attacked he found strength somewhere, and tore into the Nadir warriors facing us. You can't teach that. You can improve skill and speed and strength. But heart is something a man is born with. Or not—as with that officer. You have it, Harad. He did not."

"Aye, but it is not mine, is it?"

"What do you mean?"

"I am a Reborn. Everything I have comes from Druss the Legend. What is there of Harad?"

"I am no philosopher, my friend. And I do not understand the magic by which you were born. And, yes, there is much of Druss in you. But you are who you are. More than that, you are who you choose to be. It seems to me that the same concerns could be voiced by any man born of woman. How much of my father is in me? How much of my mother? How many of their weaknesses am I cursed with? How much of their strength can I call my own? Landis Khan tried to explain to me the process of rebirth, but I confess it shot past me like an arrow. What I did manage to hold on to was that the *physical* essence of the original person, their seed if you like, is obtained from the bones. The only difference between you and any other man is that you have only one parent and not two."

"There is nothing of my mother in me?" asked Harad. "How can that be?"

Skilgannon spread his hands. "Landis Khan spoke of seeds and eggs and arcane machines. None of it made much sense to me. What I did understand was that the rebirth produced a physical duplicate of the original. But this is my point. It is *physical*. What truly makes a man who he is? Is it the strength of his arms, or the courage in his soul? You have your own soul, Harad. You are not Druss. Live your own life."

Harad let out a long deep breath. "Aye, it is good advice. I know that. And yet . . ." The big man sighed. "I think I'll sleep now."

"I'll keep watch," said Skilgannon.

Rain began to fall, at first merely a few drops pitter-pattering on the rocks around the cave entrance. Then the clouds opened. Skilgannon eased himself back from the entrance. Rivulets of water began to stream down the cave wall as the sudden storm found cracks in the cliff face above. Skilgannon sheathed his swords and sat on a rock. As fast as it had come the storm suddenly passed, and the sky cleared. Moonlight bathed the cliffs opposite. Harad began to snore. Skilgannon moved back to the entrance.

The air was fresh, and he could smell the closeness of the nearby pine trees. High above him the stars were bright in the night sky. The same stars he recalled from his youth.

His heart felt suddenly heavy. The same stars that had shone upon him when he had first met Jianna, that had blazed above him as he had grown to manhood and taken up the cursed Swords of Night and Day. And by their light he had overseen the slaughter of every man, woman, and child in the city of Perapolis.

Another life.

He shivered suddenly, as the old memories flowed. Like the rivulets on the cave wall they seeped out from the hidden recesses of his mind.

He and the young Angostin warrior, Vakasul, had just returned from a scouting trip into the mountains. Skilgannon had been tired, and yet exultant. News had reached them of a great battle to the south. The Naashanites had fought the Zharn outside the old city of Sherak. Jianna, the Witch Queen, had crushed the Zharn army and sent them fleeing north. Such a victory was sure to have earned breathing space for the Angostins, and Skilgannon, returning once more to his home on the cliffs above the sea, felt confident for the first time in months. There were gulls wheeling in the air, and the sun was shining in a cloudless sky. Skilgannon's aches had all but disappeared; he felt at peace with himself. Vakasul had taken the horses back to the stables. Skilgannon had strode into the east wing of the house, and then through to the rear gardens. A team of gardeners were at work, pruning back flowering shrubs and preparing the soil for bedding plants. The air was rich with the scent of honeysuckle and rose. A servant brought him a cool drink, and another carried out letters that had arrived from court. These he left unopened while he enjoyed the scene in the gardens. Stepping from the broad patio, he wandered out to speak to the gardeners. One of them was planting pockets of golden blooms, edged with crimson, along the line of the path. The man glanced up as Skilgannon approached, and grinned. "I know, General! They will spread too far and block the path. But they are so pretty it will be worth it."

Skilgannon squatted down. "They are beautiful. What are they called?"

"Bride's Garland is the common name, General. Sadly, there is no scent." Skilgannon chatted to the man for a while, and then saw Vakasul approaching. He walked with the young warrior back to a shaded area of the patio, and they sat together while Skilgannon opened his letters. There was little of import. Putting down the last of them, he glanced at his companion. The warrior seemed edgy.

"What is troubling you, my friend?"

"News from the south, General. I don't know how it will affect us. After the Battle of Sherak the Witch Queen took ill and died. You think that will affect how the Naashanites deal with the Zharn?"

Then—as now—the shock of the words stunned him. The world changed in an instant. Above the garden the sky was unbearably blue, and he found himself staring up into the heavens. "Are you ill, General?" Vakasul's concern was genuine, but Skilgannon raised a hand.

"Leave me now," he said.

He could not remember the young man's departure, nor what happened to the rest of that once beautiful afternoon.

Jianna was dead. The reality was so shocking that he could find no way of dealing with it. He had not seen her in thirty years, but rarely an hour passed in his life without him thinking of her, knowing that she stood under the same sun, and breathed the same air. Only now she did not, and Skilgannon felt more alone than at any other time in his life.

The shock was too great for tears. He sat quietly, thinking back to those glorious first days when she was disguised as a common whore, her dark hair dyed yellow with red strands. Her courage in the face of peril and treachery was colossal, her spirit unconquerable. And he had loved her with such passion there had been no room for any other in his life.

What he had not realized, until the moment he heard the news of her death, was that—despite the physical distance between them—the knowledge that she was alive *somewhere* was sustaining him in his own life. Added to which, he realized, he had secretly believed that someday they would find a way to be together.

Sitting now in the cave, the anguish he felt then returned with renewed power. He found himself wondering if he could have lived his life differently. Had he stayed with her perhaps he might have softened her thirst for power and empire. His eyes misted, and then anger flickered. "This would be a good time for Jiamads to come upon you, you weeping fool!" he whispered.

"You say something?" asked Harad, rolling to his feet, ax in hand.

"Talking to myself."

"You've been alone too long," said Harad.

"A thousand years too long," agreed Skilgannon. "Is there a woman in your life?"

"No."

"What about Charis?"

"What about her?" snapped Harad, reddening.

"She told me she was a friend of yours," said Skilgannon.

"Aye, I expect we are," muttered the young logger, defensively. "Were you married?"

"Once. A long time ago."

"You have children?"

"Not by my wife. She died young. Plague."

"You never married again?"

"No."

"You must have loved her greatly then."

"I didn't love her enough, Harad." Skilgannon glanced out of the cave. "Dawn is coming. Time to tackle that cliff, I think."

Stavut stood at the far wall, clutching the spear so tightly that his knuckles were bone white. It had taken all his strength—and powerful assistance from Askari—to wrench it from the body of the Jiamad. His hands were sticky with the congealing blood that covered the long haft. In the main he kept his eyes fixed on the high opening in the cave wall, through which several beasts had already attempted to clamber through. The first he had killed with the spear, the second had been shot through the eye by Askari. A third took a shaft through its taloned hand and fell back through the opening. Stavut hoped fervently he had also fallen to a bloody death on the rocks below.

His mouth was dry. He glanced at Askari, who was resting on one knee, an arrow nocked to the composite bow. Then his gaze was drawn to the dead Jiamads. In death they looked just as terrifying. Long fangs, wicked talons, and dark fur. He shivered. There had been fourteen, Askari had said. Because she had killed one on the cliff face. Another two were dead here. *Oh good,* he thought. *Only twelve left.*

The moonlight faded. Askari put down her bow and lit an old lantern. A dim golden light filled the cave. Placing it on a rock shelf, she stretched her arms over her head and took a deep breath.

"It will be dawn soon," she said.

"Perhaps they'll go away."

She turned to stare at him, then gave a wide grin. "Always jesting, Stavi. I like that about you."

He was not jesting, but decided to accept the compliment.

Then came a scraping noise from the rear of the cave. He swung to stare at the jumbled rocks and boulders. A small pebble dislodged and tumbled to the cave floor. "What is going on?" asked Stavut.

"I'd say they have found a blocked tunnel and are trying to clear it."

"They can't, though, can they?"

Askari shrugged. "How would I know?" Bow in hand, she ran to the rear of the cave and pressed her ear to the rocks. Then she strolled back to Stavut. "I can hear them tearing at the rock. I don't think they are far away."

"Better and better," said Stavut.

"Can you shoot a bow?" she asked.

"Why? How many bows do we have?"

She stepped in close and lowered her voice. "We have only one. Our only escape is up there, through the opening and out onto the cliff face. I need to know if there are more of them still out there. I can't climb and hold the bow ready to shoot."

"I always hate disappointing women," said Stavut, "but I'd be just as likely to shoot you. Marksmanship was never my strong point."

"What is?" she snapped, turning away from him.

"Mending kettles," he said softly. Another small stone dislodged itself from the rocks at the rear of the cave and clattered to the floor. Stavut took a deep breath, then walked to the far wall beneath the opening some fifteen feet above him. The wall was jagged, with jutting sections that made for easy climbing. Something cold settled inside Stavut. His mind cleared. There were twelve beasts left. Most would be needed to clear the boulders from the rear of the cave. How many would be waiting at the other two exits, the narrow tunnel and this high window? Probably only one at each of them. All he needed to do was to climb out, grab the beast, and lever himself from the rock face, dragging the Jiamad to its death. That would clear the way for Askari to escape. And without the burden of protecting him she would likely survive. He began to climb. Askari ran alongside him, grabbing his arm and hauling him back.

"What are you doing?" she said, her dark eyes showing her

concern. He told her his plan, and she stood looking into his eyes. Then she gave a soft smile and stroked his cheek.

"No, Stavi. We fight for life as long as we can."

He sighed, then took a deep breath. "Very well. When I reach that narrow shelf below the opening I want you to throw the spear up to me."

"You can't fight with a spear up there."

"I don't intend to fight with it. Now do as I ask." Returning to the wall, he picked up the spear and, using the hem of his shirt, polished the blade. He passed the weapon to the bemused Askari and climbed swiftly until he reached the shelf of rock. Cool air was blowing through the opening. Crouching down, he half turned. Askari flipped the spear up through the air. Stavut caught the haft, then levered himself higher. The opening widened toward the outside, becoming some six feet tall and five feet long. It would make no sense for a Jiamad to be above or below the opening. From above it would not be able to reach out and grab someone who was swift enough to clamber out and begin a fast descent. And from below it could be dislodged by someone appearing above it. No, the beast—or beasts—would be either left or right of the opening. Or both, he realized glumly.

Leaning into the rock face, Stavut allowed the spear haft to slide through his fingers until the curved iron head was just below his hand. As silently as he could, he eased the spear into the opening, his keen eyes fixed to the polished head, using it as a mirror. Inching the spear forward, he saw the stars reflected on the blade. Tilting the weapon slightly, he could just make out the sheer cliff wall to the left of the opening. There was no beast there. He had to withdraw the weapon in order to climb across to the right and repeat the maneuver. Slowly he slid the spear along the length of the opening.

A massive, taloned hand swept down, grabbing the spear. Stavut jerked and almost lost his hold on the rock. The Jiamad hauled itself into the opening with incredible speed.

Stavut saw long yellow fangs and a gaping maw hurtling toward his face. He froze.

An arrow slammed into the beast's open mouth, driving through the soft palate. It reared up in shock, its head slamming into the rock above it. Another arrow punctured its throat, and it sagged down, its head mere inches from Stavut's own. He found himself staring into golden eyes. The creature was blinking fast. Blood gushed from its mouth. Then the eyes closed. The body all but filled the opening. Reaching up, Stavut tried to pull it clear, but it was too heavy. Askari, her bow looped over her shoulder, came alongside him, and together they hauled the body out. It thumped to the floor below. At the rear of the cave a larger rock came tumbling clear.

"They are almost through," said Askari, levering herself into the opening and pulling Stavut up beside her. "Come on!"

She moved toward the lip of the opening. Stavut followed her and gazed down. The sheer cliff wall fell away for around two hundred feet. Stavut shrank back, nausea almost overwhelming him. He pushed his back against the wall and sat, eyes closed.

"Come on, Stavi!"

"Can't do it," he whispered.

"We'll die here if we don't!"

"I'm sorry. You go. Go on."

"You can do it!"

He opened his eyes and sighed. "No, Askari, I cannot. My legs are trembling and I can't move them. Go! Please just go."

"If all else fails I will do exactly that," she said, easing back past him and into the cave once more. With easy grace she climbed across to the shelf of rock where Stavut had rested earlier. Here she removed her quiver of arrows, laying them alongside her. Then she lifted her bow clear and nocked a shaft to the string.

"You can't take them all," he said.

"Why not?"

"Please don't die because of me!" he begged her.

The rear cave wall suddenly sagged and fell. Dust filled the air. Two Jiamads came running into the cave. Askari shot the first through the skull. The second staggered back, a shaft in its shoulder. Then eight more swarmed forward. Stavut, realizing that Askari would not leave if he still lived, grabbed the spear, hauled it out, then leapt down to the cave floor.

Two huge Jiamads charged him. He stabbed the spear at the first, who brushed it away. Then he was flung against the cave wall, striking his head.

Merciful darkness followed.

Nine

Skilgannon went first to the body of the dead Jiamad at the base of the cliff. From the angle of entry of the shafts, they had been fired from directly above. He glanced up and, in the predawn light, could just make out the narrow line of a ledge. "That is where we have to go," he told Harad. The black-bearded logger stared up, his expression doubtful.

"Do you fear heights?" asked Skilgannon.

"Of course not," growled Harad. "I was just wondering how I can climb that, and still carry Snaga." The ax blades were too wide and too wickedly sharp for the logger to push the haft into his belt. The wrong move, or a slip, could see the pointed upper or lower blades pierce his flesh.

"We will pass it between us," said Skilgannon. Stretching to the first handhold, he then placed his foot on a jut of rock and levered himself upward. "Hand me the ax," he said. "Then you climb."

It was painstaking and slow, but they reached the ledge safely, then followed it around until they came to a chimney of rock. This proved an easier climb, and at the top they came to a dark tunnel. Skilgannon crouched down at the entrance and peered inside. Closing his eyes, he drew in a deep, slow breath through his nostrils. "The beasts passed this way," he said, softly. Then he glanced at Harad. "Every step from here must be considered carefully," he whispered.

"We find them and kill them," said Harad, with the confidence of the young.

Skilgannon looked into his gray-blue eyes. *This man is not*

Druss, he told himself. *He is young and callow, and over-confident.* "Listen to me, Harad! You killed a Jiamad back at the village. But it knocked you from your feet, and you lost your grip on the ax. Had there been a second close by it would have torn your throat out. We are about to face up to fourteen of these creatures. The chances of getting out alive are remote. So walk warily. Do not charge in unless there is no other way. Follow my lead, and stay behind me." Moving stealthily, they followed the tunnel, but it soon branched off into a series of deep, impenetrable caves. Twice Harad stumbled in the darkness. Then they heard the sound of crashing rocks from some way to their left. Skilgannon drew the Swords of Night and Day and angled toward the sound. A thin shaft of light was shining through a crack in the high, domed cavern roof. Skilgannon stood for a while, scanning the area ahead. Harad moved around him. "It's coming from ahead. Is it a landslide, do you think? I wouldn't want to get trapped in here."

"Don't speak," hissed Skilgannon. "Sound carries far in caves like this."

Harad said nothing, but stepped past Skilgannon and moved out into a wider section of tunnel.

Something dark and huge suddenly loomed over him. Harad spun, the ax slashing out, but the Jiamad was upon him and all that struck it was Snaga's haft. The Jiamad's weight bore Harad back. Losing his footing, the young logger fell, the beast upon him. Harad's left hand slammed into the creature's throat, his fingers trying to prevent the long, vicious fangs from tearing at his face. But the power in the beast was astounding. Harad twisted under it, seeking to find a way to bring Snaga to bear. It was no use. His right arm was pinned beneath the Jiamad, and the strength in his left was fading. The fangs inched nearer to his throat. Glittering silver flashed above the Jiamad, and the beast's body spasmed. It flashed again. The head came loose in Harad's hand, blood from the severed jugular gushing over the front of his jerkin and splashing his face. With a grunt he heaved the head aside, then kicked himself free of the decapitated corpse.

"I'll say it again," said Skilgannon softly. "Stay *behind* me. There is no room in the tunnels to swing that ax."

Skilgannon moved forward stealthily, swords in hand. The tunnel widened, then branched off to the left. The sound of crashing rocks was louder now, and dust filled the air. Another, taller, tunnel beckoned. Skilgannon paused at the entrance and peered around the corner. Some thirty feet away he saw light appear as a huge boulder was pushed clear of a blocked opening. In that light was a group of ten Jiamads. Three of them were throwing their weight against another massive boulder. It must have weighed several tons. A screeching sound came from the stone. Then it toppled. A chorus of growls greeted the move, and the Jiamads rushed into the wide, dawn-lit cave beyond.

Skilgannon took a deep breath. A sensible man would withdraw at this point, he knew. He glanced at Harad. "What are we waiting for?" whispered the logger.

"We can't kill them all, Harad. To go in there is to die."

"Protect the weak against the evil strong," quoted Harad. "It didn't say anything about doing it only when you think you can win."

Skilgannon gave a tight smile. "True!"

With that he swung and ran down the tunnel, Harad behind him. Just as they emerged into the cave entrance Skilgannon saw a young man, in red tunic and leggings, hurl himself down into the mass of beasts. A young woman, her features in shadow, was shooting arrows down into the surging Jiamads.

Harad gave a great shout and charged. Several of the Jiamads were swarming up the rock face trying to reach the woman. One fell, an arrow through its skull. Others roared their defiance and rushed at Harad. The great ax smashed one from its feet, its neck torn open; a second fell to a reverse cut that clove through its ribs.

Just as a third bore down on the young axman Skilgannon

leapt in, sending a slashing cut into its face. The creature stumbled back, fell, and rolled to its feet.

For a few heartbeats no one moved. The Jiamads, surprised by the sudden arrival of the newcomers, pulled back to regroup. Harad was about to charge again. Skilgannon seized the moment. "Hold, Harad!" he shouted. Then he called up to the woman. "Loose no more shafts!" His voice rang with authority, but he knew the situation was fragile. Blood had been spilled, and the tension in the cave was palpable. One wrong word. One wrong move and the killing would begin again. "Who commands here?" he said, stepping toward the seven remaining beasts.

"Shakul leads," grunted a huge Jiamad, its fur darker than the rest, and its snout more rounded. *More bear than wolf in this one,* thought Skilgannon. The creature was tense, its taloned hands clenching and unclenching.

"What are your orders, Shakul?" The beast took a step toward him, but Skilgannon did not back away. He looked up into the creature's enormous eyes. "Your orders?" he repeated.

Shakul hesitated. The beast was torn between his desire to rend flesh and kill, and his training to be obedient to the wishes of humans. "Take woman," he said, at last.

"Where?"

"Corvin. Captain."

"Corvin is dead. Both your officers are dead. Your comrades outside this cave are dead. There is no one to take the woman to. You now have a decision to make."

Skilgannon saw the beast's golden eyes flicker. His head tilted, and he gave a low growl. Skilgannon quelled the urge to speak again. It was best to keep matters simple and wait. The moment was pivotal. Shakul swung to look at the remaining Jiamads, who were standing now, calmly awaiting his orders. Then the great beast glanced at the bodies of the Jiamads on the cave floor. His head shook, as if insects were buzzing around his eyes. "You soldier?" he asked.

"I am Skilgannon."

Shakul began to sway, his golden eyes on the swords in Skilgannon's hand. His talons opened and closed. Skilgannon sensed he was about to attack.

"We could kill each other," said Skilgannon. "Or not. You choose." Shakul wavered. He glanced up at the woman with the deadly bow, then at the axman standing ready. Skilgannon waited. And the tension eased.

"Corvin dead?"

"Yes."

"You kill Corvin?"

"Yes."

"Fight no more," said Shakul. "We go."

"Do no harm to the villagers, Shakul," said Skilgannon. "Either go back to your regiment or head north. No more killing here. Do I have your word?"

"Word?" The beast was uncertain.

"Your promise. No harm to Skins."

"No harm," said the beast, at last. Lifting a mighty arm he gestured at the waiting Jiamads, and they shuffled forward past him, toward the entrance. Shakul was the last to leave. He swung toward Skilgannon and looked into his eyes. But he said nothing. Then he, too, left the cave.

By the far wall the young man in red groaned and sat up. "I'm not dead," he said.

Then the young woman climbed down from the shadows of the rock shelf and turned toward Skilgannon.

He felt as if his heart had stopped beating.

"Jianna!" he whispered.

Just before the rear wall crashed in and the Jiamads burst through, Askari had emptied her quiver, laying her remaining shafts on the shelf wall. Then she had nocked one to the string and prepared to fight for her life. There was no fear in her, no regret, just a fierce determination to survive; to kill every enemy that came at her.

When the Jiamads did rush through she realized there was

to be no escape. There were too many, and they were too swift. At best she could kill three; then the others would swarm over the rock shelf and drag her down.

She watched Stavut make his suicidal leap down into them, and saw his body hurled against the rock wall. Even then there was no regret, and fear was absent from her. Coolly she loosed three shafts and reached for a fourth.

Then the miracle happened. Two warriors rushed into the fray, one black bearded and powerful, bearing a glittering double-headed ax, the second tall and lean, bearing two shining swords, one pale gold, the other moonlight silver.

In the brief battle that followed, two Jiamads were slain, and a third cut deeply across the face. Askari nocked an arrow to the string. Then the tall warrior called out: "Hold, Harad!" He glanced up at her, and she felt the shock of his sapphire gaze. "Loose no more shafts," he ordered. Then he called for the Jiamad leader to step forward. What followed seemed almost dreamlike to Askari. The beast obeyed him, and the two talked. Then, amazingly, the Jiamads filed out of the cave. For several heartbeats she remained where she was in the high shadows, staring down at the swordsman. She had only known one lord, and that was Landis Khan. He had authority and power. But not like this man. At his word all action had ceased, the power of his personality overlaying the violence and bloodlust. His accent was strange, each word carefully enunciated. It sounded almost like poetry. She heard Stavut groan, and saw him sit up. "I am not dead," he said, the words echoing in the silence. *Trust Stavut to voice the obvious,* she thought. Replacing her shafts in her quiver, she hooked it over her shoulder and climbed down from the rock shelf. Turning toward her rescuers, she was about to thank them when she saw all color fade from the swordsman's face. He was staring at her in shock. In his handsome face she saw both pain and longing.

"Jianna?" he whispered.

The intensity of the stare was uncomfortable, and Askari

decided to press on. "I am Askari the Huntress," she said. "This is my friend Stavut. We thank you for your help."

The swordsman struggled for words, then his expression darkened. Askari thought she saw anger there. "Better see to your friend," he said coldly, then turned away and walked to the rear of the cave and vanished into the darkness beyond. The axman approached her. "I am Harad. That is . . . was . . . Skilgannon."

"It seems he finds it easier to talk to beasts than to women," she said.

"Who doesn't?" muttered Harad, with feeling. There was something in the rawness of the man's honesty that made her smile. Askari moved to Stavut, crouching down beside him and examining his head. There was a large lump just into the hairline above his temple. The skin was split and oozing blood.

"You have a hard skull, Stavi."

"I feel sick," he said, "and the cave seems to be moving."

"Lie down," she ordered him. Fetching two blankets, she rolled one for a pillow, then covered him with the second. For the first time she felt the chill in the cave and shivered. The small lantern did not give out much heat, and she prepared a fire. Once it was blazing she sat down beside it, holding out her hands to the flames. Harad joined her. He was not a talkative man, but she discovered that he and Skilgannon had come from the village. It lifted her heart to know that Kinyon had survived. But what she really desired was information about the man with the sapphire eyes.

"Is he coming back?" she asked Harad. The big man shrugged.

"Have you been friends for long?"

"No. A few days. Landis Khan asked me to show him the high country. You have any food here?"

"There is some salt-dried beef in my pack. You are welcome to it. I am not hungry."

Harad accepted the gift and sat silently chewing the meat.

The lack of conversation became irritating, and Askari stood, gathered up her bow, and left the cave, wandering down the darkened tunnel, emerging at last to the rock ledge on the cliff face. Skilgannon was there, sitting quietly in the morning sunshine.

"Your friend Harad is not a talkative man," she said.

"One of the qualities I like about him," he said.

"Have I done something to anger you?"

"Not at all," he said, with an apologetic smile. "Please join me. The view from here is pleasant." Askari settled down alongside the swordsman and stared out over the treetops and the flowing hills beyond. The sky was bright and clear, the air fresh and cool.

"What you did in that cave was astonishing."

"I was lucky. We have all been lucky," he added. He seemed friendlier now, but she noticed he did not look at her.

"Are you one of the Legend people?"

"I don't know what that means."

"From the north. The ones who hold to the ancient ways of the Drenai?"

"No. I am from Naashan, across the sea."

"I have not heard of that place. But I guessed from your voice you were from Outside."

"Something tells me you would like Naashan if you saw it." He took a deep breath. "You grew up in these mountains?" Askari nodded. "And Landis Khan visits you often?"

"He seems to have taken a liking to me," she told him. "It makes me uncomfortable."

"Do you know why the beasts were hunting you?"

"Because I killed one back at the village," she said.

He shook his head. "No. Kinyon said they came to the village seeking you."

"That makes no sense. I have no enemies. Not here and not Outside."

"Landis Khan has the answers. I shall wring them from him," he said, his voice angry once more. She found herself staring at his profile and suddenly shivered.

"Have we met before?" she asked him.

"Not in this lifetime," he answered.

The silence grew. At last Askari pushed herself to her feet. "You seem uncomfortable in my company, Skilgannon," she said, a note of sadness in her voice.

"It is not your fault," he said with a sigh. Taking a deep breath, he looked up into that familiar face. His breath caught in his throat as he did so. But he stumbled on. "A long time ago I loved a woman with all my heart. You are . . . very like her. That . . . likeness . . . stabs at my soul."

"Jianna," she said, sitting down once more. He saw her tension ease. Then she lifted her hands, pulling her hair back from her head and raising her face to the sun. It was such a simple gesture, and it tore into him with knives of fire. He had first seen it a thousand years ago, in the house he shared with the gardener, Sperian, and his wife, Molaire. Anger rose again, and he looked away, struggling for calm. He had been uneasy with the actions of Landis Khan in bringing him back from the dead. Then he had discovered Harad, and that uneasiness had coalesced into rage. Now, though, he felt as if his memories and his life had been violated. The living forms of Druss the Legend and Jianna the Witch Queen were beside him again, and far from being uplifted by the experience, he was filled with burning regrets.

"Are you a friend of Landis Khan's?" she asked him.

"A friend? No. In fact I am beginning to dislike him immensely."

"I used to like him," she said. "He came often to my mother's house, and would sit chatting to me. As a child I looked forward to his visits."

"What changed?" he asked, though he already knew the answer.

"I stopped being a child. How was it you were able to command that beast?"

"I did not command him. I gave him a choice. He chose wisely."

"He might change his mind."

"Aye, he might. And that would *not* be wise. How is your friend, Stavut?"

"He has a mighty lump on his head, and is sleeping." She laughed, the sound rich and familiar. "He is not a warrior, but he is very, very brave."

"And in love with you—according to Kinyon."

Her smile faded. "I don't know what that means. I know that I am beautiful, and that men want to possess that beauty. Why must they call it love?"

"Why does it anger you?" he countered.

"Because it is dishonest. Does the bull love the cows in the herd? No, he just desires to push his swollen penis into somewhere warm and inviting. And when he is done he walks away and chews grass. Is that love?"

"Perhaps it is. I do not know. I have never chewed grass."

Her laughter rippled out. "You are a handsome man, and you have wit. How is it that you lost this woman you *loved with all your heart*?"

"I have pondered that question for . . . a long, long time. I have no answers. Sometimes there are no answers."

"That cannot be. There are always answers."

"Why does the sun rise and fall?"

She smiled at him. "I do not know—but then that only means that I do not *know* the answer. It does not mean there *is* no answer."

"That is true."

"Did she love you?"

"Let us talk of other things," he said, forcing a smile. "When Landis Khan visited you, did he ask about your dreams?"

"Yes," she answered, surprised. "How would you know that?"

"I know Landis Khan," he hedged. "And what were those dreams?"

"Ordinary childish dreams. I dreamed of castles and palaces, and great heroes who would carry me away . . ." She faltered, and her expression changed. "I dreamed of a man with eyes the color of sapphires. I remember that now. He had eyes like yours. And he had two swords." She shivered suddenly. "Oh, this is all too silly." Pushing herself to her feet once more, she said: "I am going back to . . . to check on Stavut."

Skilgannon said nothing, and watched her walk away.

Alone again he sought to focus his thoughts. It was not easy. Jianna had always stirred his blood—virtually from the first moment he had met her. And after all the hardships, the cruelties, and her ruthless need for power, he had still yearned for her on that last day on the battlements.

Askari is not Jianna, he told himself. *She is merely a twin. And yet . . .*

Would it not be glorious to hold her close, to kiss those lips? To feel her warm flesh against his own?

Who would you be making love to? he countered. *You would be holding Askari and thinking of Jianna. Is there a worse insult to a woman than that?*

Closing his eyes, he began to breathe deeply, seeking calm. *This is not a time to let emotions run free,* he thought. *Concentrate on the important issues.*

Landis claimed to have resurrected him to fulfill an ancient prophecy. Skilgannon believed this to be true. He could also understand why Landis experimented with the process on the bones of Druss. But Jianna? When she died her body would have been returned to Naashan and buried there, thousands of miles across the ocean. Why had Landis sought her? Was she part of the prophecy? Another thought came to him. Why had he failed to restore Jianna? If Skilgannon had been trapped in the Void for his sins, then surely Jianna would have been similarly cursed? Unless her soul had been destroyed in that awful place. Skilgannon shivered. Aye, that would be it. She was a good swordswoman, and courageous. But to survive the Void called for more than that.

He rose, then moved into a series of exercises, stretching his tired muscles and seeking to free his mind. The effort relaxed his body, but his thoughts continued to prowl his consciousness with restless intensity.

Why were the forces of the Eternal hunting Askari? If she was part of the prophecy, why had Landis not told him? He sat alone for several hours, seeking answers. In the end he accepted defeat. This problem could not be solved by reason alone. There were too few facts. Only Landis had the answers. Skilgannon finally relaxed.

Tomorrow they would head back to Petar. Then all would become clear.

Unwallis had been gripped by a sense of foreboding as he rode up the long hills toward the lands of Landis Khan. Dead Jiamads were everywhere, the bodies rotting on the hillsides. Black carrion birds, gorged and fat, pecked at the corpses, while others sat in the tree branches, staring at the riders with cold, hungry glances.

The bodies should have been cleared away and burned.

The gray-haired ambassador glanced back at the column of riders behind him. Their horses were skittish with the scent of corruption in the air.

Unwallis rode on, the foreboding turning to anger as he saw the desolation in Petar itself. Smoke was still rising from burned-out buildings, and there were few people to be seen. The Eternal's Jiamads roamed the streets, and here there were more bodies, many of them human.

At the palace there were no servants to take care of the horses. Unwallis ordered the cavalry captain to find the stables and see to the mounts, then dismounted and entered the gloomy main entrance hall. No lanterns had been lit, and his footsteps echoed through the empty halls. His clothes were travel stained, his hooded gray cloak wet from a recent downpour. He had hoped for a hot bath and a relaxed meal before beginning his investigations. There was no such hope now. The place echoed like a great tomb.

Mounting the stairs, he walked past the near-decapitated body of a servant, then through to a rear upper balcony and gazed down on the gardens below. A pyre had been set there, and ash had blown across the flower beds. The last remains of Landis Khan. *No hope of resurrection for you, Landis, old friend,* he thought. Unwallis rubbed at his weary eyes. Slowly he searched the building, seeking Decado. He found five more bodies, three men and two women, lying together in an upper corridor. All carried similar slashing wounds; two had their throats sliced open, the others had been hacked in what was obviously a frenzied attack. This was what happened when matters were left in the hands of a psychopath like Decado. The town was a near ruin, the people fled or murdered, the palace a shell. Surely, he reasoned, the Eternal would not forgive this disaster. Decado was finished. There was no exultant joy in Unwallis as he considered this. The first body in the palace had been of a plump, elderly man, ashamed of going bald. He had grown his hair long above his right ear, and had swept it up and over his crown. An ordinary palace servant, skilled, no doubt, at cooking or cleaning. Unwallis had paused to stare at his face. There was a look upon it of horror and shock. He would have had no reason to believe that a berserk warrior would leap upon him and hack him to death.

Yes, it was good that the Eternal would finally see what a monster she had allowed to roam free. But not at the cost of even one old man's life.

He found Decado asleep on a couch in Landis Khan's apartments. He was unshaved, his dark clothes stained with blood. He awoke as Unwallis entered. Decado's hooded eyes were red rimmed, and he looked weary.

"What happened here?" asked Unwallis.

Decado stretched and yawned. Then he rose and moved to a nearby table, filling a silver goblet with wine. "You want a drink?"

"No." Unwallis waited. He had no power over Decado, nor any right to demand answers.

"The blind man escaped," said Decado. "The people were hiding him."

"So you sent out the Jiamads to search the town?"

"Of course. The Eternal ordered me to kill him."

"And the people panicked and fled?"

"Yes."

"So the Jiamads chased them and killed them?"

"It is what Jiamads do," said Decado, draining the goblet and refilling it.

"And you found Gamal?"

"Not yet. But I will. How far can a blind man get?"

"I don't know," said Unwallis. "Let me try to understand the situation. You killed Landis Khan, then sought Gamal and did not find him. What did the servants tell you? And where are they, by the way?"

"I had to kill a few. The rest ran."

"I see. So there is no one to supply us with food, the blind man remains at large, and a thriving, prosperous settlement has been brought to the edge of destruction. The Eternal will not be pleased, Decado. Is there any other ill news you would like to share? Where is the girl, Askari?"

"We have had no contact from Corvin."

"Corvin?" queried Unwallis.

"The officer sent to apprehend her."

"Then we don't have her, either?"

"Of course we have," snapped Decado. "He took a company of Jiamads. It is just that he has not reported back yet."

"At the risk of adding salt to the wounds, Decado, what became of Landis Khan's nephew?"

"He was not here when I came back for Landis. He, too, has gone."

Unwallis was tempted to make another dry comment, but Decado's eyes now had an almost feral glitter. Judging from the slaughter inside the palace, he had already been involved in at least one killing frenzy. Unwallis decided to soften his approach. "I expect he will be discovered in due course," he said softly. "And now, by your leave, I shall instruct the soldiers with me to begin a cleanup of the settlement. There are rather too many bodies lying around."

"As you wish," said Decado. He gave a cold smile. "This is all your fault, Unwallis. You know that?"

"No, I did not know that. By what miracle of logic did you arrive at such a conclusion?"

"If I had killed them both, as I wanted to, when Callan first insulted me, we would not have this problem."

"That sounds eminently reasonable," said Unwallis, with a short bow. "I take it you will lead the hunting party that goes after Gamal and the man you call Callan."

"What do you mean *call*?"

"The real Callan is dead. It was a ploy. I don't yet know why he sought to fool me, but I intend studying Landis Khan's notes. The man was an inveterate scribbler. The answer will be here somewhere."

"I don't care who he is. I shall cut him into pieces."

"Of course, Decado." Unwallis failed to keep a note of sarcasm from his voice.

Decado's face paled and he stepped forward. "Are you insulting me, old man?"

"Far from it. Cutting people into pieces is a skill at which you excel. A man should always stick to what he is good at. Now, if you will excuse me."

Unwallis bowed again, then turned and left the room. His heart was beating hard, and once free of the apartments, fear flowed to the surface, causing his hands to tremble. *Do not be such a fool,* he warned himself. *The man is insane. Bait him again and he will kill you.*

Not for the first time Unwallis found himself wondering just what the Eternal could possibly see in such a man. How could she treat him as a lover? He was as likely to kill her in a blind rage as any other. Unwallis smiled suddenly at his own foolishness. How many times had she died already? Death held no fear for her. Through the original brilliance of Landis Khan, and the devotion of the sly Memnon, there were always fresh hosts for the Eternal's soul.

Unwallis sought out the captain of cavalry and gave instructions for the removal of corpses. "Then send several of your men into the hills to seek out villagers. Make sure the men have friendly faces and easy personalities. Get them to tell whoever they find that it is now safe to return. And ensure that this is true. Keep the Jiamads away from them. Ideally, Captain, find some palace servants who will know how to prepare a bath."

The captain smiled. "Two of my men have already fired up the palace ovens. Give us an hour or two and I'll arrange a hot bath for you."

"You are a prince among men, Captain," said Unwallis. "I shall be in the library area downstairs. When the bath is ready, send someone to find me."

The thought of relaxing in a hot bath eased his mind, and he felt calmer as he made his way downstairs to Landis Khan's study.

He did not remain at ease for long. In the rear area, resting against a back wall, he found three picture frames containing stretched, dried, tattooed skin. The first was small, showing a black spider. The second had an eagle with flaring wings. The third was of a snarling leopard. Holding to the last Unwallis sank into a chair, his mind reeling. He gazed at the long-dead skin and shuddered. So it was true then. Landis *had* discovered the Tomb of the Damned.

"What were you thinking, Landis?" he said aloud.

Leaning back in his chair, Unwallis thought through the implications of Landis Khan's treachery. A Reborn created from the bones of Skilgannon was not, in itself, a major problem. Unless, of course, one was stupid enough to believe in ancient prophecies. Surely Landis Khan was too intelligent for such nonsense? Unwallis stared at the tattooed skin in the frame.

Bad enough that Landis Khan had hidden away a child born of the bones of the Eternal. The reasons were not hard to discern. The poor man had been hopelessly in love with her, and had been discarded, like all of her lovers and favorites. He had sought to re-create a woman who *could* love him. That treachery was understandable. But the Skilgannon question nagged at him. It was possible to be both an intelligent man and a fool, so perhaps Landis *had* believed in the old prophecy. Unwallis remembered it from childhood. A hero reborn would raid the nest of a silver eagle. He would do this after defeating a mountain giant bearing a great shield of gold.

Fascinating nonsense. Mountain giants and eagles of silver did not exist in the known world. So why did Landis Khan believe it to be true?

Unwallis gathered all the papers he could find and began to study them.

An hour passed. Then another. Darkness began to fall, and Unwallis lit a lantern. A young soldier came to him and told him a hot bath had been prepared. Unwallis rose and stretched, then took a sheaf of papers and followed the man to an empty apartment on the ground floor. Here there was a sunken bath of marble. It had taken the soldiers some time to fill it, and the water was now only lukewarm. Unwallis thanked the men, discarded his clothing, and climbed gratefully into the bath. Two more soldiers arrived, carrying buckets of steaming water, which raised the temperature briefly. Unwallis sat back and reached for the next sheet of paper.

Gamal is very weary today. His spirit-journeys into the Void have taxed his strength. It is also undeniable that entering a trance state, while his hands rest on the sword hilts, is causing him some distress. Gamal says there is evil in the blades; an old evil, some dark enchantment that grates upon his soul. However, this gives me hope, for the legends maintain that Skilgannon's swords were cursed. They are quite simply beautiful weapons to observe. Both have hilts of intricately worked ivory, set with precious gems, but the metal blades defy analysis. The Swords of Night and Day are well named. One is pale gold in color, and yet harder than the strongest steel; the other is moonlight silver. There is not a blemish or a nick on either blade.

They could have come straight from a master swordsmith. Hard to believe these swords saw any action at all.

Unwallis read on, skimming through several sheets.

We are both filled with excitement today. Through the swords Gamal has reached Skilgannon. He has been trapped in the Void for all this time. At first Gamal did not recognize him, for in the Void his skin is scaled like a lizard. He fights constantly, for he is hunted by other demonic forms. Gamal says a shining figure was with him, but disappeared when Gamal approached. I think Gamal recognized the figure, but would tell me nothing. What is, however, of greater importance is that Gamal has convinced Skilgannon to return to the world. It is not possible to convey the joy this has brought me.

Dropping the paper, Unwallis scrambled from the bath, threw a towel around his waist, and strode from the room. As he emerged into the corridor he saw two more soldiers carrying buckets of hot water.

"Are you all right, sir?"

"Where is the Lord Decado?"

"He rode out, sir, with a hunting party. Looking for some blind man, I think. You should sit down. Your face is gray."

Longbear was confused. Hunger gnawed at him, the scent of blood in the air making his stomach churn. The desire to kill and eat was growing, making his mouth salivate and his taloned fingers twitch. The woman was bleeding from several small puncture wounds to her side, caused when Longbear carried her, and the old blind Skin, from the fight. As he had run up through the wooded hills his talons had pierced her clothing, pricking the flesh beneath. She was sitting now alongside Gamal, staring back down the track, her eyes fearful. Longbear could scent the salt in the blood, and knew the flesh would be savory and filling. His empty belly rumbled.

Gamal swung his head, his blind eyes flickering toward Longbear. "How are you faring, my friend?" he asked. "Do you carry wounds?"

Longbear grunted. The voice continued to strike a chord somewhere deep in his mind. He could not place it. "No wounds," he said. "Female bleeds."

"You are hurt, Charis?"

"I am fine, sir. Why are they doing this?"

Longbear heard the terror in her voice. His golden eyes looked past her, seeing the distant smoke rise from the houses in which the Skins dwelled. The enemy had come in fast, scores of Jiamads, some on all fours, others carrying clubs or sharp blades. Longbear's troop of twenty had charged them, ripping and killing, and dying. Longbear himself slew three enemy.

The surviving six of his troop had been beaten back, fleeing through the alleyways of the town and out into the countryside. On the hillside Longbear had seen the old blind man, Gamal, and the young, golden-haired woman with him. She was leading him by the hand. In the transient safety of the trees Longbear and his survivors gathered around the pair. The woman was terrified. Not so the blind man.

"Who leads?" he had asked, his voice firm and strangely familiar. For a moment only Longbear experienced an old memory. Strange, for he was lying on a raised platform, blankets upon his body, and the old blind man was sitting beside him. Longbear had never been inside a house, let alone covered in blankets. Then the image faded.

"I am Longbear."

"That is good. Lead us away from here, Longbear."

"Where?"

"High into the hills. North."

"North?"

"Where the bears live," said the old man.

Another bizarre image flickered briefly to life. Longbear remembered walking the high hills. He was carrying a young Skin upon his shoulders. The child was laughing. A feeling

came with the memory, of great contentment and joy. Longbear shivered. Such feelings usually came when the bright
stone in his skull grew warm.

So they had set off toward the land of the bears. The female
Skin held to the old man's hand, and the pace was terribly
slow. Happily they were not followed immediately, and, as the
sun fell on the first day, they had made it into the high country.

Here came the first quarrel. Usually at sunset the stone in
Longbear's skull would begin to vibrate. He would fall into a
deep, refreshing sleep. It was close to dusk, and there was no
warmth from the stone. The other six of his comrades also
grew uneasy. They gathered together, away from the Skins.

"Dark soon. Who brings food?" asked Balla, whose appetite was always prodigious.

"Skin Place burns," said another, pointing back to a red
glow in the southern sky.

A growing sense of unease followed. Longbear squatted
down on his haunches. He had no answers. The whole world
seemed to have changed. No food was coming. The stones
were cold. And the sound of the old man's voice was stirring
fragmented memories that left him uncomfortable.

The breeze shifted. All the Jiamads tensed. The scent of
the enemy came to them. Balla, who had the keenest eyes,
ran to the edge of the trees.

"Only three," he said. "We kill! Now!"

The Jiamads rose and rushed out onto the hillside.

"No!" shouted the old man, his voice cutting through the
blood mist that had begun to descend on Longbear. "Longbear! To me!"

The others were charging down the slope. Longbear hesitated. The old man shouted again. There were only three enemy. His strength would not be needed. Padding back
through the trees he waited by the blind man. "What is happening?" asked Gamal.

Longbear glanced back. His troop was tearing into the Jiamads. Two enemy were down, the third fleeing. Then a volley of arrows soared out from the trees close by. Three of his

troop went down. A rider galloped from the trees and leapt from the saddle, a slim, dark-haired Skin, dressed all in black and wielding two bright swords. The remaining three of Longbear's Jiamads rushed the small man. Balla was the first to reach him. The swordsman ducked under Balla's flailing arms and sent a disemboweling cut across Balla's belly. Then, even before the Jiamad had fallen, he leapt toward the others. Longbear saw the dazzling swords flicker and rise and fall. Then the swordsman was standing alone. One Skin had killed three of his brethren in a matter of heartbeats.

"Speak to me!" whispered Gamal.

At first Longbear could find no words. The shock was immense. "A Skin. Two swords. All dead," he said.

"Decado! We must get away from here. Fast! Can you carry us?"

Longbear dropped his quarter staff and swept the old man up under one arm. Then he grabbed the girl and started to run. His legs were powerful, his stamina prodigious. Up through the wooded hills he ran, cutting left and right through the trees. On open ground for a while he sprinted on, over rocky outcrops, until at last even his great strength began to fade.

Releasing the old man and the girl, he looked back for the first time. Darkness had fallen and he could see little. Closing his eyes, he sniffed the wind. His nostrils quivered, separating the many scents of the forest. Some deer a little way to the west, a bighorn sheep, out of sight in a stand of rock. But he could scent no other humans, nor Jiamads.

Turning back to the human pair, he smelled the blood on the woman again. Hunger surged in him. His long tongue lolled from his mouth as he began to salivate. The woman had removed a small pack from her shoulder. From it she took a loaf of bread. As her hands delved deeper the scent of dry-cured meat came to him. Longbear watched as she produced half a round of pink meat from the pack. "I have some ham and bread, Lord," she said to Gamal.

"Give the meat to Longbear," he said, softly. "And tell him your name."

Longbear stood silently. The golden-haired woman turned to stare at him. He could scent her fear in the sweet smell of sweat breaking out on her face and arms. "Would you like some ham?" she said, moving nervously toward him and extending her arm. "My name is Charis."

Longbear did not speak to her. He snatched the ham and moved away from the pair. Squatting down, he tore at the meat, then gnawed at the bone beneath. It only partially sated his hunger.

The old man approached him. "Time for you to rest, my old friend," he said. Gently he laid his hand upon the jewel in Longbear's skull. The familiar vibration began, soothing, warming. Longbear yawned and lay down. "Sleep, Longbear. Dream no dreams."

Peace settled on the Jiamad, and he passed into darkness.

Charis sat very quietly with her back to a rock, staring at the sleeping Jiamad. The deep scratches on her side were stinging, and there was blood on the left side of her cream shirt. The night grew colder, and she drew her rust-colored, hooded cloak around her shoulders. The shivering started then, but it was not caused just by the cold. The long day had been terrifying.

It seemed somehow inconceivable to her that only that morning she had been singing a song in the palace kitchens as she and four other servants prepared the food packages for the loggers in the woods. The day had been bright and clear, a soft breeze blowing down from the mountains. Charis had been happy. Life was good.

Then she had been sent to Landis Khan's apartments with a tray of food and a jug of wine. As she reached the apartment she realized there was no goblet upon the tray. Annoyed with herself, she had swung around to return to the kitchen. Then she remembered that there were several crystal goblets in the guest rooms close by. Moving to an empty apartment, she opened the door and stepped inside, laying her tray on a table by the wall. She heard footfalls in the corridor outside and peered around the half-open door. One of Landis Khan's guests had returned, the dark-haired man with the cold eyes. *Probably need two goblets now,* she thought.

Decado entered Landis Khan's apartment. Then Charis heard voices. She would never forget the words spoken.

"You said you would not kill me," she heard Landis Khan say, his voice trembling with fear.

"And I shall not," came the voice of a woman. *"He will. Not a trace of flesh or bone to be left. Burn him to ash. I do not want him reborn."*

"As you order, so shall it be," she heard Decado reply.

"Do not make him suffer, Decado. Kill him swiftly, for he was once dear to me. Then find the blind man and kill him, too."

"The nephew, Beloved. He insulted me. I want him, too."

"Kill him, my dear," said the woman's voice. *"But no one else. Our troops will be here by morning. Try to remember that we will still need people to till the fields, and I would like servants to remain in the palace ready for my arrival. I do not want blind terror causing havoc here."*

The woman's voice had spoken once more. "You once told me you would die happy if my face was the last thing you were allowed to see. Be happy, Landis Khan."

Charis stood frozen to the spot. The she heard a gurgling scream come from Landis Khan. Fleeing the room, she raced along the corridor to the stairs leading to Gamal's apartment. She did not wait to knock, but ran inside, finding the blind man sitting on a balcony. Swiftly she told him what had transpired, her words tumbling out, almost incoherently.

"I feared it would come to this," the blind man had said with a sigh. "Fetch me my cloak, Charis, and a stout pair of shoes. Get yourself a cloak also. You shall lead me into the hills. There is someone I must find."

Now, following a day of death and bloodshed, Charis was sitting in the darkness, a terrible beast close by. The shivering worsened. Gamal came alongside her, placing his arm around her shoulder.

"I am sorry, my dear, for all that you have suffered. But I could not have made it this far without you."

Charis felt close to tears. Not this time through fear. The kindness and compassion in his voice created a shocking contrast to the horrors of the day. "Are we safe now?" she whispered.

She saw his head tilt toward the sleeping beast, and noted the concern that showed on his weary face. He took a deep breath. "No, my dear, we are not safe. Longbear was once a friend of mine, but little of that man is left in the creature. We must be careful around him. Try not to react fearfully, and do not look directly into his eyes. All animals see this as a challenge or a threat. If we can find a food source I believe there will be less cause for concern."

"Where are we going, Lord? There is nothing out here, save an old fortress and a few settlements."

"I need to find the young man who was at the palace recently."

"The one with the paintings on his skin?"

"Yes."

"He is with Harad." Thoughts of Harad calmed her. She wished he were here now. The beast they traveled with would seem far less daunting if Harad was close by. "How will we find them?"

"Tomorrow I shall ask Longbear to seek his scent. They met a few days ago. Now forgive me, child, but I am bone weary and must rest. You should try to do the same. Longbear will sleep at least until dawn."

Gamal lay down, his head resting on his arm. His breathing deepened.

Once he was asleep it occurred to Charis that she could simply stand up and walk quietly away into the night. The deadly woman who had ordered the lord's death had made it clear that no one was to be needlessly killed. She had said

something about ensuring palace servants continued their
duties. Surely if Charis was to go back, all danger would be
ended? It was an inviting thought. She gazed down at the
sleeping man. *He is old and blind,* she told herself. *What
could he do without help? How will he find Harad and the
tattooed man? The beast will do it for him,* argued an insis-
tent voice in her mind. *He said they were friends once. Leave
him. Save yourself!*

The thought was more than tempting. It was right!

Slowly she rose, so as not to disturb him. The moon
emerged from behind a cloud, and a silver glow shone on the
sleeping man. In its harsh light she saw his frailty. His eyes
were sunken, his face seamed with wrinkles so deep they appeared as scars.

He will die out here without me, she realized with cold
certainty.

In the near distance she could hear the sounds of running
water. Another thought came to her then, and she quietly
slipped away from the campsite. The stream was close by,
bubbling over rocks and tiny waterfalls. Slowly she followed
its path until she came to a wider pool, some thirty feet
across. She sat by it for a while, then stood and removed all
her clothes. Shivering, she stepped into the water and carefully waded out toward a deeper section, surrounded by
rocks. Then she stood, statue still, her hands beneath the surface. After a while she saw the sleek form of a fish swim by,
then another. Charis did not move. For what seemed an age
no fish swam close enough. But then a long, fat fish glided
over her hands. In a flash Charis swept it up, hurling it out
onto the bank, where it flopped and twisted. Then she froze
once more, waiting patiently. She failed in several more attempts, then succeeded, landing a second large fish. After
several hours, her teeth chattering with the cold, she waded
back to the bank. Drying herself with her shirt, she climbed
into her long, green skirt and threw her cloak around her
shoulders. There were six fat fish on the bank. Charis smiled.

Her father—who had taught her this technique as a child—would have been proud of her skills. Using her shirt as a makeshift pack, she carried the fish back to the campsite. Gamal and the beast were still sleeping, and Charis lay down alongside the old man and slept dreamlessly.

She awoke with the dawn. Gamal was still sleeping. She glanced at the beast, who began to stir. He rolled to his feet, sniffing the air. Charis took a calming breath and rose.

"I have food for you, Longbear," she said, her voice firm. "Do you eat fish?"

"Fish good," said the creature, his nostrils quivering.

Putting two fish aside, she carried the others to the beast, laying them on the ground. Longbear stared at her, but she avoided his eyes.

"How you catch fish?" he asked.

"With my hands. My father taught me."

He said no more, but squatted down, lifted a fish, and tore a huge chunk from it.

"Be careful of the bones," she said, then walked back to where Gamal lay. From her pack she took a small tinderbox, then began to set a fire.

Ten

Skilgannon paused on the hilltop above the village and gazed down at the people working below. He could see Harad on a rooftop, stripping away burned timbers. All around the settlement there was bustle and activity, as the survivors sought to repair the damage caused by the raid. It was futile—and yet so human—to struggle against the inevitable. More raiders would come. Skilgannon had tried to explain this to the wounded Kinyon. The enemy would send more troops to capture Askari. More deaths would follow.

"What else can we do, but rebuild?" asked Kinyon. "These are our homes."

Twenty-two of the villagers had survived the raid. They had buried the bodies of their neighbors and were now seeking to restore some semblance of normality to their community. Skilgannon admired them for it.

Leaving them to their work, he had scouted to the south, seeking signs of fresh invasion. He had found nothing. It would take time before whoever sent the raiders realized something had gone wrong. How long? A day? Two days? Then they would come again, with a larger force.

The efforts of the villagers were doomed. Their settlement would burn, their lives would be extinguished. It filled Skilgannon with both anger and sadness.

Landis Khan had told him the world had changed beyond anything Skilgannon could imagine. What nonsense that was. There was no change. True, there were more Joinings now, but the world of man was as it always had been. Violent and cruel. Greed and a lust for power dominated all endeavors. His thoughts swung to Askari. Cool and courageous, she had fought to protect young Stavut from the beasts. At her age Jianna would have done the same. How, Skilgannon wondered, could such natural heroism have become so perverted? Jianna had evolved into the Witch Queen, a terrible, cold, and malicious woman who casually ordered the deaths of thousands. Sitting on the hillside, he pondered the question. In order to regain her throne Jianna had been forced to fight, to gather armies and conquer enemies. At first she had been magnanimous in victory, offering the defeated a chance to join her. Skilgannon remembered a young prince who had accepted this offer, but then had betrayed her, pulling his men from the battlefield to join the forces of Boranius. Some months later he had been captured, with his family, trying to escape into Tantria.

Skilgannon had not been present at the execution. He was fighting in the east. But when he returned he heard what had happened. Jianna had gathered her army and addressed them. Then the traitor and his family had been brought out before them. She had his five children killed first, then his two wives. Lastly, she had approached the grief-stricken prince. "Such is the price of treachery," she told him. "Now join your family." With that she had cut his throat.

Once back with the main army Skilgannon had gone to her, unable to believe she had ordered children murdered.

"It weighs heavily on me, Olek," she had said. "Yet it was necessary. Seven innocents died. Their deaths will ensure such treachery does not occur again. In this war men must be made to realize the consequences that will follow if they betray me."

Yes, he thought, *that was the beginning.* After that more such executions followed, until, by the end, the population of an entire city was annihilated. On that day he became the Damned, for it was his men, under his orders, who carried out the slaughter.

He remembered a conversation with the Seeress, Ustarte.

"We all of us carry the seed of evil in our hearts and souls," she told him. "Even the purest, even the most holy. It is part of the human condition, born into us. We cannot root it out. All we can do—at best—is prevent it from germinating."

"And how do we do this?" he had asked her.

"We give it no sustenance. The seed will flower if it is fed on hatred, or malice. It sprouts like a cancer within the dark places of the soul."

"And what if we have already fed it? Is it then too late for us?"

"It is never too late, Olek. You have already begun to prune it back, to starve it. Jianna never will, I fear."

He had felt his heart grow heavy. "There is so much good in her, you know? She could be kind and loyal and courageous."

"And monstrous, murderous, and chilling," she added. "It is the curse of absolute power, Olek. There is no one to admonish you, no laws save those you make. We like to believe there is something special, even alien, about evil. We like to think that tyrants are different from the rest of us. That they are somehow inhuman. They are not. They are merely unchained, unfettered; free to do as they please. How often do ordinary people grow angry at neighbors, and, for a moment only, consider causing them harm? It happens all the time. What stops them from carrying out an attack? Usually it is fear of repercussion, punishment, or imprisonment. What repercussions does Jianna face for her evils? None. The more terrifying she becomes, the more powerful she appears. I pity her, Olek."

"I love her," he had said.

"And for that I pity you."

Skilgannon left the hilltop and began the descent toward the village. He could see Stavut unloading his wagon, offering goods and blankets to people whose homes had been destroyed. Askari was with him. Harad was sitting by a well. There were two people with him, a slim young man with a bruised face, and a plump blond-haired woman. Seeing Skilgannon, Harad waved and called him over.

"This is Arin and his wife, Kerena," said Harad. "They have come from Petar. Jiamads attacked the town."

"What of Landis Khan?" Skilgannon asked the young man.

"I don't know, Lord," answered Arin. "I didn't see him. I was in the woods with the loggers. We saw buildings ablaze and ran back toward the town. Then Kerena came running up the hillside. She said people were being killed by Jems. So we took off. Kerena has relatives here. We thought it would be safe." He glanced at the ruined buildings nearby. "Don't think it is, though," he added.

"You are right," Skilgannon told him. "Nowhere is safe now."

"Well, I am going back," said Harad, rising and hefting his ax.

"I'll come with you," said Skilgannon. "But first gather some food. I need to speak with Askari and Kinyon."

With that he walked away to where the huntress was sitting with Stavut, Kinyon, and several other villagers. Beckoning to Askari, he walked some distance away from the group, just out of earshot. "Harad and I are heading back to Petar," he said.

"Why? It has been overrun."

"There is a woman there Harad loves."

"That explains why *he* should go. Is there a woman you love also?"

"You need to leave, too," he said, ignoring the question.

"This is my home."

"I know that. It is also the reason it was attacked. They are looking for you. They will be back. If you are not here there is a chance—albeit remote—that they will not kill your friends. If you value their lives, then get away from here. Better still, convince Kinyon and the others to leave."

"They have nowhere to go. In the south Petar is burning. In the north there are armies of rebel Resurrectionists. And renegade Jiamads. What would you have them do?"

"Stavut has talked of the Legend people. Perhaps if they make it to their lands they can rebuild. I don't know. I have no answers. The reality is that if they stay here more Jiamads will come, with more bloodthirsty officers. They will torture and kill in order to find you."

"I don't understand this at all. Why do they seek me?"

He looked into the face he knew so well. "If Landis Khan is alive I will find out."

Harad called out to him. Turning he saw that the axman was carrying two packs.

"We are leaving now," he said. "I wish you well . . . Askari."

"You said that like a farewell. I think we might meet again."

Skilgannon strode away, took a pack from Harad, and swung it to his shoulders. He could not resist glancing back, for one last look at the tall huntress.

For most of the afternoon Skilgannon and Harad made swift progress toward the southwest, but by dusk the big ax-man was tired. He refused to stop and Skilgannon made no complaint. He held his counsel until darkness began to fall. Then he moved alongside Harad, and took hold of his arm. "Wait for a moment," he said.

Harad shrugged off the arm and plodded on.

"So tell me," said Skilgannon, softly, "how you will help Charis when you are too exhausted to lift that ax?"

Harad paused. "I will find the strength," he muttered.

"Strength is finite, axman. Now either Charis is alive, or she is dead. If she is alive, we will find her. If she is dead, we will avenge her. But staggering into an army of Joinings without rest, food, or sleep is insane. You can only help her if you are strong."

In the fading light he saw Harad's shoulders sag.

"I will rest for an hour," said Harad, reluctantly. The ax-man sank down with his back to a tree and sat, head bowed. Skilgannon doffed his pack, took out some food, and sat quietly eating. Harad, like Druss, was a man of direct action. There was no subtlety to him. A woman he loved was in danger, and he was not close enough to help her. All he could think of was closing the distance as swiftly as possible. But then what? He would walk into the occupied town seeking

Charis. It would not matter to him whether there were twenty Joinings or a thousand. Skilgannon finished his food. He was also weary, but the rest was restoring his strength. Moving alongside Harad, he said: "Time to talk and to plan."

"I'm listening," muttered Harad.

"I don't think you are."

"What does that mean?"

"There is too much anger in you. It is clouding your judgment." Skilgannon fell silent. A cold breeze began to blow down from the snow-covered mountains, and wispy clouds drifted across the bright moon.

"I do not know how to plan for this," said Harad, at last. His voice was calmer, and he leaned his head back against the trunk of the tree and closed his eyes briefly. "I fell trees. I prepare timber. I dig foundation trenches for new buildings. And I can fight. Until I met you I had never killed anything. Never needed to. Now everything has changed."

"You will change, too, Harad. Give yourself time."

"This is easy for you," said Harad. "You have no friends here. These are not your people."

"This is true," agreed Skilgannon. "There is nothing in this new world for me. Everyone I ever loved is long dead. It would make no difference, though, if everyone in Petar were precious to me. I would still be sitting here gathering my strength, and considering the possibilities."

"And all the while Charis might be in danger."

"Yes. She might. But then Petar is a large settlement. It is unlikely to have been destroyed. Therefore people will have been encouraged to return to their work. The loggers are probably back lopping trees. The palace servants will be serving new masters. If this is true then Charis is probably doing what she always does, looking after the needs of the palace guests. In short, she will not be in need of rescue. Rushing into Petar and hacking down a few Joinings before being killed would then be an act of stupidity."

"You think that is likely?" asked Harad, his voice full of renewed hope.

"I don't know. There are two other possibilities. One, she ran like Arin and his wife. If she did this, then she is out here in the wilderness somewhere. Again it would be futile, therefore, to rush into Petar. The other possibility is that she was killed." Skilgannon saw the shock register on Harad's face. "If this proves true, then there is no need for sudden and violent action. Does she know that you love her?"

"Who said that I loved her?" snapped Harad, his face reddening.

"Do you not?"

"It wouldn't matter if I did. You know what they call me? I am Harad the Bone Breaker. The Brute. I am strong, yes, but I am not handsome. I am not rich. I am not clever or witty. Charis deserves someone better."

Skilgannon smiled. "In my experience *all* women deserve someone better. My own wife certainly did."

Harad relaxed and let out a deep sigh. "I will find her," he said.

"We will find her, Harad. Now why don't you get some sleep? I'll keep watch for a few hours and then wake you."

"Aye, I could do with shutting my eyes for a while." Without another word Harad stretched out on the ground, his head on his pack. Within moments he was sleeping soundly. Skilgannon rose silently and moved away from the sleeping man. He needed to think. Something was nagging at him, tugging at the corners of his mind. It was annoying. Though many of the memories of his previous life had returned to him, so much else was jagged and unconnected. His concentration was not as focused, and he found himself constantly struggling to contain his emotions. Anger came far more swiftly than he recalled. On the other hand he was far stronger and fitter than he had been during those last years of his life. The ravages of war, wounds, fractures, and strains, had taken their toll on his fifty-year-old body. Perhaps that was the answer. As he had grown older nature made him more wary, more frugal with his strength. He had begun to lose . . . what? Passion? Desire? Recklessness? Yes, he realized, it was true. The passionate nature of youth had been replaced by the cool—apparent—wisdom of maturity. He had thought more about his actions, and planned every strategy carefully.

There is nothing wrong with your mind, he told himself. *It is merely being bombarded by the reckless energy of youth.* In order to clear his thoughts he decided to expend some of that energy.

Finding a flat area of solid ground he began a taxing series of exercises, some motionless to establish balance, others involving leaps and twirls. Finally, his face glistening with sweat, he drew the Swords of Night and Day and flowed through a series of moves, cutting and thrusting as if fighting an invisible enemy. The swordmaster Malanek had taught him scores of fighting maneuvers, and through his long life he had acquired others. The blades flashed in the moonlight. Lastly, he flipped the swords into the air. As they spun above him he dived forward, rolled on his shoulder, and came up on his knees, hands held high, fingers outstretched. The ivory hilt of the Sword of Day dropped into his left hand. The hilt of the Sword of Night brushed the fingertips of his right, the blade lancing toward his throat. His hand snapped out, catching the hilt at the second attempt. Even so the sharp blade sliced through the collar of his long topcoat. "You still have a little way to go," he told himself, aloud. Sheathing the blades, he wandered to the brow of a wooded hill. His mind was clearer, but the nagging doubt remained.

What are you missing? he asked himself.

Landis Khan had brought him back in secret. Apparently many people had sought his tomb through the centuries. Somehow—perhaps—the Eternal had found out, and the raid on Petar was retribution. Yet that did not explain the attack on Askari's village. Why would the Eternal care that the bones of a long-dead queen had been given new life?

He sat very still, the cold of winter settling on his soul. What was it Gamal had said?

She is, like you and I, Skilgannon, a Reborn. I would imag-

*ine she has lost count of the number of bodies she has worn
and discarded . . . Landis found the greatest of the artifacts,
and he and I discovered how to reactivate it. Through its
power we gave her immortality. We created the Eternal.*

And then he knew. Landis Khan had discovered the bones
of Jianna, the Witch Queen. He *had* brought her back. She,
too, had been wandering the Void. Jianna, the love of his life,
was the dread Eternal. The shock to his system was immense. He started to shiver, then felt the rise of nausea in the
pit of his stomach.

*I would imagine she has lost count of the number of bodies
she has worn and discarded.*

Somehow her immortality was maintained by taking control of new versions of herself, just as Druss had briefly
taken over Harad that night in the ruins of Dros Delnoch.
Druss, being the man he was, would not steal Harad's life.
The Witch Queen would not hesitate for a heartbeat. And
that was why they were hunting Askari. A new, young body
for the Eternal.

Skilgannon felt torn, his emotions shredded. Jianna was
alive! He could find her, be with her, change the fate that had
driven them apart.

"Are you insane?" he said aloud. The woman he had loved
was fierce and courageous, and filled with idealism. The
Eternal was a vampire who had plunged the world into chaos
and horror.

He glanced at the night sky. "Why do you torment me
still?" he raged. "Cethelin said you were a god of forgive-
ness and love. But you delight in malice and revenge."

Anger coursed through him, blind and unreasoning. Had
he not tried to atone for his sins? Had he not joined a
monastery and sought to learn the way of the Source? So who
had sent those killers to bay at the gates and threaten death to
the gentle souls inside? None other but the Source? "All my
life you have haunted me, sending violence and death to those
I loved." The gentle actor Greavas, the gardener Sperian, and
his loving wife, Molaire, had been tortured to death by Bora-

nius. Killers had come after Jianna. His entire past life had been plagued by violence and war. Now he had been dragged back into another conflict, where innocents would suffer.

His first life had seen him battling to save a princess from a dark power that sought to destroy her. Now that same princess *was* the dark power, and the victim was the physical embodiment of the princess he had loved.

The savage irony of the situation was sickening. Staring malevolently up at the stars, he shouted: "I curse you with every fiber of my being!"

Then the anger passed. He felt drained and terribly weary.

He was about to make his way back to where Harad was sleeping when he heard a sound from within the woods to his right. Instantly the Swords of Night and Day were in his hands. Skilgannon stood waiting. The undergrowth parted and the huntress, Askari, stepped from the shadows. She was carrying her recurve bow and wearing leggings of soft leather, and a hooded green shirt under a fringed doeskin jerkin. Her dark hair was held back from her face by a thin silver headband.

"Are you calmer now," she asked him, "or do you intend to behead me?"

"What are you doing here?"

"Going with you to seek Landis Khan. Or going without you. I don't much care which."

"Is Stavut with you?"

"No. He is taking his wagon back to the north. The villagers are going with him. I hope it will prove safer for them there."

"Nowhere is safe," he said.

"Kinyon often says, *The journey of life has only one destination,*" she replied with a shrug. "Everything dies."

"Not everything," he said sadly.

Stavut had offered to travel with Askari, and had been both disappointed and delighted when she had refused him. It was an odd feeling. A part of him felt a sense of loss, but he consoled himself with the thought that his own chances of survival had been increased dramatically. *Oh, Stavut,* he told himself, *you are a shallow man!*

The sun was shining as he and some twenty-two villagers set off over the mountain pass. Stavut had been amazed and relieved to discover that the Jiamads had not killed his horses, nor ripped apart the contents of his wagon. The chestnut, Longshanks, and the gray, Brightstar, had been in a paddock behind Kinyon's kitchen. Stavut had climbed the fence and called them to him. Longshanks came trotting over. The gray had pretended not to notice him. Until he began to stroke Longshanks's neck and rub his knuckles across the chestnut's long nose. Then Brightstar had moved across, dropping his head and nudging Stavut in the chest. "Yes, yes, I am pleased to see both of you," he said. "But let's not make a fuss. It is unseemly."

As he sat upon his wagon in the morning sunlight it seemed that all was better with the world. The goods he carried for trade in Petar would be worth less in Siccus, the city in which he had purchased them, but he could—just—afford the drop in profits. The most important fact was that he had escaped death and dismemberment and was still able to breathe the fresh mountain air. He felt like singing, and would have, had there not been a column of villagers strolling behind his wagon. The only audience ever to appreciate Stavut's voice were Longshanks and Brightstar—although *appreciation* might be too strong a word. Brightstar had a habit of breaking wind loudly whenever Stavut sang, but this might have been an attempt to harmonize. Stavut chuckled at the thought.

"You are in a good mood," said Kinyon from his seat in the back of the wagon. The big man was recovering well, but was still too weak to walk the grueling high road.

"Indeed I am. Try not to move around too much. There are some breakables back there."

The party stopped several times on the road to rest. Many of the villagers were carrying their most prized possessions in sacks upon their shoulders. Others were hauling hand-carts. The horses were also weary. The wagon had been extra laden with food supplies for the ten-day journey. At one point Kinyon had been forced to climb down, and Stavut had unloaded some of the heavier crates, sacks, and barrels. Even then Longshanks and Brightstar had struggled to make the last rise. Stavut and the villagers reloaded the wagon and, after another halt for rest, continued on their way.

By dusk on the first day they had reached the highest point of the mountain road and began the descent into a wooded valley. Stavut had camped here several times in the past. There was water and good grass, and a rocky hollow in which a campfire could be set without being seen from any distance.

Three cook fires were set, and the villagers gratefully settled down to rest for the night. As the moon rose, the air was rich with the smell of frying bacon, and cook pans sizzled with eggs and toasting bread. Young Arin approached Stavut. He was a tall, handsome young man, sporting a swollen black eye and a cut to his lip. Crouching down where Stavut sat, he asked: "How much longer do we travel?"

"I'd say another ten days, perhaps a little more. There are many high mountain roads. It will be tiring."

"Will it be safe?"

Stavut shrugged. "Safer than it was back in the settlement. But there are said to be roving bands of runaway Jiamads. I met a few on the way in. However, once we drop down onto the coast road we should come across Legend riders. With luck they will escort us into Siccus."

"We have never been Outside," said Arin, a worried look on his face.

"It is not so different. People still grow crops, and trade. Siccus is the city of the Legend people, so there are no Jiamads there, and no war, thank the Source."

"And they will allow us to stay?"

"I'm sure they will," said Stavut. Even as he spoke a doubt loomed in his mind. Alahir's people did not like strangers.

Kinyon approached and, with a grunt, sat down by Stavut. "The wound is sore," he said. "Healing, though."

"Good," said Stavut, still concerned about his promise to Arin.

"What are your plans for gathering food?" asked Kinyon.

"My plans?"

"Well, you *are* leading us," the big man pointed out.

"No, no, no," said Stavut, swiftly. "I am merely showing you the way to Siccus. I am not leading anyone."

Kinyon leaned in close. "Listen to me, lad. These people have been terrified. Some are injured, others have lost loved ones. Now they are leaving their homes to travel Outside—to a place of war and fear. They need to be able to put their trust in something solid. They know you, Stavut. They like you. And right now, they need a source of some comfort. The only person here who knows the ways of Outside is you. They believe you will lead them somewhere safe."

"I don't *know* anywhere safe," responded Stavut, keeping his voice down as he gazed at the faces of the villagers around the campfires.

"Even so, they have put their faith in you. *I* have put my faith in you."

Stavut thought about it. He had always avoided responsibility for others. As a sailor he had twice turned down promotion, and, as a watch officer in Siccus, he had avoided applying for more senior posts. But this was different, he reasoned. This was merely a ten-day journey to the city. Once there he could prevail upon Alahir's friendship to see the villagers settled. Then he would be free. What could be so hard about accepting a nominal role as leader?

Even as he thought it a tiny worm of doubt entered his mind. If there was one fact that life had taught Stavut, it was that Fate had a twisted sense of humor. He saw Kinyon looking at him expectantly. Stavut sighed. "Very well, Kinyon. I shall be leader."

"Good lad," said the wounded man, wincing as he pushed himself to his feet. "You won't regret it."

The words hovered over Stavut like an invisible rain cloud. *I do already,* he thought to himself.

There were many times in Stavut's young life when decisions had turned bad, but at no time had the consequences been quite as swift. After Kinyon had wandered back to reassure the villagers that Stavut was in charge, the new leader walked across the campsite to tend to his horses. As he approached them he saw they were nervous. Longshanks's ears were flat back against his skull, and he was pawing at the ground, wide eyed. The gray, Brightstar, was also jittery. They were still in their traces, the wagon brake locked in place.

"Hey, hey," said Stavut, keeping his voice calm. "Do not fret, lads. I have some grain for you."

At that moment one of the village women screamed. Longshanks tried to rear. The wagon lurched. Stavut swung around. Three Jiamads entered the campsite from the north. Others advanced from the south. The villagers gathered together. No one was armed.

In the moonlight Stavut thought he recognized the lead Jiamad, a hulking brute, obviously part bear. He was the one Skilgannon had spoken to back in the cave. What in the Seven Hells was his name?

The beast lumbered into the campsite and stood towering above the brightest of the campfires. "Leader!" he growled. "Where?"

For a moment there was no movement. Then several villagers pointed at Stavut. The young man glanced at the night sky. "You really don't like me, do you?" he said. Then, with a deep breath, he walked toward the huge Jiamad. All his life Stavut had enjoyed a gift for mimicry. He had only to hear a voice to be able to duplicate the tone and the rhythms of speech. It had caused much amusement to his shipmates when he mimicked certain officers. Now he decided to emulate Skilgannon, and—despite his growing fear—his voice rang with authority. "What are you doing here, Shakul?" he asked.

"Food," answered the great beast, his golden eyes fixing Stavut with a hard stare.

"Why do you not hunt? There are many deer in the forest."

"Too fast. They run. Eat horses."

"Not good," said Stavut.

"Not good?" echoed the beast, confused. "I smell meat. Meat good."

"What then? When the horses are eaten? How will you feed?"

"Hungry *now*!" roared Shakul, his bestial face pushing close to Stavut's own.

Stavut did not back away. "You will wait," said Stavut. "I will give you food for tonight. Tomorrow I will show you how to hunt deer. Then there will be food whenever you need it."

Shakul's great head began to sway back and forth. His taloned hands clenched and unclenched. He stared at the cowering villagers. Then his head swung back to loom over Stavut. "Hunt deer?"

"Yes. Good meat. Plentiful."

"No deer, eat horses?"

"There will be deer," said Stavut, with an assurance he did not believe. "Tell your . . . troop . . . to move away to the far side of the camp. I will bring food." Shakul stood for a moment, then turned away, gesturing to the other six Jiamads. They lumbered away to squat down to the east of the clearing. On trembling legs Stavut walked to the wagon.

Kinyon joined him. "What is happening?" asked Kinyon.

Stavut lifted the canvas cover on the wagon and pulled out several rounds of ham, passing two to Kinyon. There was also a hank of beef. "That's all the meat we have," said Kinyon.

"No, it isn't. There's you, me, and the villagers."

"What are you going to do?"

"Teach them to hunt."

"You are a hunter?"

"Let's not go into that. My confidence is frail enough as it is."

Hauling the meat to his shoulder, Stavut walked across to where the Jiamads sat, then heaved it to the ground. Kinyon dropped the rounds of ham and backed swiftly away. Stavut moved back to the horses, petting them. Brightstar, still nervous, tried to bite him. Stavut leapt back. "One more trick like that and I'll let them eat you," he told the trembling gray. He glanced back to see the Jiamads tearing at the beef, splintering the bones and gnawing at the flesh.

The meat did not last long. Stavut went to the villagers and advised them to rest. Then, heart pounding, he returned to the Jiamads, calling out to Shakul. The pack leader rose and followed Stavut, who walked to a fallen tree and sat. "Why did you not return to your regiment?" he asked.

"No officer. Dead officer we die. Kill us. Where Two Swords?"

"He will be back. Tell me how you tried to hunt the deer."

Shakul hunkered down. "Scent, chase. Too fast. You catch deer?"

"We will tomorrow," said Stavut.

Askari moved through the thick forest, alert and focused. Bards sang of the silence of the woods, but this always made her laugh. There was never silence within the trees. Breeze caused the leaves to whisper; heat or cold made the trunks of trees expand or contract, bringing groans and cracks from the bark. Animals scuttled, birds flew, insects buzzed. She ran swiftly up an old deer trail. There were tracks here, but they were not new. Ants had crawled across the deer prints, and the once sharp edges had crumbled. Up ahead a group of sparrows suddenly took flight. Askari hunkered down. Their panic was likely to have been caused by a wild cat, or a snapping branch. On the other hand it could be a sign that men— or beasts—were close by. The tall huntress crouched down and closed her eyes, listening intently. She caught the sound of dry wood crunching under a boot, and faded back into the cover of the trees. The breeze was in her face, and coming from the direction of the sound. If there were Jiamads present they would not scent her swiftly. Even so she nocked an arrow to the recurve bow. If necessary she would kill one and

head off toward the east, drawing them away from Skilgannon and Harad, who were following her trail. In her leggings
and jerkin of faded leather and her dark green, hooded shirt,
Askari was virtually invisible in the deep undergrowth. She
waited patiently. A troop of twenty Jiamads moved out of
the trees some thirty paces east of her. They were marching
in double file. Each one wore a leather breastplate emblazoned with the head of a silver eagle. Several also wore
leather helms. All carried clubs embedded with iron nails.
There were two officers with them, both walking to the rear
of the column. Askari waited until the troop had reentered
the trees, heading northeast, then rose and ran swiftly to the
far side of the trail. Here she scaled a tall tree, moving
smoothly up through the branches. From this high vantage
point she could see the valley to the south and the distant red
rooftops of Petar, some twenty miles away. Horsemen were
riding across the valley, and there were small groups of Jiamads scanning the ground. It was obvious that they were
searching for something. A rider on a pale gray horse sat unmoving, his long, dark hair blowing in the afternoon breeze.

Movement came from below her. Someone was climbing
the tree. Her bow was hooked over her shoulder, but Askari
drew a double-edged skinning knife from the buckskin
sheath at her side. Skilgannon eased aside a thick, leaf-laden
branch and levered himself up alongside her. He gazed out
over the valley. "It will not be possible to cross the valley in
daylight," she whispered. He was very close to her, and she
could smell wood smoke and sweat on his shirt. The scent
made her uncomfortable. Not because it was unpleasant. Far
from it. She tried to ease back a little from him. She saw a
small leaf had come loose and had attached itself to his dark
hair, just above the ear. It was an effort not to reach out and
brush it away.

"There are too many Jiamads searching," she said. "It
must be someone important. Maybe Landis himself."

"They will find him. The breeze is now northerly. Wherever he is they will scent him. Indeed, if we stay here they

will scent us before long." Skilgannon returned his gaze to the valley below. Askari found herself staring at his profile, and noting the sheen on his hair and the curve of his cheekbone. Closing her eyes, she drew in the scent of his clothes. When she opened them she found his sapphire eyes staring at her.

"Are you all right?"

"Of course. Why would you ask?"

"Your face is flushed."

"This shirt is too warm. I am climbing down now." She glanced at him. "There is a leaf in your hair."

Easing her way down the tree, she jumped to the ground alongside Harad. "We need to take the long route into Petar," she said. "There are Jiamads swarming over the valley."

Harad nodded. "I thought I heard something from the north," he said. "Sounded like a scream. Very faint, very distant."

Askari had heard nothing. "There are some Jiamads behind us now. However, they are searching for someone, and it is unlikely to be us. We should be able to avoid them if we move east."

Skilgannon leapt lightly to the ground beside them. "I heard a shout, or a scream," he said. "I couldn't place the direction."

"North," said Harad.

"I'm not sure it was human. It was cut off too soon. Did you hear it?" he asked Askari. She was annoyed that she had not. The scramble down the tree had been too hurried, and the swishing of the branches must have obscured the sound. She shook her head.

"Did you want to investigate it?" she asked. "Such a plan would seem foolish to me."

"I agree," said Skilgannon, "but we have a problem. Harad is looking for a friend. She may be back in the town—or she may be out here. If that scream was human then it suggests there are people in the high woods. Any one of them might know what happened to either Charis or Landis Khan. You lead off, Askari," he said. "We'll follow. Do not get too far

ahead." Askari pulled her bow clear and set off toward the
north at a lope, ducking under low branches and zigzagging
through the undergrowth. Skilgannon and Harad followed.
They had run for almost half a mile before another scream
sounded. It was a high, trembling cry, full of agony. Askari
slowed in her run and angled toward the east and a stand of
trees. Skilgannon and Harad moved up behind her as she
scaled a small rise, then crouched down in the undergrowth
at the top. Beyond it was a wide, rock-strewn hollow. There
were three bodies splayed out on the ground, and five Jiamads and a human officer were kneeling beside a fourth
man. His arm had been severed above the elbow, the limb lying some ten feet away, seeping blood to the grass. The officer had applied a clumsy tourniquet, but not to save the
man's life. Merely to keep him alive during questioning.

"Where did they go?" asked the officer. The dying man
swore at him, and spat blood toward the officer's face. A
Jiamad plunged a knife into the man's leg, twisting the
blade. The man's scream was high pitched and ended in a
gurgling cry.

"I've had enough of this," said Harad, heaving himself to
his feet.

"I agree," said Skilgannon, his voice cold. Together they
walked out into the open. Skilgannon raised his right hand
and drew the Sword of Day. With his left he took hold of the
jutting lower hilt and drew the Sword of Night.

Two of the Jiamads swung around, hearing their approach.
The beasts came to their feet with incredible speed and
charged, iron-studded clubs raised. Skilgannon darted to the
left, the Sword of Day slashing out and down, slicing
through the fur of the first beast's throat, slashing the skin
and severing the jugular. In the same movement he spun on
his heel, the Sword of Night plunging through the second
beast's leather breastplate and skewering the heart. Harad
leapt at the remaining three. Snaga hammered into the skull
of one Jiamad, the glittering blades splitting the bone and ex-
iting at the dead beast's mouth. Another Jiamad fell, a black-

feathered shaft buried in its eye socket. The last of the Jia-mads hurled itself at Harad. The giant logger leapt to meet it, ducking under the swinging club and plunging Snaga's twin points into its belly. The Jiamad's golden eyes bulged as the cold steel ripped through its breastplate. It let out a fearful howl and staggered back. Harad wrenched Snaga clear. The beast lurched forward. Harad, unable to bring the ax to bear, struck it in the snout with a straight left. Two fangs snapped off under the impact. Dazed now, the creature half turned. Snaga clove through its neck.

The officer of the Eternal was alone now. He was young and fair haired, his features handsome. But his hands were covered with the blood of a tortured man.

"Who are you looking for?" asked Skilgannon as the man drew his army saber.

"I'll tell you nothing, you renegade!"

"I believe you. Which makes you useless to me."

Skilgannon stepped in swiftly, blocked a clumsy lunge, and nearly decapitated the young man. Even before the body had hit the ground Skilgannon was kneeling beside the prisoner.

"I . . . enjoyed . . . that," said the man, blood on his lips.

Harad moved to the other side of the wounded man. "Lie still, Lathar. We'll try to stem the bleeding," he said.

"Don't! They've ruined my legs and . . . bitten off my . . . arm. Wouldn't . . . want to live . . . even if I could. Killed my brothers, too."

"Who were they looking for?" asked Skilgannon.

"The old blind lord and . . . the girl who . . . brings your food, Harad. Saw them yesterday. With a Jem. One of ours. Should have gone with them." Lathar closed his eyes and went still. Askari, who had walked over to join the men, thought he had died. Then he opened his eyes again. "That's some ax," he said. "I'd like to say it was worth it, just . . . to see you cut the bastards down. Damned well wasn't, though."

Skilgannon untied the tourniquet over the stump of the logger's left arm. Blood immediately began to flow. "Which way did they go?" he asked.

"North. Damned acorns and oaks trees," said Lathar, his voice fading. "Can't get it out . . . of my . . . head."

"Nor me," said Harad. Reaching out, he stroked the hair back from Lathar's brow. The logger's breath rattled in his throat. Then there was silence.

"A friend of yours?" asked Askari.

"No. Could have been, though," Harad told her, ruefully.

"We need to go," said Skilgannon. "The scent of the blood will carry far. There will be beasts swarming over this hollow in no time."

Even as he spoke there came the sound of howls to the south and east.

Stavut did not sleep through the long night. He sat quietly away from the villagers, seeking to summon to the surface all that he knew of hunting. This did not take long. At no time in his life had Stavut ever hunted, and he knew nothing of the movements of deer, elk, or any other wild meat-bearing creature. Yet with the dawn, he would be leading a party of carnivorous Jiamads out into the wilderness. His stomach tightened, and he spent some time berating himself.

He tried to avoid staring at the sleeping beasts. Even in repose they were massive and terrifying. If they couldn't hunt, how in the Seven Hells could he help them?

"You know, Tinker," Alahir had once said, *"if I were to put my shield in your mouth it would still rattle."*

In the darkness of this frightening night Stavut had to accept the truth of the remark. He had a fast mind, and all too often he would speak his thoughts without due consideration of the consequences. The brilliance of the instant plan to stop the Jiamads from killing his horses could not be denied. In the short term it had saved the day. In the longer term it was likely to cost him dearly. He could imagine only too well the consequences of being out in the wild lands with a group of hungry Jiamads, and no meat.

Stavut wished that Askari was close by. She knew how to hunt. She could have advised him. The huntress had talked

of deer, but, truth to tell, he had not really listened. He had
sat staring at her exquisite face and body, doing his utmost to
picture her without any clothes.

Which he began to do now.

"Are you a complete idiot?" he asked himself. "Now is not
the time."

All he could remember was that Askari would find a hide
and wait. She talked of bringing down a deer with a single
killing shot, so that panic would not affect the tenderness of
the meat. Stavut couldn't remember why a panicked deer
would taste any less tender.

He recalled far more of what she had told him about
wolves. Everyone knew they hunted in packs, but Stavut had
never realized how complex was the planning. Since wolves
did not possess the stamina and speed of a stag they would
split into groups, forming a large circle miles wide. Then the
first group would rush at the stag. It would run, and they
would chase, driving it toward the second group. Just as the
first attackers were tiring, the second would pick up the
chase, herding the stag inexorably toward a third group.
Meanwhile the first hunters would lope off to a prearranged
position, resting and regrouping their strength. Eventually
this teamwork would see the exhausted stag seeking out a
spot on high ground in which to make its last stand. By the
time it arrived there all the wolves would have gathered for
the kill.

Stavut had found it all fascinating.

Of course it wasn't helpful now. There were only seven
Jiamads. He could hardly separate them into packs, forming
circles in the hills.

At any other time Stavut would have found the problem
facing the Jiamads to be an interesting one. Here they were,
huge and powerful, and yet with no hunting skills. Most were
at least part wolf. One would have thought they would have
retained enough memory to know how to hunt. Hell, they had
hunted Stavut and Askari with a fair degree of skill. That, he
realized, had not been too difficult. Their prey was slow mov-

ing and had gone to ground in a series of caves. Out in the open the speed of the deer would give it a great advantage.

Several hours passed. In the end Stavut moved over to where the villagers slept and nudged Kinyon awake. The big man sat up and ran his thick fingers through his sandy hair. "I was having a good dream," he complained.

"Lucky you. What can you tell me about hunting?"

"I never was any good at it," said Kinyon, reaching for a water canteen and drinking deeply. "Too impatient. That's why I took up cooking."

"Good. Perhaps we can teach the Jiamads to cook pies."

Kinyon rolled from his blankets. "Let us dwell on the positives, Stavi. The Jiamads are strong and fast, and they can scent the deer."

"But they can't catch them."

"A drawback, I'll admit," said Kinyon. They talked for some time, but then the big man began to yawn, and Stavut let him return to his blankets. The merchant strolled out from the campsite and walked up the hillside, sitting down on a jutting rock.

Whatever plan he came up with would have to be simple, and rely on scent and strength.

And luck, he realized.

Eleven

Dawn was approaching as he returned to the campsite. Shakul was waiting for him, the other beasts hunkered down close by. "Hunt deer now?" asked Shakul.

"Absolutely. This may take time, and you will have to be patient."

The red-garbed merchant then walked from the campsite, the small troop of Jiamads filing after him. The wind was from the north, so Stavut headed in that direction, moving up toward higher ground. When they were some half mile from the camp he paused and called Shakul to him. "Can you scent deer?" he asked.

Shakul's great, dark head tilted up, his nostrils quivering. "Yes." He pointed northwest toward a group of wooded hills.

"Good," said Stavut. "Now we need to find a deer trail, downwind of their position."

The Jiamads stood around him, unmoving. Shakul loomed above him. "We hunt *now.*"

"How many deer have you caught so far?" asked Stavut.

"No deer. We hunt now!"

Momentarily Stavut's fear of the creatures vanished, replaced by annoyance. "You will do as I tell you—or there will be no deer. I am the Hunter. I am a great hunter. I have killed more deer than . . . than there are stars in the sky." Several of the beasts looked up at the clear blue heavens. "No, not *now,*" said Stavut. "At night. Than there are stars in the sky at night. First we find a deer trail. Downwind. So they won't scent you. Then we begin the hunt."

Shakul's head twisted to one side and jerked. Finally, after a long silence, he said: "Downwind, yes."

"Good," said Stavut. "Let's go." For the next hour they walked around the base of the high hill below the stand of trees where Shakul said there were deer. They found three trails. At the third Stavut called Shakul to him. "Now we are going to have to pick the best of your Jiamads, and set them the task of chasing the deer."

"Deer too fast."

"Exactly. But we are going to chase them *toward* us. One Jiamad must climb this trail and get behind the deer so they pick up his scent. Another must climb the far trail. They must pick up his scent also. Then the deer should run down the third trail toward where the rest of us will be waiting. Because the wind will be in our faces, the deer will not scent us. As they come out of the trees we rush them, and bring one down."

"How?" asked Shakul.

"Right, we'll take this more slowly," said Stavut, sitting down on a flat rock. "We need two of your troop, one to go up the first trail, the other to go up the second trail. They need to get behind the deer so that the deer scent them and start to run. You, me, and the others will be hidden at the foot of the third trail. The deer will run toward us. As they come close we rush out and kill one."

"Again."

Twice more Stavut explained the simple plan. Shakul squatted down, eyes closed, his head jerking from side to side. He gave a low growl. "Not there," he said, at last.

"What is not there?"

"Pack. Third trail. Not there."

"Why won't we be there?" asked Stavut, patiently.

"Long walk. All the deer will have run away."

For a moment Stavut had no clue at all what the beast was

talking about. Then it dawned on him. Shakul was right. If a Jiamad ran up the hill and scared the deer, they would instantly run. It would take around half an hour to traverse the hill and take up positions. It would take longer for the Jiamad who was to rush in from the second trail to get into position.

"Good," said Stavut. "I was wondering how long it would take you to grasp the flaw in the plan. You have done well. Now, here's the second part. The first Jiamad waits at the foot of the trail, and we send the second around to the other trail. Then we return to the killing ground. Once we are in position we'll . . . Howl! Yes, that's it. You can howl. Once. The Jiamad on the first trail can . . . er, howl back. So can the other one. Then we'll know everyone is in position and the . . . the hunt can begin."

"Again."

"Again? The rock I'm sitting on has heard enough to hunt deer."

"Rock?"

"Never mind. We'll go over it again. Then we pick the two brightest Jiamads to follow the plan. Having said that, I do appreciate that *brightest* might be the wrong word. You have anyone clever, sharp, quick witted?"

"No."

"The surprise is overwhelming. Right, let's go over it again." It seemed to Stavut that several days passed by as he sat with Shakul, but finally the huge Jiamad nodded.

"Good," he said.

It took even longer to explain the plan to the others. Stavut listened as they spoke to one other, and struggled to follow the guttural growls and grunts that interspersed the conversation. One Jiamad sat silently. He was leaner and shorter than the others, his head more elongated, his eyes wider set. His fur was a mottled gray-brown. Finally he spoke. The long tongue lolled, the words slurring, and Stavut could not quite grasp the point he was trying to make. Shakul translated. "Grava says howls will frighten deer."

"Good," said Stavut. "Excellent point. Well done. It

doesn't matter about our two . . . scouts frightening the deer. That's what we want. I shall whistle when we are in position, and the two scouts will then howl."

"Whistle?" queried Shakul.

Stavut placed two fingers in his mouth and let out a piercing whistle. "Like that!"

"Ah, good," said Shakul.

"I think Grava should be one of the scouts."

"Yes, Grava. He will run the deer toward us. I will be other scout."

Stavut tensed. That would leave him with five Jiamads he did not know. "I think you should be with the killing party," he said, swiftly.

"No, I go."

Stavut sensed there was no point arguing with the creature. "Fine," he said. "Just remember, get behind the deer and then charge at them. Force them down the third trail. Some will get away, but we'll probably catch one. Well . . . maybe not the first time. We'll see."

Without another word Shakul loped off toward the far side of the wooded hill. Grava climbed a little way up the deer trail then squatted down. With a sigh Stavut set off toward the third trail, five Jiamads moving silently behind him. As he walked he thought of all the things that could go wrong. The deer could have another trail. They might not keep to a trail, but scatter through the trees. What the hell did he know about deer anyway? His spirits sank with every step back to the killing ground. The brush was thick around the base of the hill, and he ordered the Jiamads to hide themselves. "Be ready!" he said. "You'll need to be quick."

The Jiamads spread out, then crouched down in the brush. Stavut wandered over to a fallen tree and sat down with his back to it. "This is a stupid plan, and you are an idiot," he told himself. Then he realized he had forgotten to signal Shakul and Grava. Standing up, he sent out a piercing whistle. It was answered by a howl to the north, and then another.

"Get ready!" he shouted, then hunkered down behind the fallen tree.

A whole series of bloodcurdling howls erupted from the hill. Stavut waited. A deer suddenly came into sight, bounding over the trail and veering away far to the left of the Jiamads. Then another leapt a low bush and escaped. Stavut swore. Just then seven deer, led by a tall stag, came bursting into view just above where the Jiamads were hidden. The beasts leapt from their hiding places and charged. Two deer swerved away, but the stag went down, its throat ripped open by sharp talons. Two other deer were down. A fourth swung away and tried to run back up the hillside. Shakul came into sight, moving with terrifying speed, and leapt upon the deer's back, bearing it to the ground. His jaws closed on the hapless creature's neck, snapping the spine. Stavut stood, rooted with shock. During the past few hours his fears of the huge beasts had subsided. But now he witnessed their full terrifying power, saw their faces contorted by bloodlust, witnessed the ghastly wounds that had ripped the life from the deer.

He felt unsteady on his feet, and a growing queasiness hit his stomach. Stavut swallowed hard and decided this would be a good time to return to camp. Then he noticed that none of the Jiamads was feeding. They were all staring at him. Nothing moved. Stavut became aware that something was expected of him, but he had no idea what. Then Shakul bent over a dead deer. His taloned arm flashed out, ripping aside ribs and exposing the chest cavity. Reaching in, he tore a section of lung clear, then strode over to Stavut, the bloody flesh dripping gore. "Bloodshirt eat first," said Shakul. Stavut wanted to explain that hunger was the last thing on his mind, but he sensed the importance of this gesture. Reaching out, he took the warm flesh from Shakul's taloned grasp, lifted it to his mouth, and tried to bite the greasy meat. Blood smeared his mouth and he gagged. The Jiamads sent up a roar, and then proceeded to tear into two of the dead deer.

"You great hunter," said Shakul. Stavut found himself staring at the dead stag. As fierce jaws tore into its body, its head flopped back and forth, the wide brown eyes staring at Stavut accusingly.

Shakul returned to the first carcass, pushed aside one of the Jiamads, then crouched down to eat.

On trembling legs Stavut returned to the fallen log and slumped down. Realizing he still held the ghastly flesh Shakul had given him, he hurled it away. He felt drained, but then a rather pleasant thought struck him. Not only had his idea proved successful, it had been spectacular. He had saved his horses and the villagers, and taught the Jiamads how to hunt. Not bad for a merchant with no knowledge of hunting. This day would go down as one of the few when everything had worked out perfectly. He relaxed and planned how he would regale Alahir with this adventure the next time they met. "Bloodshirt, they called me. The Great Hunter." He tried hard to picture an admiring look on Alahir's face, but couldn't quite pull it off. It didn't matter. Nothing could blight this glorious moment of achievement.

Feeling better, he rose to leave.

Just then nine Jiamads emerged from the trees to his left. They wore no shreds of uniform, but still carried long clubs embedded with iron nails.

Shakul and his troop of six saw them and rose from their feeding. They began to snarl and spread out. Only one of Shakul's Jiamads carried a club; the others had obviously ditched their weapons following the fight in the cave. If a pitched battle followed, it was possible that the new Jiamads would win it; then Stavut and the villagers would face a fresh threat.

"Let's all stay calm," Stavut heard himself say. "It is a beautiful day and the sun is shining." Slowly he walked toward the two groups. The Jiamad at the head of the newcomers was taller than the others, towering over seven feet. The fur of its face and head was black but paled to a mottled gray on its shoulders, chest, and arms. Its mouth was severely elongated, with two long incisors jutting over his lower lip. "Who are you?" asked Stavut. The creature stared hard at the small man. Its green eyes glinted with hatred.

"I kill Skins," it said, raising its club.

"We kill deer," said Stavut, swiftly. "We hunt. We feast. How long since you tasted deer meat?" He glanced at the other Jiamads. They looked scrawny, and their tongues were lolling, their nostrils quivering at the scent of fresh meat.

"We take your meat!" snarled the leader.

"And then what?" said Stavut. "Then you starve again. I can show you how to hunt."

"You die!" The club flashed out. Stavut hurled himself backward. In that moment Shakul leapt upon the leader and the two fell to the ground. Their jaws snapped at one another, their taloned claws ripping through fur and flesh. The leader lost its grip on its club and they fought with tooth and claw, snarling and growling. The fight was brief, bloody, and vicious. It ended when Shakul's massive jaws closed on the leader's throat. Shakul's head surged up. Fur and flesh parted, and the leader's jugular sprayed blood into the air. Shakul reared up above the dying beast and hammered his taloned hands into its chest, smashing ribs and ripping open a huge wound. From the wound Shakul ripped out the heart and held it high over his head.

Dashing it to the ground, Shakul tensed and made ready to charge into the eight others.

"Wait, Shakul!" shouted Stavut. "Everyone wait!" Shakul relaxed, his great head turning toward Stavut. "With a bigger pack you could hunt better. Sixteen . . . er fifteen"—he corrected himself as he saw the blood dripping from Shakul's jaws—"fifteen is a good number for a pack. Let them join you. There is enough meat here for all. You can teach them to hunt with you."

"Bloodshirt wants these *things* to live? They are enemy."

"No, Shakul. They *were* enemy. The truth is that they are runaway Jiamads like you. They will be hunted—just like you. You need each other. You will hunt better with fifteen than with seven. Let them live. Let them feed. Think on what I have said."

Shakul's great bear head tilted, and he made several small, growling sounds. Then he walked to the first of the other Jiamads. "You fight?" he growled. The beast dropped to all fours and turned its back on Shakul. One by one the others repeated the same maneuver. Shakul strode among them, growling. Then he walked back to Stavut. "It is done," he said. "They can feed. Tell them."

"Go and eat," said Stavut. The eight half-starved Jiamads rose to their feet and ran to the deer carcasses.

"Our pack now is bigger," said Shakul.

"Your pack," corrected Stavut, uneasily.

"Bloodshirt's pack," said Shakul.

A thousand soldiers, marching in lines of three, entered Petar at midday, followed by a regiment of forty-five hundred Jiamads. They were followed by fifty supply wagons, with a hundred more on the road some way behind. Three hundred cavalrymen, in white-plumed helms and armor of polished iron, escorted the Eternal up the slope toward the palace of Landis Khan.

Jianna, the former Witch Queen of Naashan, rode a strange horse, pure white and eighteen hands tall, its head adorned with two horns that curled back over its ears like those of a mountain goat. The Eternal's helm, shaped from gleaming silver, sported identical horns, and sunlight glinted from the delicate chain-mail shoulder guard she wore over a sleeveless shirt of thin, black leather. The slim and beautiful woman on the horned horse drew rein and stared out over the settlement, her dark eyes angry as she took in the burned-out buildings and the remains of funeral pyres. There were some people moving around the settlement, but little sign of the thriving town it had been only a few days before.

Touching her heels to the flanks of her mount, she rode on toward the palace.

Unwallis was waiting for her at the entrance. He bowed

deeply. In the sunlight he looked old, the lines on his face deeply chiseled, his eyes weary. For a brief moment Jianna remembered the young man she had taken to her bed half a century before. He had been witty and good company, though she could recall nothing of his skills as a lover. Unwallis had merely been one of hundreds of fleeting affairs to lift the boredom. Most had been disappointing, some had offered ephemeral joys, a few had made a mark on her memories. Landis Khan's devotion had been appealing at first, but had soon become cloying.

The hooves of the horned horse clattered on the stone paving slabs before the entrance. The Eternal drew up before Unwallis, who bowed once more. He was dressed in an ankle-length tunic of gray, embroidered at the shoulder with the head of a silver eagle.

The Eternal felt a moment of regret. She had last seen this clothing worn by Landis Khan ten years ago at the palace in Diranan.

I should have killed him then, she thought.

Jianna stepped down from the saddle. A cavalryman rode alongside, taking the reins of the horned horse and leading it away.

"You look like death," she told Unwallis.

"As ever, my queen, you look radiant," he responded.

Jianna did not feel radiant. This current body was approaching forty years of age, and though there were few visible signs of age, she could feel them. The long ride had been tiring, and her lower back was aching. She looked into Unwallis's eyes. The man was more nervous than she had expected.

"Where is Decado?"

"In the wilderness somewhere, Highness. Still seeking Gamal."

"What happened here?"

"I was not here for the . . . the problems, Highness. Decado says the villagers sought to hide Gamal. He found it necessary to kill a few. The rest panicked and fled. Jiamads ran riot. Houses burned. It is as you see. Some villagers have been encouraged to return. More will do so—assuming there is not more violence. I have had rooms prepared for you, Highness. There are still no servants, but some semblance of normality is returning."

Despite his attempt at forced neutrality, Jianna caught the implied criticism. Decado had bungled this simple task, producing exactly the result she had warned him against. It was almost time to put him aside. Even as she thought it she realized that Decado would not be like her other lovers. He would not tolerate being dismissed. *Ah well,* she thought, *it will have to be death then.* When Memnon arrived she would discuss it with him.

"You have a bath prepared?" she asked Unwallis.

"Yes, Highness, the water is being prepared as we speak. However . . ."

And there was that look of nervousness again.

"What is it?"

"Something you should see. A matter of some urgency, I believe."

"Show me," she ordered him. Unwallis bowed once more, then led Jianna into the palace and down to the long library. Moving through it, he brought her to the small study Landis Khan had used.

A lantern was burning in the windowless room, and the heat was oppressive. Upon the desk lay a picture frame. For the first time in centuries Jianna felt a shock so great that it caused her legs to tremble. Reaching out, she supported herself on the desk, and stood staring down at the tattooed skin stretched out in the frame.

"He found Skilgannon, Highness. I believe he brought him back."

She laid her hand tenderly on the tattooed eagle. "A Reborn?"

"More than that. In his notes Landis talks of Gamal finding Skilgannon's soul."

Jianna struggled to contain her feelings. Her mind swam with images, her emotions surging. Keeping her voice as calm as she could, she turned toward Unwallis. "This is all fascinating," she told him. "We will talk later. First I will bathe. Send a rider out to meet the Black Wagon. Memnon should be here by dusk."

On leaden legs Jianna followed Unwallis to a first-floor bathroom. Soldiers were moving back and forth, pouring hot water into a blue-veined bath of marble. Unwallis walked to a nearby shelf upon which stood jars of perfumed oils. Lifting each of the glass lids, he sniffed deeply before deciding on the scent of lavender. Carrying it to the water's edge, the gray-haired ambassador poured a small amount of oil into the steaming water. The bath was only half full, the water lapping at the second of four steps. Dipping his hand into the bath, he withdrew it swiftly. "Fetch more buckets of cold water," he told the soldiers.

Jianna moved out onto a wide balcony overlooking the mountains. Reaching up, she lifted clear her horned helm, laying it on a wicker table. Her long, dark hair fell free. She wanted to ask so many questions, but they would show how important she regarded the rebirth of Skilgannon. There could be no show of such weakness with anyone—even one as loyal as Unwallis.

She thought of the last time she had seen Olek Skilgannon. He had fought a vicious duel with the traitor Boranius and was standing on a battlement, high above the rocks below. A madwoman also stood there, armed with an ornate black crossbow. She had tried to jump, but Skilgannon had leapt from the high ramparts, catching her, and then making a wild grab for a jutting rock. Jianna had run to the battlement's edge and peered down. He was hanging on grimly, but he could not hold her. Her weight was dragging them both to their deaths.

"Let the girl go. I'll haul you up."

"I cannot."

"Damn you, Olek! You'll both die!"

"She is . . . the last survivor . . . of Perapolis." His blood-covered hand was giving way. He grunted and tried to cling on.

Jianna climbed over the ramparts, lowering herself to the thin ledge. Holding to a crenellation, she reached down, clamping her hand over his wrist. "Now we all go, idiot!" she said. Then the weight lessened. Looking down she saw that Druss the Legend had climbed out of the window of the Roof Hall and was standing on the ledge below, supporting the unconscious girl. "Let her go, laddie! I have her." Freed of the weight, Skilgannon swung his left arm over the lip of stone and, as Jianna made way for him, climbed back to the battlement.

Jianna took his hand and wiped away the blood. His fingers were deeply gashed, and more blood pumped from the wounds. "We almost died. Was she worth it?" she asked, softly.

"Worth more than the Witch Queen and the Damned? I would say so."

"Then you are still the fool, Olek," she snapped. "I have no time for fools." Yet she did not move away.

"We need to say good-bye," he whispered.

"I don't want to say it," she told him. Leaning in, he kissed her lips. Malanek and several soldiers arrived on the battlement. They stood back respectfully as Jianna put her arms around Skilgannon's neck.

"We are both fools," she whispered.

With that she had swung away from him. She had looked back only once as she rode from the citadel. High on the ramparts Skilgannon was standing with Druss.

She never saw him again, though she had followed his adventures.

At the last, when she learned he was preparing to face the might of the Zharn, she had led a Naashanite army against them, crushing two of their armies. She had thought it might give him a chance to survive.

She never knew in life whether she had succeeded. On the night after the battle she had felt unwell. Pains struck her chest, flowing down her left arm. Her strength had failed, and she had taken to her bed. At some point, though she could not now recall it, her life had flickered and failed.

On the balcony she shivered, remembering the dread times in the vastness of the Void. Demons had sought to kill her, and for a while she believed they would succeed. Then had come help from a bizarre quarter. Surrounded by scaled beasts, with black eyes and taloned fingers, a bright light had appeared. Fire swept through the demons, killing several and scattering the others. Jianna had stood very still, her dagger raised. From the smoke came the Old Woman. *"Love blinds us to peril,"* said the hag, with a harsh laugh.

"You said that when I killed you," Jianna told her. *"I didn't know what it meant then, and I do not now."*

"Come sit in my cave, child, and we will talk."

"If you want revenge do it now. I am in no mood for conversation."

"Revenge? Ah, Jianna, my dove. I would never have harmed you in life, and I will not harm your spirit now. What did I mean, after you plunged the Sword of Fire into my back? I meant that I had loved you for all your life. As I loved your mother. You are blood of my blood. You are my descendant, child. The last of the line of Hewla. Now come with me. I will keep you safe."

"You tried to kill Olek. He was the great love of my life."

"No, he wasn't, Jianna. Be honest with yourself. You loved power more. Otherwise you would have given it all up just to be with him. The woman in you loved him, the queen in you knew he was a danger. And so he proved. You were unwell in the palace, before leading the army against the Zharn. Your own physicians warned you to stay home and rest. You ignored them, in a vain bid to save him. He died anyway, child."

"Did he win, though?"

"Of course he won. He was Skilgannon."

"Then he is here? Somewhere?"

Fire flashed from the Old Woman's fingers. A demon screeched, and darkness fell again.

"Let us talk somewhere safer."

Jianna had followed her up a steep hillside and into a deep cave. The Old Woman gestured at the entrance, and a wall of

*flame closed over it. By its light she sat on a rock shelf and
stared at Jianna. "It is as well there are no mirrors here,
Jianna. I fear you would not like what you would see."*

"What do you mean?"

"Look at your arm."

*In the firelight Jianna saw that, like the beasts that had at-
tacked her, her skin was gray and scaled. "Why do I look like
this?" she asked, sheathing the dagger and reaching up to
feel the ridged skin of her face.*

*"The evil that we do follows us. Here our spirit mirrors
our true selves."*

*"You are not scaled, and yet you lived a life of appalling
evil."*

*"Magic still operates here, child, though not as powerfully
as in the world of flesh. But I am scaled and grotesque. I
merely disguised it so that you would not recoil and run from
me. Or worse, strike me down with the dagger I gave you."*

*"What happens now? Is there somewhere we must go to
escape this horror?"*

*The Old Woman shook her head. "Nowhere for souls like
us, kinswoman. This is where we dwell now. Yet I have hopes
for you. Your bones were placed in a vault beneath the statue
of you in the palace gardens. Those bones may be the key to
returning to the flesh. We will see. We will survive."*

"The bath is ready, Highness," said Unwallis.

Jianna strode back into the bathroom and removed her
clothes. Then she climbed into the perfumed water.

"So what became of the reborn Skilgannon?" she asked.
"Did Decado kill him?"

"He was gone, Highness, when Decado came for Landis.
He is somewhere in the forests with another Reborn."

"Another?"

"Apparently Landis experimented with bones found in a
locket in Skilgannon's tomb."

"His wife, Dayan," said Jianna. "It was his dream to bring
her back to life."

"No, Highness. It was a man. Landis described him as a

brooding giant, immensely powerful and short tempered. The last notes talk of a double-headed silver ax that Landis asked Skilgannon to give to the man. This, too, was found in the tomb."

"The ax is called Snaga," said Jianna. "The man who wielded it in life was known as Druss the Legend." Leaning back in the bath, she suddenly laughed. "Ah, Landis, you were such a clever, clever man."

Jianna relaxed for a while, then rose from the bath. Unwallis was waiting with a long, soft towel, which he held out for her. Taking it from him, she swirled it around her shoulders and walked back to the balcony. The air was cool on her wet skin.

"Do you still desire me, Unwallis?" she called back to him.

"I do, Majesty, but I fear I am a little too old to perform as I should."

"Then we shall take it gently, for I am in need of a little distraction."

"I am sure Decado will return shortly."

"Are you frightened of him, Unwallis?" she asked, moving closer to the statesman and laying her hands upon his shoulders.

"Yes, Highness."

"And this will stop you making love to me?" Her hand slid down the front of his tunic.

"Apparently not," he said.

As night fell Askari, Harad, and Skilgannon had still not found the blind man and Charis. Askari had discovered tracks. At first she had believed there was a Jiamad on their trail, but she had soon realized the beast traveled with them. In places its footprints overlaid those of the two humans, but in others their tracks overlaid its. They were heading northwest and not moving at any great speed. Even so, with the coming of night it was foolish to press on. They could lose the trail at any time. So Askari found a secluded spot for a night camp, and they settled down, without a fire, to wait for the dawn. Harad stretched out without a word and went to sleep. Skilgannon sat apart, his expression bleak and distant. He had seemed changed since that moment on the hillside, when she watched and listened as he railed at the heavens. There was such rage in him, such power. And before that, as she had watched silently, she had seen him dance, twisting and leaping with extraordinary grace. The contrast had been stark. Even more so now that she had seen him fight. He had killed the Jiamads with cold precision, and murdered the officer without a second thought. He was—in every way—a dangerous man, and Askari felt uncomfortable with his brooding silence.

"What is it that makes a good swordsman?" she asked him, in a bid to start a conversation. His expression flickered as his thoughts were interrupted. At first she thought he was going to tell her to leave him alone, but he seemed to relax.

"A combination of strengths," he told her. "Some learned, some gifted by nature. Speed of hand and a good eye, balance. An ability to close off fears and free the mind."

"Are there tricks you learn?"

"Tricks?"

"Yes. Like when shooting a bow. The secret is to loose the shaft between breaths, so there is no movement in the upper chest. If you hold your breath you will be too tense. If you breathe in, or out, there will be movement that affects the steadiness of the arm. Therefore you breathe out, slowly, and then, with the lungs empty, you let fly."

"Yes, I see. With the blade, and against another master, one must seek the *Illusion of Elsewhere*. The mind empties of all distractions, like heat, cold, pain, hunger, fear. The body is then freed to do what it has been trained for. A swordsman will have learned scores of moves, variations of attack, counterattack, and defense. He will flow into the combat like a dancer."

Askari glanced down at the sleeping Harad. His huge hand was curled around the haft of the silver ax.

"How would a swordsman fare against a man with such an ax?"

"That would depend on who was wielding it. There is only one sure fact about such a combat. It would not take long. To kill an axman one must come within range of his ax. If he has speed and skill he will bury the blades in you before you can strike and step back. A good swordsman would kill the axman, because the ax is a heavy offensive weapon, and ill suited to defense. But *that* ax was once carried by a Legend. I know of no swordsman who could have bested him and survived. At least none ever did."

"What happened to him?"

"He was killed in a battle, not far from here. He was sixty years old, and he still fought like a giant."

"You speak as if you knew him."

Harad grunted and sat up. "How is anyone expected to sleep with such chatter?" he grumbled. Scratching his thick, black beard, he asked, "Is there any food left?"

"No," said Askari. "We carried only enough to bring us to Petar. Tomorrow I will find meat, but we may have to eat it raw. The smell of roasting flesh will carry on the breeze."

The sound of horses' hooves came to them, and they fell silent. Skilgannon beckoned Harad to stay where he was, then he and Askari rose smoothly to their feet and edged toward the undergrowth to the south of the hollow. The ground rose here, and they carefully made their way to the rim. Below, on a wide track, they saw six horsemen following a lean Jiamad. The breeze was blowing toward the two watchers, and there was no way the beast could scent them. It dropped to all fours and sniffed the track. Then it pointed to the northwest, and the small group moved on.

Skilgannon and Askari made their way back to the hollow. Harad was standing, ax in hand, waiting for them. "Riders," said Skilgannon. "They have moved on. We must follow."

"Why?" asked Harad.

"The lead rider was a killer named Decado. I think he is hunting Gamal."

"Landis Khan told me of Decado," said Askari. "He said he was terrifying. He carries two swords, like you. He has killed many men. Landis said no one alive could best him with a blade."

"That is not the problem now," said Skilgannon. "First we must follow them. They cannot suspect they have enemies behind. The wind is with us at the moment, but we must move without undue noise. Askari, you set off first. Leave sign on the trail so that we can follow in the dark. With luck they will lose the trail, or stop for the night. If either should prove true we will bypass them and seek out Gamal before they do."

"And if not?" asked Harad.

"Then we kill them all. You and Askari will take out the Jiamad tracker and the riders. I will deal with Decado."

Askari looked uncertain. "You need to know that Decado is not human," she said. "He is one of those soulless Reborns, brought back from hell. Landis told me this." Touching her brow and chest in the Sign of the Blessed Priestess, she went on. "They are cursed creatures who only look like men. They have demon power and are unconquerable."

Harad's face darkened. Skilgannon's reply was cold. "Let us hope you are right," he told Askari.

"I don't understand."

"You will, but this is not the time to discuss it. Set off and we will follow."

Askari hooked her bow over her shoulder, then turned and loped off toward the northwest.

Skilgannon glanced at Harad, whose expression was thunderous. "She is merely mouthing superstition. It means nothing."

"What if she's right?"

"She's not. You think a man without a soul would seek to rescue a woman in danger?"

"I don't know what to think." Harad sighed, yet Skilgannon saw him relax. "A week ago I was a logger. My biggest concern was meeting the quota and earning enough to pay for my winter supplies. Now? Now I have a dead hero's ax and I have fought and killed."

Skilgannon said nothing for a moment. He looked into the familiar ice-blue eyes. "The real concern is that you are enjoying it. Is that not so?"

"Yes, I am," admitted Harad. "And that's why I fear the girl is right."

"We are closest to life when we are vying with death," Skilgannon told him. "The blood runs hot, the air smells sweet, the sky becomes an unbearably beautiful blue. Battle is intoxicating. That is why the ghastly vileness of war has always been so popular. Now let us follow Askari."

It was close to midnight and the pain had moved from the ever-present thudding in his temples to a sharp, nausea-inducing agony behind his eyes. Decado drew rein on a flat shelf of land high on a hillside and, in dismounting, almost fell from the saddle. He staggered for several paces, then slumped down. His stomach heaved, and fresh pain surged through him. From a small pouch at his side he drew out a small glass vial. With trembling fingers he broke the wax seal and drank. He had long ago learned to tolerate the vile, metallic taste. Without a word to the riders he swung the Swords of Blood and Fire from his shoulders and laid them by his side. Then he stretched out on the ground.

Bright colors flashed across his closed lids. His senses grew sharper. The smell of the horses was stronger now, and he could hear their breathing, interspersed with the creaking of leather saddles as the riders fidgeted. The pain grew more intense, as it always did when the poison seeped into his body. Sharp cramps clawed at his belly, and a tingling began in his arms and fingers. Lying very still, he waited. Sometimes the visions were harsh and frightening, causing fresh upsurges of pain. At other times they would be gentle and reassuring and he would slip away into peaceful dreams of better days.

He had long ago given up hoping for these. They either came or they didn't. There was nothing he could do to encourage them.

The scent of the grass grew stronger, and the breeze seemed full of perfume.

Memnon's pale, golden features appeared in his mind, his jet-black hair drawn back from his thin face, his large, dark, almond-shaped eyes staring at him intently. He was sitting by Decado's bedside. Heavy black curtains were drawn across the windows, the only light coming from two flickering lanterns. "Are you feeling better, child?" asked Memnon.

Decado remembered that long-ago night. He had been eleven years old, and the awful headache had lasted for several days. He had tried to knock himself unconscious by head butting a stone wall, but had merely gashed his brow, making the pain worse.

Now he was lying in a broad bed, a cool breeze whispering through a narrow gap in the curtains. His head was resting on a satin pillow. The freedom from pain made him want to weep for joy. "The pain is gone, sir," he said. Memnon patted the boy's arm. Decado had flinched. Memnon's hands were curiously webbed, his fingers long, his nails dark, as if painted. They were also mutilated. The little finger of each hand had been amputated.

Memnon had noticed the boy's unease and withdrawn his hand. "Do you remember what happened when the pain began?"

Decado had struggled to recall the incident. He had been playing with Tobin and his friends in the open fields behind the apple orchard. The sun had been very bright, and Decado had found it made his eyes water. There had been an argument, but he couldn't recall what it was about. Then Tobin had thrown an apple at him. It had struck him on the cheek. After that the other boys had pitched in, hurling fruit at him. It was not an unusual scenario. Decado was slim and small, and often the object of bullying.

"Do you remember?" said Memnon, again.

"I was hit by an apple," the boy told him.

"And after that?"

"I passed out."

"Do you remember the knife?"

"Tobin's knife?"

The master nodded.

"Yes, sir, it is a little knife with a curved blade. Tobin's father gave it to him."

"What color was the blade?"

"It was red, Master," said Decado. "Red and wet." Even as he spoke an image came to him, sharp and vivid. He saw his own fist, smeared with blood, the dagger blade dripping gore. "I don't understand. And how did I come to be here?"

"It is not important, my boy. You will stay with me for a while. Then we will journey to Diranan."

Within a day the familiar head pain had begun again, but this time Memnon had given him the black draft. He had gagged and been violently sick, but enough of the noxious substance reached his belly for it to ease the agony. Decado had slept for several hours.

For several days he had remained in the palace. Memnon gave him books to read, but they were dull, full of stories about men with swords and shields, fighting and killing. Decado had no interest in such things. At the orphanage he had become fascinated with the craft of pottery, the shaping of wet clay into useful and beautiful objects. He had been most proud of a jug he had made, with the handle shaped like a lizard. It had cracked in the glazing process, but his tutor—the elderly Caridas—had been most complimentary about his skill. "You are an artist, Decado," he had said.

It was to Caridas that Decado had always gone when the bullying was at its worst. "Why do they torment me?" he had asked the old man.

"Sadly, it is the nature of children. Do you ever think of fighting back?"

"I don't want to hurt anyone."

"And that is why they feel safe when they attack you, Decado. There is no fear in them, for you will not cause them harm. They see themselves as wolves, and you as the deer.

Perhaps they would react differently were you to find a little
bit of wolf in yourself."

"I don't want to be a wolf."

"Then you should avoid their company, Decado."

On the surface it was good advice, but the village was
small and there were few places a young boy could go that
did not bring him into contact with other children. Decado
spent much of his time with Caridas the Potter, and found
himself looking forward to the times he would be taken to
Lord Memnon's palace, in the hills outside the village. At
least twice a year Memnon would journey west from Diranan. Decado did not know why the courtier should be interested in him, nor did he care. The weeklong visits to
Memnon were free of stress and fear. The lord would talk to
him about his dreams and his hopes, and would set him little
physical tests that were always diverting. Most were simple,
and Decado failed to see why Memnon found them fascinating. He would ask Decado to hold out his hand, palm downward. Then he would take a small stick and hold it below the
boy's hand. "When I drop this I want you to catch it," he said.

Decado had done so. It was not difficult. Memnon, holding
the stick between both index fingers, would release it.
Decado's hand snapped downward, catching the stick almost
before gravity had exerted its influence. "Wonderful!" said
Memnon.

It was baffling. What was wonderful about catching a
stick? Decado had put this point to the lord. Memnon bade
him wait, then called in several of his servants. One by one
he set them the same task. No one caught the stick. It fell
from Memnon's fingers, their fingers scrabbled for it, catching nothing but air.

"Reaction time," Memnon had said, after the servants had
gone. "You see the stick fall, you send a message to your arm
and hand, then—and only then—do you instruct the hand to
catch the stick. In that time the stick is already falling away
from reach. But not for you, Decado. Your reactions are
lightning swift. This is good."

Decado failed to see how this—until now—unrealized skill could have any benefit. One did not have to catch falling clay in order to make a pot. However, the tests engaged Memnon's interest, and as long as he was interested he would continue to invite Decado to spend time with him. It was a fair trade. Decado was free from the bullies, and all he had to do was catch sticks, or juggle knives, or pluck insects from the air. In the evenings Memnon would ask him about his dreams, or talk about the Eternal and the wars being fought. Decado found talk of war unsettling. There was a man in the village, a friend of Caridas, who had lost an arm during a battle. He had once, according to Caridas, been a fine potter. Now he was a cripple, bitter and lost.

On the last morning before the journey to Diranan, Decado had asked Memnon if he could go and say good-bye to Caridas. The lord shook his head.

"Best not, child."

"He is my friend."

"You will make new friends."

On the journey the head pains had started again. Memnon gave him more of the black draft, and Decado had fallen into a dream-filled sleep.

As he awoke he remembered the incident in the orchard. The boys had been laughing as they threw hard fruit at him. The dreadful pain in his head had increased, and he had rushed at Tobin. At some point he had snatched Tobin's dagger from its sheath and slashed the blade across the boy's throat. Blood had bubbled and sprayed from the wound. Decado had shrieked like an animal and leapt on another boy, bearing him to the ground and plunging the small dagger again and again between his shoulder blades. At first the boy had struggled and screamed, but then there was silence.

Someone had grabbed Decado and hauled him off the boy. Decado had spun, the blade flashing out and plunging through Caridas's right eye. The old man cried out and fell back. His body had twisted and convulsed. Then it, too, lay still alongside Tobin and the other boy.

In the back of the long coach Decado had screamed. Memnon, who had been reading a parchment, put it aside and leaned over the boy.

"What is it, child?"

"I killed Caridas!" he said. "I killed others."

"I know," said Memnon, soothingly. "I am very proud of you."

Twelve

Askari eased her way up the slope, keeping downwind of the Jiamad traveling with the riders. Even so she knew that the creature would also have keen hearing, and each time she moved she waited for the breeze to blow, rustling the leaves in the trees above her and the undergrowth around her. It was slow going. At one point she thought she would lose sight of the riders, but now they had stopped halfway up the slope, some fifty paces from her hiding place. One rider had stepped down from the saddle, staggered, and then slumped to the ground. It seemed that he was ill. The other cavalrymen sat their horses for a while, then, without conversation, dismounted and stood quietly. The small Jiamad squatted down on its haunches waiting for orders.

The man on the ground cried out in pain, startling the horses. The riders calmed them. Then a tall man approached the one in pain, crouching down alongside him and speaking softly. After that the riders drew back, remounted, and set off toward the north, the Jiamad in the lead. Askari waited. They had tethered the wounded man's horse to a bush and left him behind. He groaned again, then cried out.

What was wrong with the man?

Askari rose from her hiding place, drew her hunting knife, and silently approached him.

He was young, dark haired, and—even though his face was contorted in pain—he was handsome. Beside him lay a single scabbard, from which jutted the ivory hilts of two swords. This, then, was the demonic Decado. Moonlight

shone on the blade in Askari's hand. It would be the work of
but a moment to plunge that blade through his vile throat.
Askari knelt beside him, ready to slash open his jugular.

His eyes flickered open. "I am sorry, my love," he said. "I
tried. The red mist came. I could not hold it back. Landis is
dead, though, his ashes scattered. The blind man is close. I
will find him."

Askari's knife slid up to the man's pale throat, the blade
resting against the pulse point. "Do not be angry with me,
Jianna," he said. Then his eyes closed.

Jianna!

The name Skilgannon had used when first he saw her.
Askari readied herself for the death blow once more.

And could not do it. As a huntress she had killed for meat
and skin. As a hunted victim she had killed to protect herself
and Stavut. This, however, would be murder. Sheathing her
blade, she looked down at the pale, pain-filled face. Once
more his eyes opened. His hand reached up and lightly
stroked the skin of her cheek. Instinctively she brushed the
hand away. He looked hurt, and almost childlike. "What
must I do?" he asked.

"Go back to Petar," she said.

"What of the blind man? You wanted him dead."

"Not anymore. Leave him. Go back."

He struggled to rise, groaned in pain, and fell back. Askari
took his arm, hauling him to his feet. He sagged against her,
and she felt him gently kiss her cheek. "Go now!" she said.
Decado took a deep breath, then picked up the sword scabbard and looped it over his shoulder. Askari helped him to his
horse, half lifting him to the saddle. "Go!" she shouted, slapping her hand to the gray's rump. The gelding set off down
the hillside. She thought Decado would fall, but he held to
the saddle.

And then he was gone.

Askari sighed. *I should have killed him,* she thought. She
shivered. Too late now to worry about it, she decided. Scouting around, she found several sticks of dry deadwood. Ar-

ranging them in the shape of an arrow pointing north, she set off after the hunting party. As she moved higher up the slope, the woods grew more dense. The riders had kept to a narrow deer trail, and Askari followed it for around half a mile. Then it swung toward the west. This was a problem. The breeze had shifted and was now blowing from the east. If she continued along it, she would no longer be downwind of the Jiamad leading them. It would pick up her scent. If it doubled back through the shadow-shrouded trees, she would have no warning of its approach. Lifting the bow from her shoulder, she nocked a shaft to the string. *You are Askari the Huntress,* she told herself. *If it comes you will kill it.*

Then she set off once more.

The trail, which had been rising, now dipped down toward a heavily wooded valley. She found where the horses had left the trail, moving down the slope, and caught a glimpse of the last two riders far below, entering the trees. They were around a quarter of a mile ahead.

Askari squatted down to think through her route. Straight ahead would put her on open ground, but to skirt around the bare hillside would take too long. As she considered the question she heard movement in the undergrowth behind her. Spinning around, she drew back the bowstring. Skilgannon moved into sight, Harad behind him. Askari eased the pressure on the string. Swiftly she told Skilgannon of the route the riders had taken. He listened quietly. Then his sapphire gaze locked to her eyes. "We saw a rider heading south," he said.

"That was Decado."

He nodded. "On the hillside I followed your tracks. You met a man there."

"Yes."

"The footprints showed you stood very close to him."

"You read spoor well. I helped him to his horse."

"Why would you do that, Askari?"

She heard the note of suspicion in his voice, and found herself growing irritated. "I do not answer to you," she snapped.

"Do you know him?" he persisted, his voice cool.

"No. He was lying on the ground, in pain and delirious. I found I could not kill him."

"Why did he not seek to kill you?"

"He thought I was someone else. Like you, he called me Jianna. Then he kissed my cheek and asked me what he should do. I told him to go back to Petar." She saw the shock register and his steady gaze faltered.

"We will talk more of this later," he said. "For now let us find these riders."

Rising to his feet, he set off down the slope. Harad set off after him without a word to Askari.

The huntress followed them.

The moon shone brightly as they neared the trees. Then came a high-pitched shriek of pain, and the distant sounds of snarling beasts and terrified horses.

For most of the day Longbear had carried the old blind man while Charis stumbled behind. Her skirt was torn from the stand of brambles they had traveled through, to try to gain a march on the mounted men following, and her legs were covered with scratches from the sharp thorns. Charis was wearier than she had ever been. Her legs felt leaden, her thighs sore, her calves burning. The higher they climbed the more she felt that she could not breathe swiftly enough to fill her lungs. There was no conversation. Gamal was old and frail, his strength long gone. His face was gray with exhaustion, and there was an unhealthy blue pallor to his lips. Longbear had told them the night before that a Jiamad was leading the pursuers, and that the soldiers hunting them were horsemen. The chances of escape were slight.

Out in the open a bitter wind was blowing from the snow-covered mountains, and even in the cover of the trees Charis began to shiver. Longbear laid Gamal on the ground, then turned and stared back over the ground they had covered. Far below Charis could see horsemen emerging from the trees.

Several of the riders carried long lances, and the last of the sunlight gleamed upon their silver breastplates and plumed helms.

Gamal was awake now. Reaching up, he laid his hand on Longbear's furry arm. "Save yourself," he said. "Go now. They are not hunting you."

"You die soon," muttered the beast.

"I know."

Longbear growled, then straightened. "I go," he said. Without another word he moved off into the trees. Charis sat beside Gamal. The old man was shivering, so she drew him into an embrace, rubbing his back and holding him against her.

The light was failing, the temperature dropping. Charis leaned back against the tree. The six riders below were on open ground now, and she could see the dark figure of a Jiamad loping ahead of the group, heading unerringly along the trail they had walked an hour before. "You go, too," whispered Gamal. "Longbear was right. I am dying. I have a cancer. Even without Decado I would have lived for a few days only. Save yourself, Charis."

"I am too tired to run," she said. "You just rest."

She saw three running figures emerge some way behind the riders, then cut to the left entering the trees. They were so far away she could not see whether they were soldiers or Jiamads. *What does it matter?* she thought. *Nothing matters anymore.*

Still holding to the old man, she looked up. Darkness had come swiftly, and already bright stars were gleaming in the sky. Her father had said that stars were merely holes in the heavens through which the bright, glorious light of the Source shone down on humanity. Kerena had said this was nonsense. Her father had told her they were the ghosts of dead heroes. The Source had blessed them and given them a place in the sky until they could be returned to the earth. Sometimes, if one was lucky, it was possible to see a hero flash across the sky upon his return. Charis had seen two such miracles. One night, sitting on the flat roof of the bakery, she had seen a star shooting across the sky. It was so bright it must have been a great hero.

There were no shooting stars tonight.

Gamal's head felt heavy on her shoulder, and she eased her position. The old man was sleeping now.

She found herself thinking of Harad, and hoping that he had survived the attack on Petar. She guessed he probably would. Even a Jiamad would think twice before attacking her Harad.

A stooping Jiamad came into sight. It did not approach her, but squatted down some thirty feet away. Then the horsemen came. They drew rein and sat staring at the girl and the sleeping blind man. For a moment no one moved.

"Well?" Charis called out. "Which one of you *heroes* is going to step down and kill an old blind man?" She saw the riders glance at one another. One man eased his horse forward.

"No one here would choose to kill him," he said. "But his death has been ordered by the Eternal. Step away from him. I have no orders concerning you."

"A pox on your orders," she sneered. "I am going nowhere."

"So be it," he said, swinging his leg over the saddle and preparing to dismount.

Just then Longbear charged from the trees, letting out a mighty roar. Several of the horses reared. The soldier who had been dismounting was hurled to the ground, his panicked horse racing past Charis. Longbear rushed at the horses, his talons slashing through the neck of the nearest. Blood sprayed in the air, and the horse reared and fell, hurling its rider to the ground. One of the soldiers brought his lance to bear and kicked his mount forward. It charged at Longbear, just as he was rushing toward the enemy Jiamad. The lance took Longbear high in the shoulder, plunging deep before snapping. With a roar of pain and fury Longbear swung and leapt at the rider. As he did so the enemy Jiamad jumped on his back, burying fangs deep into Longbear's neck. Another lancer charged. His weapon speared the back of his own Jiamad, shattering the beast's spine. The Jiamad fell from

Longbear, who spun and charged at the rider. The lancer tried to turn his mount, but Longbear's talons ripped into his side, dragging him from the saddle. The rider's helm came loose and tumbled to the ground. Longbear's jaws crunched down on the man's head, crushing the skull. Another lance hammered into him. This, too, broke. The great beast stumbled, blood pouring from the wounds in his back and the torn flesh of his throat.

Charis watched in horror as the five remaining soldiers closed in on the dying beast. Three of them had dismounted, allowing their horses to run free. Two others were baiting Longbear, holding him at bay by stabbing their lances toward him. The beast roared again, but the sound had no power. He tried to rush at the dismounted soldiers, but lost his footing. As Longbear fell they charged him, burying their lances deep. The beast gave one final cry, high and piercing and grotesquely human. Then he died.

One of the riders still mounted steered his horse toward where Charis sat. Amazingly Gamal had not woken during the battle. *Perhaps he is already dead,* thought Charis, *and will be spared the pain of plunging sword blades.*

The rider approached Charis. His face was pale and angry. "You knew that beast was close. Now you will die, too, you bitch!" he said.

His head jerked to the right, a black arrow thudding through his temple. He sat very still for a moment, his face showing his shock. Then he dropped his lance and started to reach up. His body slumped forward over the horse's neck.

The four surviving soldiers swung away from the fallen beast, the men on foot drawing their sabers and straining to see where the shaft had come from.

They did not have long to wait.

Three people emerged from the trees to the left. Charis saw that Harad was one of them, and her heart lifted. The second was Callan, the tattooed man from the palace. He looked different now, harder, his eyes cold. In his hands were two glittering swords. Beyond them was a dark-haired woman, dressed in a fringed buckskin shirt and dark leggings. She held a curved bow in her hands, an arrow nocked to the string.

Harad moved toward the soldiers, carrying a huge ax, but the tattooed man called him back. Then Callan stepped forward.

"There is no need for any more to die," he told the swordsmen. "Gather your horses and be on your way."

"We have orders," said the young man who had spoken to Charis earlier. "The blind man is a condemned traitor. He has been sentenced to death."

"Your orders are now meaningless. You cannot fulfill them."

"Large talk. Let's see you back it with action." The man ran at Callan. He did not seek to avoid the swordsman. Instead he merely blocked the thrusting sword and rolled his wrist. The soldier's sword flew from his hand. Before he could move, Callan's own blade was resting lightly on his throat. The second soldier rushed in. Still keeping his left-hand sword against the first soldier's jugular, he parried the first clumsy thrust and once more rolled his own weapon around the enemy's blade. The soldier cried out as Callan's sword sliced across his knuckles. The cry was cut off as the shining blade swept up and touched his throat.

It was all so fast Charis could not quite take in what had happened. Callan's swords had moved with lightning speed. Then he spoke again.

"Are we done?" he asked, coldly. "Can we end this farce now?"

"I cannot disobey my orders," said the first man.

"I understand," said Callan. His sword flickered. Blood gushed from the severed artery in the man's throat. A look of stunned surprise hit his features. He stumbled back, half turned, then pitched to the ground.

For Charis the moment was more shocking than the bloodthirsty attack by Longbear. This was cold and horrible. Murder without emotion. No one moved, and Callan spoke again.

"Can *you* disobey your orders?" he asked the second man.

"Oh yes. Absolutely."

"Very wise. What about you two?" he asked the others.

Both men nodded. "Then gather your horses."

They did so with some speed. Callan watched as they rode away. Harad moved to her side, laying his ax upon the grass. "Are you hurt?" he asked.

"No. It is so good to see you." She looked into his pale eyes, her gaze soaking in the familiar features. She relaxed then and smiled. "You came after me."

"Of course I did. I'm here, aren't I?"

"Why did you do that?"

"I have a feeling you're going to make me wish I hadn't," he muttered.

Callan came alongside and knelt by Gamal. The old man was unconscious. Callan laid his fingers on Gamal's throat, feeling for a pulse. "He's not dead, is he?" asked Charis, fearfully.

"No." Callan squeezed the man's hand. "Gamal, can you hear me. It is Skilgannon."

At first there was no movement; then a juddering sigh came from Gamal's lips. "Skilgannon?" he whispered, his blind opal eyes flickering open.

"Yes."

"The soldiers?"

"They have gone."

"Help me to sit. There is much to tell, and not a great deal of time left to me."

"It is not safe here," said Skilgannon. He turned to Harad. "Will you carry him? We must find a more defensible position. Those riders will seek out comrades and then return."

Harad passed the ax to Skilgannon and lifted the old man into his arms. Then the group set off toward the higher country. Askari found a campsite on a high shelf of rocky ground under an overhanging cliff. There was a depression in the cliff face out of the wind, and Harad laid Gamal down. The old man's face was gray, and there was a faint blue tinge to his lips. Skilgannon knelt beside him. "You need to rest," he said.

Gamal shook his head. "It would do me no good. This body will not survive the night." A spasm of pain showed in his face, and he groaned. "I shall not be here for the end," he said. "And I cannot speak to you in this form. The pain is too great. It cuts across the thought processes. Will you journey with me, Skilgannon?"

"He is delirious," said Askari. "He makes no sense."

"Yes, he does," said Skilgannon, softly. "I once did this journey with another." Returning his attention to the dying man, he asked: "What would you have me do?"

"Lay your body down and take my hand."

Skilgannon stretched out, then he rose on one elbow. "Let no one touch me or disturb me," he commanded the others. "Leave me to wake in my own time." Then he lay back, reached out, and took Gamal's hand.

His vision swam, bright colors flashing before his mind's eye. There was a sense of falling, spinning, and a great roaring sound washed across his consciousness. Then there was darkness. A light grew. Skilgannon blinked and sat up. The roaring was still there, and he turned to see a waterfall. It was a magnificent sight, the water gushing over black basaltic rock and falling several hundred feet into a wide lake. There was a black stone bridge above the waterfall, high and curving. Sunlight on the water spray around it created a rainbow over the bridge.

"It is so beautiful," said a voice. Skilgannon glanced to his right. A handsome young man sat there, his hair long and blond, his eyes blue.

"Gamal?"

"Indeed so. I long ago decided that—if it was in my power—I would be here at the point of my death. There is something about this place that feeds my soul."

"It is not a dream place then?"

Gamal smiled. "Well, yes, it is at the moment. But it exists in the real world."

"How did they build a bridge across it?" asked Skilgannon.

"No one built it. Ten thousand years ago—perhaps more—a great volcano erupted. A huge river of molten lava swept across the land. It burned a tunnel through the rock face, then swept on down through the valley. The bridge is just the upper section of a cliff that was once here. A long time ago, before one of the many falls and rebirths of the world, there was a race who believed that the rainbow bridge was a connection between their world and the place of the gods. It is easy to see why."

"At most other times I would be fascinated to know more," said Skilgannon. "However—as you yourself said—we have little time."

The young man nodded. "This is true. First let me tell you about the Eternal—"

"She is Jianna, a woman I loved more than life. I know. Now I must destroy her."

"No!" said Gamal. "That you must not do! She would return instantly."

"How is that possible?"

"Once more Landis is at fault here," said Gamal, sadly. "The Eternal's Reborns are linked to her. Landis believed the process of the Eternal's rebirth would be more efficient if there was some way to make the process of soul transference immediate upon the Eternal's death. As it was we had to locate the Reborn and bring her to Diranan, and the palace, and then perform the exchange. This was obviously fraught with difficulty. What if the Reborn, sensing her fate, chose to run away? What if the Eternal died and was destroyed in the Void by some demon? Landis spent many years attempting to refine the process. In the end, though, it was Memnon who supplied the answer."

"Memnon?"

"I will come to him, Skilgannon. He has a brilliant mind, and is also possessed of great psychic power. When one of the Eternal's duplicates was born Memnon had a tiny jewel inserted under the skin at the base of the infant's skull. This

jewel carries a spell. If the Eternal dies, her spirit would automatically flow to the eldest of the duplicates, wherever
they might be. As far as I know this has been achieved twice.
So you must not seek to kill her. It would be a waste of time.
There will be more than twenty Reborns scattered around the
empire."

"I understand," said Skilgannon. "Now tell me of Memnon."

"He is the Lord of the Shadows—a Jiamad, but of a
unique kind. Landis created him a long time ago. It was part
of an attempt to find a formula for longer natural life, to
counteract the aging process. Landis had begun to loathe
the idea of raising duplicates, only to kill their souls in order for the original to live on. He saw it—quite rightly—as
evil. So he experimented with Joinings, seeking one who
could regenerate more efficiently than nature might intend.
He was very successful. His experiments gave many of us
longer, healthier lives. Then, a hundred years ago, came
Memnon. At first we thought him a triumph. Despite being
created from animal and human he was in almost every way
a perfect baby. Not a trace of Jiamad. As a child he possessed rare gifts. He could restore faded blooms to health.
He could draw wild creatures to him. An amazing child."
Gamal sighed. "His intelligence was—is—phenomenal.
By the age of thirteen he was assisting Landis in experiments. He had mastered the machines of the ancients. By
twenty he had moved beyond even Landis. The Eternal favored him, allowing him to experiment on more and more
humans. Many of them died terrible, agonizing deaths.
None of this concerned Memnon at all. The pain of others
passed him by. He has no conscience, no sense of what we
consider good or evil. His one redeeming feature is his devotion to the Eternal."

"One of her lovers, I expect," said Skilgannon, an edge of
bitterness in his voice.

"No, not Memnon. I said he was *almost* perfect. There is
no way he could perform any meaningful sexual act. Landis
believed that was the reason for his lack of passion. He never

grows angry, or sad. Memnon just is. He created the Shadows. They will be coming after you before long, Skilgannon. Make sure there is always light around you. They favor the dark. Bright light burns their eyes."

"They are Jiamads?" asked Skilgannon.

"Of a kind. They have no fur. They are skinny—almost skeletal—and they move with bewildering speed. So fast that if a swordsman were to thrust his blade at one, the sword would cut only air. They have two curved fangs, which inject poison into the victim. It is not deadly, but causes temporary paralysis. They also carry daggers, the blades dipped in similar poison."

"Apart from light, what other weaknesses do they have?"

"They lack stamina. After an attack they will find some safe, dark place to rest. And, as I said, their eyes are sensitive. Their vision is not strong. In the forest you will hear them. They emit loud, extremely high-pitched shrieks. In some way this allows them to *see* objects. I do not understand how this works. Neither did poor Landis."

"I take it that he is dead."

"Yes, Decado killed him. Despite his centuries of life Landis was a romantic. He believed in Ustarte's prophecy."

"And you do not?" said Skilgannon.

"The simple answer is that I do not know. I cannot see how one warrior—even one such as you—can end the reign of the Eternal. Even if you did, what would it matter? The artifacts exist. They will always exist. They survived for thousands of years, their powers almost dormant. Nadir shamans found a way to harness the energies radiating from these sleeping machines below the ground. They did not know the artifacts were there, but, like Memnon, they were attuned to the energies pulsing from them. They acted as conduits for that power. All the physical magic in this blighted world emanates from these artifacts."

"So what changed?" asked Skilgannon.

"The Temple of the Resurrection. An abbot found a way to awaken them. The power in the artifacts swelled. All over this continent and beyond. So you see, Skilgannon, the physical death of the Eternal will do nothing to change the unhappy state of the world."

"What did he do, this abbot?"

The young Gamal shrugged. "Much is lost in myth now, but he found a passageway inside the holy mountain, and then there was light. I cannot say. I was not there."

"Then the answer lies at the temple."

Gamal smiled. "Perhaps it would—if it were still there. Almost five hundred years ago the temple vanished."

"It was inside a mountain," said Skilgannon. "It could not vanish. There must have been a more powerful ward spell placed on it."

"No, Skilgannon. I have walked on the open land where the temple mountain once was. There is nothing there. It is an odd place now. Nothing grows there. The land twists and changes. Metal reacts in a bizarre way. I had copper coins in my pouch. They began to jingle together. I remember feeling nauseous, and could not maintain my balance. My companion and I left the area as soon as we could. Once clear I looked in my pouch. Five coins had somehow welded themselves together. I had to cut my belt loose, for the brass buckle was mangled and bent. Believe me, Skilgannon. The temple is gone. The mountain is gone."

"But the power remains," said Skilgannon softly.

"Yes."

For a while they sat in silence, Skilgannon thinking through what Gamal had said. Gamal suddenly sighed. "It is beginning," he said. "I can feel the pull of the Void."

"Are you frightened?"

"A little. My life has not been one spent in philanthropic pursuits. I have been selfish, and my actions have resulted in deaths of innocent people. Yet the Void is not unknown to me. I have traveled there often. It is where you and I met."

"I have no memory of such a meeting."

"As I told you, the Void is a place of spirit, and you now live in the world of flesh. The memories will return one day.

I wonder if I will find Landis. I was fond of him. It would be good to see him again."

Suddenly all noise from the waterfall ceased, and the blue sky faded to black. A chill wind blew. Gamal looked fearful, and was staring at a point over Skilgannon's shoulder. Skilgannon rose to his feet and turned. A tall man was standing close by, dressed in pale robes of shimmering silver. He was dark haired and androgynously good looking. His skin was pale gold, his cheekbones high, his eyes large, dark, and almond shaped, like the peoples of the Chiatze.

"What are you doing here, Memnon?" asked Gamal.

"I have come to say farewell to an old friend," the man replied, his voice gentle.

"We were not friends."

"Sadly, that is true. I was attempting to be polite. Go ahead and die, Gamal. It is Skilgannon I wished to speak to."

"No! He will not die here, Memnon." Gamal rose swiftly to his feet and reached toward Skilgannon. "Take my hand. Now!"

Memnon's arm snapped forward. Gamal disappeared. "He chose a pleasant spot," said Memnon, moving forward to walk past Skilgannon and stare at the towering waterfall.

"Did you kill him?" asked Skilgannon.

Memnon shrugged. "Let us hope so. And before you consider attacking me you should understand that such violence will have no effect here. There is no pain. No blow of yours will concuss me or damage my form. This is merely a dream place. Would you like to hear the water rushing? I find it an annoying distraction, but if you wish I will restore it."

Skilgannon stepped in, his left fist hammering into what should have been Memnon's face. The blow passed through the man. "Ah, I see you are a man who needs to discover his own realities. So now that we understand the situation, let us sit and talk. A fire would be pleasant." Memnon gestured to the ground and a small circle of stones appeared. Flames leapt up from within them. "The Eternal has spoken of you often. She has such fond memories of you."

"What is it you want from me?" asked Skilgannon.

"Landis should never have brought you back. It was a mistake. I am here to rectify it. However, your passing will be without pain."

"How do you intend to kill me?"

"Ah, did Gamal not indicate to you the dangers of these kinds of journeys? How remiss of him. Let me explain. The essence of your life force is now here. For short periods such departures from the flesh can be tolerated. After a few hours, though, the body begins to die. Time here does not flow in the same way as beyond. I would say that your new form is already fighting for life. So what would you like to talk about, in the brief time that we have?"

Skilgannon closed his eyes. He pictured the shallow depression in the rocks where his body lay, and tried to will his spirit to return. When he opened his eyes the dark-haired Chiatze was staring at him.

"You are not as godlike as the Eternal described you," said Memnon. "True, you have beautiful eyes, but you are merely a man. I suppose that is what legends do. They exaggerate and amplify. However, she loved you, and I suppose that does color the memories. Even so you do not seem like a man who would butcher the inhabitants of an entire city."

"Looks can be deceiving," said Skilgannon.

"Quite so. Excuse me for a moment." Memnon faded from view. Alone now Skilgannon sought again to awaken, but to no avail. He walked to the water's edge and found a sharp stone, which he tried to cut into his palm, thinking that pain might awaken him. There was no pain. The skin cut and bled, then resealed instantly.

Memnon reappeared. "I apologize for leaving you. I wanted to see how close the pursuers were to your little group. Their deaths will not be long after yours—and considerably more painful I would say."

Harad was standing on the shelf of rock, staring out over the land, Charis beside him. Askari had left some time before, to scout for any sign of their enemies returning. The sun was setting, the sky red as blood. Brilliantly lit clouds hovered above the western mountains, themselves dramatically colorful with their bases crimson, their flanks a mixture of coral and black, their rounded peaks white as snow. "It is so beautiful," said Charis, taking Harad's arm, and resting her head on his shoulder. "Look at those clouds."

"I am looking at the clouds. I think it will rain tomorrow."

"Oh, Harad," she said. He heard the disappointment in her voice and felt a sense of loss as she withdrew her arm and moved away from him.

"They are beautiful," he said, swiftly.

"You don't see it, though, do you?" she said, turning toward him. "You look at clouds and you think of rain. A deer is just meat on four legs. A tree is something to chop down to make a table, or a chair."

"Aye, well that's all true, isn't it?"

"Of course it's true, you clod! There is so much more, though. I wish you could see it."

"Why? What difference does it make what I see?"

Charis did not answer. She rubbed at her tired eyes, and then pushed her hand through her golden hair, pushing it back from her face. "I am really tired," she said. "I think I'll go and rest."

"I understand beauty," he said, softly. "When you just brushed your fingers through your hair. That was beautiful. Sometimes, on a cold autumn day, after the rain, when the sun shines through the broken clouds, that is beautiful, too. When you live alone in the mountains you tend to deal in realities, like food and shelter and comforts. Clouds bring rain, deer is meat."

"Well," she said, with a smile. "You used up a whole winter of words there."

"I didn't want you to go away," he told her, his face reddening.

"Why did you come after me, Harad?" she asked, stepping in close.

"Thought you might need me."

"And I did. Not just because I was in danger. I needed you before that. Did you never wonder why I always brought your food?"

"I thought it was because you enjoyed irritating me."

Her face darkened. "Did it not occur to you that I might have been attracted to you?"

"To me?" he said, shocked.

"Yes, to you, you dimwit! Did I not ask you to the Feast? Did I not promise to teach you to dance?"

Harad struggled in vain to bring his thoughts into focus. It was as if the sea were roaring between his ears. "I'm not a handsome man," he said, at last. "It never entered my mind that you . . . I don't . . . I don't know what to say."

"Tell me you love me. Or you don't," she added, swiftly.

Harad drew in a deep breath; then he relaxed and gave a broad smile. "Of course I love you. When I thought you might have been . . . hurt," he said, unwilling to voice the real fear, "I thought I would go out of my mind."

"Then perhaps you should kiss me," she said, moving in close.

At that moment there came a strangled cry of pure agony from behind them. Harad swung around. The old man, Gamal, was writhing on the ground. His body spasmed, and there was blood upon his lips. Charis ran to him, kneeling by his side. Gamal's face was a mask of agony. "The swords!" he groaned. "Skilgannon!" Then he screamed in pain. His body convulsed, and more blood sprayed from his mouth as he cried out.

"Help me, Harad!" pleaded Charis.

The axman knelt down beside Gamal. The old man sagged unconscious into Harad's arms. The big man lowered him gently to the ground.

Charis held her fingers to Gamal's throat. The pulse flickered briefly for a few moments, then stopped. Charis sighed, and a tear fell to her cheek. "I liked him," she said.

She began to weep and Harad sat close to her, his huge arm

around her shoulder. He felt a touch of guilt, for, despite her distress, Harad himself felt content. In fact more content than at any time he could remember. The woman he loved was nestled in close to him. He could feel her warmth, and smell the scent of her hair. The moment was blissful. For the first time in days the glittering ax was forgotten. All that mattered was that he comforted this woman in his arms.

Charis relaxed, her head against his chest. "He was a kindly old man," she said. "It was so cruel to hunt him in this way."

Harad said nothing. The old man had been one of the lords, one of the creators of beasts. Harad had little sympathy for his passing.

"I am so glad you are here, Harad."

"Where else would I be?"

Charis sighed and moved back a little from him. She leaned in and closed the dead man's eyes. "Your friend is still asleep. Should we wake him?"

"He said not to." A sense of emptiness touched Harad as Charis drew away from him. A flicker of anger replaced it. Then she smiled at him, and the anger melted away.

"Where did you find that big ax?"

"It was a gift," he told her.

"It is a horrible weapon." She shuddered. "Why do we need such things?"

"What sort of question is that?" he responded. "Without the ax I would have been killed. Then I couldn't have been here to help you."

"I meant why do people *want* to make such weapons. Why do we fight each other?"

"I don't know. I never know answers to the questions you ask. Everything is so complicated when you are around. It makes my head swim." Yet there was no irritation now. Harad wondered if there ever would be again. He gazed at her face. She had never been more beautiful.

"I'm really frightened, Harad," she said, suddenly. "All

I've wanted for the last two years is for us to be together. Now we are. And people are trying to kill us."

His pale eyes glittered. "No one is going to kill you, Charis. They'd have to get past me. I may not be handsome, and I'm not a great thinker, but I *am* a fighter. Ten days ago that was not a virtue. Now it is. We'll get away from here. We'll find a place. With the Legend people, maybe, to the north. Or high in the mountains, away from Jems and armies."

Askari came running over the lip of the rock shelf. "They are closing in," she said. "Around twenty riders and four Jems. Not seen their kind before. They move on four legs, like hounds, but they are big. Almost as big as ponies." She glanced at the dead man, then at Skilgannon. "Best wake him," she said.

Harad leaned over and shook Skilgannon. There was no response.

Charis touched his face. "The skin is cold," she whispered. "I think he's dead."

Askari knelt on the other side of Skilgannon and shook him roughly. Charis touched his throat. "There is a heart-beat," she said. "It is very faint."

The sound of a distant howl came to them. Charis shivered. "Doesn't sound like a wolf," she said. "It makes the blood run cold."

"Wait till you see them," said Askari. "Your blood will turn to ice!" She shook Skilgannon again. "We have to get away from here," she told Harad. "Can you carry him?"

Harad grabbed Skilgannon's arm and hauled him upright. Askari ran to the edge of the rock shelf. "Too late," she called back. "The beasts are coming."

Harad laid Skilgannon down, then took up Snaga and moved out into the moonlight. He followed Askari for some fifty paces to the edge of the slope.

Four huge beasts were bounding up the trail.

Askari nocked an arrow to her bow.

The grotesque hounds came rushing up the hillside. Harad had once seen a lion in the high country, but these creatures were far bigger. For the first time in his life he knew fear. Not for himself, but for the fact that Charis was behind him, and if the beasts got past him, she would be torn to pieces. The fear was replaced by a sudden blazing fury. These creatures were threatening the woman he loved. He hefted the ax and waited. Askari let fly. The shaft flashed through the air, thudding into the chest of the first beast. It howled in pain and swerved, but then came on. A second arrow plunged into its gaping maw. Its jaws snapped shut, snapping the shaft. Then it continued its run.

Harad leapt out to meet the charge. Snaga hammered into the beast with terrible force, half severing the head. Harad wrenched it clear. A second creature leapt at him. A shaft plunged into its side. Snaga clove into the jaws, splitting the skull. A third Jiamad leapt over Harad as he killed the second beast, and ran on toward the cave. The fourth stumbled and fell as a shaft from Askari tore into its throat.

Harad ran back toward where he had left Charis. The last beast had almost reached the campsite. Harad could never make it in time. He ran up the hill as fast as he could. As he came over the lip of the rock he saw the beast, sprawled on the ground. Skilgannon was standing there, the Swords of Night and Day in his hands.

Without a word to the swordsman Harad ran to the campsite beyond. Charis was standing in the shadows. Dropping the ax he swept her into his arms, holding her close. Then he let out a sigh of pure relief.

He turned to Skilgannon. "Thank the Source you woke in time," he said.

Skilgannon merely nodded. Harad saw that he looked exhausted. Releasing Charis, he moved to the swordsman. "Are you all right?"

"Weak," said Skilgannon. He staggered and almost fell.

Harad caught him. "Rest a moment," he said.

"No time for that," said Askari, running into the camp. "The riders are already in sight. We need to get higher into the tree line."

Skilgannon sheathed his swords, then swung to Charis. "You saved me," he said. "I would have died there."

Then he followed Askari out into the open. Harad took Charis by the hand, and they moved after the huntress and the swordsman. The twenty riders were still some way distant. Harad glanced up at the tree line. It was at least half a mile away. Skilgannon and Askari were already running. Harad and Charis followed them. Skilgannon stumbled twice, then fell to his knees. Harad hauled him to his feet, then ducked down and lifted the exhausted swordsman onto his shoulder. Then he ran again. Charis and Askari were far ahead, but Harad pounded on. The slope was steep, and there was scree underfoot. Even Harad's great strength began to fail. His breath coming in ragged gasps, he forced himself on. He could hear the pounding of hooves getting closer.

An arrow sang past him, and he heard a horse whinny in pain.

Then he was into the trees. Askari sent another shaft down into the riders. It sank into the shoulder of a bearded horseman. The other soldiers hauled on their reins and turned their mounts, riding back down the slope.

Harad laid Skilgannon down. The man was unconscious again, but breathing normally.

Charis came alongside and felt his pulse. "He's just sleeping now," she said. "When I woke him he could barely stand. I don't know how he found the strength to kill that awful creature."

"How did you wake him?" asked Harad.

"The swords," she told him. "You remember when Gamal woke. He shouted: 'The swords. Skilgannon.' When you ran out to fight the Jems I drew one of his swords and put it in his hand. His body jerked and he cried out. I helped him to stand, then we saw the beast coming. He drew the other sword, the golden one, and stepped out to meet it. I thought there was no way he could survive. He is an amazing man."

"I killed two of them and *he's* the amazing man?" grumbled Harad, good-naturedly.

"Are you jealous?"

"Yes."

"Good!"

Askari kept watch, and Charis slept for a while. Harad dozed beside her. After an hour Skilgannon woke. He sat up. The movement roused Harad.

"How are you feeling now?"

"Stronger. Thank you, Harad. I couldn't have made it."

"It was a pleasure. So what do we do now?"

"You should take your lady and find somewhere safe. As for me? I'm going to fulfill a prophecy."

Alahir was glad to be away from the encampment. The army of Agrias had swelled to around twelve thousand now—more than a third of them Jiamads. They were camped on high ground near a deserted and ruined city that had once been the capital of the Sathuli lands. Every day more troops arrived, along with an endless stream of supply wagons. Alahir found the encampment too noisy and far too unpleasant on the nose. Latrine trenches had been dug, but Jiamads tended to squat wherever and whenever they felt the need, and the stench was overpowering.

The tall cavalryman led his troop of fifty riders over a ridge, heading south. It was not a routine patrol, hunting runaways and scouting for any sign of enemy movement. Agrias had said the Eternal was moving her forces into the lands of Landis Khan, and there were reports of enemy cavalry moving through the mountain passes. So all the riders wore full armor, heavy, hooded mail shirts and breastplates, and horsehair-crested battle helms with long bronze nasal guards. Each man possessed a recurve bow with fifty shafts, a heavy cavalry saber, and a short sword in a scabbard fitted to the left shoulder. Agrias had said the final battle was ap-

proaching. His words were full of confidence at the outcome, but Alahir didn't like the look in the man's eyes. There
was fear there. He had expected a huge uprising to follow his
rebellion, and it had not materialized. Alahir wouldn't have
cared one way or another who won, save that his own homeland was at risk.

The Last of the Drenai.

It was not just a romantic phrase to Alahir. It meant everything to the young soldier. The lands around the city of Siccus had been ruled by the descendants of the Drenai for more
than three hundred years. The borders were closed, and
though they paid lip service to the Eternal, sending taxes and
maintaining her laws, the old ways remained paramount.
Honor, nobility of spirit, courage, and a love of the homeland were the first virtues instilled in the young. This was
followed by lessons in Drenai history, to make the young citizens aware of the great ones in whose footsteps they would
be expected to walk. Karnak the One Eyed, who had held
Dros Purdol against impossible odds; Egel, the first earl of
Bronze, builder of the great fortresses. Adaran, who had
won the War of the Twins, and Banalion, the White Wolf,
who had fought his way back from the disasters of the last
Ventrian wars and helped to rebuild a shattered empire.
There were stories of villains, too, not all of them power-
hungry foreigners seeking to destroy the greatness of the
Drenai. There was Waylander the Assassin, who had sold his
soul to the enemy and murdered the Drenai king, and Lascarin the Thief, who had stolen the legendary Armor of
Bronze. Stories of men like these were told to stem the arrogance that might flower instead of pride in a Drenai youngster's heart.

Alahir smiled. The tales of many heroes had been im-
parted to him, but few had touched his heart as had the tale
of Druss the Legend.

He sighed and rode on.

The day was a bright one. The heavy clouds of the night
before had moved on, and the air was clean and crisp.

They scouted for several hours, then Alahir headed to a campsite they had used before, and the men dismounted, picketed the horses, and prepared cook fires for the midday meal. Alahir was happy to be out of the saddle. His own favorite horse, Napalas, a speckled gray, had thrown a shoe, and he was riding a mount loaned to him by his aide, Bagalan. The beast was skittish. If Alahir's cloak flared in the breeze the horse would rear and try to bolt. Several times he had glanced at his aide, and the youngster was trying hard not to chuckle.

"It is the last time I borrow a horse of yours," he said as they dismounted.

"He has great speed," said the dark-haired youngster, trying to keep the smile from his face. "He's just a little nervous." The boy was a practical joker of some renown, and Alahir had only himself to blame for trusting the lad. "Anyway, you always said you could ride anything you could throw a saddle on."

Alahir untied the chin straps of his helm and lifted it clear. Then he brushed his hand over the white horsehair plume, knocking the dust clear. Removing his sword belt, he pushed back his mail hood, sat down on the ground, and stretched out.

"Are you tired, Uncle?" asked Bagalan, sitting alongside him.

"Don't call me Uncle."

"Why is it you are always so scratchy after a night with the whores?"

"I am not scratchy. And the whores were . . . were fine."

"The one you went off with had a face like a goat."

Alahir sighed and sat up. "I was drunk. I do not remember what she looked like. In fact I don't care what she looked like. My sister promised me you would be a fine aide. She obviously has your sense of humor. Now go and get me some stew." The young man chuckled and moved off toward one of the cook fires. The boy was right. He was scratchy, and the camp whores were ugly. But the two facts were not connected.

His sergeant, a twenty-year veteran named Gilden, approached him. "You want some time alone?" he asked. Alahir looked up into the man's thin, bearded face. Two white scars ran through the beard from the right cheekbone down to the chin, permanent reminders of a clash with renegade Jiamads three years before. Gilden also had scars on his chest, arms, and legs. But none on his back. Not a man to run in the face of an enemy.

"No, sit. *Your* company is always welcome."

Gilden removed his sword and sat on the ground. "The boy is all right, Captain. Just a little brash. You were much the same ten years ago."

"Ten years ago I thought I was saving the homeland. I believed I could change the world."

"You were eighteen. You're supposed to feel like that at eighteen."

"You felt like that?"

Gilden spread his hands. "Too long ago to remember. I don't like what's happening now, though. Bad feel to it."

Alahir nodded. There was no need for elucidation. Agrias had begun talking about the need to protect the port areas around Siccus against enemy invasion from the sea. The whole point of serving the man was to prevent the war reaching the homeland, to protect the borders and keep Jiamads out.

"The council will argue against the plan," said Alahir, at last.

"Old men. Once strong, now fragile. Lukan argued against Agrias. He was the best of them. True Drenai. Heart and soul. Deserved better than a knife in the back for his efforts."

"Shadowmen serving the Eternal. Nothing to do with Agrias," replied Alahir, doubtfully.

"Maybe. Even so there is no one to stand against him now." Gilden swore, which was rare. Alahir glanced at him.

"Problems for another day," said Alahir.

"Never did study much, save for Drenai history," said Gilden. "But I know that civilizations rise and fall and die away. The Sathuli used to inhabit this region. Where are they now? Dust. All but forgotten. The Nadir hordes swept across these lands and butchered them all. And where are the Nadir? Dust. All my life I've fought to keep the Drenai alive. Yet we are dying, Alahir. Slowly. If not Agrias, then it will be the Eternal. A pox on them both!"

"No argument there. I agree the future looks bleak," he said, seeking to find something hopeful to say to the man, "but it has been bleak before, and we are still here. Think of Dros Delnoch, when Ulric's Nadir were before it. Hundreds of thousands of warriors, and only a handful of soldiers and volunteer farmers. They held, though, and the Drenai lived on."

"They had Druss."

"And we have you and me—and five thousand like us. If we have to go down, Gil, we'll carve a legend of our own."

"Aye, that we will." Alahir saw the man relax. Gilden suddenly smiled. "That was the ugliest whore I've ever seen. She had a face like a horse."

"Goat," corrected Alahir.

"Ah, I see," put in Gilden. "I'd forgotten you're from farming country. Sing love songs about goats up there?"

"Only the pretty ones," replied Alahir.

Thirteen

The long ride back to Petar helped clear Decado's head. The pain finally faded away, and the freedom from it was almost as blissful as a kiss from the Eternal.

There were people moving through the streets of the town, and a semblance of normality had returned. There were no Jiamads in sight, but he saw several groups of soldiers walking among the citizenry.

At Landis Khan's palace he dismounted, handed the reins of the horse to a servant, and walked up the steps to the great doors. Once inside he saw two female servants carrying a heavy rug. They were young women, and quite pretty. One of them glanced up. He smiled. The girl cried out, dropped her end of the rug, and fled. The second girl also let go of the rug and backed away, her eyes wide, her face pale. "I am not going to hurt you," said Decado. The girl turned, gathered up her long skirt, and ran after her friend. Decado looked down at the embroidered rug, which had partially unrolled. It was stained with dried blood.

He wandered up to his rooms, wondering how long it would be before the Eternal returned from the high country. Now that his head was clearer he found it strange she should have been there at all. It was rare for her to travel without her guards. And she had been dressed strangely. In disguise, he guessed. The outfit suited her, the leather leggings emphasizing the sleekness of her figure. Once in his rooms he removed the scabbarded Swords of Blood and Fire, laying them on a couch, then stripped off his travel-stained clothes. He needed a bath, but no servants were close by. Even if there were, he realized, they would run from him. Pulling on a clean shirt and leggings, he searched the room for some wine. There was nothing here.

Tugging on his boots, he walked to the door. At that moment there came a tap at the wood frame outside.

"Come in," he ordered, hoping it was a servant. Instead it was the old statesman Unwallis. Decado gazed at him curiously. The man seemed different, younger. Lines of stress had vanished from his face. Though his hair was still iron gray there was a brightness to his eyes, and the smile he offered was warm and friendly.

"Welcome back, Decado," he said. "How was your mission?"

"I fell ill. The Eternal ordered me back here. Let me know when she returns."

"Returns?"

"I saw her in the high country. She said to come back to Petar."

"Er . . . She is here, in Landis Khan's old apartments."

"That's not possible. She could not have returned before me."

Decado saw the confusion in Unwallis. The statesman stood silently for a moment. "May I come in? We should sit down and talk."

"There's nothing to talk about."

"Decado, my boy, there is everything to talk about. The Eternal arrived here two days ago. She has not left the palace." He sighed. "Is it possible you dreamed it? I know of the head pains, and the narcotics Memnon supplies. They are very powerful."

"Yes, they are," snapped Decado. "But I always know the difference between dreams and reality. She was there, dressed as a hunter. She even had a bow." He went on to explain that he had been following the trail of the blind man, but had been struck down by terrible pain in the head. Then he described how she came to him and ordered him back to Petar. Unwallis listened intently.

"So," he said, at last, "there were some things Landis did not note down. Fascinating."

"What are you talking about?"

"She was not the Eternal. That is the only point you need to realize. I take it you did not find the nephew?"

"No."

"Then you should know he is not the nephew. Landis Khan rebirthed the bones of Skilgannon. He also found the man's soul and reunited it. The man you were chasing is the legendary Skilgannon himself."

Decado walked back into the apartment and sat down on a wide couch. The Swords of Blood and Fire were beside him, and he absently reached out and laid his hand on one of the hilts. Unwallis moved into the room and sat beside him. "The woman you saw is a Reborn. Landis obviously stole some bones from the Eternal's last resurrection two decades ago."

"I need to see Jianna," said Decado. "I need to explain . . ."

"Of course—but may I suggest that you bathe first? The days of travel have left you . . . somewhat pungent, Decado. Servants are preparing a bath downstairs."

Decado, still shaken by what the statesman told him, nodded. "Yes, that is a good idea. Thank you, Unwallis."

"A pleasure, my boy. Come. I will have fresh clothes brought for you."

"Just lead on!" snapped the swordsman. There was something about the urbane statesman that always riled him. Perhaps it was the knowledge that he had once been a lover of the Eternal. Decado didn't know—but he did know she did not want Unwallis killed. This was a problem for the young swordsman. Often he had no control over such matters. Just like the first time in the orchard. He would hear a roaring in his ears, and then—apparently—pass out. Only he did not pass out. He would *awaken* some time later to discover either bloodstains on his clothing, or the corpses of those he had slain. Only later would the memories return, and with them the shame of his murderous rage. Memnon called it the Sleep of Death and had offered advice on how to prevent, or at worst delay the onset of the Sleep. Curiously it involved being more aggressive with people. According to Memnon the condition was triggered by Decado's attempts to hold in his rage. "Let it out a little at a time with angry words," Memnon had advised. Mostly it worked, though as Decado followed Unwallis down the long corridor he saw more bloodstains on the rugs there, and he remembered the unfortunate servants who had fallen victim to his insanity. A deep depression settled on the young man, and he focused on the wall murals they passed, hoping his concentration on works of art would prevent the images of the terrified victims. It was a vain hope.

They reached the lower levels and Decado followed Unwallis into a small, lantern-lit bathhouse. There was already hot water in the deep marble bath. Decado sighed. If only he could wash away the sins of his flesh as simply as he could sponge away the dust and the dirt on his body.

"I will leave you to relax, my boy," said Unwallis, stepping to the long, garden window and pulling shut the heavy drapes.

"I . . . thank you," said Decado. "I am sorry that I have been so boorish in your company." Unwallis looked shocked. He stood waiting for some barbed comment. When he realized none was to come, he smiled.

"Enjoy the bath," he said. Decado removed his clothes and laid them on a chair, placing his scabbarded swords on top of them. Then he moved toward the bath. There was a mirror on the wall, and his anger returned. Decado did not like mirrors. He could not stand to look at himself. The eyes always accused, as if the man in the mirror were someone else entirely. Someone who knew him and, in knowing him, loathed him. Almost against his wishes he stared back at the slender, naked man.

"You do not deserve to live," the mirror man told him.

"I know," he replied. Stepping forward, he lifted the mirror from the wall, intending to smash it. Yet he did not. He had destroyed so much in his young life. Instead he placed the mirror on the floor, resting it against a table on which clean, white towels had been laid.

Then he entered the bath. The warmth was welcome. The water was lightly perfumed. Decado sank beneath the surface, running his fingers through his hair to wash off the dust. Then he surfaced and looked around for some soap. He saw several small blocks in a wicker basket to his right. As he reached for one he froze. In the mirror he had placed against the table he saw the reflection of a crossbowman, stealthily moving from the door behind him.

The weapon came up. Decado hurled himself to his left. The twang of the twisted string came to him just before the bolt splashed into the water. Decado heaved himself from the bath and rolled to his feet.

The crossbowman, a slim dark-haired young man, threw aside his weapon and drew a dagger from his belt. Decado darted toward him. Even as he did so he saw the heavy drapes over the garden window drawn back, and two more armed men ran in. The first assassin rushed forward, dagger extended. Decado flung himself to the floor, swinging around to kick the man's legs from under him. The assassin fell heavily, cracking his head on the marble floor.

Decado came up fast. A second man came at him. Decado leapt feetfirst, his heel slamming into the man's chin, hurling him back. Rising, Decado ran for the Swords of Blood and Fire. Two more killers had entered the room. They were soldiers, and carried both swords and daggers. Decado drew his swords and ran to meet them. The newcomers were terrified. One tried to run, the other slashed his saber at the swordsman. The Sword of Blood clove into his neck, severing the jugular and slicing through muscle, sinew, and bone. The fleeing soldier had reached the door, but, as he pulled it open, the Sword of Fire plunged through his back. The soldier gave a gurgling cry and slid down the door. Decado spun. The second attacker was unconscious. The first groaned and tried to sit. Blood was smeared above his left eye and flowing down over his right.

Decado ran to the drapes, pulling them shut, then moved to the injured man, pushing him to his back. Resting the Sword of Blood against the man's throat, he said, "Who sent you?"

"The Eternal has spoken the words of your death," said the man. "What choice did I have but to obey?"

"You lie!"

"I am not an imbecile, Decado. You think I *wanted* to come after you? The Eternal ordered me. Personally. Unwallis was with her, and the Shadowlord."

"I don't understand," said Decado, stepping back from the surprised man. "She . . . loves me."

"I don't understand, either," said the man, rubbing blood from his eye. "Are you going to kill me? Or can I go?"

"Sit over there while I think," said Decado, gesturing to a chair. Moving to his clothes, he dressed swiftly. Then he returned to the soldier. "What exactly did she say to you?"

"I was summoned by my captain, and sent in to see her. She asked me if I was good with a crossbow. I said I was. She said she wanted the death to be clean and fast. Then the Shadowlord said I was to cut off your finger and bring it to him. Don't ask me why."

"I don't need to. What happened then?"

"Nothing," said the man, but he looked away.

"Be careful, my friend, for your life depends on this."

The other attacker groaned and started to rise. Decado stepped in, slashing a blade through the back of the man's neck. The soldier slumped to his face, twitched once, then lay still.

"Oh, careful, is it?" said the first man, his expression hardening at the murder of his comrade. "You won't let me live anyway."

"Then you would have nothing to lose by speaking. You would gain a little more time. However, I am telling you the truth. Speak freely and I will let you live."

The prisoner considered his words, then shrugged. "She said some stuff about you, Decado. Not complimentary. She told Memnon he'd made a mistake with you, and she didn't want him repeating it."

"Exactly what did she say?"

The man took a deep breath. "She said you were insane, and she told me to forget the finger. We were to carry your body out into the garden and burn it to ash."

"Take off your clothes," said Decado.

"What for?"

The Sword of Fire nicked a cut into the man's neck. "So that you can live. Be swift!"

The man undressed. "Now get in the bath."

The slim soldier looked nonplussed, but he slowly waded down into the water. "Good," said Decado. "Now come out, and pick up the two sabers your friends dropped."

"I can't fight you!"

"You don't have to fight me. Just do as I say."

Decado followed him across the room to prevent any sudden flight. The naked man took up the two swords. "Now what?"

"Now you can leave—through the garden."

"Without any clothes on?"

"Alive, though."

"You're going to stab me in the back."

"Just leave," said Decado, tapping the man's shoulder with the flat of his blade.

"Whatever you say."

The man walked to the heavy drape and pulled it back. Then he opened the garden door and stepped outside. Something moved past him in a blur. He cried out and fell back into the bathhouse. Dropping the swords he began to crawl, but his body spasmed. A pale shape appeared in the doorway, large round eyes narrowed against the lantern light. Its thin face was corpse gray, and its lipless mouth hung open. A wide, curved single tooth jutted from its maw. It was stained with blood.

The Sword of Fire lanced out from behind the curtain,

spearing through both the creature's temples. Decado dragged the blade clear, then walked back to the twitching soldier. "You are not dying," he said. "You will be paralyzed for an hour or two. After that you will be dead. The Eternal does not appreciate failure."

The man passed out. Decado stood silently, trying to think of what to do. The one joyous, true, and perfect part of his life had been his time with the Eternal. Now she had betrayed him. Decado felt the pain of it, and a cold anger began. He considered striding through the palace and cutting out her heart. Then he would kill Unwallis and . . . Memnon?

The Shadowlord had been like a father to him, helping him with his pain and his rages. And the soldier had said he wanted a piece of bone, and that could only have been used to bring Decado back.

Decado needed time to think.

Swords in hand, he left the bathhouse. The gardens were empty, and he walked around the rear of the building until he reached the stable. There he chose a sturdy chestnut gelding, saddled it, and rode from the palace grounds.

The battle was short and fierce. Enemy lancers, some two hundred strong, hidden in the woods on the slopes of the mountains, had suddenly charged Alahir's troop. They had obviously expected the surprise of their attack to disconcert the Legend riders. The enemy were charging from the high ground. All the advantages were theirs. Alahir yelled an order, and his fifty men coolly swung their mounts and lifted bows from saddle pommels. The first volley sent horses and men tumbling to the ground. The charge faltered as the charging men, behind the fallen, swerved their mounts to avoid running down their own wounded. A second volley tore into them. Then a third.

Hurling aside their bows, the Legend riders drew their sabers and heeled their mounts forward. In close-order battle the long lances were of little use, and the enemy let them fall, drawing their own swords. But the impetus of their charge was lost, and they were now facing grim and deadly opponents, who slashed and cut their way through the enemy center. Alahir was relieved to find that his mount—afraid of shadows and swirling cloaks—showed no fear in the battle. He followed his every physical command.

Alahir saw the enemy officer, on a pure white stallion, and heeled his horse toward him. A lancer tried to block his path. Alahir ducked under his slashing blade. The lancer was wearing a heavy breastplate and mail, but his arms were unprotected. Alahir's saber flashed out, hacking into the man's forearm and snapping the bone. The lancer's sword fell from his hand, and Alahir swept past him. The officer beyond, still holding to his lance, made a feeble stab at the warrior closing on him. Alahir struck the lance with his saber, diverting it, then, as their horses crashed together, hammered his saber against the man's bronze helm. The officer swayed in the saddle. Alahir struck him twice more; the second time the saber cut through the man's ear and down through his neck. He pitched from the saddle. His white horse galloped away. Even in the chaos of a battle Alahir found himself wishing he had time to catch it. It was a Ventrian purebred and deserved better than the wretch who rode him.

Pushing thoughts of horses from his mind, Alahir swung to find a fresh opponent—but the remaining lancers were fleeing in panic. The younger and less battle hardened of his men began to give chase. Alahir bellowed an order, and they drew rein.

Alahir gazed around the corpse-littered battlefield. Around seventy lancers lay dead or wounded. Alahir scanned the area, seeking out fallen Legend riders. He saw eight bodies, lying unmoving, and nine more men, unhorsed and carrying heavy wounds. Gilden rode alongside. The sergeant had a deep cut on his cheek, almost exactly between the white scars. Blood was flowing freely from it and running over his mail shirt.

"What orders?" he asked.

"Deal with our wounded first, then find two prisoners who will survive a trip back to camp. Then we'll push on." He pointed up the mountain slopes. "There's a fine view of the south up there, and we'll see how many troops they are funneling through the passes."

Leaning to his left, Gilden spat blood from his mouth. "Luckily they weren't great fighters."

"They were good enough," said Alahir, grimly. "They just weren't Drenai."

Gilden smiled, which opened the wide cut on his cheek. He swore.

"Get someone to stitch that," said Alahir.

"What do you want to do about the prisoners we don't need?"

"Let them go—without their mounts."

"Agrias won't like that."

"Do I look as though I care?"

"No."

In the distance Alahir saw a huge flock of birds suddenly take to the sky, and his mount reared. A deep groan came from the earth. Alahir's horse bolted. Several other riders were unhorsed. Alahir kept a firm grip on the reins and let the panicked beast have his head for a while, then he gently steered him to the left, seeking to head him back to his troops. Ahead of him a cloud of dust swirled up from the earth, followed instantly by a tremendous thunderclap. The horse, totally panicked now, galloped on. Alahir saw a jagged black line appear on the flatland some fifty yards ahead, as if a giant, invisible sword was scoring the earth. Then the ground suddenly split and a chasm began to open.

Alahir's first instinct was to kick his feet from the stirrups and roll clear of the horse. However, the memory of Egar's paralyzing fall still haunted him, his friend lying on the damp earth, unable to move his limbs. If Alahir were to die, it would not be because he fell from the saddle. The horse thundered on. The dust was billowing now, and Alahir had no way to tell how wide the chasm had become.

As the galloping horse closed on the yawning gap, Alahir let out a Drenai battle cry. The terrified horse leapt. For a frozen moment Alahir believed they would not survive. It was as if he and his mount were hanging in the air over a colossal drop. Time stood still. Then the horse's front hooves struck solid ground. He landed awkwardly, and stumbled. Alahir was half thrown from the saddle, but hauled himself back. The horse came to a stop and stood trembling. Alahir patted his sleek neck, then stared back at the chasm. It was closing behind him. Clouds of dust swirled up once more. In the distance he saw huge trees tumble to the mountainside. Touching heels to the still-trembling horse, he rode back to where his men were clustered together. Most of them had dismounted and were holding the reins of their frightened mounts.

His young aide, Bagalan, looking shocked and pale, called out to him. "What is happening?"

"Earthquake," replied Alahir. "Speak calmly. The horses are frightened enough." He was surprised to hear that his voice showed no sign of the fear pumping through his body. His legs felt weak, and he decided not to dismount for a while, but sat, staring up at the ruined woods above. Some of the wounded enemy lancers were also standing, alongside their conquerors, all thoughts of war vanished.

For a short while there was silence among the gathered men. As the dust began to settle Alahir rode to where Gilden was sitting on the ground, having the wound to his face stitched by another rider. "Forget prisoners," said Alahir. "Get them to dig a grave for our dead, then let them all go."

Gilden raised a hand in acknowledgment.

Turning his horse, he rode back to Bagalan. The youngster was still pale, and there was a bloody cut on his forearm. Alahir dismounted. From his saddlebag he drew out a leather pouch. Flipping it open, he took out a curved needle. "Sit down," he said. "I'll stitch that wound."

The lad sank to the ground. Bagalan looked up at him. "Why did you leap that chasm?" he asked. Alahir threaded the needle and took hold of his aide's arm. At first the question seemed odd; then he realized how it must have looked.

He had turned the horse and headed directly at the great split in the earth. Looking up, he saw other men staring at him. He chuckled and shook his head.

"Because it was there, boy," he said, inserting the needle into the torn flesh, and drawing the thread through. Once back in camp, with a few flasks of wine being shared, he would tell them the truth.

Or maybe not, he decided.

Alahir supervised the burial of the eight dead Legend warriors. First they removed the armor. The Drenai were a poor people now, and the cunningly crafted chain mail was too expensive to bury. The head mail coifs and shoulder protectors alone contained hundreds of hand-fashioned rings, involving months of work. The knee-length hauberks, the ring-mail gorgets, the chain leg mail, the helms, swords, and bows would cost more than the average Drenai land worker would earn in several years. Armor was therefore passed from father to son.

Stripped of weapons, each man had copper coins placed over his eyes, held in place by a black strip of silk. Then they were wrapped in their red cloaks and laid carefuly in the mass grave dug out by the enemy lancers. The grave was marked so that the bodies could be recovered later and taken away for a more suitable funeral, where songs would be sung, and their deeds spoken of.

All the dead were well known to Alahir. He had grown up with two of them. And another had been one of his history teachers. This last, a stern man named Graygin, had been nearing sixty, and had tried to hide the fact that the rheumatic had begun to eat away at the joints of his arms. Alahir had known of the condition. *I should have sent him home,* he thought.

"The fields are green, the sky blue, where these men ride," he said, as the warriors gathered around the grave. "They will be welcomed in the Fabled Hall, for they were men, and the sons of men. We will all see them again. Keep them in your minds and your hearts." He sighed. "When this patrol is over we will gather them up and speak the stories of their lives." Pulling his mail shirt hood into place, he donned his plumed helm. "Now it is time to ride," he told them.

Throughout the afternoon they rode a twisting trail, higher and higher into the mountains. Alahir had sent scouts ahead, and they reported no sign of enemy activity. On one section they found the bodies of three lancers, crushed by falling rocks. Trees were down, cutting off the trail in places, and the riders had to dismount and haul them aside or make difficult detours over rock-strewn slopes.

Gilden, his face stitched and bloody, angled his mount alongside Alahir as they topped a steep slope. "Land's pretty twisted now. Can't tell where we are," he said.

"We'll see better when we crest that rise," replied Alahir, pointing southwest. A strong breeze was blowing. It was chill with snow from the upper peaks. Alahir shivered.

Turn to the east, said a voice in his mind.

Alahir tensed in the saddle. Gilden spotted the movement. "Are you all right?"

"I'm fine. The horse spooked." Alahir felt anger swell in his heart. He had thought he had silenced the voices years ago, when he had refused to answer them. They had brought him nothing but humiliation and mocking laughter. As a child he would answer them out loud, and other children would stare at him, at first confused, but then would come the jeers.

"Alahir's talking to ghosts again!"

Stupid Alahir. Alahir the Loon. "The poor boy is unhinged," he heard an old woman tell his mother. So he had stopped speaking to them, and stopped listening to them. Gradually they died away. In truth he had never really expected them to stay away for good. His grandfather had gone mad, people said. He had dressed in rags, covered his face in mud, and moved about on all fours wailing like a hound. His great-grandfather, on his mother's side, had also been insane. Gandias had walled up his wife and two of his sons, and had taken to murdering travelers on the high road above Siccus. It was even said he drank their blood. His trial had produced shocking evidence of his debauchery. When he had been taken to the scaffold Gandias had shrieked and begged, insisting that the voices had told him to do these dreadful things, and that he was not to blame.

So when Alahir started hearing voices, his mother was terrified. One night Alahir had crept downstairs and listened to a conversation between mother and father. "Madness runs in families," he heard her say. "What if he is another Gandias?"

"He's just a boy with an overactive imagination," his father told her. "He will grow out of it."

Alahir never forgot that conversation. It was why he had never married. If he was to go mad like Gandias, he would do so as a single man. No wife of his would be walled up to die in a dark, airless room.

As the years passed he had grown a little more confident about the voices. Never convinced he was free, but allowing his hopes to grow.

Now they were back.

Turn east, Alahir. There is something you must see.

"You need to step down from the saddle, man," said Gilden. "Your face is whiter than snow." Gilden reached out to take his arm.

"I'm fine!" snapped Alahir, snatching his arm out of reach. The movement was so sudden that Alahir's skittish horse reared and sprang to the left, moving out onto a steep scree slope. Immediately he began to slide. Alahir fought to keep the animal's head up as he scrambled for footing. There were few riders better than the Drenai captain, but even he almost lost control. Finally firmer ground appeared under the horse's hooves, and he scrambled safely to a rock shelf some two hundred feet below the other riders. Alahir looked up at the worried faces above him and waved to show he was all right. Then he rode on, seeking a path back to the high trail.

Irritation flared as he was forced to continue along a rock trail running east, away from his men.

Ahead of him was a sheer wall of rock that had been split open by the earthquake. Several tons of earth had been displaced, and a score of trees leveled. As he rode by he glanced at the desolation. His eye was caught by an odd sight. Just beyond the huge mound of fallen earth he saw a wide lintel stone above a half-buried doorway. It made no sense. Who would build a doorway into a mountain?

Alahir knew he should get back to his men. The enemy lancers may have regrouped or been reinforced. And yet . . . The doorway beckoned to him. How long must it have been hidden here, to have been covered so completely?

Dismounting, he trailed the reins of his mount and climbed over the earth mound. On closer inspection the lintel stone was beautifully carved, and an inscription had been engraved upon it. It was full of earth, and Alahir scraped some of it away with his dagger. He soon realized it was in a language unknown to him. Considering the history of the land, he decided the inscription must have been Sathuli. Possibly a tomb of some kind. His interest waned.

Then the voice came again.

Go inside, Alahir.

"Leave me alone, damn you!"

If you wish it I will never speak again. But go inside. The hope of the Drenai lies within.

No other inducement would have caused him to lever himself into the dark of the tomb, but his heart and mind had been filled with worry for his people for too long now. With a sigh he removed his crested helm, laid it on the earth, then climbed inside. Beyond the entrance was a tunnel going off into the dark. Alahir moved along it. Some fifty paces ahead he saw a shaft of light shining down through a crack in the ceiling. Alahir made his way toward it.

The shaft was illuminating a great block of what at first seemed to be ice, shimmering and glistening. Squinting against the glare, Alahir approached the block. It was too perfectly shaped to be ice. More like a gigantic cube of glass. Then he saw what it contained and his breath caught in his throat.

On a wooden stand within the block was a suit of armor, beautifully crafted in bronze. It had overlapping scales of plate, and the breastplate was emblazoned with a golden eagle, wings spread, flaring up and over the chest. There were scaled gauntlets, and a winged helm crested with an eagle's head. Beneath the breastplate was a bronze ring-mail shirt and leggings with hinged kneecaps. Then there was the sword, the hilt double-handed, the guard a pair of flaring wings, the blade gold. It shone in the shaft of light as if it were crafted from fire.

Alahir's mouth was dry.

He stepped forward on trembling legs. His booted foot crunched down on old bones, and he glanced down to see the desiccated remains of a man. Shreds of dry cloth clung to the bones.

"Who was he?" he asked.

Lascarin the Thief. He saved the Armor of Bronze and brought it here, before the horror that was the last battle.

Alahir knew the story of that battle. Every Drenai child did. The civil war had raged for nine years, culminating in a fierce exchange at Dros Delnoch. The fortress had been built to withstand an assault from the north and was virtually open to attack from the south. The defenders had been vastly outnumbered, and, three days before the last battle, the thief Lascarin had stolen the Armor of Bronze. Two days later an earthquake ripped through the fortress, bringing two of the walls down and killing more than a thousand men. The surviving defenders had taken their families and fled north to the colony of Siccus. These were Alahir's ancestors.

"Why did he steal the armor?" asked Alahir.

He did not steal it. He saved it.

"Who are you?"

One who cares, Alahir. One whose voice can echo across Time's vast valleys.

"You are a ghost?"

In a manner of speaking. I am alive as I speak to you, but in your time I am long dead. I cannot speak for long, Alahir, so question me not. You know what you see here, and you know what it means. This is the Armor of Bronze, crafted for Egel, worn by Regnak as he stood beside Druss the Legend. You stand before your own destiny. For this Armor is yours, Alahir, by Blood and by Right. You are the earl of Bronze, and it falls to you to help save your people.

"I have less than fifty riders. The armies of Agrias are a hundred times larger. And even were I to defeat him there would still be the Eternal."

There is a man coming to you. He carries the Swords of Night and Day. Ride with him, Alahir.

"And this will save my people?"

I cannot say for certain. There is much I do not know. I will try to speak again, but for now I must leave you. My strength is waning. Draw the sword, Alahir. Draw the sword.

"Wait!" he shouted. His words echoed, and then there was silence.

Draw the sword, the voice had said. Not an easy task when it was encased in crystal. Alahir reached out toward the hilt. His hand slid through the crystal as if it were mist.

He shivered.

Then drew the golden sword from the crystal. It was lighter than it looked, and yet perfectly balanced, the golden blade glittering in the shaft of sunlight. Alahir sighed—and returned it to its scabbard.

Askari found a deep cave in which the travelers could shelter from the wind, and the four of them hunkered down in its mouth and risked a fire. Skilgannon had been withdrawn since the death of Gamal, and had spoken little. Harad and Charis seemed oblivious to everything except each other. They would walk hand in hand, and at night wander off to be alone. Askari, too, had left the brooding Skilgannon and gone scouting. Her thoughts were troubled as she found the cave. So much had happened in these last few days. Her entire world had been torn asunder. Her settlement was ruined and deserted, her friends fled or slain. Landis Khan was dead. Above all this, though, the handsome swordsman filled her mind. She found herself watching him, noting with satisfaction the easy grace of his movements, the calm, assured style of his speech. It was difficult to look into those sapphire eyes without reddening. It was as if he could read her thoughts, and they were not thoughts considered seemly.

Desire was not a stranger to Askari. She had desired Stavut, and before him a tall, young woodsman who used to travel to the settlement for supplies. Her feelings for Skilgannon, however, were vastly different. A glance from him would set her heart beating faster. She sensed in him a similar desire, and yet, for some reason, he fought it. Askari could not understand such reticence.

As they settled down by the fire she saw him staring out over the mountains, his face expressionless, his eyes distant.

"What are you thinking?" she asked. For a moment she thought he had not heard her. Then he sighed.

"I was thinking of a temple that no longer exists," he said.

"Why?"

"It holds the key to everything."

"You are a strange man."

"Yes," he admitted, "strange indeed. You spoke of Reborns earlier. You said I should beware Decado, because he is soulless."

"I remember. You gave an odd answer."

"Not so odd, Askari. I am Skilgannon. Once I was called the Damned. I led armies, destroyed cities. Cities that are now dust, and forgotten by history."

"I don't understand," she said. "How could that be?"

He gave a rueful smile. "Because I am a Reborn. I died a thousand years ago. Landis Khan brought me back . . . from hell," he added.

She looked at him closely, hoping he was lying for some

reason. She saw in his face that he was not. "Why are you telling me this?" she asked.

"I was brought back for a purpose—one that even Landis did not fully understand. One that I certainly do not yet understand. I need to find that temple. The answers are there."

"You did not answer my question."

"It is not easy to answer." He glanced back to where Harad and Charis were sitting together in the rear of the cave, holding hands and leaning in close. "Harad is also a Reborn."

"No!"

"I am afraid so. You think he has no soul?"

"Landis Khan brought him back?" she asked.

"Landis Khan could not bring back the man he was. He tried. He went to Harad when he was a child and asked about his dreams, hoping, I think, to gain some insight to who he might have been in that previous life."

Askari looked into those sapphire eyes and this time did not redden. "He asked me about my dreams also," she pointed out.

He nodded. "Then do you need your question answered?"

A cold knot appeared in the pit of her stomach. The ramifications of his words were too ghastly to contemplate. Anger flared.

"You are suggesting that I am a soulless Reborn?"

"I said nothing about souls. And I am suggesting nothing. I *know* you are a Reborn. That is why they are hunting you. That is why Decado called you Jianna."

"I don't believe it! I know who I am. I am Askari."

"Yes, you are," he said, softly. Then, as best he could, he told her of the process Landis Khan had described to him, the placing of shards of bone in an arcane machine, and the impregnation of a willing surrogate. "You were born, as any child is. You were nursed and raised. But the essence of your physical being comes from Jianna the Eternal. Everything about you is identical to her. It is why she has *become* the

Eternal. Young women are bred from her essence and born. As the years pass the Eternal casts off each aging body, and takes . . . steals . . . a new form."

"She casts out their souls from their bodies?"

"Yes."

"Where do they go?"

"To the horror of the Void and, perhaps, through it. I do not know."

"And this is her plan for me?"

"I don't think so. I think Landis Khan wanted you for himself. It is my belief that he loved the Eternal, and that she discarded him. You were his future. That is why he wanted to take you to distant lands."

Askari looked at him closely. Anger was still strong in her, but she could no longer deny the obvious. He had called her Jianna when first they met. Decado had also been convinced of her identity. Inner turmoil raged and she felt the need to strike out. "So," she said, at last, "when Landis Khan created you, he did it the same way?"

"I would imagine so."

"Your body would have been born and then grown to manhood. Then the soul was cast out and you were brought back to . . . how did you put it . . . steal the body?" She saw the shock register. The sapphire eyes closed and a look of pain crossed his features.

"How stupid of me," he said. "It did not cross my mind. I have been too self-absorbed. Of course. A young man was bred to be slaughtered so that I could return." She saw his pain and felt a stab of guilt that she had caused it, and her anger passed.

"Why did he bring you back?"

"He thought I could end the reign of the Eternal. He tried to tell me his actions were to protect his people. They were not. It was all so that he could find a place to be with you, without fear that Jianna would find him."

"Did he think you would kill her?"

"I don't know what he thought. He was relying on an old

prophecy. It referred to my swords, and some magical silver eagle. That was why he sought my tomb."

"I know of the silver eagle," she said. "It flies among the stars, granting wishes to righteous wizards. An old hunter told me the tale on the night he gave me my first longbow. The ancient gods crafted it from silver and blessed it with life. Then they hurled it into the sky and it flies around the world, forever, chasing the moon and feeding on the sun."

He smiled. "Ah well, then perhaps that is my destiny. To be cast into the sky to seek its nest." Then the smile faded. "The truth is, I do not yet know my destiny. What I do know is that I must fight her, and do everything in my power to end her reign."

"Can you?" asked Askari.

"Once there was a time when I believed there was no deed beyond me. I was younger then. Now I am a fifty-four-year-old man in a young body, striding through a world that is alien to me. I cannot undo the evil that Jianna has wrought. But I knew the woman who made the prophecy, and I trust her. Therefore there must be some way I can win."

"And you believe this . . . this lost temple is the answer?"

"Yes. All the magic seems to have flowed from it. I went there once. I saw the ancient artifacts, and the glittering lights in the walls, with no flame in them. I stayed there for a month. It seemed to me that all the priests there were wizards, in one form or another."

"You say it is no longer there?"

"Gamal told me the entire mountain in which the temple was carved has disappeared. All that remains is open land, where metal twists out of shape and natural laws hold no sway."

"Mountains cannot disappear," she said.

"My thoughts exactly." He laughed then, the sound rich and full of humor. "But then I am a thousand-year-old dead man in a world full of monsters. Who am I to deny the power of magic?"

Just then huge flocks of birds took off from the trees be-

low the cave, soaring into the sky like a black cloud. The
wind died down, and an eerie silence settled over the land.
Askari pushed herself to her feet. "That is not natural," she
said.

A low rumble came from the ground beneath them. Skilgannon surged to his feet. "Earthquake!" he shouted. "Get
out of the cave! Harad! Get out into the open!" Hauling
Askari to her feet, he held tightly to her hand and they began
to run. The earth twisted beneath their feet. Skilgannon staggered. Askari fell against him. From above them came a
great crashing. Rocks and boulders began to tumble down
the cliff—then a huge section of stone sheared away. Harad
and Charis came running from the cave. A massive rock
crashed down mere feet from where they stood. Charis fell.
The black-bearded axman picked her up and began to sprint
for open ground. More boulders tumbled, then an avalanche
began. Skilgannon ran down the slope, seeking out a place of
safety. There was none to be found. So he ran on for a while.
Boulders came flying past him. Finally he swung around.
"What are you doing?" shouted Askari.

"We can't avoid what we can't see," he told her.

A hugh rock, twice the height of a man, came hurtling toward them. Skilgannon darted to the left. The rock crashed
into a tree, snapping the trunk. The ground lurched—and
opened beneath Askari. Even as she fell Skilgannon dived,
his hand stretching out. Her fingers clutched at his wrist. For
a moment it seemed her weight would drag him over the
edge of the huge crack in the earth. But he held on. Using her
feet Askari scrambled up from the yawning gap. Skilgannon
hauled her to solid ground. With a grinding roar the earth
closed. Dust spewed up around them. Trees were tumbling
around them, and with the dust clouds and the shifting earth
there was no way to avoid disaster. Skilgannon drew Askari
in close, holding tightly to her. Helpless against the fury of
nature she suddenly relaxed, laying her face against his
cheek. And they stood, waiting for the end.

Then silence came again, and the dust slowly settled.

"We are still alive," said Askari, genuinely surprised. All around them were fallen trees and massive boulders. One tree had crashed into the earth no more than ten feet from where they stood.

"So it would appear," he said, releasing his hold on her. A sense of emptiness touched Askari as his arms fell away from her. "Where is Harad?" he said, suddenly. Together they ran back over the ruined land, searching through the fallen trees. Skilgannon found Harad pinned beneath the trunk of an elm. Touching the axman's throat he felt a pulse, strong and steady. He had been hit by the upper part of the tree, and thrown from his feet. Skilgannon had no way to test for broken bones or internal injuries. Calling out to Askari he tried to lift the tree from the unconscious axman. It was too heavy. Even with Askari's help he could raise it only a few inches. "You take the weight again," Askari told him, "and I will try to pull Harad clear."

Crouching down he grasped the trunk, and waited for Askari to get into position alongside Harad. "Ready!" she said. Skilgannon took a deep breath, then heaved at the trunk. Askari grabbed Harad's jerkin and hauled at the huge body. Skilgannon strained to hold the trunk, as inch by inch Askari eased Harad from beneath it. "Clear!" she said.

Gratefully Skilgannon released his hold. His arms were trembling, and he saw there were cuts upon his palms. Ignoring the pain, he ran to Harad. "There is no blood in his mouth," he said. "That is a good sign. And his pulse is strong. With luck he is merely bruised and stunned." He glanced around. "We must find Charis."

"I found her," said Askari, softly. "Let us see to Harad."

Fourteen

When Harad opened his eyes he was surprised to feel no pain. He remembered the tree falling, and trying to push Charis away from it. He had hurled himself back, and the trunk had hammered into him, smashing him to the earth. His head had struck a rock, and he had been knocked unconscious for the first time in his life.

Now he felt fine, though the earthquake seemed to have caused incredible changes to the landscape. The sky was uniformly gray, and there were no trees growing anywhere. He sat up. In fact there were no trees at all, neither standing nor fallen. Puzzled, he looked around. He saw Charis sitting with Skilgannon, and a bigger man just beyond them. There was something familiar about the huge figure. He was wearing a black leather jerkin, with metal plates upon the shoulders and a round helm. And he was carrying Harad's ax. None of this made any sense to Harad, and he looked at Skilgannon.

"What is happening?" he asked.

The man glanced back at the silver-bearded axman, who moved forward and knelt beside Harad. "How are you feeling, laddie?"

"Good." Harad looked up into the ice-blue eyes. Then at the helm with the axes-and-skull motif. "You are Druss."

"Aye, that I am."

Charis moved alongside him, laying her hand upon his cheek. "You should not be here, my love," she said.

"I should be where you are. Always." He looked at Skilgannon. The warrior was dressed differently, in leggings and a tunic. There was no sign of his swords, and he looked more like a farm worker than a warrior. "I don't understand any of this. Where is Askari?" he asked the man.

"I do not know any Askari."

"Have you gone mad? We are traveling together."

"I do not know you either, my friend. My name is Geoval. My home is . . . was . . . on the coast. Now it is here, in this gray horror."

"Then I have gone mad," said Harad. "Or this is a dream?"

"Aye, laddie, it is a dream of sorts," said Druss. "There is no easy way to say this, so I'll be blunt. Charis was killed on the mountainside. This is why she is here, in the Void. Why *you* are here is another matter."

Suddenly something screeched down from the sky. Harad saw it and surged to his feet. The winged creature swept toward Druss, talons extended. The axman reared up and hammered Snaga through its ribs. The demon disappeared instantly. "Where were we?" said Druss. "Ah, yes. You should not be here, Harad. The life force is strong in you. Trust me, laddie, you cannot stay."

Harad backed away from the axman, then moved to Charis's side. Taking her hand he raised it to his lips and kissed it. "This is wrong," he said. "It is all wrong. We will go back together. We will end this dream. Then we will make the life we planned." Charis stepped into his embrace and kissed his bearded cheek.

"I cannot go back," she said. "Oh, I so wish I could." There were tears in her eyes. "You don't remember, do you? Believe me, Harad, my dear, there is no way for me to return. You will understand when you go back."

"I'll not go back without you."

"No, Harad. Please don't say that. You are not dead. You have a life to live."

"Without you I might as well be dead. And if I am not dead, then why am I here?"

"It was love that brought you," said Druss. "I can understand that. A man should be prepared to face death for the woman he loves. Charis is right, though. This is not the place for you. Charis can feel the Golden Valley reaching out to her. I shall escort her there. And you—you can hear life calling you. I know you are resisting it, Harad. But the call will get stronger."

Harad's head dropped, and he kissed Charis tenderly. "You are my life," he said. "I don't want to go on without you. I won't!"

"Love doesn't die, Harad," she whispered. "And I will be waiting for you in that valley."

He wanted to answer her, but felt strangely light-headed. A sense of weightlessness flowed through him. "Not yet!" he shouted.

Then his weight returned, and he felt solid earth beneath his back and mountain air filling his lungs.

Harad opened his eyes. Skilgannon was beside him to the right—the real Skilgannon, an ivory sword hilt jutting above his shoulder. Askari was sitting by his left. "Thought we'd lost you," said the warrior. "Your pulse faded for a while."

"Where is Charis?"

"She died, Harad. I am sorry. Askari and I buried her."

Harad tried to sit, but pain stabbed through his right side. He swore and sank back. Skilgannon spoke. "You are badly bruised, my friend, and may even have snapped a rib or two. You need to rest."

"How did she die? I pushed her away from the falling tree."

"A falling boulder struck her," said Skilgannon. "Death was instantaneous."

Harad looked at the swordsman. "I saw your twin in the Void. He was with Druss. His name is Geoval. He lived near the coast."

"Druss told me he was protecting someone there." Skilgannon sighed. "Landis Khan killed him in order to give me his body. We exchanged places in the Void." He laid his hand on Harad's shoulder. "Get some sleep. It will be night soon."

"It will always be night for me, from now on," said Harad.

Skilgannon moved away from the axman. Askari joined him, and together they walked through the ruined wood.

"That was a good lie to tell him," she said.

"It was what a friend of mine once called a velvet lie. The truth would have crushed him."

They paused by the graveside, and Skilgannon lifted Snaga from the ground. One of the blades was smeared with dried blood. He plunged it into the earth, then pulled up a section of long grass and rubbed at the blade until all sign of the stain had vanished. "We like to think of life as a constant," he said. "Yet it can be ended in a heartbeat."

"I know," she said, "but that was a cruel way to die."

"They are all cruel, in their own way. And it wasn't a complete lie. When the ax flew from Harad's hand I think it struck the boulder and ricocheted. She would have known nothing. It was a swift, painless death."

"Yet pointless."

"Most deaths are," he said. "Even those that seem to have purpose. I died seeking to save a people I had grown to love. Now the nation no longer exists. The Angostin are part of the dust of history. Ultimately my sacrifice was worth nothing. But then, ultimately, all the works of man are as nothing."

"I don't agree," said Askari. "When I was a child I remember Kinyon rescuing a little boy from a cliff face. He was trapped on a ledge, around a hundred feet above the ground. Kinyon climbed that rock face. It was raining, the holds were slippery. He almost fell several times. Yet he reached the child, swung him to his back, and made the long climb down. The boy died the following spring, of a fever. Does that mean Kinyon's bravery was for nothing?"

"No, of course not," he said. "My old swordmaster used to talk about the Now. It is all there is. The past is a memory, the future a dream, the present a reality. All we can ever do is live in the Now, and try to ensure that our deeds are worthy.

Kinyon's deed was worthy." He sighed. "You are right to chide me. What counts is how we live *now,* not whether in a thousand years civilizations will fall."

"So what will we do *now*?"

"We?"

"You don't want me with you?"

"I don't want you killed."

"If we can end the reign of the Eternal, then I won't be," she said. "I don't know much about destiny, and I don't care about the Eternal and her magic. I never did. All I wanted was to live in the high country, to hunt, to swim, to eat, to laugh. It seems to me, though, that we are here for a reason. You, me, Harad. Three Reborns, all from the same period in time. So tell me again of the prophecy, and let us try to make sense of it."

"There is no sense to any of it," he snapped. "Whatever Ustarte prophesied has become a piece of doggerel verse. *Hero Reborn, torn from the gray, reunited with Swords, of Night and of Day*. Landis Khan did not tell me the rest of it, save, as I said, that it involved killing a mountain giant with a golden shield, and stealing an egg from a silver eagle."

"Perhaps the key to the riddle is in the tale of the eagle," she suggested.

"A magical bird that flies around the sun?"

"Feeds on the sun," she corrected, "and flies around the moon."

"Granting wishes to wizards," he said. "I was listening."

"Only with part of your mind. All legends have a base in fact. Kinyon told me that. They just get elaborated. They distort as they grow."

"There's truth in that," he said. He laughed. "When Landis Khan first woke me I went to his library and studied all that was known about my life. I had no memory then, and wanted to learn about myself. Much of what I did was there, but hidden beneath ludicrous tales of flying horses and fire-breathing dragons. Yes, you are right. We need to examine the fables. Tell me again all you can recall about the eagle."

He listened as she spoke. "Why wizards?" he said, suddenly. "What?"

"Why would the bird grant wishes only to wizards? Why not heroes? Why not farmers?"

"I don't know. *Righteous* wizards, so the story goes. What are you thinking?"

"Wizards understand the nature of magic. They use magic to weave spells. So it is not a question of the bird making a choice to grant wishes. It is the wizards who *take* magic from the bird." He fell silent, thinking it through. "The eagle is not alive. It is merely a source of power the wizards call upon. It is silver," he went on. "Created. An artifact, just like the machines in the temple, and back at Landis Khan's palace." He paused and shook his head. "What am I saying? A machine that floats in the sky and, somehow, sends power to the earth. It makes no sense. How would they send it into the sky? And why would it not fall back down?"

"The *why* is not important now," she said. "Any more than your winged horse. The eagle is the answer. And the egg that you must steal."

"Or destroy," he said. He swore softly. "There is something we are missing. Something central. If the eagle was placed in the sky by the ancients, and if all magic began in that moment, why is it only in this time that the artifacts of the ancients can be used again? We had a few Joinings in my day—Jiamads, as you call them. They were created by Nadir shamans. But nothing on the scale we see now."

Skilgannon paused by a fallen log and sat down. "This is making my head spin," he told her. "We are building theories about something implausible and impossible. A metal bird that had great power, lost it, and then had it returned. And what of the giants with golden shields?" He suddenly froze.

"What is it?" she asked him.

"The shield of gold. I have seen it. It is not carried by a mountain giant, but sits upon a giant mountain, above the Temple of the Resurrection. It is huge. The priests called it the Mirror of Heaven. It is coming back to me now. A young man I knew took me to the temple. He talked of it on the way, about abbots in the ancient days, and of the Mirror. They called it a mirror because when it first appeared, lights blazed within the darkened halls. Lights with no flame, like captured sunlight. They believed the Mirror somehow reflected sunlight into the mountain. That was when the ancient artifacts had their magic renewed. I think I have it now. The metal bird always had magic, but only when the Mirror appeared did that magic flow freely back from the sky. It also explains the vanity."

"Vanity?" queried Askari. "What are you talking about?"

"Landis Khan said the eagle was vain—in love with its own reflection. The eagle gazes at itself in the Mirror of Heaven. Only then does the magic flow."

"And it flows into the egg," she said.

"Exactly. And it is from the egg that the artifacts somehow draw their power. If I destroy the egg, the machines will be useless again. No more Reborns. And the Eternal will be human, and face death like the rest of us." He took a deep breath. "I must find the temple."

"*We* must find the temple," she corrected him. "How far is it from here?"

"That is hard to say. I did not travel to it from this direction. I took a ship from Mellicane, a city on the eastern coast. It journeyed to an estuary on this side of the ocean, on the River Rostrias."

"Kinyon would know. Originally he came from the north."

Another hunt had ended successfully, and Stavut sat contentedly by the fire, cutting slices of roast venison. Shakul and nine of his pack were stretched out on the ground nearby, bellies distended, sleeping soundly. A second pack of eighteen Jiamads had returned earlier. Led by the small, mottled-gray Grava, they had also been successful, though it had taken Stavut a little while to grasp this. Grava's speech was horribly mangled by his overlong tongue, and Stavut had to struggle to understand a word he said. It was no sur-

prise, however, that Grava yet again had returned with two
more Jiamads than he had started with. Before long, thought
Stavut, every runaway Jem in the high country would be part
of Bloodshirt's pack.

He grinned. The fear of the beasts had long since departed. Indeed, he found he actually enjoyed their company,
and had taken to wandering off for longer periods. In some
ways this was good. Kinyon and the villagers had become
increasingly concerned, and, despite all of Stavut's best efforts, remained frightened and wary around the huge creatures. There had even been some talk of returning to their
village and taking a chance on the land not being invaded.
Stavut had soon stopped this line of conversation. "Skilgannon says the enemy will come back. I don't think he's a man
given to exaggeration. The best way is forward. I am sure
Alahir will help us."

Surprisingly there had been little argument. People just
nodded and wandered away. In fact very few people argued
with Stavut now. Probably, he reasoned, because he had
proved to be such a good provider and leader.

When Grava returned with the two newcomers he had
pushed them to stand before Bloodshirt. Stavut had stood
and stared coolly at the Jiamads. It had become a ritual, and
Stavut enjoyed the drama of it. "You wish to join Bloodshirt's pack?" he asked them.

They were a scrawny pair, one heavily round shouldered,
almost hunchbacked, the second tall and thin, his fur almost
black. They stared at him, then looked at Grava, who said
something unintelligible, but in a harsh growl.

"Serve Bloodshirt," said the hunchback.

"Your names?" asked Stavut.

"Ironfist," the hunchback answered. "This Blackrock," he
added, pointing to his skinny, black-furred companion.

"You will hunt with us. You will kill no Skins."

They both nodded.

"Do not forget it. Now go."

They shuffled away. Grava said something else, which

Stavut did not understand, but it ended in a gargling sound that Stavut recognized as laughter, so he smiled and nodded. Then he settled down by the fire. Shakul awoke and stretched. Then he broke wind loudly.

"Charming," said Stavut.

"Good sleep," said Shakul. "No dreams."

"The best kind." Stavut scratched at the dark stubble on his chin. Normally he was clean shaven, but lately he had decided a beard would suit Bloodshirt. "Time to be getting back to the villagers," he said. "They will be glad of the fresh meat."

Shakul lifted his head and sniffed the air. "They have gone," he said.

"Gone? What do you mean?"

"Head south."

"They wouldn't do that."

Shakul shrugged, then leaned down toward the joint of roasted venison. "Burned," he said, shaking his head.

"When did they go?"

"We leave, they leave," said Shakul.

That was yesterday morning. "Why would they do that?" said Stavut.

"Fear us," said Shakul. "Fear Bloodshirt." Stavut looked into the beast's golden eyes, and at the huge fangs in the immense face. There was nothing now about Shakul that caused him any fear. But, of course, that would not—could not—apply to the villagers. He knew then that their lack of argument had nothing to do with his leadership, but everything to do with their terror of the beasts, and an increased fear of Stavut himself.

"I would never have harmed them," he said. Shakul's head came up. The wind was southerly, and he tipped his head, his nostrils quivering.

"Many Skins," he said. "Horses. Jems."

"Soldiers?" queried Stavut.

"They hunt us?" responded Shakul, his eyes glinting.

"I wouldn't think so. Where are they?"

"South. Your Skins see them soon."

Stavut swore. "We must get to them. If it is an enemy raiding party, they will be in danger."

"Useless Skins," said Shakul. "Don't hunt. Do nothing. Better without them."

"That's true," agreed Stavut, "but, as you say, they are *my* Skins. We help them."

Shakul rose and let out a howl, which brought the other Jiamads to their feet. "Run fast," said Shakul. "Bloodshirt slow. Shakul carry Bloodshirt."

The suggestion put Stavut in a quandary. He knew it was the only sensible choice. The Jiamads could move at terrifying speed, and if they waited for him it would be a long, slow, and pointless journey. If the villagers were in danger now, that peril would be long past by the time the group reached them. On the other hand there were only two ways Shakul could run and carry Stavut. Either like a babe in arms, or with Stavut clinging to the fur on his back. The first would be ludicrous, and would—Stavut believed—severely dent his authority among the beasts. The second would be equally risible, for Stavut's arms were not powerful, and he knew he could not hang on to the fur for a long journey. This left the prospect of falling off a number of times, and then having to revert to the first ghastly option, that of being carried like a babe.

"Right," said Stavut, buying time to think. "Let's be sure of what we are all doing. We are seeking my comrades, who may be in danger. If they are, we must rescue them. I want no one rushing in. We get close enough to see what the situation is, then I shall give orders. Is this understood?"

"Yes," said Shakul. "Now leave?"

Stavut gazed around the pack. There were more than forty Jiamads now. Some still carried iron-studded clubs, others heavy swords. A few retained long staffs. Several of them still wore wide baldrics on their shoulders, from which hung empty scabbards. Stavut crossed to two of them and told them to remove their baldrics. The beasts did so without question, handing them to Stavut. Both had broad brass buckles. Undoing them, he buckled them together and walked back to Shakul. "Bend forward," he said. Shakul obeyed instantly. Stavut slipped the double-sized baldric over his head. Shakul was larger than any of the other Jiamads, and the leather hung to just above his hips. "Stand still," said Stavut, lifting his leg and placing it on the lowest part of the loop. Then he stood and took hold of the long fur on Shakul's massive shoulders. "Now we go!" he said.

Shakul took off at a great pace, and Stavut was briefly thrown back. He clung on grimly, seeking to read the rhythm of the great beast's running style. Within a very short space of time he began to feel sick. It was almost as bad as the first time he had gone to sea. With iron resolve he willed his belly to hold on to its contents and tried to think of other things as the run continued. This was hard, for with each heavy running step Shakul took Stavut's belly heaved.

Just when he felt he could hold on no longer he saw a sight that took all thoughts of sickness from him.

Shakul ran into the campsite he had left yesterday. His wagon was still there, his beloved horses, Longshanks and Brightstar—or what was left of them—still tethered. "Stop!" shouted Stavut. Shakul came to a stop and Stavut leapt down. His legs almost gave way, and the ground seemed to be moving. Stavut gazed down at the dead beasts. He saw a movement in the trees nearby, and two gray wolves padded back from sight. The villagers had left his wagon behind, not thinking that, with the brake applied, the tethered horses would have no way to escape a wolf pack.

Shakul loomed alongside him. "I loved those horses," Stavut told him. The great beast looked nonplussed. Stavut sighed. Two Jiamads approached the dead beasts. Shakul snarled at them, ordering them back.

"Time to move on," said Stavut.

This time he felt no sickness. His heart was heavy, and all he wanted was to find the villagers safe. Then he would turn the pack over to Shakul, seek out new horses, and head north.

He realized Shakul was speaking to him, and leaned forward to catch what he was saying.

"Blood in air," said Shakul. "Skin blood."

The trio rested up for most of that day, and the one following. Harad said little. He sat by Charis's grave, his expression bleak, his eyes distant. Skilgannon did not intrude on his grief, and Askari left the two men, setting off to hunt for food. She returned at dusk on the second day with three hares, which she skinned. "The meat is better when left to hang for a while," she said as they ate.

Skilgannon thanked her for the meal, then walked out into the moonlight. His mind flowed back to the dream meeting with Memnon. Now, there was a dangerous man. No anger, no hatred; a cold mind and eyes that glittered with intelligence. He was an enemy to fear.

He suddenly laughed aloud. All across this war-torn land there were enemies to fear, armies of Joinings, cavalry, foot soldiers, archers. Memnon was merely one more to add to the list, along with Jianna and Decado—and who knew who else.

He glanced back to where Harad sat by the fire and sighed. The young man had lost the woman he loved, and his world was in ruins. Skilgannon felt for him, recalling the cold day he had heard of Jianna's death. Would Harad ever be the man he once was? Skilgannon wondered. He had not touched the ax all day. It lay against the cliff wall, forgotten. Askari strolled out. "You want to be alone?" she asked.

"No. We must set out tomorrow and find Kinyon. Or if not Kinyon, then someone who can offer directions to the Rostrias. I am sure that if I find the river, I can locate the temple."

They heard a horse whinny in the darkness. Askari reached for her bow and nocked a shaft. A figure rode into sight.

It was Decado.

His clothing was travel stained, a layer of dust upon the black jerkin he wore. He seemed surprised to see them, and drew rein.

Askari drew back on the string, but Skilgannon reached out and touched her arm. "Do not kill him yet," he said.

"Nice of you," said Decado, lifting his leg over the saddle pommel and jumping lightly to the ground. His dark eyes stared hard at Skilgannon. "So, you are my ancestor. To be honest I see no resemblance."

"I do," Skilgannon told him. "It is in the haunted look, and the fear of the blades."

"I fear nothing," said Decado. "Not you, not the beauty with the bow, not the Shadows. Nothing."

"A poor lie," Skilgannon replied. "You fear losing those blades. You do not like them out of your sight. When you sit in the evenings you make sure they are beside you. You reach out and touch them endlessly. In the mornings the first action you take is to caress the hilts."

Decado gave a cold smile. "True," he said, reaching up and pressing an emerald stud on the ivory hilt jutting over his shoulder. With one smooth pull the Sword of Fire slid from its scabbard. Skilgannon stepped back and drew his own blades.

"You have come a long way just to die here, boy," said Skilgannon.

Decado's second blade appeared in his hand. "A man has to die somewhere. Keep the bow nocked," he said to Askari, "and move back away from us. Stand as close to the cliff wall as you can."

Skilgannon's eyes narrowed. It was an odd thing to say. He watched Decado loosen the muscles of his arms, sweeping the swords back and forth. "You see the clouds gathering?" said Decado.

Skilgannon glanced at the sky.

"Be ready when they cover the moon," said Decado. "I don't know how good you are, kinsman, but death is very close if you are less than superb."

"You think you are that good?"

Decado smiled. "Oh, I know how good *I* am, but it is not me you need to concern yourself with at this moment. The

Shadows are here." Harad, ax in hand, had moved out into the open.

Darkness came swiftly. Skilgannon closed his eyes, slipping into the Illusion of Elsewhere. There came a sudden hissing sound, like a breeze blowing through a window crack. Skilgannon spun, the Sword of Night slicing through the air. The blade struck something metallic, which then fell against his shoulder. He heard Askari cry out. Then came a high-pitched screech of pain. The darkness was total. Skilgannon leapt to his right, then spun again, blades extended. He heard the slightest whisper of movement. Instantly he dropped to one knee and slashed out with the Sword of Day. The blade struck something soft, then cut through. The clouds began to clear the moon. Sight returned. Skilgannon blinked. For a fraction of a heartbeat he saw a pale form some twenty feet away. Then it was gone—only to appear alongside him. A dark dagger plunged toward his chest. The Sword of Night swept up. The creature ducked and moved with incredible speed. The Sword of Day snaked out, the very tip of the blade slicing across the creature's throat. It sped away, staggered, then fell.

Moonlight shone down, illuminating the open ground. Harad was down, as was Askari. Decado looked at Skilgannon and smiled. "Quick, aren't they?"

There were three skeletal bodies lying on the earth. Snaga was embedded in one, a second lay close to Decado, and the third was the one slain by Skilgannon. "And now do we fight?" he asked Decado.

"If you really want to," replied the swordsman. "For myself I would like to sit beside a fire and relax. Perhaps stroke my sword hilts for a while."

"How many more of these creatures are there?"

"None close, I think. They travel in threes. More will come, though."

Skilgannon moved alongside Askari and knelt down. Her face was unnaturally pale, her eyes open. Reaching out, he touched her throat. There was a faint pulse. "She is not dead," said Decado. "The venom in their darts and daggers merely paralyzes. Close her eyes for her, and let her sleep. She will awake in an hour or so, with a ghastly headache."

Decado stepped to where Harad lay. "Now, that is a strange sight," he said. "I would have wagered all I have that a huge clod with an ax would not have been able to kill a shadow." Placing a booted foot under Harad, he flipped the axman to his back. Sheathing his swords, he dropped to one knee and closed Harad's eyes. Then, ignoring the fallen man, he walked over to the dying fire and added a few sticks. Skilgannon joined him.

"Why did you aid us?" he asked.

"Actually, kinsman, it was the other way around. The Shadows were hunting me. So how does it feel to be alive again after all these centuries?"

"Why were they hunting you?"

"I fell out of favor with the Eternal. She ordered my death. Strange really. She only had to ask me and I would have killed myself for her." Decado sighed. "According to legend you loved her, too, so you'll know what I mean."

"What do you intend to do now?" said Skilgannon, ignoring the comment.

"Well," said Decado, "I could follow your historic example and join a monastery. I don't think so, though. My namesake did that, too, you know. He was after your time. He became a warrior of the Thirty, in the days of Tenaka Khan. He was known as the Ice Killer—the greatest swordsman of his age. Of any age. I suppose he would have been your . . . what . . . great-great-grandson. Something like that. Nice to know blood can run true, don't you think?"

"You have merely said what you are *not* going to do," pointed out Skilgannon.

"I have not made up my mind."

"Let me know when you do."

"You'll be the first, kinsman."

Skilgannon cleaned his blades then sheathed them.

"Our swords are very similar," said Decado. "Is that how you knew of my obsession?"

"Yes. It is the same for me. These blades are possessed, Decado. They make us more violent. They have the capacity to unhinge us, turn us into madmen. They call for blood and death. It is hard to resist them. Yours are more dangerous than mine. The Swords of Night and Day were created by a witch named Hewla. She was extraordinarily talented, but the blades she made were merely copies of a more ancient and deadly pair. You carry those. The Swords of Blood and Fire."

"I was a killer before I carried them," said Decado, sadly. "I cannot blame the swords for what I became." He looked up at Skilgannon. "Jianna told me you killed the last man to carry these. She talked of you often. I found myself growing jealous of a man long dead. I used to hope that someone would bring you back—just so that I could kill you, and show the world you were not as great as they believed."

"And now?"

"Pretty much the same," said Decado with a smile.

Askari felt a tingling sensation in her fingers. Then feeling returned. Slowly she opened her right hand, pressing the tip of her index finger against the thumb. The tingling swept up along her right forearm. She lay quietly, her head throbbing as slowly her body came once more under her control. With a groan she sat up. Skilgannon moved to her side. "Welcome back," he said.

"What were they?"

"Decado called them Shadows. A different form of Jiamad."

"I have never seen anything move so fast. One moment it was yards away, the next—" She glanced down at her green shirt. There was a small hole in the shoulder, drying blood upon it. "—it bit me. As I fell I saw it spin and fly at Harad. Is he all right?"

"He killed it, but it stunned him also. He is still sleeping."

"Oh, it is not sleep," she said, with a sudden shiver. "I heard everything. Your conversation with Decado, the crackling of wood upon the fire. I just could not move." By the fire Decado stirred. Rolling smoothly to his feet, he swung his black scabbard over his shoulders and moved alongside Skilgannon and Askari. She found the intensity of his gaze disturbing. "Stop staring at me," she said.

Decado laughed. "Hard not to. The resemblance is . . . uncanny."

"And that is all it is," she snapped. "I am not like her."

On the far side of the fire Harad sat up. Then he pushed himself to his feet, staggered, and walked out into the open. Skilgannon rose and followed him. Askari remained with Decado. "Now it is you staring at me," he said.

"I have heard tales of you. None of them good. You must be a very sad and bitter man."

"Nonsense. I am as happy as anyone else."

"I cannot believe that."

"It is true. My childhood was a time of great joy and laughter. I was the most popular child in my village. And now I am known for my wit and my charm. You have any food here?"

"No."

"Ah well, no matter."

"How did those creatures move so fast?" she asked him.

"It is mostly beyond my understanding. They are fashioned, I understand, from creatures with hollow bones, very light. Bats, birds, something like that. Terrifying, aren't they?"

"No," she said. "They do what they are bred to do. They are merely dangerous. *You* are terrifying." She struggled to stand. Instantly Decado reached out a hand to support her. She brushed it away angrily. "Do not touch me!"

"Are you afraid you might be more like her than you think?"

"Meaning?"

"She enjoyed my touch."

"Perhaps that is because you are so alike," said Askari. "You are both monsters."

"There is that," he agreed amiably.

"And, if she enjoyed your touch so greatly why does she now want you dead?"

"A lovers' spat," he said. "You know how it is. Boy meets girl, girl wants boy dead. An everyday story, really."

Despite the lightness of tone she saw the pain in his eyes. For a moment only she felt sympathy. The feeling was replaced by a burst of anger. "Well, for once I hope she gets what she wants. You are evil, and the world would be better off without you in it."

"True enough," he answered.

Walking away from her, he went to his horse and stepped into the saddle. Askari followed him out. Skilgannon and Harad were standing close by.

"I expect we shall meet again," said Decado.

"As enemies or friends?" Skilgannon asked him.

"Who knows? If you are heading north, be aware that a large company of soldiers and Jems is ahead of you. Advance column for the main army. The last battle against Agrias is close now. Jianna wants to end the war this side of the ocean."

With that he turned his mount and rode off.

"I don't like him," said Harad.

"He doesn't like himself," Askari told him. "Which shows he is capable of good judgment."

Skilgannon smiled. "Even so I am glad he was here when the Shadows attacked. What did you talk about?"

"Jianna. I told him I was not like her." She looked into his sapphire eyes. "I am not, am I?"

"I cannot give you the answer you want to hear," he said. "When I first knew her she was just like you. Brave—indeed fearless—and loyal and beautiful. She was her own woman, with a strong, independent mind. We used to talk about how we would change the world. When she became queen of Naashan she would make the land like a garden, and every citizen would live in peace and prosperity. These were her dreams."

"So why did she change?"

"She became queen of Naashan," he said, simply.

"I don't understand."

"It took me a while," he told her. "Mostly people obey the laws of their respective lands for one simple reason. If they break them they will suffer for it. The thought of suffering deters them from wrongdoing. It is an age-old principle. Kill someone, and you yourself will be killed. Rob someone and you will be punished. You might lose a hand, or be branded upon the brow, or indeed hanged. The question is, what happens when *you* are the law, when *your* actions are unchallenged, *your* decisions final and beyond appeal? When you are surrounded by people who agree with your every word and every deed? You become like a god, Askari. It is but a small step from that to tyranny."

"I would not be like that. I know the difference between right and wrong."

"I believe you. I also believe that if Jianna had been born in the high mountains and grown to womanhood here, she would have said the same. That is beside the point, though. You are not Jianna. You were not raised in a duplicitous court. You did not see your parents murdered by traitors. You did not have to fight huge battles in order to win back a kingdom. I do not defend what she became. I will not simplify it, either, by holding to the view that she was merely a devil in human flesh, or a monster."

"That is because you love her!" she said, anger flaring again.

"Perhaps so. But I will do all in my power to end her reign, even if by doing so I condemn her to death. I can do no more than that."

"No," she said, her voice softening. "No one could ask more than that."

Stavut sat alone, the horror of the day clinging to him like the blood-drenched shirt he wore. He had wandered away from the pack, needing to be alone. The sun was setting in a bloodred sky, and Stavut thought how apt it was that such a day should end with a crimson sky. The color of rage.

Tears formed, flowing down his bearded cheek. He brushed them away, and his hand came away stained red.

For however long he lived this would be the Day of the Beast in his memory. He would never forget it, not one dreadful part of it.

The pack had run for hours, eating up the miles in a steady fast lope. Then they had come to a line of wooded hills, and Shakul had paused. "What is it?" asked Stavut.

"Fight finished," said Shakul. Stavut glanced at the other beasts. They all had their heads high, sniffing the air. "Much blood," added Shakul.

"Show me," Stavut ordered him.

Shakul ran on, up the slope and through the trees, the pack following. They came to a stretch of open ground. Bodies were everywhere. Stavut stepped down from Shakul's back and walked among the corpses. He saw Kinyon first, his head crushed. Arin, the logger from Harad's settlement, was pinned against a tree, a broken lance impaling him to the trunk. His wife, Kerena, was close by. Her throat had been cut, but not before she had been brutally raped by the soldiers. She was lying on her back, her skirt over her breasts, her legs splayed. Other women had been equally abused before being slain. There was no point checking for survivors. All of the men had been hacked to death, save Arin.

Shakul loomed alongside him. "Four Jems," he said. "Stood by trees."

"What?"

"We go now?"

"Go? Yes, we go. We find the soldiers responsible for this." A cold anger began in the pit of Stavut's belly, a rage unlike anything he had ever experienced. "We find them. We kill them. Every one."

"As Bloodshirt says," muttered Shakul.

"How far away are they?"

"Not far. Catch soon."

"Then let's be going." Stavut reached up and took hold of the baldric. Shakul crouched down, allowing Stavut to place his foot in the loop. Then the great beast reared up, Stavut on his back, and let out a howl. He began to run. As he did so his right arm swept out, and he called an order. Some fifteen of the pack veered off to the right. Shakul barked out a second order, and another group headed toward the left. The pack ran on silently.

Stavut ducked down as Shakul plowed through thick undergrowth and low-hanging branches. Then he slowed and pointed ahead. A column of men were marching over the brow of a hill, some quarter of a mile ahead. "How many?" asked Stavut.

Shakul lifted up his huge, taloned hands, opening and closing them three times. "Few more, few less," he said.

Then they ran again, pounding up the hillside. As they crested the hill they saw the troop still marching ahead of them, oblivious to the danger. Then one of the soldiers swung around and shouted a warning. The troop drew their weapons and tried to form a defensive wall. There was no time. The Jiamads tore into them. Stavut was thrown clear of Shakul. He hit the ground hard and rolled. A swordsman loomed over him. Shakul's talons tore the man's face away. Blood bubbled from his ruined throat, and he fell. Stavut grabbed the man's sword and ran into the fray, hacking and stabbing. An officer on a tall horse was leading the men. When he saw the carnage he tried to flee. Grava hurtled across the grass and leapt at the man's mount, ripping its neck open. The horse reared, hurling the rider to the earth. Stavut ran across the killing ground, slashing his sword into the bodies of men trying to flee. Not one escaped. Their skulls were crushed or bitten through, or their backbones shattered by iron-shod clubs. Stavut paused and looked around. A few men were still moving, trying to crawl. The beasts leapt upon them, long fangs slicing into thin necks.

Then Stavut saw the officer, lying very still. Grava was

close by, his long, curved fangs tearing chunks of flesh from the body of the dead horse. Stavut walked to the officer, a young man, slim and handsome, his chin beard carefully shaped and trimmed. "I have information," said the man. "Agrias will find it very useful, if you take me to him."

"I don't serve Agrias," said Stavut.

"I . . . don't understand. Who do you serve?"

"A man named Kinyon, and a young girl called Kerena. And others whose names I don't recall now. I don't suppose you asked their names before you killed them and raped their women." Stavut raised the bloody sword.

"No wait!" shrieked the officer, lifting his arm high. Stavut's blade slashed down, smashing the man's forearm and cutting deeply through muscle and sinew. The officer screamed. "Mercy! I beg you!"

"Mercy? You'll get what you gave, you whoreson!" The sword slashed down again, clanging against the man's breastplate, then ricocheting down to slice into his thigh. He began to scramble backward. Stavut followed him, the sword hammering again and again, sometimes striking the metal armor, but more often cutting into flesh and bone. A massive blow caught the young officer on the side of the face, shattering several teeth and opening up a long cut down to the chin. The man rolled to his side, curling his legs up in a fetal position, and began to sob and cry. Stavut hacked at him. Then Shakul grabbed his arm, pulling him back and pushing him to the ground. The huge beast crouched over the mewing man and slashed his throat swiftly. The officer sank to the ground. Then Shakul moved away. Stavut sat very still, suddenly weary.

He had avenged the villagers. Only it didn't help. They were still dead, their dreams soaking into the earth with their blood. Kinyon, a big man who only wanted to cook for others, to have them visit his little kitchen and tell him his pies were delicious. Kerena, who wanted five children and a little house on the high hills overlooking Petar. Their deaths had been cruel and meaningless. Stavut sighed. As had the deaths of these soldiers.

Pushing himself to his feet, he saw Shakul standing with the four Jiamads that had marched with the troop. "Why are they still alive?" he asked, moving alongside Shakul.

"You want dead? I kill."

"Why did you not kill them already?"

"Bigger pack, better hunt."

"They killed my people."

"No, Bloodshirt. Stood by trees." Stavut recalled the scene of the horror, and realized there were no fang or talon marks on the dead. "I kill now?" asked Shakul. The four Jiamads backed away, raising their clubs.

"No," said Stavut, wearily. Then he sighed. "Why do they want to join us?"

"Be free," said Shakul. "Run. Hunt. Feast. Sleep. No Skins."

"I am a Skin."

Shakul gave a low, rumbling, broken series of grunts that Stavut had discovered was a version of laughter. "You Bloodshirt."

Stavut realized it was a compliment. He was about to reply when he saw blood on Shakul's side. "You are wounded," he said.

"Not wound," said Shakul. "Boot." He pointed to Stavut's feet. The fur had been ripped away by Stavut's boot during the long run. Yet the beast had said nothing.

"I am sorry, my friend," he said. Then he took a deep breath and walked to stand before the towering enemy Jiamads. "You wish to run with Bloodshirt's pack? To be free in the mountains?"

They stared at him with cold, golden eyes. "Run free," said one. "Yes."

"Then join us. There will be no killing of Skins . . . unless I order it. There will be no fighting among us. You understand. We are all brothers. Family," he said. He recognized the look of noncomprehension on their faces. "You will not stand alone. Your enemies are my enemies. They are Shakul's enemies and Grava's enemies. We are friends. We are . . ." He swung to Shakul. "How can I make this clear to them?"

"We are pack!" said Shakul. "Bloodshirt's pack."

The Jiamads nodded vigorously. "We are pack!" they echoed. Then all of the beasts began to howl and stamp their feet. The sound went on for some time, then faded away. Shakul approached Stavut. "Where now, Bloodshirt?"

"Back to where we camped. We'll rest up for a day or two."

The journey back was slower for Stavut. Shakul sent some of the others on ahead, but he and Grava walked alongside the human. Stavut felt wearier than at any point in his life, but he refused the offer of being carried.

Back at the campsite the Jiamads retrieved the meat they had hung in the high tree branches, and began to eat. Stavut had no appetite.

He sat alone, the events of the day going around and around in his head.

I am an educated man, he thought. *Civilized.* And yet it was not the Jiamads who tortured and killed the villagers, and not the Jiamads who hacked and cut at a defenseless man on the ground. In fact it was a Jiamad who stopped him, and put an end to the officer's misery.

This would always be the Day of the Beast to Stavut. And shame burned in him that he had been the beast.

Fifteen

Gilden was growing worried as he led the riders down a treacherous slope toward the east. Alahir had been gone too long, and he feared some disaster had befallen him. The veteran soldier had every faith in Alahir's skills with bow or blade, but in the mountains a horse could stumble, pitching its rider over the edge of a precipice, or fall, trapping the rider. One man had been killed last year when his horse fell and rolled, the saddle pommel crushing his breastbone. No matter how skilled the rider, or how brave, accidents could kill.

The young aide, Bagalan, rode alongside Gilden as the trail widened. By rights he should be leading the troop, for he was the only officer present. But the lad was canny, and knew Gilden had the experience. So he stayed silent and followed Gilden's lead. The elder man drew rein, scanning the ground ahead. Bagalan leaned over to him. "Why did you never accept a commission?" he asked, suddenly. "I know Alahir has twice tried to make you an officer."

"Family tradition," answered Gilden, straight faced. "Peasant stock. We hate officers. If I took a commission my father would never speak to me again."

"Gods!" said the boy. "Is he still alive? He must be a hundred and twenty."

"Sixty-eight," snapped Gilden. "And if that skittish horse of yours has killed Alahir you won't forget what I'll do to you if *you* live a hundred and twenty years."

"I'm sorry about that," said the young man. "It was stupid—but I wasn't expecting earthquakes."

A burly rider eased his way alongside Gilden. "That slope looks treacherous," he said, indicating the scree-covered ground ahead.

"It does," agreed Gilden. "So you'd better scout it."

"Why me?"

"You know how it goes, Barik. The least useful gets the most dangerous assignments."

Barik gave a broad grin, showing a broken front tooth. "I see. Not because you owe me a month's wages then?"

"That did have a small part to play in my decision."

"Nothing worse than a bad loser," replied Barik, touching heels to his mount and carefully picking out a path through the scree. Twice the horse slithered, but Barik was probably the best rider in the troop, and Gilden had little doubt he would find a way down.

"You follow him," he told Bagalan. "I was lying when I said he was the least useful. I'm not lying when I say it to you."

"No way to speak to an officer, grandfather," said Bagalan. The boy chuckled and set off after Barik.

I should be a grandfather, thought Gilden. *I should be sitting on the two acres of land my service has paid for. I should be watching my crops grow, and my horses feed. There should be children at my feet.*

And a wife?

The thought sprang unbidden.

Gilden had been wed twice, outliving the first. The second had been a mistake. Loneliness had clouded his judgment. She had begun an affair with a neighbor, and Gilden had challenged him and killed him in a saber duel. He still regretted that. He had liked the man. After that he had gone to the public square and snapped the Marriage Wand, giving the pieces to the Source priest there. His wife had married a merchant and now lived on his ship.

So no grandchildren, and the farmland he had been awarded for his twenty years was being managed by tenants, and he sat in his saddle, waiting to negotiate a dangerous slope.

Gilden sighed, raised his arm, and led his troops out onto the slope. Barik and Bagalan had made it to firmer ground. Gilden followed the trail they had set, and soon joined them. Both men looked tense and said nothing. Gilden glanced down the trail and saw Alahir's horse standing, reins trailing.

"Well," said the sergeant, "let's find out the worst."

The earthquake had felled several trees ahead, but Gilden rode at them with speed, leaping his mount over the obstructions until he drew level with the waiting horse. He glanced up at the rockslide ahead and saw Alahir sitting there.

"Nice afternoon for a nap," said Gilden, trying to keep the relief from his voice. Alahir did not respond. One by one the other riders gathered at the foot of the slide. "Are you all right?" called Gilden.

"Something you need to see," Alahir told him. "Come up. Bring Barik and Bagalan with you. The others can take turns later."

Gilden dismounted and scrambled up the slope. "What's wrong with you, lad?" he asked.

"Nothing and everything. You'll understand. Follow me."

Alahir led the three Drenai soldiers through the half-covered entrance and along the corridor beyond. Once into the inner chamber all three men stopped and stared at the Armor of Bronze.

"That cannot be what I think it is," said Gilden, at last.

"It is," Alahir told him.

"No, it is a hoax of some kind," said Barik. "You don't stumble on the answer to your dreams in a rockslide."

"I have always wanted to know what it really looked like," said Alahir, his tone reverential. "I never dreamed it would be so beautiful."

"What good is it, though?" asked Bagalan. "Locked in crystal."

"It is not crystal," Alahir told him. "It is some sort of illusion. Go to it. I have already done so."

Bagalan strolled over to the huge, shimmering crystal and thrust out his hand toward the winged helm. He cried out as his fingers cracked against the cold, hard block. He stared accusingly at Alahir. "I could have broken my hand." Gilden walked to the block, and reached out. The surface was cool and firm and seamless. Carefully he ran his hand over the entire front of the block. There was no opening. Alahir stepped forward, and Gilden could see the reluctance in his every movement. Slowly the captain reached out his hand. It passed through the crystal, his fingers curling round the winged hilt. The sword slid free of the scabbard.

"How in the name of the Source did you do that?" asked Bagalan, still rubbing at his bruised fingers.

Alahir sighed and passed the blade to Gilden. Then he moved across the chamber and sat down on a shelf of rock. "It is all wrong," he said.

Gilden sat beside him. "Tell it all, lad. What is going on here?"

He listened as Alahir talked of the voice that led him to the Armor, and how she had said he should don it. Then he stopped. "There is more," prompted Gilden.

"She said I was the earl of Bronze, by blood and by right."

"And that has dispirited you?"

"Of course it has," said Alahir. "I'm not a Druss the Legend, Gil. I'm just a soldier. I was third from last in my class at the academy. You're a better swordsman, and Barik a finer archer. The voice was wrong. I'd follow the earl of Bronze into fire. I'd willingly give my life for the Drenai. But I am not good enough for this."

"You are probably right," Gilden told him. "We are none of us worthy of our ancestors. They were giants. You said it yourself, lad, only yesterday. They had Druss, we have you and me. You say you'd ride through fire for the earl of Bronze. There's not one of us who wouldn't ride into hell itself if you gave the order." Clapping Alahir on the shoulder, he rose. "Now come on, do as she bid—whoever she was. Don the Armor. I'll help you."

Alahir returned to the block and removed the scaled breastplate with the flaring eagle motif, then the mail shirt and leggings, and the winged helm. Removing his own chain mail, he donned the shirt. Gilden lifted the breastplate. Alahir opened his arms, allowing Gilden to buckle it into place. Then he added the wrist guards and the gauntlets. Gilden settled the scabbard belt around his waist, thrusting the sword back into its bronze sheath. Lastly, Alahir lifted the winged helm. He was about to place it on his head when he stopped. "I feel like I am desecrating something holy," he said.

"You are not, lad. You are honoring it. Put on the helm."

Alahir settled it into place. As the voice had promised, it all fit perfectly.

A rumble began in the stone beneath their feet. Dust fell from the ceiling, and a huge chunk of rock fell—and bounced from the now empty crystal block.

"Another earthquake!" shouted Barik.

"Everyone out!" ordered Alahir.

They ran back through the tunnel. Gilden fell. Alahir hoisted him to his feet. Just before they reached the entrance there came what sounded like a clap of thunder from behind them. The entire roof collapsed.

Then the side wall of the tunnel split open, a massive slab of rock sliding away.

Gilden, Barik, and Bagalan all scrambled out onto the open slope. The tremor faded away and Gilden saw the rest of the troop standing below them, looking up in awe. He turned. Standing in the new cave mouth, dust billowing around him, was a golden figure. Gilden knew it was Alahir. He had helped him don the armor. Yet now, in the bright sunlight, it seemed that a hero of legend had emerged from the bowels of the earth, his arrival heralded by an earthquake. He was Alahir no longer.

This golden man on the mountainside was the earl of Bronze.

Memnon stood quietly in Landis Khan's upper apartments as the Eternal and Unwallis spoke. It always fascinated the slender minister to see how men reacted around the Eternal. Whenever he did so he found himself grateful for his own lack of sexual desire. Men became such fools as they moved into the orbit of her beauty. Memnon had always rather admired Unwallis. The man had a fine intellect, but it was so obvious that the Eternal had taken him once more to her bed. He fawned around her like an aging puppy. It had, though, Memnon conceded, improved his dress sense. Clothes were Memnon's second obsession, delicate silks, rich satins, fine wools; brilliant and beautiful dyes. He adored designing new tunics and gowns, employing the finest embroiderers and artists. Since becoming the Eternal's lover for the second time Unwallis had put aside the gray, lackluster clothes that were his trademark and was now wearing a quite delightful shirt tunic of blue silk over cream leggings and gray boots. It seemed to Memnon that the boots were an inspired choice, complementing the silver-gray of Unwallis's hair.

The Eternal had taken less care with her appearance, but then when someone had such natural beauty it would not matter were she to dress in sackcloth. Her knee-length tunic was simple white wool, the only adornment being a filigree gold belt with small ornaments hanging from it. Several of them were quite exquisitely fashioned, but, Memnon decided, would look better on the backdrop of a darker dress, or gown.

Pushing such thoughts from his mind he stood quietly, arms folded, his fingers stroking the soft sleeves of his own ankle-length gown of rich blue silk.

Unwallis was concerned about the prophecy. He had studied more of Landis Khan's notes and had become convinced—as had Landis—that Skilgannon could threaten the reign of the Eternal. Jianna did not share his conviction. "He is one man. No army, no magic. Even with the Swords of Night and Day he could not overcome a regiment of Jiamads, nor even a troop of lancers."

"The prophecy says—" began Unwallis.

"A pox on prophecies," she snapped. "This one is merely wish fulfillment. Can you not see it? An ancient crone talks of Skilgannon's return, so Landis Khan brings him back. Even Landis had no idea how the prophecy could be fulfilled. You think Skilgannon will know?"

"What I do know, Highness, is that the Blessed Priestess was a genuine seer."

Jianna laughed. "Would you really like to know what she was? I met her once. She was a Joining—a Jiamad—created by men. She wore gloves to disguise her talons, and long-sleeved gowns to hide the fur. And yes, she was gifted—but not gifted enough to read a future a thousand years after her death." She swung to Memnon. "And what of Decado? I take it from your expression that he is not dead?"

"No, Highness. He met with Skilgannon, and together they killed three of my Shadows."

She turned her dark gaze on him. "Your invincible Shadows? Three of them?"

He thought she was going to become angry. Instead she smiled. As always the shock of her smile caused his breath to catch in his throat. It was exquisite, stunning. Even without the vile drawback of sexual arousal Memnon felt the extraordinary power of her beauty. "It is amusing, Highness?" he managed to ask.

"Only to me. The man I knew would not be killed by such creatures."

"Decado warned him. They were ready. The next time it will be different."

"There will be no next time. I do not want Olek killed. You

understand me, Memnon? That man was—is—the love of my life. If I can speak to him he will return to me."

"Of course, Highness. The Shadows were following Decado. It was mere happenstance that he was with Skilgannon and the others."

"Is he still with them?"

"No, Highness, he rode north."

"And Olek?"

"A woman with them was killed in the earthquake. They buried her and also headed north."

"Not my Reborn?"

"No, Highness. A peasant from Petar."

"Good. What is their destination?"

"Skilgannon seeks the lost temple," Memnon told her.

"Of course he does. Haven't we all? He will find the twisted crater that remains. Then he will seek to come after me. He will not succeed. Even if he reaches me he will be unable to kill me. I know him. I know his love for me."

"Then you also know how resourceful he is," put in Unwallis.

Memnon watched the Eternal closely, seeing her smile fade and her dark eyes narrowing. "Yes, I do, Unwallis. And you are right to remind me of it. Skilgannon is unlike any other man I ever knew. He failed at nothing. Even at the tender age of sixteen he evaded the skills of trackers and assassins. By twenty-one he had won every battle he fought. Once, with only a handful of men, he assaulted a citadel and killed a man I believed to be the finest swordsman alive. He should not be underestimated—especially by me. Send a regiment of Eternal Guardsman and their Jiamads to the temple site. They can take ship from Draspartha."

"Yes, Highness."

"Now to more immediate matters. The army should cross the mountains within the next three days. I will ride with them. We will crush Agrias once and for all." She turned to Unwallis. "Now leave me. I wish to talk to Memnon."

He looked crestfallen, but merely bowed and backed away.

As the door closed behind him Jianna raised her arms above her head and stretched. Then she sighed. "We will talk on the balcony," she said. Memnon followed her out into the fading light. She beckoned him to a wicker chair. He waited for her to seat herself, then slightly raised his gown and perched on the edge of his chair. He had no wish to stretch the gown and spoil the line.

"Has he bedded her yet?" she asked.

He noted the jealousy in her voice. It was surprising. He had never known her to show such emotion. "No, Highness. It is obvious they have great attraction for one another, but there has been nothing . . . carnal."

She laughed. "You make the word *carnal* sound like something stuck to the bottom of a boot." The smile faded. "So, she is a virgin still. Good. I always enjoy being a virgin again." Jianna sat silently for a while. Then she spoke again. "When you watched him did he speak of me?"

Memnon had known this moment would arrive. He had planned to lie, but now that he observed the depth of her feelings for the man he decided the truth would be far more potent. "Yes, Highness. I don't think you would like to hear it, however."

"I will judge that! Speak!"

"The Reborn now knows of her origins. She asked Skilgannon about you. He said you had been corrupted by power, and had become evil, and that he would do all in his power to end your reign."

"Yes, that is my Olek! A true romantic. Good and evil as separate as night and day. It will be so good to see him again."

Her response shocked him. "You are not angry?"

"I might as well be angry at the sun for shining too brightly. Olek is an unusual man. He had great intelligence, and yet he insists on seeing the world in a basically simple way. He looks at my Reborns and no doubt says that I steal their bodies and banish their souls. Quite true. However, I look at those Reborns and say, *But they would not exist, save for my bones and my blood. Without me they would have had no life at all. They would never have been born. Therefore I have gifted them with twenty years of life they would otherwise never have experienced. I have loaned them a part of my life. When the loan period is up I take it back.* Equally true. Do you think I am evil, Memnon?"

"I do not know what evil is," he answered.

"When you send out your Shadows to kill a rival, is that evil?"

"I expect the rival would think so. Would you mind if I stood, Highness?"

"Not at all."

Memnon rose and smoothed his hands down the sides of his gown. "The material stretches badly," he explained.

Reaching up, she took hold of his mutilated hand. "How are your Reborns faring?"

"All dead, but one. And he will not last the winter."

"No more mutilations, Memnon. You are having difficulty walking now. How many toes have you taken?"

"Two from each foot. I must find a way, Highness. Or I, too, shall be dead."

"Not for some years yet, my dear. There is still time."

"There is something wrong, and I cannot find it. The artifacts are flawless, and everything is fine until the children reach eight, sometimes nine. Then the cancers begin. They are eaten alive by them."

"I recall that you yourself were the only survivor of the . . . the family created by Landis. Those children also died. In the end he used all the bones he found."

"That is a great shame," he said. "Perhaps with them I could create a more perfect duplicate."

"I do not think so. The bones were not human, Memnon."

"What?" He was shocked. "Landis told me he found the remains of a great wizard from the past."

"Yes, he did. There was enormous excitement. According to legends the wizard, a man named Zhujow, made a pact with a demon lord. He was being hunted by a knight named Rulander. Zhujow called on the demon to give him the power to defeat the knight. The demon did just that. He changed Zhujow into a Joining. Rulander still slew him. It was the bones of the Joining Landis discovered. That is why it was so difficult for him to refine the process and produce you. I still do not know how he did it, but I recall the horrors of his first attempts. One child clawed its way from the womb of the mother. Both died. Others were born hideously deformed and had to be destroyed. Then you arrived. Almost perfect."

"Why was I never told this before, Highness?"

"When you were young Landis believed the knowledge would have a detrimental effect on you. As you grew older—" She shrugged. "—the subject just never arose. Is it helpful to know?"

"It could be. It might explain why the children's bodies become so unstable. I need to study more. Unwallis has become fascinated by Landis Khan's journals of his experiments with Skilgannon. For myself I prefer the more detailed journals I have discovered in the artifact chambers. These are more concerned with the various refinements he made."

"Well, make sure you get enough rest," she said, releasing his hand.

"Thank you, Highness, for your concern. As you know, my demise will not affect the passage of your soul to the first of the Reborns."

"That is not what I meant. You are dear to me, Memnon. I want you to be well."

He was momentarily touched by her concern. But then he thought, *Decado was dear to you, too.* The Eternal was beautiful, and kind, and considerate, when it suited her. And chilling and deadly when the mood took her.

"I shall rest now, Highness, by your leave."

"Do that. On your way out you will see a handsome soldier, with blond hair, guarding my door. Send him to me."

Memnon did not go to his bed. Instead he walked from the palace, cutting through the gardens to the stables at the rear. Beyond them was a long black wagon, high sided, with a curving roof. The six-wheeled vehicle was more than twenty feet long. There were no windows, but a series of covered slits could be seen along both sides. The entrance was at the rear. The sun had sunk behind the mountains, and although the sky was still blue no direct sunlight shone upon the wagon doorway. Memnon pulled on a lever beside the door, and three steps slid into view. Mounting the first, he tapped on the door. "Close your eyes, my children," he said. Swiftly he opened the door and moved inside, pulling shut the door behind him.

The darkness within was absolute. A soft chittering sound began. Memnon felt the Shadows moving around him. "Three of your brothers are no more," he said, his voice a mere whisper. "They failed. They have brought shame upon us. Their deaths must be avenged."

Reaching out his hands, he continued. "Touch me, my children. Touch me and *see* the enemies whose deaths are required." Eyes closed, he summoned images of Decado and Skilgannon to his mind, holding to them, as each of the seven Shadows closed around him, their touch as light as a morning breeze. "First there must be Decado. You know his scent. Then the other, the carrier of two swords. He is a danger to us all. Kill him, and any with him. Devour their hearts. And hide the bodies where none will find them. Tonight there will be clouds. You must travel far. I will commune with you, and lead you to the prey. Now close your eyes, my children, for I must open the door and there is still daylight beyond."

Memnon left the wagon swiftly and returned to his apartments. A servant girl with frightened eyes brought him food and a goblet of red wine. She had not served him before and did not know of his distaste for liquor of any kind.

As he ate he considered the events of the day. The Eternal's desire to keep Skilgannon alive was a mystery to him. It was also ill advised. Of course some prophecies would prove false. Equally some would prove true, and it was foolish to allow an enemy to walk free. Memnon would keep his death secret. Eventually the Eternal would tire of looking for him, and all would be as it was.

Not all, he hoped.

The deaths of his Reborns were proving bitter and frightening. How was it that children fashioned from his own bones should prove so frail? Why indeed had he not died as a child?

Lighting a lantern, he gathered up yet more of the papers he had discovered in the artifacts chamber and began to study them. They were interesting. Landis Khan had had a fine mind, and many of his theories of the artifacts were thought provoking. Yet nothing he found cast any new light on the problem he faced. Pushing the papers aside, he lay back on a couch, staring up at the ornate ceiling.

As he drifted toward exhausted sleep he released his mind, floating clear of his weary frame. His spirit floated along deserted corridors and down to the servants' quarters, where young women were gathered, preparing food for the soldiers who guarded the palace. Their conversation was dull and predictable and he flowed past them, down into the artifact chambers below the palace. Here his two aides were also studying Landis Khan's journals. Patiacus, bald and round shouldered, sat hunched by a table reading slowly. The younger Oranin suddenly leaned back and rubbed at his eyes. "A clever man," he said.

"Too clever," responded Patiacus. "His ashes are scattered through the gardens."

"Why do you think he spent so much time drawing necklaces?"

"Necklaces?"

"These notes are full of them. He talks of structures and debilities and instabilities. I cannot understand a tenth of it."

"Look for references to the Lord Memnon," advised Patiacus. "That is what is important."

Oranin rose from his chair and ran his hand over his close-cropped red hair. "There are hundreds of these journals. It will take weeks."

"You have other plans?" asked Patiacus.

"There is a plump serving girl with inviting eyes. I think she likes me."

"Then she has no taste," observed Patiacus. "Now stop interrupting me."

The two men returned to their work. It was obvious to Memnon, and not for the first time, that the two men liked one another. In a way he could not explain Memnon found this dispiriting. Affection was an emotion he had never experienced. There had never been anyone that Memnon had truly liked. At first he thought most people were like him, learning how to socialize, establishing working relationships, knowing when to smile and when to be solemn. But he was older and wiser now, and knew that he was different from those others in so many subtle ways. Mostly he tried to convince himself that his lack of emotional response to people was an asset. At times like this his confidence in that belief was less sure.

Returning to his body, he sat up and drank a little water.

People believed he was devoted to the Eternal. Once, when floating unobserved above Unwallis, he listened as the statesman told a colleague: "It is his only redeeming human quality."

Yet even this was not true. He looked upon the Eternal as he looked upon his clothes. Beautiful to gaze upon, to observe, to enjoy.

"Do you think I am evil, Memnon?" she had asked.

"I do not know what evil is," he had replied.

It was not strictly true. Evil was anything that hampered or obstructed his life and his plans. Good was anything that facilitated his desires.

He felt the weariness of his body and decided to float free

once more. In spirit form there was no exhaustion, no heavy weariness. He floated up to the royal apartments and watched as Jianna entertained the young cavalry officer, their bodies locked together, sweat glistening on their skin. Then he moved away and saw Unwallis pacing the corridor outside, his eyes angry.

This relaxed Memnon. Who could possibly desire to know such jealousy? Who could want to be locked in such a sweaty embrace with a stranger?

Leaving the palace, his spirit soared up and over the mountains.

The machines of the ancients were incredibly complex, their component parts a mystery. It was not even possible to ascertain the method of their construction. The metals were extraordinarily fine and light, alloys, Memnon guessed, of gold and other metals unknown in this time. When the power was in them they functioned automatically, following a pattern laid down by ancient wizards, whose knowledge was as far above Memnon's as could be imagined. They were perfect. Which made the failures of Memnon's own Reborns all the more galling. His Reborns should have been exact duplicates of himself. Why they should be prone to cancerous growths in childhood was a mystery that filled his mind. He could not recall ever being ill. His own body seemed capable of fighting off any infection or disease.

Pausing in his flight, he realized he had flown to the site of the lost temple. He gazed down at the two mountain passes leading to what had once been the Mountain of the Resurrection. Now there was just an empty bowl of land, full of twisted shrubs. He saw the wind blow a dust cloud toward the bowl. The cloud disappeared as it reached it.

How Skilgannon's heart would sink when he saw this place.

He thought of the man he had encountered in Gamal's dream place. Jianna was right. There was a fierce intelligence in his eyes, and there was no doubt he was possessed of an indomitable spirit. Memnon had observed the peasant girl placing the swords in his hands, and had seen him awaken. He was weak and disoriented—and yet still he summoned the strength to kill the beast that came at him.

Memnon turned south, soaring high above the River Rostrias and back toward the distant mountains. He passed over valleys and hills, forests and streams, seeking out the swordsman. At one point he saw a group of Joinings and a small man in a red tunic. It was an incongruous sight. Two Joinings were hauling a wagon. At any other time such a sight would have piqued his interest. He flew on, scanning the forest trails.

Then he saw a flickering campfire set in a wooded hollow. It was well placed and could not have been seen from ground level. Memnon floated down to hover above the trio sitting quietly by the fire. He gazed at Skilgannon. The man's expression was stern and distant. Close by the Eternal Reborn kept glancing at him. Beyond them both was the huge peasant with the ancient ax.

"How did you die . . . the first time?" he heard the woman ask.

"Painfully," replied Skilgannon. He glanced across at the peasant. "How are you faring, Harad?"

"I'm hungry," answered the man. He looked up. "Did you see Druss in the Void when you were there?"

"I do not remember. It is all hazy now."

"Why did you not pass to the Golden Valley he spoke of?"

"The evils of my life prevented me. All I remember is that I did not look as you see me now. My arms were scaled. There were no mirrors there, but I would guess my face was scaled also. The evil do not cross the Valley."

"What do they do?" asked the woman.

"They fight to survive."

"But they are already dead," said the woman. "What more can happen to them?"

Skilgannon shrugged. "I do not have the answer to that. When you kill a beast in the Void it simply disappears. Ceases to exist perhaps."

"And these beasts attack those who . . . who are not scaled?" asked Harad.

"Yes."

"Hardly seems fair," pointed out the woman. "Someone good dies, enters the Void, and is then killed again by a demon."

Skilgannon laughed. "Fair? In my previous life I heard that so often. I would like to meet the man who first suggested that life was fair. It is not. It is just life. Some people are lucky. Some are not. Fairness has nothing to do with it. And if that is the situation in life, then why should the Void operate any differently?"

"Do you fear returning to it?"

"Would it make a difference?" he responded. "I do not fear the inevitable."

"Druss said he would take Charis to the Golden Valley," said Harad.

"Then he will," said Skilgannon. "Be assured of that."

"I wish that I had been killed with her," said Harad. "We would be together then."

"One day you will be together," said the woman.

That day will be soon, thought Memnon. Judging by the distance his spirit had traveled, it would take the Shadows no more than three nights to reach them. Memnon was about to return to his body when the woman spoke again, this time to Skilgannon.

"Do you regret loving the Eternal?"

He smiled. "One fact I learned in my life is that we should never regret love. In many ways it is what defines us. In that respect I have been lucky. I have been loved, and I have loved. Ultimately that is all that counts. The dreams of men all come to dust. If I did not know that in my first life, I know it now. Nothing remains of the world I knew—not even its history. All is fable and shadow."

"The Eternal remains," she said.

"For now," he told her.

"You really believe we can end her reign?"

"Askari, there are many areas of my life that have fallen
short of what could have been. There were—and there are—
men more clever, more powerful, more wise than I. But I
have never been defeated in life or in war. Ustarte—whom
you call the Blessed Priestess—said I would change this
world. And I trust her wisdom."

Arrogant man, thought Memnon, but then he looked into
the sapphire eyes.

And felt a stab of fear.

Gilden rode down the slope and onto the flatland. The
troop was some little way behind him, and Gilden had volun-
teered to scout the area. Some way ahead was a thick,
wooded area that could conceal enemy troops. Gilden rode
slowly toward it, his bow in his left hand, an arrow nocked.
As he approached the trees the wind changed. His mount's
ears pricked up, and it veered to the left. Calming the horse,
he stared into the wood. At first there was nothing to be seen.
Then came a movement, as the undergrowth rustled. A Jiamad stepped out and stood staring at the rider. It was a big
beast, maybe seven and a half feet tall, with a massive
breadth of shoulder. Gently pulling back on the reins, Gilden
walked his horse backward, creating space between himself
and the monster. Over short distances a Jiamad could run
down a horse. Another Jiamad appeared. Then another. They
made no hostile move toward him, but they watched him.
None of them was wearing a baldric or other indications of
army apparel. It was likely they were runaways.

Suddenly a familiar voice called out: "Is that you,
Gilden?" Before he could answer he saw the young merchant Stavut emerge from the trees. He strolled past the
beasts and out into the open. "Good to see you. Is Alahir with
you?"

It was like a dream. There was no sense to it. "What are
you doing here?" asked Gilden, staring at the merchant. His
clothes were filthy, stained with what looked like dried
blood. He was unshaven but as jaunty as ever.

"It is a long story. You can relax. Not one of my lads will attack you."

"Your lads?"

"As I said, it is a long story. I've been teaching them how to hunt."

Gilden's horse backed away as more Jiamads emerged from the trees. Gilden watched them. There were more than forty beasts. "These are all yours?"

"Not mine exactly. They are free, you see."

"Oh yes, I see. I also see you have blood on your clothes. Did you get that bringing down a deer, Stavut?"

Stavut sighed. "No. We were in a battle. We killed the soldiers who had massacred some villagers. It was not pretty."

"Why don't you climb up behind me, Stavut?" said Gilden, softly. "I'll ride you away from here. We'll see Alahir together."

"Can't leave my lads," said Stavut. "Did you know there is an army marching from the south? We saw them. Must be twenty, thirty thousand strong. That's why we are moving north. Keeping out of their way."

If Gilden had been surprised to find Stavut with a pack of beasts he was even more amazed moments later. Two huge Jiamads came into sight, pulling Stavut's wagon behind them. They paused at the tree line. Stavut turned. "Wolves killed my horses," he said.

"I don't understand any of this," admitted Gilden. "I think you should ride with me. You may think these beasts are tame, Stavut, but you are in great danger. You can't trust them. They are vermin."

"Vermin? Did you know they don't even like killing people?" said Stavut, his eyes angry. "They don't taste good. They kill us because they are bred to do that, trained to do that, ordered to do that. By men. Vermin? *We* are the vermin, Gilden. I am not in danger from them. Go and tell Alahir we need to talk. We'll wait here."

Gilden took a deep breath. "You are not thinking straight, boy. Our job is to kill these monsters. What do you think is going to happen when Alahir gets here? You think he's going to talk? Of course he isn't. He hates these beasts as much as any of us. Come on, Stavut! See sense. Just ride with me."

"I would be glad to see Alahir. He is my friend. As you are, Gilden. I wanted to tell him of the army approaching. However, you can do that. I shall stay with my lads." Stavut turned as if to walk away. Then he swung back. "We will do you no harm. We are merely moving north. You come after us, Gilden, and you will regret it."

"You are siding with them against us? Are you mad?"

"Put up your bow and ride away, Gilden."

"You know we will be back."

"I'll tell you what I know," hissed Stavut. "I know your patrols usually number around fifty *men*. I have fifty *Jiamads*. Now it may just be that you Legend riders are all great heroes, with the strength of ten. But we just wiped out around your number of the Eternal's soldiers. Killed them all. We lost no one. Come after us at your peril."

"You would send these beasts against your friends?" said Gilden, aghast.

Gilden looked into Stavut's eyes and saw they were glittering strangely. "You come after my lads," he said, "and I'll rip your heart out myself."

"I shall remember that, renegade, when next we meet," said Gilden, tugging on the reins and riding back to the hills.

Skilgannon could scarce believe it when he saw the horse. It was pure white and beautiful, strong limbed, with powerful hindquarters. Its neck was long, its eyes fierce and proud. It was standing with six other mounts, all saddled, with no riders in sight.

Telling Askari and Harad to remain where they were, for fear of causing the horses to bolt, Skilgannon walked slowly down the hillside toward them. He could not take his eyes off the white stallion. He had not seen such a horse in this world, and knew instantly it was a Ventrian purebred. In his own time it would have cost hundreds of gold Raq. It was a mount for princes, kings, or conquerors.

As he approached he saw all the mounts staring at him, ears pulled back. Slowly he sat on the grass and began to speak to them, in a soft, soothing voice. "How is it that you are here, my beauties?" he said. "And where are the lucky men who rode you? Hmmm?" Reaching down, he tugged a handful of long grass from the earth, then another. Keeping his movements slow and unthreatening, he angled toward the mounts, holding out the grass. "You should be eating grain," he said, "but this will have to suffice." His easy manner calmed them, though the great white horse—he estimated almost seventeen hands tall—eyed him warily. "Come, eat with me, Greatheart," he said, offering the grass. The horse dipped its head and took the grass from his hand. Skilgannon stroked its sleek neck and noted there was dried blood upon the ornate, silver-mounted saddle. Two of the other horses carried cuts, and one had a broken arrow hanging loosely from the skin of its flanks. "Ah, you have been in a battle," said Skilgannon. "And your riders were slain, or unhorsed." Moving alongside the white, he carried on stroking it while taking hold of the long, snowy mane. Then he raised his foot into the stirrup. The white immediately reared and bolted. Skilgannon heaved himself up and swung his leg over the saddle, seeking out the second stirrup. The speed of the gallop both astonished and exhilarated Skilgannon. In his previous life he had possessed some truly great horses, and this stallion would take its place among the best of them. He had no idea yet as to the beast's temperament, but its power was outstanding. Gently, but firmly, he guided the horse into a wide turn, heading back up the hill toward the waiting Askari and Harad. Drawing on the rein brought an instant response. The horse slowed and stood quietly. Just as Skilgannon relaxed it leapt and bucked. He was almost unseated, but clung on. The stallion bolted once more, leaping and twisting. Then it slowed once more. Skilgannon sensed what was coming. Kicking his feet from the stirrups just as the horse rolled, he leapt clear. As the stallion struggled to regain its feet, Skilgannon vaulted back into the saddle. "Nice try, Greatheart," he said, patting the stallion's long sleek neck. "Are we done now? Do we know each other yet?"

They did not. The stallion bounded off again.

Askari watched in silent wonder, struck by the awesome beauty of the horse and the almost uncanny skill of the rider. She had ridden only twice in her life, and had enjoyed the experience. However, the horse she had borrowed from Kinyon was a swayback more used to pulling carts. There was no comparison between old Shavu and this magnificent creature. She glanced at Harad. "Have you ever seen a more beautiful horse?"

"It is big," he said.

"Have you ever ridden?"

He smiled. "Once when I was a lad. Didn't like it. Couldn't find the rhythm. After an hour I was wearing my arse round my shoulders."

Askari laughed, then leaned in and kissed Harad's bearded cheek.

"What was that for?"

"Good to see you smile, Harad," she told him.

His face darkened, and she thought she had offended him. Then she saw he was staring down the hillside. A group of heavily armed riders had emerged from the trees and had spread out as they rode toward Skilgannon.

The Armor of Bronze, wrapped in blankets, was being carried on the back of one of the spare mounts, and Alahir had once more donned his own armor. The chain-mail hauberk had been worn by his grandfather at the Battle of Larness, and by his father at the Siege of Raboas. The coif head-and-neck protector had been a gift from his uncle, the warrior Elingel, and he had worn it proudly during the Four Year War that saw the end of the Gothir Successors. His saber was the oldest piece in his armory, and was said to date back to the War of the Twins, though this conflict was now considered to be mostly fable. Alahir felt more comfortable in his own armor.

Not in a physical way, he realized. The Armor of Bronze, as the voice had promised, fitted him perfectly. It was lighter than his own chain mail. Truth was, it just felt wrong to be wearing it. Regnak, the Great Earl, had first donned this at Dros Delnoch, in the mighty war that claimed the life of Druss the Legend. Other heroes had donned it. That a farmer's son from the high country should now be in possession of it seemed almost sacrilegious. He was also uncomfortable with the way the men reacted to him; men he had known since childhood seemed in awe, and responded to his every word with undue courtesy.

Alahir had become a man apart. And he didn't like it.

After the second quake they had all waited for him to make a decision as to their actions now. Were they to ride back to camp, or was there some wondrous plan that the new earl now had for them? It was all too much for Alahir.

Then he remembered the white horse.

Was it an omen? Was this horse meant to be ridden by the new earl of Bronze?

Alahir had no idea, but tracking a runaway stallion at least gave the men something to think about. Indeed it gave Alahir time to think about all that had happened.

He was no nearer a conclusion when Gilden came riding back over the brow of the hill. The veteran rode up and saluted—something Alahir could never remember him doing before.

"What are you doing back here, Gil?" he asked. "Is there trouble ahead?"

"Could be. I just saw your friend Stavut."

Alahir's mood brightened. Stavut was a clever man. He might offer some answers to the problems Alahir faced.

"Why did you not bring him with you? This is dangerous land for a merchant."

Gilden removed his helm, pushed back his coif, and brushed his fingers through his sweat-streaked gray hair. "I

offered to. You should know he's traveling with a large pack
of Jiamad runaways. Calls them *my lads*. I tried to tell him
it's our job to hunt them down, and you know what he said?
He said he'd cut my heart out himself if anyone attacked
them. What do you think of that?"

"Stavut said that? We are talking about the same Stavut?
Small man, wagon, scared rigid of Jiamads?"

"Aye, the same. Only he's not scared now. Must have
fifty of the beasts with him. Been teaching them to hunt, he
told me."

Alahir burst out laughing. "What is so funny?" asked
Gilden, eyes narrowing.

"This is a good jest, Gil. And you sold it well. I never realized you had such a dry sense of humor. So where is he? Is
he following you?"

"I wish it were a jest. His clothes are covered in dried
blood. He even has two Jiamads pulling his wagon—and
don't you dare laugh again. This is all true. What are we to
do? Our orders are clear when we come across Jems."

"Our orders no longer apply, Gil. Not since we found the
Armor."

"It's not right letting those beasts walk free. I think Stavut
is deranged. They'll kill him as soon as hunger takes them."

"I hate the creatures as much as you, Gil. But he was in no
danger when you saw him. What else did he say?"

"He said there's an army moving from the south, thousands of men. Looks like the final confrontation is coming."

"Let's find the horse, then we'll swing north."

"Whatever you say," replied Gilden, glumly.

The troop rode on for just under an hour, entering a thinly
wooded area of flatland. As they emerged onto open ground
they saw the white horse and its rider. Alahir's breath caught
in his throat. The beast was majestic, thundering across the
land, seeking to unseat the man. The rider also was magnificent, reading the stallion's every move. When the horse
rolled, and the rider leapt clear, only to vault back into the
saddle as it rose, Alahir felt like applauding. Every man in

the troop watched with admiration as the contest of wills continued. At last the horse realized it had met its match, and the rider put it through a series of sharp turns and sudden sprints. Only then did he look up and see the Legend riders. Patting the horse's neck he rode toward them, drawing rein and sitting silently. Alahir stared at the man. His face was lean and handsome, his eyes ferociously blue. He did not seem ill at ease. Heeling his own mount forward, Alahir spoke. "Thank you for finding my horse," he said.

"It is not your horse," said the man. The words were not spoken angrily; nor was there any sense of confrontation. They were just spoken, matter-of-factly.

"How do you arrive at that conclusion?"

The man smiled and pointed to the riders around Alahir. "You all have the same saddle designs, stirrup protectors, horns from which to hang your bows. This saddle has no such designs. Added to which there was blood upon it. My guess is the rider was killed."

"Very astute," said Alahir, "and entirely right. However, the horse is mine by right of conquest, since I killed its rider."

"Ah well," replied the man, "that sets an interesting precedent. Are you intending to conquer me also?"

"You think we cannot?"

"I would be a fool to believe I could beat forty armed soldiers. No, there is no doubt that the survivors would claim the horse." His voice hardened. "You, however, would not be among the survivors. Nor the two riding with you. I am not sure how many others I could take with me on the Swans' Path. Three or four probably. Even so it might be worth the risk. It is a fine horse."

Alahir laughed. "Then you think we *should* attack you for it?"

"Depends how much you want the horse."

At that moment two other people came into view, a staggeringly beautiful young woman, dark haired and slim, carrying a recurve bow, and a huge, black-bearded warrior bearing a massive ax.

"Stay back," the rider told them, "and do nothing."

Alahir stared at the woman, and the bow she carried. "Would you be Askari?" he asked.

"I am. How would you know that?"

"I chose that bow myself. Stavut wanted a fine present for you."

"You are Alahir?"

"Indeed I am, beautiful lady," he replied, bowing low.

She laughed. "He said you were ugly and crookbacked and had lost all your teeth."

Gilden edged alongside him. "Have you seen the ax?" he said. Alahir looked more closely at the weapon carried by the massive young man. He said nothing for a moment.

"Are there runes upon that blade?" he asked the man.

"Aye, in silver."

"May I see it?"

"Step down first," said the man. "I'll not be passing my weapon to armed men."

Alahir dismounted and walked over to the man, who held up the ax so that the runes on the haft could be seen.

"Does it say what I think it might?" called out Gilden.

"It does." Walking back to his horse, he stepped into the saddle and returned his attention to the man with the sapphire eyes.

"This is a day of surprises," he said. "Would you do me a kindness, and show me the weapons you would have used to defend your right to the horse?"

The man's arms swept up and back, and two gleaming swords flashed in the sunlight. One was gold, the other moonlight silver.

"The man with two swords," said Alahir. "We are to follow where you lead."

Sixteen

Askari, nursing a thudding headache, sat with Harad as Skilgannon, Alahir, and many of the riders gathered round and talked. Much of the conversation was lost on the huntress, dealing as it did with Drenai history, old legends, and new prophecies. Her attention waned still further when Alahir produced a brilliantly burnished helm of bronze and showed it to Skilgannon. Armor was not one of her interests. Beside her Harad was becoming irritated by the number of men wishing to see the ax. Many of them reached out reverentially and touched the haft.

One young man squatted down before them and just stared at the weapon. Askari, her patience wearing as thin as Harad's, said: "It is an ax—not a holy relic."

"It is *the* ax," he replied, not taking his eyes from the weapon.

"Well, you have seen it. Now leave us in peace," snapped Harad.

The conversation among the leaders turned to more recent events, and Askari heard Stavut's name mentioned. A grizzled veteran soldier was talking about the merchant now keeping company with a troop of Jiamads. Askari listened in amazement. Stavut, who was terrified of wolves and noises in the dark, was now leading a pack of monsters? It was ludicrous. There must have been a mistake. He was supposed to be leading her friends to a place of safety. Rising, she walked to where the men were talking and questioned the veteran. He told her what had transpired, including the story Stavut

had outlined, of a battle to avenge the deaths of people he
cared about.

"Which way was he heading?" she asked.

"Northeast."

Askari moved back from the men, swept up her bow and
quiver, and walked away through the trees. Harad followed
her. "Where are you going?" he asked.

"To find Stavut."

"I'll come with you."

"No disrespect, Harad, but you can't move as fast as I can."
With that she set off at a run, cutting through the trees and
back toward the north. Once away from the group she felt her
tensions ease. The headache she had suffered for the last few
hours drifted away. There were perhaps three hours of good
daylight left as she loped across the grassland toward a distant
wood. If Stavut was with a pack of Jiamads, then their tracks
should not be hard to find. As she ran, eyes scanning the
ground, she thought of what she had heard. Stavut covered in
blood. Something had obviously happened that had unhinged
the young man. Though brave, he was not a warrior, as she
had seen during the fight in the cave. No, Stavut was a sensitive fellow, with charm, wit, and a good heart. So why was he
with the beasts? Perhaps they had taken him hostage or were
keeping him for . . . for food? She shuddered at the thought.

Askari ran on, moving now toward the east, seeking to cut
across the trail left by the beasts. The tracks would tell the
story better than she could imagine it. The search took far
longer than she had estimated, and there was less than an
hour's daylight remaining when she came upon the trail. She
was tired now, having been on the move at speed for around
two hours. Carefully she studied the spoor. It was difficult to
estimate the numbers of beasts, for the tracks overlapped one
another, but it seemed there must be more than thirty of
them. Stavut's boot prints were clear, here and there. One
huge Jiamad was walking alongside him. Guarding the prisoner? Now with a clear trail Askari ran again, heading northeast. The ground rose steadily toward a high stand of pine.

The wind was blowing from the west, so the Jems would not be able to pick up her scent. Even so she moved more warily. The last thing she needed was to run straight into their camp.

Askari ran on. As she neared the tree line she heard a horse whinny. Coming to a stop, she nocked an arrow to her bow. From the trees ahead she saw Decado ride into sight. He waved and smiled. "You are a long way from your friends, beauty," he said.

"And you are a short way from death," she said.

"Pish! We are all a short way from death." Lifting his leg over the saddle horn, he jumped lightly to the ground. "So what brings you here?" he asked, walking to a jutting rock and sitting down.

"Does it not concern you that I might kill you?" she asked.

"You didn't kill me that first night, beauty. You just let me go. Why was that?"

"Obviously a mistake," she told him.

"Probably."

"And stop calling me beauty. I am not her."

"Confusing, though," he said. He winced suddenly and rubbed at his eyes.

"What is wrong with you?"

"Nothing of note. I get head pains sometimes. Mostly they are bearable. Sometimes—as when you found me—they are . . . not so bearable. This one is—happily—not so debilitating. So, why are you here?"

"I am looking for a friend."

"Ah well, lucky you, for you have found one."

"You are not my friend, Decado. I am speaking of a true friend, a man named Stavut."

"The one walking with the Jiamads?"

"Yes. You have seen them?"

"Indeed I have. I came upon them earlier. Thought I would have to fight my way clear. Happily he has them well disciplined, so there was no trouble."

"He is not a prisoner then?"

"It would be an unusual definition of the word *prisoner*.

He commands them, and they obey. Strange man. A little deranged, I think."

Askari laughed then. Decado smiled. "I have amused you?"

"That you, of all people, should accuse another of being deranged."

"Yes, ironic isn't it? Of course I could argue that it gives me a better insight." He looked at her quizzically. "No offense, but I don't suppose you'd consider getting naked with me. It would help relieve my headache."

"I don't believe you! I loathe you, Decado. What on earth would make you think I'd want to sleep with you?"

"I wasn't talking about sleep. Just sex. However, a simple no would have been sufficient." He glanced up at the sky. "Are you still thinking of finding your friend?"

"Of course."

"You won't do it before dark on foot. Climb up behind me and I'll take you to them." Rising from the rock, he walked to his horse, stepped into the saddle, then held out his hand to her.

"Why should I trust you?"

"I can't think of a single good reason."

"Nor I," she said, with a smile.

Returning the arrow to its quiver, she took his hand. Decado slipped his foot from the stirrup, and Askari levered herself up to sit behind him.

The meeting with Gilden had depressed Stavut considerably. He liked the man and, more, respected him. Gilden was brave, honorable, and good-hearted. Yet the hatred in his face when he talked of the "vermin" had shocked Stavut. As he walked on, the ground rising higher and higher toward the northeast, he kept thinking of Gilden's savage reaction. It wouldn't have surprised Stavut a few weeks ago, he realized. In fact he, too, had felt the same about Jiamads. But then he had never known any. Now he knew there was no evil in them. They were savage in the same way as the wolf or the lion. They killed to eat. There was no hatred in them, no malice.

Last night he had witnessed a fight develop between Shakul and another huge beast. It had begun so swiftly Stavut had no chance to intervene. The two beasts had rushed at one another, snarling and biting. At first Shakul had been pushed back, but then he struck his opponent with a ferocious right hand. The beast staggered. Shakul leapt upon him, bearing him to the ground. He hit him twice more, open-handed, the sound sickening. The beast slumped. Then Shakul rose above him, standing very still. The dazed Jiamad slowly moved to all fours, then nuzzled the ground at Shakul's feet. The other members of the pack gathered around. Then each began to stamp his feet on the ground.

Shakul walked back to where Stavut stood, mesmerized by the scene. "What was that about?" he asked.

"Place," said Shakul. "Place in pack."

"I don't understand."

"Shakul's place."

"He wanted to take your place as . . . what?"

Shakul's huge hand touched Stavut's shoulder. "Bloodshirt," he said. Then he tapped his own chest. "Shakul." He pointed to the beast he had fought. "Broga." Then at Grava, who was sitting close by.

Stavut understood then. The pack order was decided by battle. This left him suddenly uneasy. "Does this mean you and I will fight one day?"

Shakul's shoulders heaved as he made the staccato growl Stavut understood to be laughter. Then he walked away.

Throughout the morning the pack pushed on. Stavut had no idea how fast the army of the Eternal marched, nor indeed whether they had anything to fear from them. It was likely they would merely pass through the land. However, Stavut had no wish to depend on luck. His view was to put as much distance between the army and the pack as possible. Unfortunately this meant climbing higher into the mountains. The Jiamads were taking turns now hauling his wagon, but the trail was becoming more and more difficult. It was also narrowing. To Stavut's right there was a fearsome drop. As he walked, he stayed close to the cliff wall on his left. Shakul came alongside him, staring at him.

"Bloodshirt sick?"

"No. Frightened. I hate heights," he said, pointing to the edge.

Shakul walked to the lip of the precipice and stared over and down. "Long way," he said.

Then he marched on, scouting the path ahead. Grava came alongside, his long tongue lolling from his mouth. He said something utterly unintelligible. Stavut nodded. "Good point," he replied. Grava nodded and spoke again. Happily, he wandered off before Stavut was forced to admit he didn't understand a word.

The pack moved on. Up ahead came the sound of falling rocks. Stavut raised his arm and halted the pack. Grava ran forward to check for danger. When he returned Stavut could see he was agitated. He ran to Stavut and began to speak. "Slow down," said Stavut. "I can't understand you."

Grava did so, but Stavut could only make out one word. *Shakul.*

He followed Grava back to where a rockslide had struck the trail. A section of the ledge had fallen away. Grava moved to the edge and pointed down. Stavut inched his way forward, then dropped to hands and knees. His stomach churning, he peered over. Some thirty feet down Shakul was clinging to an overhang, unable to lever himself up. Stavut swore—then remembered there was rope in the wagon. Easing back from the ledge, he ran to where three Jiamads were heroically pulling the wagon up the slope. Climbing to the driver's seat, he applied the brake, then clambered over to the back, searching through the packages, pushing aside small barrels and bales of cloth. At last he came up with the rope. Looping it over his shoulder, he ran back to where Grava and some others were gathered. Calling one of the most powerful of the Jiamads to him, he looped one end of the rope over the beast's shoulder. "I am going to throw the rope to Shakul," he said. "When he grabs it you pull him up. Understand?"

"Pull up," answered the beast. Unlooping the rope, he walked to the edge.

"I am throwing a rope down," he shouted to Shakul.

Grava came alongside, shaking his head.

"What?" asked Stavut. Grava lifted his hands in a clawing motion and spoke, very slowly. Stavut made him repeat his words several times before he understood. Shakul could not let go. Stavut moved to the cliff edge once more, and understood what Grava was trying to say. Shakul's arms were fully extended, his weight enormous. If he tried to let go and reach for the rope he would fall. "Can you climb down to him?" Stavut asked Grava. The beast stepped back, shaking his head.

Stavut swore again, then took hold of the end of the rope and made a large loop. Then he threw the rope over the edge. Glancing back at the beast holding the other end of the rope, he said: "When I shout, you pull up."

"Pull up," said the beast.

"Brilliant!" muttered Stavut.

Taking a deep breath, he took hold of the dangling rope and lowered himself over the edge. "Do not look down," he told himself. "That's what Askari says." Carefully he lowered himself down the rock face. Footholds were plentiful, and he had little difficulty reaching Shakul. As he climbed down alongside the Jiamad, he saw fear in Shakul's eyes.

"Long way!" he gasped.

"I am going to loop the rope around your waist. You hang on!"

This was the moment that Stavut realized he was going to have to look down. His stomach tightened. Slowly he moved his head, his eyes fastened to the black fur on Shakul's massive legs and dangling feet. Carefully Stavut lowered himself farther, lifting the loop over the legs and up toward the hips. A cold wind blew across the cliff face. Small stones tumbled down. Shakul's left hand slipped, then scrabbled to hold on. Stavut pulled the rope up over the beast's hips, then shouted: "Pull up!"

Nothing happened.

Only then did he realize he had given the rope to Broga—the beast Shakul had fought the night before. *You idiot,* he told himself. The one creature in the pack who wanted Shakul displaced now had Shakul's life in his hands. "Pull the rope!" Stavut shouted again.

Shakul fell from the ledge, dislodging Stavut.

The rope went tight. Shakul's arm shot out, talons slicing through Stavut's shirt and raking the skin beneath. Then they both hung over the dizzying drop. The shirt began to tear.

Grava's head peered over the edge. "Pull us up!" yelled Stavut.

The rope tightened once more, and slowly, inch by inch, they were hauled up the cliff face. Once above the overhang Shakul managed to gain footholds. As they neared the top Grava reached over and grabbed Stavut, pulling him to safety. Stavut moved away from the cliff edge, then turned toward Broga. There was blood on his hands where the rope had burned him. Yet he had not let go.

"Good work," said Stavut, patting the beast on the arm.

"Broga pull up," he said, dropping the rope and licking his bloodied palms. Stavut wandered away. His legs were trembling now, and he felt sick. To take his mind off vomiting he gathered up the rope, looping it over his forearm. Only when he was almost done did he realize that one end was still tied around Shakul. Walking to the beast, he undid the knot.

"An adventure, eh?" said Stavut.

"We move now," said Shakul. "Find place. Eat. Sleep."

"No, no," said Stavut, "you are embarrassing me with such a show of gratitude."

Shakul stared at him, nonplussed. "Again?" he said.

Stavut grinned. "It doesn't matter. Let's find a place to rest, eat, and sleep."

Shakul nodded, then ambled off once more down the trail.

As Stavut sat quietly by the small campfire, he kept glancing at Shakul. It seemed to him that the beast had been behaving strangely since the incident on the cliff. He had snarled and snapped at the others, and was now squatting alone beneath an overhanging tree branch. A group of the others, led by Grava, had left for a hunt. The rest, including the massive Braga, were sleeping. Stavut was also tired, but the stinging pain from the deep scratches where Shakul's talons had pierced his shirt was keeping him awake. Rising from the fire, he walked over to Shakul. The beast's golden eyes looked up at him. Stavut sat down.

"What is wrong, my friend? Are you hurt?"

"Not hurt. Shakul sleep now." The beast closed his eyes.

"I know you are not sleeping," said Stavut.

Shakul snarled suddenly, causing Stavut to jerk back. Then the beast blinked, and his shoulders sagged. He glanced at the others. Some of them, hearing the snarl, had stirred and were watching the pair. Shakul settled back. Realizing there was no drama, the others returned to sleep. Stavut sighed. "Talk to me, my friend. What is troubling you?"

"Big fear," said Shakul, his voice low. "Long way down."

And Stavut knew what the problem was. Shakul was both embarrassed and shocked by his fear. The great beast had not experienced such terror before, and this had left him uneasy.

"Nothing wrong with fear," said Stavut, at last. "It is how we deal with it that counts. A friend taught me that." He laughed. "You and he wouldn't get on. Though in fact I think you are quite similar."

"Shakul was coward," said the beast, his head sagging.

"Nonsense! Every living thing knows fear. Listen to me, Shakul. When you were hanging on that rock face you were frightened. And so you should have been. It was a long way to fall. But when I was dislodged you caught me. You saved me. Shakul is not a coward. Shakul is brave. I know this. Bloodshirt knows this."

Shakul's head began to twist from side to side, his body rocking. Stavut waited. "Big fear," he said, at last.

"Me, too. But we survived, you and I. We live. We will hunt and we will eat."

"Bloodshirt came for Shakul," said the beast.

"Yes. We are friends."

"Friends?"

"We are pack," corrected Stavut, with a grin. "I am sure you would have done the same for me."

"No," said Shakul. "Long way down."

"Whatever! Are you feeling better now?"

Shakul's head came up. His nostrils quivered. "Horse. Skins," he said.

"Soldiers?"

"Same Skin Bloodshirt meet." He sniffed the air again. "One other. Female."

"Gilden? The soldier with the bow?"

"Other Skin."

Stavut remembered the dark-eyed young man, the one wearing swords like Skilgannon's. Stavut hadn't liked him much. Rising to his feet, he said: "Where are they coming from?"

Shakul pointed to the south. Stavut strolled across the campsite and waited. He heard a horse whinny in fear. Then the rider came into sight through the trees. The horse was skittish as the smell of the beasts came to it, but the rider was skilled and kept it calm. A dark-haired woman jumped down from behind the rider. Stavut's heart leapt. It was Askari.

He ran forward to greet her, smiling broadly. "Oh, it is good to see you," he said.

"What are you doing here?" she asked him, gazing around at the beasts, who had now awoken and were staring balefully at the newcomers.

"Long story—and a sad one."

The rider dismounted. Holding to the reins of his horse, he walked forward. "I shall leave you now, beauty," he said to Askari. "Can we part as friends?"

"We are not enemies, Decado," she said.

"Good." He delved into the pocket of his jerkin and came up with a small golden locket on a thin chain. "Take this," he said, extending his hand.

"I don't want gifts."

"It is a peace token. No more than that."

Askari took it, and Stavut saw that there was a small, blue gem at the center of the locket. It was a valuable piece, though there was no reason that a country girl like Askari would know that. He felt anger welling, but kept his expression calm.

"It is very pretty. Thank you, Decado. Where will you go?"

"I shall find Skilgannon. I'll tell him where you are."

"You are going to join us?"

"Why not? In a way he and I are kin." With that the swordsman, without a glance at Stavut, stepped smoothly into the saddle and rode from the woods.

"I do not like that man," said Stavut.

"Never mind him," said Askari. "What has happened to you, Stavi?"

Askari looked at her friend, trying to see some sign of the merchant she had known. His dapper red clothes were stained with blood and dirt, his dark hair matted and filthy, his face, now unshaven, smeared with dried blood. She looked into his eyes and saw little there that she remembered.

"Happened to me? So much, Askari," he told her.

"And my people?"

Stavut sighed, and his shoulders sagged. "All dead. Killed by soldiers of the Eternal. We hunted them down, though. None survived."

"Walk with me, Stavi," she said, setting off toward a rippling stream close by. He followed her, and as he walked he told her of the arrival of Shakul and the others, and how he had taught them to hunt. Then of the villagers fleeing back toward the settlement. Askari listened, but said little. She followed the line of the stream until she reached higher ground, where the water bubbled over white rocks, tumbling down into a broader pool. Then she turned to him. "I'd like to see you without the blood and dirt," she said. "Come, let us see if the water is deep enough to swim in." Laying her bow and quiver on the bank, she stripped off her green, hooded shirt, and her leggings. Stavut stood, watching her.

"I cannot swim," he said.

"Then you can wade." Naked she stood before him. "Stavi, the stench of you could fell an ox. Now get out of those clothes." He stood very still, but did not resist as she stepped in closer and lifted his bloodied tunic over his head. Then she saw the deep scratches. "Did one of the beasts do that to you?"

"To stop me falling from a cliff. Saved my life."

"You have other clothes in the wagon, yes?"

"Yes."

"Then let us discard these."

A huge beast pushed its way through the undergrowth and stood staring at Askari. She remembered it as one of the creatures that had attacked her in the cave, the one Skilgannon had spoken to. It was around eight feet tall, and its golden eyes were staring at her coldly.

"This is my friend Shakul," said Stavut, walking to the beast and slapping him on the shoulder. "Shakul, this is my friend Askari." Then he paused. "Oh, I expect you remember her."

Shakul said nothing. "Ah, I can see you are going to get along famously," said Stavut. "I sense a real bonding taking place."

Askari approached the beast, her heart hammering. "I have told him he should bathe," she said, trying to keep her voice light. "But he won't get into the water." The beast's huge head began to sway back and forth. Then he suddenly grabbed Stavut and hurled him into the pool. He landed with a huge splash and came up spluttering. The beast let out a series of short, staccato grunts, then turned away and wandered back through the undergrowth. "Well, thank you for that," Stavut called from the pool. "It is freezing in here."

Askari ran down to the pool's edge and waded in. He was right. The water was deliciously cold. Reaching Stavut, she told him to duck under the surface once more. Then she rubbed at his hair until the dirt and the blood were gone. Finally she looked once more into his face. The sun was setting, turning the mountains to gold. "Are you still in there, Stavi?" she asked him, her voice soft, her hands cupping his face.

"I am here. A little wiser, maybe. A little sadder. But I am here."

Leaning in, she kissed him on the lips and drew him into an embrace. "That is the kiss I owe you," she said.

"There is not enough fletching thread in the world to merit that," he told her.

She laughed and kissed him again. Stepping back, he gave a broad smile and was Stavi again. Then he looked past her and laughed aloud. "Can no one get any privacy here?" he called. Askari turned. The sound of the rushing water had masked the approach of the pack, and she saw the pool was ringed by beasts, all staring at them. "Go away, you rascals!" said Stavut, still smiling. The Jiamads turned at once and vanished into the woods.

Wading back to her, he opened his arms. "I think that is enough for now," she told him. "Come, let us find you some fresh clothes."

A little later, with Stavut in clean leggings and yet another crimson tunic shirt, they sat by the fire. Askari, with a blanket around her shoulders as she waited for her clothes to dry, gazed around the campsite. Some of the beasts were feeding; others stretched out, sleeping. The sun was down now, the light fading fast. Stavut told her of his climb down to rescue Shakul, and how the beast had been embarrassed by fear.

"You talk of him as a friend, Stavi," she said, her voice low, "but they do not understand friendship. Landis Khan spoke of the beasts often. He was a man who liked to talk. He said that the merging of beast and man eliminated the best of both species. You lead because you offer them something. There is no affection there, no loyalty. No understanding of genuine love. No compassion."

"You are wrong. I know this. There is, in them, something

far greater than anything we have allowed to develop. Put aside your prejudices for a moment. Shakul came after us because he was curious. When you told him I would not enter the pool he threw me in. That sound you heard from him was laughter. You see? It was a practical joke. And when Shakul was hanging from the cliff face, the beast that pulled him up was one he had fought the night before to reestablish his place in the pack."

"That is what I am saying," she insisted. "They fight for place and position. No loyalty."

"Men do the same. But men will assassinate rivals, or plot to see them removed from power. When Shakul fought Braga there was no blood spilled. There is no animosity between them. Rank is merely decided on strength, because the pack leadership needs to be strong. These creatures have never been allowed to develop. They have been subject to iron discipline, and used only for war and death. Out here they are forming bonds and learning to cooperate. They no longer need me, Askari. If what you said was true then Shakul would just kill me and lead the pack himself."

Askari was unconvinced. Stavut added wood to the fire. "You are happy among them, aren't you?" she said.

He grinned at her. "Yes, I am. I couldn't begin to tell you why. I am watching them grow. I am seeing their joy at running free. It is a wonderful feeling."

Askari relaxed. This *was* the Stavut she knew, an intuitive man, generous and sweet natured. She gazed at him fondly, then realized it was more than fondness she felt for him. The kiss had lingered long in her mind. He saw her looking at him. "What are you thinking?" he asked her.

"Nothing," she said.

Stavut laughed then. "When a woman says that, a man knows he is in deep trouble."

Her eyes narrowed. "I forgot that you have known many women."

"Yes, I have," he said. "But I would not trade that kiss in the pool for all the wealth in the world."

She relaxed. "Sometimes you do know how to say the right words."

"Would you like to take another walk with me?" he asked her.

"I think that I would."

Rising, he held out his hand, and together they walked into the woods.

Memnon had seen death before. Many times. Yet the feeling he had now was most odd. His spirit floated above the narrow bed, and he stared down at the dying child. The boy's thin face was drawn and pale, his skin glistening, his breathing ragged. His mother was at the bedside holding the child's hand. Tears were streaming down her face. Behind her, his hand on her shoulder, stood the man who believed himself to be the father. His face was set, his eyes red rimmed. Memnon saw the boy shudder, then all movement ceased. The mother cried out and threw herself across the dead child.

"There, there, my love," said the father. "There, there."

The mother's wailing grated on Memnon's nerves, irritating him. Also he could no longer see the boy's face. He floated to the right. Now he could see the child in profile. It was a sad face, a lost face.

His face.

That is all the feeling is, thought Memnon. *A remembrance of a childhood that lacked warmth.* It was not the death he mourned. And yet the strange feeling remained, a hollow emptiness. *It is a regret,* he told himself. *That is all. An experiment failed.* The mother took the boy's face in her hands and kissed both his cheeks. Memnon could not remember anyone ever kissing his cheek. Nor, had he died as this child had, would anyone have wept over him. But then he had chosen these parents well. The man was a merchant, dealing in linen and cotton. The woman was a seamstress, and well known for her gentle nature. They lived by the sea on the Lentrian coast. Memnon had thought the air would be good for a growing boy.

He had grown now, as far as he would ever grow. An immense sadness touched him then.

An experiment failed, he told himself again.

The father walked across the room and picked up a pottery jug. "No more of these useless potions," he said. "No more." In a sudden fit of anger he hurled the jar across the room. It smashed against the far wall, scattering seeds and dried leaves, which settled on the rug beneath the window. Light shone on them.

Memnon floated closer and stared down at the seeds, recognizing them. Sadness disappeared.

His spirit fled back to the flesh, and he surged upright. Rising too fast, he staggered and almost fell. Usually he lay still for a while, until his body and spirit came into balance. He made it to the door of his room and stood for a moment, holding to the frame and drawing in deep breaths. Then he opened the door and walked down to Landis Khan's laboratory. A heavy weariness lay upon him. The last few days had been tiring, especially the long ride into the high country, where he had summoned several of his Shadows to meet him. Memnon did not like to be far from the comforts of a good palace.

In the laboratory his two assistants were still working. Patiacus looked up from the notes he was studying, then rose and bowed. Redheaded Oranin scrambled to his feet, dropping his notes. He, too, bowed deeply.

"Have you discovered anything?" asked Memnon, his voice soft and friendly.

"Much of general interest, Lord," replied Patiacus, "but nothing as yet of a nature specific to your request."

"In time it will become clear." He turned to Oranin. "It is getting late, young man. Go and have some food. Get some rest. It will be a long day tomorrow."

"Thank you, Lord." The young apprentice bowed again, then backed away to the door.

After he had gone Memnon walked to Patiacus and patted him on the shoulder. "Sit down, my friend. Let us talk."

"Yes, Lord. What did you wish to talk about?"

"The child died tonight. It was very touching. Tears and wailing."

"I am sorry, my lord."

"Yes. As am I." Memnon moved behind him, his hands resting on the man's shoulders. "How is your knowledge of herbs these days? Do you maintain your previous interest?"

"I have little time for such matters now, Lord."

"Was it interesting as an apothecary?"

"It was interesting enough, Lord. Not as fascinating as the work I do now."

"I would imagine not." Removing one hand from Patiacus's shoulder, he drew a small needle dagger from a sheath hidden beneath his shirt. Reaching around, he held the blade in front of Patiacus's face. The man jerked back. "If this blade has been smeared with the resin obtained from Abalsin stem, Swaggerroot, and Corin seed, what would the effect be, were I to cut you with it?"

"Death, my lord."

"Instant death?"

"Convulsions, swelling of the glands in the throat and the groin. Excruciating pain. Then death."

"Very good," said Memnon, patting the man's shoulder. "Excellent. You have a fine mind, Patiacus. I have always respected that. Good memory, and excellent attention to detail."

"You are frightening me, my lord."

Memnon glanced down. Sweat was glistening on the man's bald head. "Oh, do not fear, Patiacus. The blade does not carry the poisons I described. Though it is very sharp." Lifting the knife, he made a tiny cut in the skin of the cranium. Patiacus cried out and struggled to rise. Memnon's hand came down firmly on his shoulder, pushing him back in his chair. "We do need to talk, you and I." Sheathing the blade, he moved past Patiacus and pulled up a chair.

The assistant was sweating freely now. "About what, Lord?"

"About service, Patiacus. Loyalty, if you will. Whom do you serve?"

"You, my lord."

"True, but not accurate. Do you not also serve the Eternal?"

"Yes, of course. But you are my master."

"I am indeed. I am also infinitely more clever than you. I say that not with any undue pride, merely stating a fact. Yet despite my greater intelligence I have been most foolish. The child who died, where did he live?"

"On the coast. Lentria, I believe you said."

"Yes, I did. With whom did he live?"

"A merchant, you said. Cotton."

"Exactly. Did you mention this fact to anyone else?"

"Of course not, Lord."

"Ah, a lie, Patiacus. Your eyes flickered as you spoke it. So, whom did you tell?"

"I did not lie," answered Patiacus, straining to hold to Memnon's gaze.

"This time your eyes widened, showing the effort you were making to keep them still. My dear Patiacus, you are not doing very well. How are you feeling?"

"I am . . . feeling very warm, Lord. And still frightened."

"Can you move your legs?"

Patiacus glanced down and jerked once more. "You have poisoned me!"

"Yes, but it is not deadly. It is Shadow venom. Not in its pure form. It is diluted. The paralysis will be that much slower. Also—and more importantly—you will be able to talk. You will not be able to move, but you will feel. There should be a tingling in your fingers now. It is the sign that your arms and upper body are becoming immobile."

"I don't know what you want from me."

"There is a mixture of seed and leaf that you used for me in the past, to kill those who sought me harm. You recall. The Slow Killer. The mixture could be boiled and administered within a stew, or even placed in a sweetened tisane, you said. It was almost tasteless, save for the trace of tannin. Death could take weeks, sometimes months, depending on the amount administered."

Patiacus's arm flopped out as he struggled to rise. His body spasmed, and he slid from the chair. Memnon grabbed the collar of his tunic and hauled him out from beneath the table. "Imagine my surprise, Patiacus, when I saw that the boy's parents had been administering the same seed and leaf to their son, thinking it to be medicine."

"Not I, Lord. Please!" begged Patiacus, his words slurring.

"Not you? Let me think. Someone wanted to kill a merchant's son in a small town on the coast. In order to do this they decided to prepare the Slow Killer and convince the parents it was a potion for good health. Does that not seem to you to be overly complicated, Patiacus? If someone wanted the boy dead, they could just as easily have stabbed him. The question then becomes, why did they not? The answer is fairly obvious. They wanted the death to appear natural. The lumps under his skin would be thought to be cancerous. Is the merchant so feared that his vengeance might be the reason for the complexity? I think not. And then, my dear friend, there are the others. All my Reborns have died in the same way. Can you account for that?"

"I am your loyal servant. I swear it!"

"You are beginning to irritate me. Let us move to the specifics of your predicament. I am going to kill you, Patiacus. There is no question of a change of heart. I am going to spend the entire night causing you the most dreadful pain. I shall use flame, a metal file, a hammer, and any other item that comes to mind. I shall rend your flesh and smash your bones. Is that clear?"

"Oh please, Lord. I beg you!"

"Begging is not going to change anything. Tell me why you have been killing my children, and I might kill you swiftly."

"You are making a mistake!"

Memnon smiled. "I am glad you said that. For an awful moment I thought you were going to tell me right away. You just lie there, Patiacus, while I fetch what I need."

Seventeen

Gilden eased his mount up a steep slope, halting just below the crest of the hill. He had no wish to be skylined and seen, so he dismounted and removed his helm before creeping up to the crest. When he looked over, his breath caught in his throat. Stavut had been right.

On the plain below were thousands of marching men and columns of horses. Bringing up the rear were two regiments of Jiamads. The army stretched all the way back to a distant line of hills. Gilden hunkered down and tried to gauge the numbers of the enemy. He estimated there to be at least twenty thousand fighting men, plus the two thousand Jiamads. In the vanguard he saw the riders of the Eternal Guard, in their armor of black and silver. Like the Legend riders they wore elaborate chain-mail hauberks, coifs, and gorgets. They also carried sabers and lances, and round bucklers on their left forearms. The thousand men of the Eternal Guard were the elite of the Eternal's army, handpicked for their valor in other regiments.

Then he saw the Eternal herself, dressed in armor of bright silver, riding a white horse. Narrowing his eyes, he sought to focus more sharply. It seemed the horse had protruding horns on its brow. Gilden eased himself back from the slope and mounted his own chestnut. Swinging the beast, he set off slowly toward the north. He would have preferred to ride at speed, but was wary of his horse throwing up dust on the dry hillside. When he reached lower ground, he eased the beast into a run.

There was no doubt now that the last battle was approaching. Agrias would be hard pressed to hold off such a force. Especially without the Legend riders. Alahir had sent Bagalan back to gather the other two hundred fighting men, ordering him to rendezvous in three days at the small town of Corisle, eighty miles north. The town's income derived from its situation close to the merging of three rivers. Due north, along the ancient canal, lay the Rostrias; west was a narrow, silt-heavy waterway that once flowed freely down to Siccus on the coast. East was another ancient canal that had been created in the far past to ferry supplies to the copper mines in the old Sathuli territories. From Corisle the plan was to hire barges that would carry the riders to the Rostrias, and along the river, before disembarking toward the site of the mysterious temple Skilgannon spoke of. The journey—if all went smoothly—would take many days.

Gilden was unhappy with the plan. More so now that he had seen the Eternal's army. The battles would rage into Drenai land, and, as far as Gilden was concerned, *that* was where the Legend riders should meet the foe. Others agreed with him, and the conversation became heated.

Then Skilgannon spoke: "I understand your concerns," he told them. "I also understand the desire to protect the homeland. It does you credit. We could ride for Siccus, and fight, seeking to hold off the Eternal. We might even succeed in turning back one of her armies. One of her *ten* armies. However, we would ultimately fail, because her resources are so much greater than those of your people. She can summon thousands of Jiamads, scores of regiments. If Ustarte's prophecy is true, then we can win the war *only* by destroying the source of all her power. It is my belief the answer lies at the temple."

"A temple you say is no longer there," put in Gilden.

"That is so," accepted Skilgannon. "However, since the artifacts of the elders still generate magic, the power source must still be operating. The first time I visited the temple it could not be seen. I had already ridden past it many times in my search. A ward spell had been placed over it, which fooled the eye. I cannot say to you, Gilden, that we will succeed. This may be a fool's errand. But I trust Ustarte. I believe it was she who spoke to Alahir, leading him to the Armor. It was she who urged him to follow me."

"A pox on prophecies," said Gilden. "Why could she not just have told us what to do?"

"Not an easy question to answer," said Skilgannon. "When I spoke with her she talked of there being many futures. Each decision we make changes those futures. We could go to the temple. We could travel to Siccus. We could stay here and do nothing. Some could go, some could stay. Each decision would result in scores of possible outcomes. Nothing is certain. My guess is that Ustarte saw a great number of possibilities for us. She dared not push us in any one direction, for fear of inadvertently sending us on the wrong path. The decisions are ours to make, for that is our destiny."

"Well, *that* just shot over my head like an arrow," said Gilden. "Perhaps there is a future where the Eternal vanishes in a puff of dust." The comment eased the tension, and the men chuckled.

"The key," said Skilgannon as the laughter died down, "has to be in the source of the magic. Destroy that and there will be no more Jiamads, no more Reborns, and—ultimately—no more Eternal. This will become once more a world of men. Think of it this way. If a bear is savaging your cattle, you do not wait in the pastures for its next attack. You seek out its lair and you kill it. The temple is the lair. That is where the war will be won."

"As much as I appreciate discussion," said Alahir, "I know of only one certain fact. The voice told me to follow where Skilgannon led. She said the hope of the Drenai rested on us. I will ride to the temple. Alone if need be."

"Damn it, man, you won't be alone!" said Gilden. "It hurts me you would say such a thing. We're all with you. I'd ride into a lake of hellfire if you ordered it."

Bagalan laughed. "You didn't follow him into the pleasure

den last week. Left him alone, I recall, with a goat-faced whore."

"Ah well," replied Gilden, smiling broadly, "he wasn't the earl of Bronze then."

The conversation had moved on to more prosaic matters, like provisions for the journey, and how they would pay for passage on the long barges that ferried supplies and men along the coast. The discussion was interrupted by the arrival of a scout, followed by a dark-haired swordsman on a tall chestnut.

"This man claims to know Skilgannon," said the scout.

Skilgannon rose. "What do you want here, Decado?"

At the mention of the name a sudden silence fell over the warriors. Every rider had heard of the famous killer.

"I came to join you, kinsman, and to tell you that Askari is currently in the camp of the Beastmaster. She called him Stavi, I recall."

"What are you talking about?" asked Skilgannon.

"Her friend. A merchant, I think she said."

"Stavut is with beasts?"

Gilden stepped in and explained what had passed between him and Stavut the previous day.

"How many Jiamads does he have?" asked Skilgannon.

"I'd say around fifty," Decado told him.

"They could be useful."

"We don't need animals," said Gilden. "We are warriors. We fight as men."

Skilgannon shook his head. "We don't yet know what we need. Successful war involves using all the weapons at one's disposal. That is how we came to train horses, Gilden. We saw they would make us faster and more mobile. The Eternal will have sent a force to stop us. You think they will all be men? These are strange days. The Armor of Bronze has returned, and the ax of Druss the Legend. I am here—and I died a thousand years ago. Now a gentle merchant has somehow gathered an army of beasts, who could aid us in any battle. If I can use them, I will."

Skilgannon had walked to the white stallion and saddled it. Then he mounted and rode back to Decado. "Where are they?" he asked.

"About ten miles due east and a little north. You'll see a ridge, and just beyond it a line of trees. They are camped there."

Skilgannon swung to Alahir. "Head toward the town you spoke of. I will catch up with you. The Eternal's army is marching through the mountains, so make sure you keep scouts ahead."

Without another word he rode from the campsite. Decado dismounted. "A little food would not go amiss," he said. No one spoke to him, though at the orders of Alahir a warrior fetched him a bowl of broth and some dried beef. Decado took it a little way from the others and sat down to eat.

"They say he is a maniac," Gilden told Alahir, keeping his voice low.

"A maniac with excellent hearing," called out Decado. "Move farther away if you wish to discuss my merits. Better still, wait for a few moments, for I shall be asleep by then." Finishing his meal, the swordsman stretched out on the ground.

Gilden and Alahir walked to the far side of the campsite. "I have heard the tales of him," said Alahir. "Cold and deadly, and utterly without mercy. However, he is a swordsman and a warrior. He could be useful."

"Beasts and madmen. Not very glorious, Alahir, my friend."

"I am not interested in glory," said Alahir, with a sigh. "I just want the Drenai to survive."

Gilden recalled the conversation as he rode. There had been a weight of sadness in Alahir's voice, and more than a little fear. As a Legend rider Alahir was expected to fight for his homeland.

As the earl of Bronze he would be expected to perform miracles.

*   *   *

As he rode away into the night Skilgannon's mood was somber. The young Legend riders were fine men; brave. Bright eyed and eager to fight for their homeland. Such was always the way with the young. They had looked at him and seen someone of their own age, believing him to be filled with the same aspirations and ambitions. For the first time Skilgannon felt like a fraud. He wondered then about what was lost and what—if anything—was gained by the passage of the years. He was an old man in a young man's body, and his thoughts of the world were sullied by his deeds in a previous lifetime. He had promised the Legend riders that if they won, it would once more become a world of men. He had made it sound as if this were something to be desired; some noble cause worth dying for.

He rode now under stars a thousand years older than when first he had seen them. And what had changed in this wondrous world of men? The strong still sought to dominate the weak. Armies still raged across the lands, killing and burning. *What will truly change if we win?* he wondered. The wheel of good and evil would spin on. Sometimes good would triumph for a while, but then the wheel would spin again.

The cold reality was that, even if he destroyed the source of magic, one day another source would be found.

By that token, he told himself, a man would never seek to counter the evils in his day. He would shrug and talk of spinning wheels. Perhaps, he thought, the wisdom of the old inevitably leads to a philosophy of despair and acquiescence.

Pushing such thoughts from his mind, he rode on, enjoying the power and the grace of the stallion. Moonlight gleamed on its bright flanks. Not the best horse on which to pass unnoticed, he thought, with a grin. His spirits lifted. In life a man could do no more than fight for what he believed to be right, without thought to future generations or the ultimate folly of man's dreams.

His thoughts swung to Decado. The man was a disturbing

presence, and Skilgannon was unsure about trusting him. His story about being hunted by the Eternal might have been false. He could have been sent as a spy, or as an assassin. Skilgannon did not want to have to fight him. With two swordsmen of such skill it was unlikely that even the victor would escape unscathed.

Ahead he saw the ridge Decado had mentioned, and headed the stallion toward the trees.

As he rode up the hill a huge Jiamad came into sight. It stood and watched him. Controlling the urge to draw his swords, he guided the stallion closer. The horse was nervous, and began to stamp its foot and edge sideways. "Steady now, Greatheart," said Skilgannon.

As he came closer he recognized the Jiamad as the leader of the attack in the cave.

"Well met, Shakul," he said. "How are you faring?"

"Run free. It is good."

"I have come to see my friend, Stavut."

"Bloodshirt with woman."

Skilgannon dismounted. It was hard to tell from the growling delivery whether Shakul was happy or irritated by Askari's arrival.

"Am I welcome in your camp?"

Shakul did not respond. Instead he turned and lumbered back into the trees. Holding firm to the reins of his mount, Skilgannon walked after him. Some fifty paces beyond the tree line he came to the camp. Many of the Jiamads were asleep. Others were sitting close to one another, speaking in low grunts.

Stavut was sitting by a campfire, Askari beside him. Skilgannon tethered his horse and walked across to them. He noted that Stavut was holding Askari's hand, and surmised that their meeting had been a joyful one. A touch of jealousy stung him. Moving to the fire, he sat down. "Good to see you, Stavut."

The young merchant looked at him without warmth. "I'll not take my lads into your battles," he said. "Know *that* straight from the outset."

"What he meant," said Askari dryly, "was that it is good to see you, too."

Stavut blushed. "It *is* good to see you," he said. "I'm sorry if I sounded brusque, but Askari has been telling me of your plan to find the temple. I don't want my lads put in any danger."

Skilgannon nodded. "Can we take this one step at a time? When last I saw you it was in the company of Kinyon and the villagers. Now you are being called the Beastmaster. I would be fascinated to know how all this occurred."

Stavut sighed and launched into his tale. It was told starkly and simply. Skilgannon listened, then leaned back. "I am sorry about the villagers," he said. "But it was their choice to return home. You have nothing to blame yourself for."

"Nice of you to say so, but I *do* blame myself. I should have realized they were fearful of the lads—and of me. I should have taken steps to put them at their ease."

"I cannot fault you for that," said Skilgannon. "We all carry our guilts. So what will you do now?"

"I . . . we . . . haven't made any plans."

"Is that true?" Skilgannon asked Askari. "No plans?"

"I shall go with you to the temple, as I said," she told him.

"What?" burst out Stavut. "You can't!"

"I can't?" she responded, her voice cold, her expression icy.

Stavut looked crestfallen. "What I meant . . . oh never mind! Why do you have to go?"

"Because her life is at risk as long as the Eternal holds power. She is a Reborn, Stavut, like me. Askari was created from the bones of the Eternal herself. That is *why* she is the Eternal. She steals fresh bodies as her own decays. My purpose in this world is to stop her. To end the magic. If I succeed then Askari is safe from her."

"Then of course I'll come with you. I'll leave the lads with Shakul. He can lead the pack. They can be safe here. There is plenty of game, and no reason for soldiers to hunt them."

From all around them the beasts began to move forward, squatting in a circle around the fire. Shakul leaned in toward Stavut. "Bloodshirt leave?" he asked.

"You will be pack leader, Shakul. I have to go."

"We are pack," Shakul reminded him.

"Yes, we are. But where I go there will be danger, and fighting, and death. This is my fight. Mine, Askari's, Skilgannon's. It is a fight for . . . for Skins. It is not your fight. I don't want to see any of you hurt. You understand?"

"Not hurt," said Shakul, his great head swaying. Easing his huge bulk forward, he peered at Skilgannon.

"Not take Bloodshirt," he said.

"He is not taking me," said Stavut. "I am going willingly. I don't want to leave you lads. Truly I don't. You are the best friends I ever had. I am fond of all of you. But I must go."

Shakul stared hard at Skilgannon. "Big fight?" he said.

"I think so, Shakul."

The beast lifted his head and sniffed the air. "Many soldiers. Jems. Horses."

"There is an army moving south of us," said Skilgannon.

Shakul heaved himself upright and moved back from the fire. The other beasts crowded around him. Skilgannon looked at Stavut. "What are they doing?"

"Making a decision," said Stavut, "and—if it is what I think it is—I am going to hate you, Skilgannon."

They sat in silence for a while as the beasts continued to speak in low, incomprehensible grunts. Then Shakul came back to the fire. All the other Jiamads formed a circle around the humans.

"Make choice," said Shakul. "Go with Bloodshirt."

Stavut's head dropped. "I don't want you to be in danger," he said.

"We are pack!" said Shakul, stamping his foot. One by one the others joined in, and Skilgannon felt the earth tremble beneath him.

It was close to midnight, and Skilgannon was sitting with his back against a tree. He had tried to sleep, but Stavut's words continued to haunt him. It was obvious that he felt strongly about the Jiamads—his lads—but it was not just that affection that concerned Skilgannon. It was the deceit he had perpetrated on the merchant. In making their decision to travel with Stavut, the Jiamads had surprised the swordsman. They had shown loyalty and friendship. Stavut had talked of watching them develop, forming bonds, playing practical jokes, laughing. This was a far cry from the savage, soulless creatures Skilgannon had believed them to be. He thought then of Longbear. According to Charis, Gamal had sent him away, but he had charged back and died to defend the humans.

This made the deceit even harder to bear.

Skilgannon had talked of ending the magic, and thereby the reign of the Eternal. What he had not said was that, in doing so, it was possible that the Jiamads, melded by magic, would die in their thousands. This meant that Shakul and his pack might unknowingly be fighting for their own doom.

Guilt nagged at the man Skilgannon, but the strategist Skilgannon knew that the Jiamads could mean the difference between success and failure. In war, he told himself, hard decisions had to be made.

And how does this make me different from the Eternal? he wondered.

Sadness touched him, merging with the guilt. He thought of the elderly abbot, Cethelin, a man who believed love was the way to change the world. The man had been prepared to die, cut down by a vengeful mob, rather than compromise his beliefs. Skilgannon had not allowed his sacrifice—and had butchered the ringleaders. Those moments of horrifying violence had ended his own attempts to become a monk, and had left Cethelin alive, but heartbroken.

Skilgannon had promised the Legend riders he would help them change the world. It was a lie. The world would not be changed by swords. In theory Cethelin was right. The greatest change could only occur when all men refused to take up swords; when war was seen not as glorious, but as obscene.

It would never happen, he knew. He glanced around the campsite at the sleeping beasts. *We are Pack,* Shakul had said. It was not only wolves and Jiamads that followed this hierarchical pattern. Man was the same. The strongest male would fight to rise in the pack, to dominate lesser males. It could be seen endlessly in the natural play of children. The weak and the sensitive were brushed aside by the brutish and the powerful.

Just then, in the far distance, he heard a high-pitched series of unnatural cries. On the far side of the camp Shakul stirred and sat up. Skilgannon rose to his feet and walked to his horse. Askari rolled from her bed and called out to him. "Where are you going?"

"The Shadows are abroad," he said. "There is no room to fight here."

Askari rose and stood by as he hefted the saddle onto the stallion's back. Tightening the cinch, he looked at Askari and smiled. "Do not look so concerned. I shall ride out to open ground and deal with them."

"I'll come with you."

"No."

"You are an arrogant man, Skilgannon. These creatures move with terrifying speed. You are not a god, you know."

"No, I am not. But I am a killer." Stepping into the saddle, he touched heels to the stallion's flanks.

Skilgannon rode out of the woods and down the hill to the flatland, constantly scanning the surrounding countryside. A quarter of a mile to the west there was a rounded hillock. From its summit he would have a clear field of vision. Against creatures of such speed he needed to be able to see them coming. Skilgannon dismounted at the top and tethered the stallion. Then he eased himself through a series of exercises, loosening his muscles and preparing his mind. The moon was low in the sky, and there was little breeze. Drawing his swords, he waited.

You are an arrogant man, Skilgannon.

This was true. *The Shadows may not even be coming for me,* he realized. They could be looking for Decado, or Alahir, or even Askari. This thought was an uncomfortable one. If the latter was true, then he had left her unprotected. The Jiamads may be huge and powerful, but they were cumbersome and would not prevent an attack. On the other hand the Shadows paralyzed their victims. They would not have the strength to carry Askari away from the likes of Shakul. This reasoning calmed him. She would be safe with them.

And if it was Decado they were hunting? Well, in many ways that would be a problem solved.

His exercises complete, he continued to cast his gaze over the grassland, seeking not to focus on any one spot, but allowing his peripheral vision to pick up movement. Slowly the moonlight began to fade. He glanced at the sky. There were few clouds and the stars were bright, but the moon itself would soon be behind the distant peaks.

The stallion suddenly reared, its tethered front feet thumping down on the hillock. "I know, Greatheart," he said, softly. "They are coming."

Yet still there was nothing to be seen on the swaying grassland.

As Malanek had taught him so many centuries before, he slipped into the Illusion of Elsewhere, freeing his body to act and react instantly without need for conscious thought. This simple mind trick enabled him to cut down reaction time. His eyes continued to watch the land, but his mind concentrated on a single memory from the past. He saw himself standing with Druss the Legend on the high parapet of Boranius's tower, after the rescue of the child Elanin. Druss had been fifty years old, his beard more gray than black, his eyes a piercing winter blue. The golden-haired little girl had been standing beside him, her small hand engulfed by his own huge fist. He had talked of returning to his cabin in the mountains, and retiring from wars and battles. Skilgannon had laughed.

"I am serious, laddie. I'll hang Snaga on the wall and put my helm and jerkin and gauntlets into a chest. By heaven, I'll even padlock it and throw away the key."

"So," said Skilgannon, "I have witnessed the last battle of Druss the Legend?"

"Druss the Legend? You know I have always hated to be called that."

"I'm hungry, Uncle Druss," said Elanin, tugging on his arm.

"Now *that* is a title I do like," said the old warrior, lifting the child into his arms. "That is who I will be. Druss the Uncle. Druss the Farmer. And a pox on prophecies!"

"What prophecy?"

Druss had grinned. "A long time ago a seer told me I would die in battle at Dros Delnoch. It was always nonsense. Delnoch is the greatest fortress ever built, six massive walls and a keep. There's not an army in the world could take it—and not a leader insane enough to try."

The grassland still seemed empty, and Druss's last words echoed through his mind. *A pox on prophecies,* he had said. And yet, ten years later, the sixty-year-old Druss had stood on the walls of Dros Delnoch, defying one of the largest armies ever seen in the world.

Skilgannon had been in a tavern in Gulgothir when he had heard Druss was back, training the recruits at Delnoch. He had seen the Great Khan riding out with his army two days before, and had known the fortress would fall. Ulric was a brilliant strategist and a charismatic leader. The armies of the Drenai had been largely dismantled by a political leadership that believed this was the best way to avoid war. It was a reasonable theory. Lessen the strength of the army and you gave the clearest indication to neighboring countries that you were not planning to invade them. The problem with the theory was that it required potential enemies to be equally reasonable. For all his great skills and his enormous courage Ulric was not a reasonable man. And his problems were uniquely different from those of the rich Drenai southerners. Ulric had a vast army. Armies need to be fed and paid. The larger the force, the greater the drain on the treasury. Huge armies needed plunder. Ulric had already destroyed the

Gothir. The Drenai, by reducing their fighting forces, were now virtually defenseless against him. One decrepit fortress, manned by raw recruits, farmers, and peasants, against a horde of Nadir warriors, fearless and valiant. There was only one outcome.

Skilgannon had been emotionally torn when he heard Druss was among those defenders. He loved the old man, but he also owed Ulric his life. The man had risked everything to save him when they had fought together. Two friends on opposite sides. Skilgannon could not help them both, save by staying clear of the conflict.

The decision was a heavy burden to bear.

A flicker of movement on the grassland caused his head to turn. There was nothing to be seen. He glanced at the stallion. Its ears were flat back against its skull now, and it was tense and nervous.

Returning his gaze to the darkening grassland, he saw a small, dark patch of earth some two hundred paces from him. Movement flickered again to his left, but he kept his eyes on the dark patch. Suddenly it moved, with blistering speed. Skilgannon saw then that it was a slender figure in a hooded dark robe. Another movement to his right. They moved so fast it seemed they disappeared from one place only to appear in another, as if they were moving through invisible gateways.

Skilgannon walked several steps away from his horse, giving himself room to swing his blades. He could not beat these creatures for speed, so he watched them move across the flatland, heading inexorably for the hillock, and gauged their style of movement. Their attack was designed to confound the eye. One would move and drop to the ground. Another would move fractions of a heartbeat after the first. The victim would continue to seek out movement, and never quite be able to focus on any one Shadow. By now Skilgannon knew there were three of the creatures. He felt his heartbeat quicken with the thought of battle, and quelled the rising excitement. If they were to pierce him with the para-

lyzing darts, or get close enough to bite, then he didn't want
the venom to be pumped swiftly through his system by a fast
heartbeat. Many years ago when his father's retainer, Sperian, had been bitten by a snake, he had lain very still while
his wife, Molaire, ran for the local apothecary. The nine-
year-old Skilgannon had sat beside Sperian, who closed his
eyes and breathed slowly and deeply. Later, after the apothecary had administered an antidote, Skilgannon asked him
how he could have stayed so calm. "Only way to stay alive,
boy. Fear causes the heart to beat faster, and that pushes the
poison around the blood faster. Don't want that. Too much
of it in the heart itself and that's it. Life's over."

Moonlight had almost gone now and Skilgannon calmly
awaited the attack.

It came suddenly. Something bright flashed before his
eyes. The Sword of Day swept up. A dart cannoned from the
blade, spinning off across the hillock. Skilgannon dived to
his left. A second dart missed his face by inches. Rolling to
his feet he lunged—the sword cutting into a dark robe, and
slicing through it. Skilgannon rolled again, coming up fast.

The Sword of Night swept out, biting through flesh and
bone. Skilgannon had not even seen the creature's approach.
The cut had been an automatic response. The Shadow fell
writhing to the ground. Something sharp bit into Skilgannon's shoulder. He staggered back, feeling the venom in his
system. He stood very still, then toppled to his knees, his
arms outstretched, his sword tips resting on the earth. Staying calm, he slowed his heartbeat once more, concentrating
deeply. He did not blink or move. The remaining two creatures came into sight, no longer darting. They watched him.
Then they moved forward, lips drawn back. One had a thick,
single curved fang, which jutted over its lower lip; the other
boasted two slender fangs. Their mouths widened as they approached him, squatting down. The Swords of Night and
Day swept up. One sliced through the first creature's throat,
the second almost missed as the Shadow hurled itself backward. But the Sword of Night cut through its ribs and across

its stomach, disemboweling it. The creature tried to run, then stumbled and fell, twitching, to the earth.

Skilgannon's limbs were getting heavy now. The Swords dropped from his fingers.

Numbness crept through his limbs. Slowly he toppled sideways, not able to feel the cold grass against his cheek. Despite the paralysis he felt a sense of exultation. The three Shadows were dead, and he had won again!

His eyes were still open—and he saw a fourth Shadow moving up the hillside.

You are an arrogant man, Skilgannon.

Oh how true it felt at that precise moment.

The Shadow approached him and squatted down, staring at him with baleful eyes. Then it drew a wickedly curved dagger. "Eat your heart," it said.

Skilgannon could not reply. In a bewildering instant the creature was suddenly looming over him, the dagger resting on Skilgannon's chest. He could see the dagger, but could no longer see the creature above him. He heard it grunt, though, as it slumped across him. He wondered what was happening. Was it biting through his paralyzed, unfeeling neck?

Then its body was hauled away and dumped unceremoniously on the ground. Skilgannon could see that a long shaft had shattered its temple, the point emerging on the other side.

Askari sat down beside him. "Well, well," she said, brightly, "what have we here? It cannot be the legendary, invincible warrior. The man who fights alone and never loses. The man who needs no help. Must be someone who looks like him."

The ground drifted away from him, and Skilgannon became aware he was being lifted. His body was hauled up, his head falling against Shakul's chest.

"You are going to have the worst headache of your life when you awaken, Skilgannon. However, you deserve it," said Askari, leaning in toward him and closing his eyes.

* * *

Once back in his apartments Memnon removed his clothes and washed the blood from his hands and arms. His satin shirt was ruined. Bloodstains rarely completely vanished from the fragile cloth. It was a shame, for the shirt was one of his favorites, dark blue, with gold trim. Once he had cleaned himself and donned fresh clothing, he called for a servant to summon Oranin.

The young man arrived an hour later, bowing deeply and offering profuse apologies. "I was not in my room, Lord, so it took them some time to find me."

"No matter," said Memnon. "You will be working alone for a while. I require you to search through the journals, looking for any reference to the technique Landis Khan used to create me. You understand?"

"Of course, Lord. Is Patiacus returning to Diranan?"

"Patiacus is dead. He betrayed me. Parts of him are still littering the laboratory floor. Clean them up yourself. The sight of his remains would disturb the servants. I shall be leaving tomorrow, to join the Eternal. You will work diligently while I am gone. I expect to see a successful conclusion to your studies."

"And you shall, Lord," said Oranin, bowing once more. "Might I ask how Patiacus betrayed you?"

"Why?"

"So that I do not make the same mistake," replied the man, with transparent honesty.

Memnon sighed. "It was not a small oversight, Oranin. I did not kill him out of pique. He poisoned my Reborns. I should have expected something of the kind. Always been a problem of mine to see the best in people."

"Why would he do such a thing?" asked Oranin, appalled.

"On the orders of the Eternal. It is so obvious, really. As a mortal I could serve her diligently. As an Immortal I might have become a threat. Understandable. I don't doubt, had the situation been reversed, that I, too, might have come to the same conclusion."

"You are not angry with her, Lord?"

"I do not become angry, Oranin. She is the Eternal. It is not for me to question her on grounds of loyalty, or treachery. The virtues of the one are ephemeral, the vices of the other debatable. It is merely the nature of politics, Oranin. Go now, and do as I have bid."

Alone once more Memnon stretched out on the sofa and closed his eyes. It took him time to release his spirit, but once he had done so he soared up over the palace and sped north. He hovered for a while over the tent of the Eternal. Guards patrolled outside, while inside she slept. He gazed at her face, enjoying the exquisite beauty of her. Then he moved on.

Some twenty miles north of the encamped army he found Decado, asleep in the midst of a group of soldiers. There was no sign of Skilgannon. Memnon circled the area, at last heading east over wide grassland. He almost missed the dead Shadows, only seeing the bodies at the last moment when one of them screeched in pain. Memnon floated down above it. Its skinny legs were drawn up, its clawed, blood-covered hands seeking to stem the flow of blood from its gutted belly.

Four bodies there were—one with an arrow through the skull.

It was unheard of. Four Shadows killed in a single night. He floated closer. Three had been killed by a sharp blade, the last by a shaft. They would not have attacked had the victim not been alone, or vulnerable. Far off to the right Memnon saw a twinkling campfire. His spirit sped to it.

There were Jiamads there, and several humans. One was the Eternal's Reborn, the other a bearded man in clothes of bright crimson. Memnon admired the tunic shirt, which was beautifully cut, though the cloth was not of the highest quality. The third human was Skilgannon, who was lying down, apparently asleep.

"Might have been better had they killed him," said the man in the red shirt.

"Don't say that, Stavi!"

"I didn't mean it. Well . . . not entirely. Because of him my lads are going into danger."

"That is not fair. They are going because of you. You could always stay here. After we succeed I will come back and find you."

"I love the optimism. You are going to find a temple that no longer exists and destroy the source of a magic you don't understand. What does it really look like, this thing you call an egg? How will you know it when you see it? Silver eagles, magic shields! None of it makes any sense."

"It does, as Skilgannon explained it to me. The ancients could and did work miracles that we no longer understand. They created the magic. It doesn't matter how it works, the fact is that it does. Now bear with me. The artifacts of the elders were just that, for a long while. Empty and dead. Suddenly they had life. Something woke them, powered them. Something at the temple. The legend says that all this power comes from the silver eagle in the sky."

"Metal birds," muttered the man, scornfully.

"Forget birds. Something metal was raised into the sky by the ancients. Whatever it was gave them the power to work magic. Now somewhere, way back in the olden days, that power suddenly stopped. It no longer reached the artifacts. They all stopped. They . . . slept . . . would be the best way to describe it. Then something happened, and the power returned. You understand?"

"I understand this is making my head hurt."

"Think of it this way. There is a cup that is empty. It does nothing. It sits. It has no uses. Then someone goes to a well and fills the cup with water. Now it is useful again. You can drink from it."

"The power source is someone with a jug?"

"No, it is the water, stupid. The water makes the cup useful. Inside the temple there is something that fills the artifacts. We will destroy it. The artifacts will become useless.

No more Reborns. No more Jiamads. No more Eternal. She will age and die like the rest of us."

"All right," said the man in the red shirt. "Suppose all you say is true. You still have to find a temple that is no longer there."

"It must be there, Stavi. It is the source of the power. And the power still operates. If it were truly gone the artifacts would already have become useless."

"This is all very well," he said, taking her hand. "But I would think more clearly if you were to take a little walk in the woods with me."

"You would *not* think more clearly," she said. "You would fall asleep with a smile on your face."

"So would you," he countered.

"That is true."

Hand in hand they crept through the sleeping Jiamads and away into the woods.

Memnon did not follow. He had seen people rut before.

Instead he flew back to the palace. There was so much to think on, and so many plans to initiate.

There were times in Jianna's long life when she considered boredom to be almost terminal. Intrigue had long since lost the fascination she had felt for it when young, and the new queen of Naashan. Manipulation, coercion, seduction had been exciting then, and each small victory had been something to celebrate. This last hundred years particularly had seen those skills honed to a perfection she felt she should have been proud of. Instead the practice of them had become a chore. There was a time when she had found men fascinating and intricate. Now they were—at best—merely diverting. Their needs and their values were always the same, their strengths and their weaknesses easy to manipulate.

It was one reason her heart yearned for Skilgannon; why she had sought his body for so many centuries. The prophecy meant nothing to her. She had lost count of the number of prophecies concerning her that had come to nothing over the centuries. It was not that some of the seers did not possess genuine talent. It was merely that a level of wish fulfillment entered their heads, coloring the visions they had. No, Skilgannon was unique among the men she had known. He had loved her fully and completely—loved her enough, indeed, to walk away from her. Even after all these years the shock of his departure remained a jagged wound in her heart.

He would have enjoyed this victory.

Agrias, apparently outnumbered and outmatched, had pulled back his army toward the ruins of an ancient city. Jianna's forces had swept forward through a valley between a line of wooded hills, pursuing the fleeing enemy. It had been a trap, and beautifully worked. Agrias had sent out three regiments, two of men, one of Jiamads. The beasts had attacked from the high woods to the west, the enemy infantry sweeping down from the east. The third regiment of lancers had emerged at the rear of Jianna's forces, completing the circle. It was a splendid ploy, which she had much enjoyed. Sadly for Agrias she had also anticipated the maneuver and held back the regiments of Eternal Guard, the finest fighting men on the planet. Highly trained and superbly disciplined, they had fallen on the enemy rear, scattering the lancers. Jianna's own Jiamads had torn into the enemy ranks. The encircling maneuver had been the only potent weapon in Agrias's arsenal. When it failed, the spirit of his troops was broken. They had fought well for a little while, but then panic set in, and they fled the field. In the rout that followed, thousands were slain.

Agrias himself was taken, and the War in the North was over in just under twelve days. There were still pockets of resistance to overcome, mainly in the Drenai lands to the west. This, however, was a relatively simple matter. The Legend riders had a few thousand doughty fighters, but no Jiamads, and no reserves to call upon.

Jianna opened the flaps of her tent and stepped out into the moonlight. The two Guardsmen saluted. Several of her generals were waiting outside, and she saw Unwallis walking across the campsite toward her tent. He had been hurt by her rejection of him. It amazed her that he could have considered becoming a regular lover again. The man was old and lacked the stamina she had once enjoyed in his company. It was not a mistake she would make again.

Agrippon, the senior general of her Eternals, bowed as her gaze fell upon him. Jianna liked him. She had tried to seduce him several years ago, but he was a married man and ferociously loyal to his wife. She felt that with a little extra effort she could have broken down this resistance, for he was obviously besotted by her, but she rather liked his stolid honesty and his attempt to be true. So she had drawn back, and now treated him with sisterly affection. Summoning him to her tent, she told the Guard to admit no one else until she ordered it.

"Sit down, Agrippon," she bade him. "What are the figures?"

"Just over a thousand dead. Eleven thousand enemy corpses—not counting their beasts."

"And my Guard?"

"We lost only sixty-seven men, with another three hundred bearing light wounds."

"Excellent."

"As indeed was your battle plan, Highness." The compliment was clumsily made, but she sensed his sincerity. Agrippon was not a man given to compliments.

She gazed at the black-bearded soldier and wondered if she should reconsider her sisterly demeanor. The battle had been exciting, and Jianna felt the need to have the tension relieved. He grew uncomfortable under her direct gaze and rose from his seat.

"Will that be all, Highness?"

"Yes, thank you, Agrippon. Convey my congratulations to your officers. Will you have Unwallis attend me?"

"Of course, Highness," he said, bowing.

After the general had left, the statesman ducked under the tent flap. He, too, bowed.

"How did you enjoy your first battle?" she asked him. He had ridden alongside her at the center of the army, looking faintly ludicrous in a gilded breastplate and overlarge helm.

"It was terrifying, Highness, but having survived it, I wouldn't have missed it for all the wine in Lentria. I thought we were trapped."

She laughed. "It would take someone with more skill than Agrias to trap me."

"Yes, Highness. Might I ask what your plans are for him? I thought—"

"You thought I would have had him killed immediately."

"Indeed, Highness. He has been a thorn in our sides for many years now."

"I expect he is contemplating his situation even as we speak. We will allow that contemplation to continue."

"Exquisitely cruel, Highness," he said, with a sigh. "He is an imaginative man, and will be considering all the horrors that could come his way."

"Indeed so. You wanted to see me. Do you have news?"

"We have been questioning some of the captured officers. It seems that the Legend riders attached to Agrias—some three hundred of them—left his service two weeks ago. One of the riders is fond of a local whore. She was, in turn, fond of the particular officer we questioned."

"For the sake of my sanity," said Jianna, sharply, "can we cease talking of *fondness*. I am not a Temple Maiden. The whore was humping both men, and probably a score of others. What did she say?"

"That the leader of the Legend riders had found some mysterious armor, important to them. In bronze. And that a mystic voice had compelled him to leave Agrias's service and follow a man with two swords."

"The Armor of Bronze," said Jianna. "It was a legend even in my own time." She shivered suddenly. "I do not like this, Unwallis. Too many damned portents. A reborn Druss the

Legend carrying his ax, Skilgannon rediscovered, and now the Armor of Bronze. Perhaps that cursed prophecy is not so far-fetched."

"The regiment of Eternal Guard you sent should be close to the temple site by now. And there are two hundred Jiamads with them. Some of the latest and most powerful. Even with a few hundred Legend riders Skilgannon will lose."

"That would be a first," said Jianna. "Leave me now, Unwallis. I need to think."

"Yes, Highness," he said, with a deep bow. He looked at her and suddenly smiled. "May I say something?"

She sighed. "Make it brief."

"My thoughts are clearer now, and I apologize that my behavior has been . . . foolish. Your gift to me at the palace was exquisite, and I am very grateful. I feel, though, that my attitude since has caused a breach between us. I would like that breach to be sealed. I am, once more, merely Unwallis. And your friend, Highness."

Jianna was touched, and felt herself relax. "You are a good friend." Stepping forward, she kissed his cheek.

He reddened, bowed once more, and departed. Jianna walked to the rear of her tent and opened a small, ornate box of carved ebony. From it she took an ancient bronze amulet, covered now in green verdigris. Holding tightly to it, she whispered Memnon's name.

At first there was no response; then it was as if a breeze whispered into the tent, though none of the lanterns flickered. Jianna felt cold and shivered once more. By the far wall an image formed, at first like a shadow against the white, silk-covered canvas. Then it shimmered and Memnon's image appeared, pale and translucent.

"There is a problem, Highness?" he asked.

"Skilgannon is close to the temple site. He has a small force with him."

"I know this, Highness. Legend riders, and a troop of Jiamads. Be not concerned."

"Can we not bring the plan forward?"

"No, Highness. Timing is essential. Vital, in fact. All will be as you wish it to be. When my messenger comes to you, leave the camp and follow him. I will appear to you then, and ensure that all is well."

"The Eternal Guard will not attack until the time is right."

"I am with the general. He understands fully what we intend. Be at ease, Highness. Enjoy your victory. There will be another for you to savor very shortly."

Eighteen

For Harad the long, slow trip on the barges was a time for quiet grief. He sat on the narrow deck, surrounded by Jiamads, and watched the land drift slowly by. Harad had chosen to travel with the beasts because they didn't talk much, and he found the lightness and banter of the Legend riders hard to bear. Almost everything had been hard to bear since Charis's death. Harad even felt surprise when he heard birdsong coming from the rushes on the eastern bank. It seemed somehow inconceivable that birds should still be singing, or that the sun still shone from a clear blue sky. The weight of his grief was colossal. But he did not share it, even with Askari, who would occasionally join him, and sit in merciful silence.

They had hired five barges, each pulled by oxen for the first forty miles of the journey. After that, so Skilgannon had been told by the merchant, they would leave the oxen behind and navigate the wider waterways through the mountains until they met the River Rostrias. The soldiers had surrendered all their coin, and Stavut had sold his wagon and contents. Even so they had been far short of the hiring charge, and the provisions necessary for the trip.

Stavut had haggled with the master merchant for some hours while Decado steadily lost patience. He was all for commandeering the vessels. Skilgannon urged him to stay calm. The master merchant was also the local commander of the Corisle militia, and though it would not have been difficult to overcome them Skilgannon wanted to avoid unnecessary deaths. Harad had looked closely at Decado. He seemed paler than usual, and kept rubbing his eyes.

Stavut left the merchant and walked back to where Skilgannon was waiting with Decado, Alahir, and the others at the flimsy dock. "He says he would be prepared to take your stallion to conclude payment for the trip and the provisions," Stavut told Skilgannon.

Skilgannon stood silently for a moment, then approached the merchant. The man was tall and slim, his eyes deep set. He wore a shirt of embroidered blue satin, and his long, gray hair was held back from his face by an ornate headband of filigree silver. "You are a man who knows horses," said Skilgannon.

"I breed them for the Eternal Guard," said the merchant. "They are fastidious about the quality of the horses they ride. Do we have an agreement?"

"We do not," said Skilgannon. "The horse is worth more than your barges."

"Then, sadly, I do not see how we can accommodate you."

Skilgannon chuckled. "The Eternal's army is marching on Agrias. Soon there will be a major battle to the west. Knowing the Eternal as I do, she will not lose this battle. You are a servant of Agrias. Your position here will soon become perilous. And yet you quibble over a few coins?"

"It is a merchant's nature to quibble over coins. It is how we become rich and buy satin shirts. The problem of who governs this area is one for another day. For today I have five barges, ready to carry you to the Rostrias. I have already offered my best price."

Decado, who had been listening, stepped forward. "Let me cut his miserable throat, then we can take the damned barges." Even as he spoke he drew one of his swords and moved toward the merchant. The Sword of Night swept into Skilgannon's hand, the blade flashing out to bar Decado's path.

"Let us not be hasty, kinsman," said Skilgannon softly. For a moment Harad thought Decado was going to attack Skilgannon. Instead he stepped back, his eyes wide and glittering strangely.

"Why do you want him to live?" asked Decado. "I don't understand."

"I like him."

Decado shook his head in disbelief and stalked away.

"Reassuring to be liked, I am sure," said the merchant. "But the price remains the same."

"I will rent you the stallion," said Skilgannon. "You will loan me one of your own mounts. I would prefer a gelding. You can use the stallion as a stud until my return. Then I shall claim it."

"How long will you be gone?"

"Some weeks at the least."

"A dangerous mission?"

Skilgannon laughed aloud. "Indeed it is, master merchant. I might not survive."

"Oh perish the thought," said the man, rising and holding out his hand. "It will be as you say. I shall have a gelding brought over immediately. The barges will leave at first light. If your beasts cause any damage to my vessels I shall seek redress upon your return."

On the evening of the second day of travel, with the sun sinking, Harad went to his usual spot at the rear of the barge to find Decado sitting there. Askari was behind him, gently rubbing his temples. Stavut was close by. Harad eased himself past them without a word and found a place to sit, his back against a sack of grain. Decado was deathly pale.

"What is wrong with him?" he asked Askari.

"I don't know. It was the same when first I found him."

Decado sighed. "The two of you do know I am here, don't you?"

Askari laughed. "You are feeling a little better."

"Yes, the pain is fading a little."

"You should eat something," said Stavut.

"A waste of time and energy. I might just as well get the food and throw it over the side. No, my stomach will hold nothing until the pain passes. I will be all right. I know the rhythms of these attacks. This was not so bad. It will soon be gone."

"You get them often?" asked Stavut.

"They come and go." He looked up at Askari, and there was adoration in his gaze. It made Harad uncomfortable, and he glanced at Stavut. The red-garbed merchant looked away, then rose.

"We should go and get some food," he said, reaching out and taking Askari's hand.

After they had gone, Harad leaned his head back on the grain sack and closed his eyes.

"I hear your woman died," said Decado.

Harad's eyes snapped open. The last person he wanted to talk to about Charis was this demented swordsman.

"Nice-looking girl. Beautiful eyes," said Decado. "I remember thinking how lucky you were. Brave, too. Had she not rescued Gamal from the palace I would have killed him that first night. Took nerve." He glanced at Snaga. "I am surprised you still want to handle that weapon."

"Why would I not?"

Decado did not reply for a moment. "You don't know what I am talking about, do you?" he said, at last.

"No."

"Askari told me that when the tree struck you the ax flew from your hand. It was the ax that killed Charis. Now that is what you call bad luck." Decado stretched himself out on the deck and drew his cloak over his shoulders.

Harad sat very still, his grief now returned redoubled. If he had kept hold of the weapon Charis would still be alive.

It was as if he had killed her himself.

Skilgannon stood at the prow of the lead barge, enjoying the cool night breeze on his face. It had been a long time since he had led an army, and the weight of responsibility sat heavily on him. Most of the problems he faced were familiar to him. Most men with no military experience believed that

an army needed only courage and discipline to win a battle.
Those with a little more insight might add that the quality of
training, weapons, and armor would be important. Both
views were correct in part. Without these assets no army
would survive for long. Yet in his long life Skilgannon had
seen armies with fine weapons, good training, and strong
leadership fall apart on a battlefield when faced by troops
less well armed. Morale was the real key to success. Low
morale would strip away the confidence of the best fighter,
and, more often than not, good morale resulted from good
provisions. Hunger caused discontent. The food he had purchased from the merchant would feed the force for some ten
days. After that it would be down to foraging. Not a simple
exercise in the desert environment they were heading for.
The horses would need good water, the men full bellies. This
problem was even more pressing for the Jiamads. Their ap-
petites were prodigious.

A secondary morale problem was also worrying him. The
Legend riders loathed the Jiamads, and the beasts, in turn,
sensing the hatred, were nervous and ill at ease. At the moment
the problem was not serious, for the beasts traveled in separate
barges. At night, when the Legend riders took their mounts
ashore for exercise and grazing, the Jiamads stayed well clear
of them. Skilgannon had tried to talk to Alahir about the hos-
tility, but he, too, was locked into age-old prejudices. Jiamads
were demon spawn. Jiamads were evil. Jiamads frightened the
horses. It was equally difficult with Stavut, who seemed to
consider his "lads" as merely large puppies. And then there
was Harad. Skilgannon had not known Druss as a young man;
nor had he spoken to him at any length about the death of his
wife. He had no idea how the tragedy had affected the Drenai
hero. Had he, too, become unhinged when the tragedy struck?
Harad spoke little to anyone now, save perhaps Askari.

Skilgannon wandered along the now empty deck and
down the wide gangplank to the shore. The Legend riders
had gathered some hundred or so paces east and were sitting

around campfires, laughing and talking. The Jiamads had wandered off with Stavut. The countryside was still lush, and Skilgannon had seen game in the hills. Askari was sitting with Decado on the riverbank. The swordsman was yet another concern for Skilgannon. Back at the merchant's office Skilgannon had seen a look in the young man's eyes that was disturbing. There had been a need in Decado to kill. For a brief moment Skilgannon had believed he would have to fight him. Then the moment had passed.

It might come again.

Skilgannon strolled toward the campfires. As he did so, Stavut and a group of Joinings emerged from the woods some little way to the west. The grazing horses picked up the scent of the Jiamads and immediately began to run. Legend riders surged up and rushed out into the meadow, seeking to calm them.

In the confusion that followed, three Legend riders approached Stavut and a heated argument broke out. Skilgannon moved swiftly toward them as other riders gathered. "Are you a complete idiot?" shouted one of the riders. "Your vermin scare horses. How could you be so stupid?" He leaned in toward Stavut, his manner threatening. A huge beast snarled and rushed at him, hurling the man from his feet. A great roar went up from the Jiamads. Legend riders grabbed their bows. Others drew swords and rushed forward.

Skilgannon raced in. "Stand fast!" he yelled.

The moment was tense. Many of the riders now had their bows bent. Skilgannon walked out to stand between the riders and the beasts. "This has gone far enough," he said, his voice ringing out. "And I am becoming sick of the stupidity around me. Yes, Stavut should have known better than to bring his pack so close to the horses. But you"—he pointed to the man hurled to the ground—"showed even greater stupidity. Worse, it was a complete lack of judgment. How dare you use the word *vermin*? Stavut's pack *chose* to come on this quest. You understand the meaning of the word? *Choice.*

He told them to stay behind, because this was not their fight. They chose to support *you,* to fight alongside *you.* To die in *your* war. And this is how you repay them? Calling them vermin. You should be ashamed of yourself." One by one the bows were put down, the arrows returned to their quivers. "I'll tell you something else. I lived during the time you are all so desperate to bring back. I walked with Druss the Legend. I fought alongside him. At a citadel, full of Nadir warriors and renegade Naashanites. There were not many of us. There were two brothers, a Drenai warrior named Diagoras, and a woman with a crossbow. There was Druss. There was me. And there was a Jiamad. We all fought together. Druss the Legend did not call the Jiamad *vermin.* He did not shy away from him. He did not look at him with disgust. Druss judged all creatures by their deeds. If he was here when the word *vermin* was used it would have been Druss who downed the idiot who spoke the word." He paused for a moment and looked at the still-angry men. "I don't want to hear how many of your friends have been killed by Jiamads, or how your grandfathers made blood oaths to keep Jiamads from the sacred lands of the Drenai. This world is ancient. It has always had its share of evil. Evil, I think, was born in the heart of the first man. You don't find evil in a leopard, or a bear, or a sparrow, or a hawk. We carry it. Men carry it. Out there," he said, gesturing toward the north, "is a place of magic. If we can find it, and locate the source of it, we can prevent the Eternal—or anyone else—from ever creating another man-beast. *That* is what we need to focus upon." He could see from their faces that his words had failed to sway them. And there was nothing more to say.

Skilgannon fell silent, and Alahir walked out from his riders and approached the towering Shakul. "I am Alahir, of the Legend riders," he said. Shakul's head swayed from side to side.

"This is my friend Shakul," said Stavut. The beasts milled around, uncertain and nervous. Stavut took Alahir to one side and spoke to him in a low whisper. Alahir suddenly laughed and turned to his men.

"Follow our lead," he said. Then he and Stavut began to rhythmically stamp their feet on the ground. With looks of bemusement, the Legend riders copied the movement. Then Alahir called out: "We are Pack! All of you say it! Together now!"

The response was at first weak and sporadic. "Louder, you whoresons!" shouted Alahir, laughing as he gave the order.

"We are Pack! We are Pack!" The chant boomed out over the meadows.

"Shakul!" yelled Stavut. "What are we?"

Shakul began to stamp his foot. One by one the beasts copied him. "We are Pack!" roared Shakul, then let out a ferocious howl. The Jiamads raised their heads and howled with him.

"Let's hear some Drenai howls!" shouted Alahir. Cupping his hands over his mouth, he let out a piercing wolf call. Laughing now, the Legend riders began to whoop and howl. The horses scattered once more, but no one seemed to care.

Skilgannon looked around and smiled. For the first time in days he felt the tension ease from his body.

As Skilgannon walked back to where the barges were moored, Alahir joined him. "What you said back there, was it true?" he asked.

"I do not lie, Alahir."

"Druss fought alongside a Jiamad?"

"We called them Joinings back then, but they were the same. A Nadir shaman had performed a melding on one of Druss's oldest friends, a man named Orastes."

"Ah well," said Alahir, "that is different then."

"What is?" inquired Skilgannon.

"The Jiamad was once a man Druss knew."

Skilgannon took a deep, calming breath. "Where is the difference, Alahir? Shakul was once a man. All of them were."

"Aye," agreed Alahir, "but criminals and suchlike. Theirs is a punishment for crimes committed."

Skilgannon paused. He had no wish to insult the man, and

he was grateful for the action he had taken. He looked at the young warrior. "I know you are not a stupid man, Alahir. But what you just said shows a remarkable naïveté. Do you believe the Eternal is evil?"

"Of course. Her actions prove it."

"Exactly. Why then do you suppose an evil leader would use only criminals for melding? Shakul was melded for the Eternal's army. Yes, he might have been a thief, or a murderer. Or simply a good man who spoke against the Eternal?"

"I see where you are going. Yes, forgive me, Skilgannon. I am a stupid man."

Skilgannon laughed. "When you consider this venture, I think we both qualify for an award in stupidity. Do not be so hard on yourself. We all get locked into prejudices. In my time and my country the Drenai were considered to be arrogant, selfish conquerors who needed to be taught a lesson in humility. Had I been a little older I, too, might have been part of Gorben's army, taking on the Drenai at Skeln Pass. You look at the beasts, their awesome power, and their ferocious ugliness, and you wonder just what they could have done to deserve such a fate. For surely, if there is a Source watching us all, they must have done something. I don't doubt the first Jiamads might have been criminals. After that, with the need for more and more to fill her armies, I expect they were mostly peasants, rounded up in villages. I tell you, Alahir, I was moved when I saw the pack volunteer to travel with Stavut. It made me think there just may be a chance for humanity to change one day. That a group of beasts could show such loyalty and affection inspired me."

"Ah well, everybody likes Stavut. He has a rare gift for comradeship."

Once back at the barges Skilgannon bade Alahir good night and wandered down to the last barge. He found Harad sitting at the stern, Snaga in his hands. He looked up as Skilgannon climbed to the deck. "You should have told me," said Harad, tossing the ax to the deck. The points of the butterfly blades bit into the wood and the haft stood upright, quivering with the impact.

"What difference would it have made?" said Skilgannon, sensing what he spoke of. "She died in an earthquake. She died instantly."

"Aye, but by my ax!" The anguish in his words was painful to hear.

"I knew a man once who was killed by a pebble, flicked up from the hoof of a passing horse. The man was a tough warrior who had survived a dozen battles. The stone struck him in the temple."

"There is a point to this?" demanded Harad.

"We rarely get to choose the manner of our passing. You did not kill Charis. The earthquake killed her. Listen to me, Harad, guilt always follows bereavement. It is a natural part of the process. Someone we love dies and the first question we ask ourselves is: Could we have done anything to prevent it? And even if we couldn't the guilt remains. Did we love them enough? Did we give them enough of our time? We remember arguments or rows, or tears or misunderstandings. And every one of them comes back to us like a knife in the heart. You are not alone in your suffering. Every man or woman old enough to know someone who has died feels the same. For me it was my wife. She was pregnant and happy. Then the plague struck. For years I suffered, knowing that I had not loved her enough. I traveled the world with a shard of her bone and a lock of her hair, seeking the very place we are now trying to find. I wanted to bring her back, to repay her for the days of love she had given me. Charis loved you, Harad. The gift of love is priceless. You are a better man for having loved her, and for having been loved by her. Let the grief flow by all means. But rid yourself of the guilt. You have nothing to feel guilty about."

Harad sat silently for a moment, then he let out a sigh. "I will think on what you have said," he told Skilgannon. Leaning forward, he wrenched the ax from the deck. "Why are we in these damned barges?" he asked. "I could walk to the desert faster than this."

"Tomorrow you will see. Alahir says the waterway opens out into a great submerged canyon. We will have to leave the oxen behind, for there is no land for them to walk. There are sheer mountains all around. Alahir claims it is the fastest way to the Rostrias. If we had to ride it would take another two weeks to skirt the mountains."

"I have another question," said Harad.

"Ask it."

"What happens if we do stop the source of the magic?"

Skilgannon was puzzled. "The Eternal will be able to create no more Jiamads or Reborns. Have I not said this before?"

"Yes, you have. I meant what *happens* to the Jiamads?"

"I really don't know. They are melded by magic. It could be that removing it would cause the meld to come apart. Or it could be that nothing will happen to them. You are concerned about the welfare of the beasts?"

"As a matter of fact I am," said Harad. "But I was thinking more about you, and me, and Askari."

"I don't follow you."

"Were we not also created by magic? Are we not, in our own way, just as unnatural as the Jems? Perhaps destroying the source will kill us, too."

"That is a thought I could have done without," admitted Skilgannon. He looked at Harad. "Does it make a difference?"

"No," said the axman. "We are doing this to protect the weak from the evil strong. We are following the code. Have you any idea of how to find this temple?"

"I know where it *was,"* said Skilgannon. "We'll start from there."

Seventy years before, when Unwallis had first traveled to Diranan, one of the first important people he had met had been Agrias. His position as the queen's favorite, and chief councilor, had seemed unassailable. Fiercely intelligent, handsome, and multitalented, Agrias had radiated power and authority. Unwallis had stammered foolishly upon being introduced, muttered some dreadful banality, and then stood like a country bumpkin as Agrias and his entourage swept on through the palace.

Physically Agrias had not changed. He still looked young. He was still handsome and tall. But now he radiated nothing but fear as he was dragged before the Eternal. For five days he had been kept tied in a covered pit amid the ruins. He was hauled out on the fifth morning, blinking and squinting against the sunlight, his long pale robe soiled with his own excrement. Unwallis wanted to look away, but there was something magnetic about the man's disintegration.

When he saw the Eternal, sitting on a high-backed chair and flanked by the senior officers of her Eternal Guard, Agrias struggled to find some last shreds of dignity. As the Guard released their hold on his bound arms, he drew himself upright. "No pretty compliments for me, Agrias?" said the Eternal. "Are you not going to tell me how my hair gleams in the sunshine in raven beauty? Or how to gaze upon my face fills your heart with light?"

"You, my dear," said Agrias, rediscovering his manhood, "may look beautiful on the surface, but beneath the smooth skin there are the rotting bones of the long dead, and a stench of corruption."

A Guard struck him violently on the side of the head. Agrias staggered but did not fall. A trickle of blood seeped from a cut in his temple. He suddenly laughed.

"Oh do share your good humor," said the Eternal. "Amuse us while you still can."

"When I was a young priest," said Agrias, "I was gifted with visions. These faded as I grew older and became enamored of power and material wealth."

"Wonderful," said the Eternal. "I do so love a morality tale. Does it have a happy ending?"

"There are no happy endings for the likes of you and me, gorgeous one."

"Ah! That compliment brings back happy memories. You have won a few extra moments of life, Agrias. Pray continue."

"As I said, I once had a talent for prophecy. Last night, as I sat in the charming apartments you set aside for me, I had another. I cannot say that it entirely lifted my spirits, for my own death was part of it. Doom is upon you, Jianna. The world is about to change. The Armor of Bronze is once more gleaming in the sunshine. And heroes long dead will consign your empire to dust. You are about to become a legend, a creature of the past. Future generations will listen in horror to your tale. They will shiver and reach for talismans at the mention of your name."

Jianna clapped her hands. "I already know that Alahir and his Legend riders deserted you when they found an ancient relic. The story you have built around their desertion is diverting, but not as fascinating as I had hoped." Her voice hardened. "I am glad you liked the apartments I put aside for you. Even now bricks and mortar are being brought so that we can give you a more permanent roof. You will have no need of doorways or windows. You can spend your last days, or perhaps weeks, in quiet, lonely contemplation of your treachery."

Unwallis shivered at the sentence. The man was to be buried alive. Now he looked away, not wishing to dwell on the stricken expression of the former minister. As Agrias was dragged away his courage broke. "Kill me now!" he screamed. "For mercy's sake!" He was cuffed to silence.

Unwallis eased himself back through the watching crowd of soldiers.

Seventy years ago there had been two great men serving the Eternal, Landis Khan and Agrias. Both had now been dealt with. Landis was dead, his body burned, his ashes scattered. Now Agrias would die in a filthy pit amid the ruins of an ancient city. There had been others, who had not scaled the heights of Agrias and Landis, but who nevertheless were great men. Gamal, hunted down and murdered, Perisis, poi-

soned after he quit the Eternal's service, Joran, killed by
Memnon's Shadows. The list went on and on.

He remembered the day Landis Khan had left Diranan for
the lands granted to him by the Eternal. He had wondered
then if the Shadows would be dispatched after him. He and
Landis had spoken briefly on that last morning as servants
packed Landis's belongings. "Why are you leaving, my
friend?"

"I am tired, Unwallis. I want to rest and look at the mountains. I cannot face another war."

"There is no war."

"No, but there will be. Agrias to the north, Pendashal
across the ocean. One or the other. Perhaps both."

"Have you told the Eternal of your fears?"

Landis had smiled. "You think she does not know?"

"I don't understand."

"She is bored, Unwallis. War is the only recreation that
truly fires her blood."

Unwallis had dropped his voice. "She *wants* a war?"

"Think about it. Before sending Agrias north she abused
him in front of the court, heaping ridicule on his achieve-
ments. She shamed him, then, by way of apology, she
granted him the lands beyond the Delnoch mountains. You
know Agrias as well as I. He is unforgiving and vengeful. He
is also powerful and charismatic. He has his own generals,
his own artifacts. He can produce Jiamads. He can recruit
men. If you were the lord of this realm, would you let him
live?"

"I suppose not," agreed Unwallis.

"Indeed not," insisted Landis. "Now I have been granted
lands adjoining his. I will not play this game, however. I
will take no part in the coming war. Look after yourself,
Unwallis."

Looking back, Unwallis wondered how a man as intuitive
and intelligent as Landis could have believed his later actions
would fool the Eternal.

Unwallis trudged across the campsite to where his own tent had been placed. It was far smaller than that of the Eternal, and Unwallis had to stoop to enter it. There was barely room for the folding bed. He sat down upon it, then lay back and closed his eyes. It was as if a light had shone on a dark place in his mind, and he saw now so clearly. The first indication had come during the battle—or to be more precise, the dreadful moment when Jianna had drawn her grotesque horse alongside his and told him they were riding into a trap. Her eyes had shone with excitement, and he knew then that the Eternal *enjoyed* flirting with death. It seemed so obvious now why she engineered treachery and promoted men who would ultimately betray her. Eternal life bored her to tears. That was why she had ordered Memnon not to kill Skilgannon—not because she loved him, but precisely because he was a threat.

In effect poor Agrias was to be buried alive for doing exactly what the Eternal wanted.

How evil is that, wondered Unwallis.

Then there was Decado. She had ignored his excesses for years, but when the time came refused to consider poison, which would have taken his life swiftly and without the danger of escape. Now he was with Skilgannon, making the threat to Jianna even more potent.

The Armor of Bronze was even more mysterious. Unwallis recalled a time some fifty years ago when the Eternal had become interested in archaic sites. She had traveled then with an arcanist named Kilvanen, a shy man with only one abiding passion—seeking to unveil the secrets of the past. Unwallis had liked him. Unlike most of his contemporaries the arcanist was not power hungry; nor did he seek to rise through the Eternal's ranks. Unwallis felt comfortable in his company, and enjoyed the man's tales of digging and scrabbling through ancient earth in search of history's clues. He had become ill after a dig in the Sathuli lands. Unwallis had visited him. Kilvanen was not a rich man, and had few servants. He lived in a pleasant house on the hills north of the city. Unwallis had decided to offer him the services of his own physician, but when he arrived at the house he knew it was too late for medicines or potions. Kilvanen was all skin and bone, his skin pale and dry, his eyes bright with the coming of death. Unwallis asked him if he was in pain, but Kilvanen shook his head. "The Eternal has sent me strong narcotics," he said. "Thank her for me when you see her."

Then they had talked. Kilvanen drifted away into drug-induced sleep, then awoke and began to talk about his work. One story stayed with Unwallis. Kilvanen had discovered a secret chamber on a mountainside. In it, upon a wooden stand, was a suit of incredible armor, gleaming bronze. Kilvanen had known immediately what it was. It represented the greatest find of his life. He had rushed back to the camp to inform the Eternal, and together, holding lanterns, they had eased their way through the narrow tunnel that led to the armor. She had drawn the sword and touched the gleaming breastplate. "Before we remove it," Kilvanen had said, "we need to examine the chamber and see if there are any other clues as to why it was brought here."

"I would imagine he would know," said Jianna, pointing to the bones on the ground.

"My guess is that this was Lascarin the Thief," Kilvanen had told her. He then outlined the story of the theft of the legendary armor. At the rear of the chamber was a doorway leading to a blocked tunnel. Kilvanen had walked along it. Behind him the Eternal had cried out. Kilvanen rushed back.

The Armor was now encased in a block of glittering crystal.

"What happened, Highness?" he asked her.

"It just appeared. Did you touch anything in the tunnel?"

"No, Highness."

"How curious." Then, according to Kilvanen, she had walked to the crystal and reached out for the sword. Her hand had passed through the block, and she had drawn the blade cleanly. She had laughed then. "It is merely an illusion," she said, returning the blade to its scabbard. Kilvanen had approached the block—only to find it solid as glass. For a time they talked about the magical phenomenon. Finally Jianna gestured for Kilvanen to draw the blade. This time there was no resistance, and the arcanist pulled the weapon clear. "Now put it back," she told him. After he had done so Jianna reached toward the glittering helm—only to find her fingers could not pierce the crystal. She had laughed. "A clever spell," she had said. "The crack in the rock through which we arrived was not here when this chamber was built. The only entrance was the tunnel, into which you walked. It is the tunnel that activates the crystal barrier, and the sword that causes it to become illusion. This is so fascinating."

For Kilvanen it had been the most rewarding moment of his life. His joy had been short lived. Jianna had ordered the opening sealed, leaving the Armor of Bronze untouched. Kilvanen had pleaded with her, but she had been adamant that not only was the Armor to remain where it was, but Kilvanen should tell no one of its existence. There was little chance of that. Kilvanen took ill almost as soon as they returned to the capital. He was dead within three weeks.

It was only later, when some of the Eternal's other detractors died in the same way, that Unwallis realized she had killed the arcanist.

The Armor of Bronze, the great rallying symbol of the Drenai, was back.

Could it be, he wondered, that somehow the Eternal had engineered this also? That she had sought to make Skilgannon just a little more powerful, in order to heighten the risk?

That evening, in her tent, Jianna communed with Memnon. "I want to see Olek," she told the translucent image of the dark-eyed mage.

"I can show you him, Highness."

"I want him to see me, too. Can you help with this from such a distance?"

"Distance is no object, Highness. Hold the talisman firm in your hand and lie back. I will guide your spirit to him. He will see you."

Lying down on her bed, the bronze amulet in her hand, she closed her eyes. A cool breeze whispered across her, and she felt the mildly sickening wrench that always accompanied these flights of the spirit, as if a harsh hand had dragged her from her body. Then she was in the air, her spirit being drawn toward the northeast. She flowed over mountains and plains, and through a winding river canyon. Below her she saw five long barges, their sides painted bright crimson. They were anchored in the lee of a towering cliff face.

"He is in the lead barge, Highness," came the voice of Memnon. "He may be sleeping."

"Show me," she said, feeling a sense of rising excitement.

Her spirit was drawn closer to the boat. There were horses upon it, and sleeping men. At the prow stood Skilgannon, the Swords of Night and Day on his back. He was everything she remembered, and a great sadness touched her. He was tall and dark, his eyes brilliant blue, his face handsome. He looked just as he had that last day at the citadel, when they had kissed for the last time. "Bring me closer to him, Memnon."

Slowly her spirit floated over the deck, past the sleeping Drenai. She was now only a few feet from him. He was staring at the rearing cliffs, his eyes distant. Jianna knew that look. He was thinking and planning, examining every possibility that could thwart his mission.

"Ah, Olek," she said. "I have missed you."

"He did not hear you," said the voice of Memnon. "I need a moment, Highness, to bring your image to life."

Jianna waited.

Skilgannon suddenly stepped back, his face a mask of astonishment.

"I have dreamed of this moment for a thousand years," she said. "But never did I think we would meet as enemies." He said nothing, but she saw the surprise replaced by longing, and his expression softened.

"What is it you want here?" he said softly.

"To be friends again, Olek. To talk as we once did."

For a long moment he said nothing. Then he sighed. "Shall we talk of the day you chided that boy you caught pulling wings from a butterfly? Or of your dreams of gathering the finest surgeons and apothecaries to a central university, in order to advance the cause of medicine? Or perhaps the promises you made to make life more prosperous and happy for all the citizens of Naashan?"

"Why must you always be so argumentative, Olek? You could at least say you are glad to see me."

"Aye, it would be true, too," he admitted. "When you died the sun ceased to shine for me."

"Then come to me, Olek. Together we will build that university you spoke of. We will put in place all the plans we ever made."

"And you would be Sashan for me again?" he asked. His soft use of the name they had concocted when she had masqueraded as a whore to escape capture lanced into her. It brought back memories so distant they had all but disappeared from her consciousness.

"I would love that, Olek."

"It cannot be," he said, harshly. "Sashan is dead, Jianna. As indeed you and I are dead. We should not be here."

"Then you will not come to me?"

"I intend to end your reign."

"You would kill me, Olek?"

"No," he admitted, "I could never do that. But I can destroy the Eternal."

"You were a great general, Olek. You taught me much. I have a regiment of Eternal Guard on their way to the temple site. And two hundred of our strongest Jiamads. You think this ragtag group of misfits and dreamers can oppose them? Even with you and Decado? Even with Druss's ax and the Armor of Bronze? A thousand battle-hardened veterans, Olek. You really want to proceed with this folly? You really want all these boys to die?"

"I think you should go now," he said. "There is no more for

us to say. I love you. I have always loved you. But you are my enemy now, and I will bring you down."

He turned away from her then, and gripped the boat rail.

"I love you, too," she said.

Memnon's voice whispered into her mind. "Is it finished now, Highness?" he asked.

"Yes," she told him.

The world spun and she gasped as the weight of her body returned. Replacing the bronze amulet in its ornate box, she walked from her tent into the moonlight. She sent a sentry to find Agrippon. The officer had obviously not been sleeping, for he arrived swiftly.

"Dig up Agrias," she said.

"Highness?"

"I have changed my mind. Bring him out."

"At once, Highness."

Jianna returned to her tent and filled a goblet with rich, red wine. She did not often drink, but tonight she wanted that warm, enveloping mist that would soften the sharp pangs of her regrets.

She had not set out to become the Eternal, back on that distant day when her new eyes opened to a world of blue skies and fresh, sweet air. That was when she had first seen Landis Khan. In those early days in the temple she had merely been glad to be back in the world of the flesh, enjoying the long-forgotten delights of eating, sleeping, feeling the sun on her face, the wind in her hair. And she had been fascinated by the temple and its artifacts. There had been no thought of building armies or regaining thrones. She learned within the first few days of her new existence that the old empire of Naashan had survived a mere fifty years after her death, and that now her old palace was a ruin. At first she had thought it would be good to travel across the sea and gaze once more on familiar mountains. Common sense told her that this was not wise. The new world was much like the old, torn by wars, greed, and the lust of men. A woman without wealth, traveling alone, would be prey to any bandit chief, slaver, or mercenary warlord.

The decision that set her on her current path had been made with the best intentions. Landis Khan told her that a former priest, now a renegade warlord, had gathered a force and was said to be marching on the temple, desiring its power and the wealth it contained. The priests were terrified. The ward spell that protected them could be pierced by the renegade. Jianna asked them why they were not making plans to defend themselves. Landis Khan pointed out that the men here were academics, and not warriors. They commanded no soldiers and no defense force.

By this time Landis Khan was her lover and would do anything to please her. She told him that the answer lay in hiring mercenaries from among the bandits who roamed the wild lands. He was aghast at the thought. "Anyone who tried to approach them would be taken and tortured," he said. "These are savage, unholy creatures."

"Who is the worst of them?" she had asked.

"Abadai. He is vicious and cruel."

"How many men does he have?"

"I have no idea. Nor do I want to know."

"How old is he?"

"In his middle years. He has been raiding the caravans and sacking towns for three decades at least."

"Then he will do," said Jianna. Two days later, on a borrowed horse and armed with a saber, Jianna had ridden from the temple. She still had a crystal-clear memory of the moment she glanced back and saw nothing but a mountain behind her. No sign of the great doors, or the many windows. Merely blank rock. Even the great, golden mirror atop the peak was no longer visible.

She pushed on, following the directions Landis had reluctantly given her. He had even offered to come with her, and she had seen the gratitude in his eyes when she refused. By late afternoon, high in the mountains, she saw the first of Abadai's riders. There were three of them sitting their horses on the trail ahead. Jianna realized that from their position they must have been watching her for some time. As she rode closer she saw the hunger and the lust in their eyes. The men were of Nadir extraction, with high cheekbones and almond-shaped eyes. They wore breastplates of baked leather and carried long lances.

Jianna drew rein. "I am seeking Abadai," she said.

"I am Abadai," answered one of the men. "Step down and let us talk."

"You are far too ugly to be Abadai." The other riders smiled at her insult—the smiles vanishing as the first man glared at them.

"You will regret those words," he said.

"Regret is pointless," she told him. "Now either take me to Abadai, or—" The saber flashed into her hand. "—or just try to take me."

The lance head dropped and he yelled a wild battle cry as he heeled his horse forward. Jianna swayed to her left as the lance blade thrust at her, then her sword arm lashed out, the blade slicing through the back of the man's neck as he passed. His horse rode on for several steps. Then he pitched from the saddle.

"Do I have to kill you all?" she asked the two warriors, noting their expressions of shock. "Or will you take me to Abadai?"

"We'll take you," said one. "You should know that the man you killed was Abadai's brother."

The camp was a ramshackle affair, the tents old and patched. Naked children ran across the stony ground, and the women she saw were scrawny and undernourished. Raiding had obviously not been so profitable recently.

The men drew up outside a tent larger than the others. One of them called out, and a squat, powerful, middle-aged man stepped out. His harsh face was deeply lined, his eyes black and cruel. The riders spoke to him in a language Jianna did not know, and she sat quietly waiting.

At last Abadai turned his dark eyes on her. "Speak," he

said. "When you have finished I will decide whether to kill you quickly or slowly."

"You will not kill me, Abadai," she said, stepping down from the saddle and lifting her saddlebag clear. Draping it over her shoulder, she walked to face him.

"And why will I not?"

"I hold your dreams in my hand, warrior. I can give you what your heart most desires. I can also give your people what they most desire."

"And what is it that I most desire?" he asked.

Jianna smiled and stepped in close, her mouth next to the warrior's ear. "To be young again," she whispered.

He laughed then. "And perhaps I could grow wings, so that I could attack my enemies from the air, like an eagle?"

"Invite me into your tent and I shall prove the truth of my promise."

"Why should I even talk to you? There is a blood feud now between us. You killed my brother."

"You will not mourn him. I doubt you even liked him. The man was an idiot. You are not. However, if my words prove false, or if you decide to take your revenge anyway, it can wait until after we have spoken. You know the old saying? Revenge, like wine, needs time to mature. Then it tastes all the sweeter."

Abadai laughed. "You are an unusual woman. Is it merely extreme youth that makes you so reckless?"

"Youth, Abadai? I am five hundred years old. Now invite me inside, for the sun is hot, and I am thirsty."

Jianna smiled as she remembered that long-ago day. Sipping her wine, she thought of Skilgannon. He would have been proud of her. There would have been no look of contempt in his eyes. She sighed. That look was hard to bear. It did not matter that he was a romantic and could never understand the need for ruthlessness in a monarch. It did not matter . . .

Yet it did.

In all her long life Jianna had needed admiration from only one person.

The man now out to destroy her.

She shivered, drained her goblet, poured another, and sought refuge in a past untainted by soaring ambition.

Landis Khan had given her a regenerative potion that the priests used to fend off sickness. It was, he said, a life extender. Not as powerful as having a reborn body, but it strengthened the immune system and revitalized glands and muscles that had begun to wither with age.

She had walked into Abadai's filthy tent and sat down on a rug at the center, her saber across her lap, her saddlebag by her side. Abadai sat cross-legged opposite her. "Your words need to be golden," he said.

She smiled. Reaching into her saddlebag, she produced the potion. It was contained in a bottle of purple glass, stoppered with wax. "Drink this," she said, offering it to him.

"What is it?"

"It might be poison. Or it might give you a hint of what youth was once like." Abadai returned the smile, but it was more of a grimace. He called out to the riders who were waiting outside. Ducking under the tent flap, they entered.

"I am about to drink a potion," he said. "If it kills me then I want the bitch cut into pieces. Her suffering should be long."

The riders glanced at one another and looked nervous. Jianna leaned forward. "They don't want to embarrass themselves, Abadai, but they would be happier if you called in more men. However, that will not be necessary," she said, lifting her saber and tossing it to one of the warriors. Abadai shook his head and suddenly chuckled.

"I am beginning to like you very much," he told her, his gaze resting on her long legs.

"I have that effect on men," she said.

Abadai took the purple bottle, broke the seal, and drank the contents in a single swallow. Then he sat very still watching her. "I feel nothing," he said.

"You will, warrior. Now here is the second part of my promise." Delving once more into the bag, she produced a heavy pouch, tossing it to the leader. He tipped the contents into his palm. Gold coins tumbled from his fingers. The other two warriors scrambled forward to get a closer look at the treasure. Abadai waved them back. He looked at her now with different eyes.

"This is the kind of promise I can understand," he said. "What is it for?"

"I need an army. Not too large. Perhaps two hundred good fighting men, a few archers."

Abadai took a deep breath, then levered himself to his feet. Stretching out his arms, he clenched his fists. Jianna looked at him. The deep lines on his face were softening, the iron gray of his hair growing darker. "I feel . . . strong," he said. Jianna, who had only heard from Landis about the power of the potion, was almost as surprised as the warlord. The effect was startling. Masking her surprise, she glanced at the two warriors. They were standing openmouthed.

Abadai waved them away. As they left the tent he sat down once more. "You have been true to your word, girl. Where do you come from?"

"The Temple of the Resurrection."

His eyes widened, and he was about to reply when he stopped and laughed. "I was about to say it was a myth. But I am here, younger and stronger. How young do I look?" he asked, suddenly.

"You have lost at least ten years," she said. "I will supply fifty more gold coins before the fight, and fifty after we win. How many men do you have?"

"Sixty or so. There were more . . ." He shrugged. "This has been a bad year. Two bands struck out on their own."

"You know where they are?"

"Of course."

"Then send for them. When they are gathered, show them the gold. I will supply you with one extra coin for every man. This needs to be accomplished with speed, Abadai. The force we are facing will be in the mountains within the week."

"And they are?"

"Mercenaries—much as you yourself. They are led by a former priest of the Resurrection and will be traveling down from the city of Gassima."

"How many men does this priest have?"

She shrugged and spread her hands. "I would think no more than a few hundred. Perhaps less. All plunder from the bodies will belong to you, and all horses taken."

Drawing in a deep breath, he stared at her with undisguised longing. "You fire my blood, girl. Share my bed and we will spit hands on the agreement."

Jianna laughed. "After we win, Abadai, I will come to you. You will need the extra youth and vitality I have given you. And perhaps more." Rising from the rug, she gathered up her saddlebag, slinging it over her shoulder. "When you have the men assembled, ride west until you see the hanging rock. You know where I mean?"

"Of course I know. Close to the old oasis."

"The very same. I will join you there."

"You were right," he said as she reached the tent flap. Jianna glanced back. "He was my idiot brother. I came close to killing him myself a couple of times."

The battle with the priest's force had been short, bloody, and decisive. Unfortunately the man had escaped with a handful of riders. But most of his three hundred mercenaries lay dead on the desert floor. Abadai and his warriors had rushed around the battlefield, butchering wounded survivors and stripping them of rings, trinkets, clothes, and boots.

That night, as she had promised, she spent with the bandit leader. His lovemaking was fierce and urgent, lacking finesse and subtlety. Yet it was sublime when compared to the fumbling adoration of Landis Khan.

And so had begun the journey that would culminate in empire. Fearing the priest would return with a larger force, the priests had authorized Jianna to gather an army. With this she had marched to Gassima and sacked the city. Once more the priest escaped, heading south. Jianna pursued him. The priest sought refuge with a bandit warlord in the Sathuli mountains. Jianna gathered more fighters and crushed his army also. As her fame grew, her force swelled. She had become a power in the land. By the time the priest was caught and killed, he had become incidental to the greater purpose. The day of the Eternal had dawned.

The wine jug was empty. Jianna called out to her Guard, ordering them to bring her another. Agrippon himself brought it. "Well," she said, "where is Agrias?"

"He had strangled himself with the cord of his robe, Highness."

"The idiot. He always had a poor sense of timing," she said. "Send for Unwallis."

Alone once more she allowed the memories of the years to slide before her mind's eye. As the army grew larger it became more and more necessary to widen the scope of its activities. More and more towns and cities came under her sway. Until, at last, even the fading empire of the Drenai fell before her, their ambassadors bending the knee, pledging allegiance. She had transferred the seat of her power to Diranan, taking Landis Khan and Agrias, and many of the priests and their artifacts of power, with her.

There had been many insurrections, a score of small wars. Yet always her empire swelled. As she grew older, and even the restorative potions began to lose their magic, Landis Khan had suggested repeating the process by which they had brought her back: raising duplicates of her.

Was that when I became evil? she wondered. Anger flared. *You are seeing yourself through Skilgannon's eyes,* she chided herself.

Or perhaps through the eyes of the last abbot, she realized. She had returned to the temple with Landis, seeking more artifacts. Landis wanted to study in the great library. The abbot had come down, she thought, to greet them. Instead he stood in the great doorway and refused them leave to enter. Jianna had been shocked.

"You have corrupted this temple," he said. "You have made a mockery of everything we have worked for over the centuries. You have built an empire of evil, and seduced once good men like Landis to follow in your footsteps. You will not enter here, Jianna."

Before she could answer he had stepped back inside, and the doors had swung shut. Furious, Jianna had ridden, with her fifty Eternal Guardsmen, to the closest garrison. Gathering several hundred men, she had returned—only to find the temple gone. Two riders rode over the rim of the crater that remained. They died horribly, the metal of their armor twisting around them, tearing into their flesh.

The arrival of Unwallis brought her thoughts back to the present. The statesman was disheveled, his eyes heavy with sleep. "Is there a problem, Highness?" he asked.

"I felt in need of the company of a friend," she said. "Be at ease, I do not intend to seduce you. Just sit with me."

"What has happened?" he asked.

"I saw Skilgannon. And now I must kill him." She laughed then. "It is curious, Unwallis, but a part of me wants to be at his side, fighting the good fight against the evil Eternal. How foolish is that?"

"A part of you is doing just that," he said.

"An interesting riddle? Perhaps you would explain."

"I might be wrong, Highness, but did you not send the Legend riders to him?"

She looked at him closely, then shook her head and smiled. "I always forget how clever you are, my dear. But this is your crowning moment. How could you possibly know that? Did Memnon tell you?"

"No, Highness. I knew that you and Kilvanen found the Armor of Bronze. It seemed rather too coincidental that a wandering Drenai rider should discover the site."

"And what conclusions do you draw?" she asked him.

"The wars with Agrias here, and Pendashal in the east, are of your own making. You crave excitement, and, in reality, there is no one who can truly defeat you. Once I realized that, then I knew the discovery of the Armor was not happenstance."

"Ah, Unwallis, if you had only been a soldier, or developed some strategic skills."

"I am happy I did not, Highness, for perhaps then I would have been buried alive like poor Agrias. As it is I fear my candor will cost me my life."

"Then why risk it?"

"Sometimes," he said, "the truth just has to be spoken, no matter what the consequences. Landis Khan was a friend of mine. He knew of your manipulations. He also knew you were hoping he would join Agrias. The two of them might have really tested you."

"His plans were rather more dangerous to me," she said.

"I think he surprised you with those. Even so, you have sought to give Skilgannon a greater chance than he would have had."

"He deserves it," she said, refilling her goblet. "I never had a braver or more dedicated friend. Olek risked his life many times for me. Without him I would never have escaped the city. My father's murderers would have caught me and killed me, as they did my mother. Skilgannon lost his friends and his youth to my cause. Through the darkest times—when we thought we were finished—he stayed loyal. He won battles no other general could have. Outnumbered, sometimes outmaneuvered, occasionally even—in those early days—outclassed, he won. He was unstoppable. His men revered him. They fought with utter belief in his ultimate victory. It was a sight to behold."

"And this is the man you have given an army to? Do you want to be defeated, Highness?"

"Sometimes," she said, her voice slurring. "Come to my bed, Unwallis. I don't want sex. I just want to fall asleep next to a friend."

"Then you are not going to have me killed?"

"Ask me in the morning," she told him.

Nineteen

Skilgannon headed his chestnut gelding up the steep, rocky slope, pausing below the crest and dismounting. Leaving the gelding's reins trailing, he eased his way to the top and gazed out over the rugged, arid lands that stretched from the mountains to the sea. Unlike the deserts across the ocean there was no heat to speak of here. It was a desert simply because the ground lacked topsoil, consisting almost entirely of rock. Harsh winds blew across the plateau, and what plants could grow in this inhospitable place were thin and spiky. The few trees were dry, the wood snapping and crumbling under the faintest of pressure.

Skilgannon's throat was dry, his hair gray with rock dust. His eyes felt gritty. Seeing that the land below was empty of movement, he waved the others forward. Decado and Alahir rode their horses up.

"No sign of them yet," said Skilgannon.

"Why would she warn you?" asked Decado.

"I cannot answer that."

"Maybe the bitch was lying," said Alahir. Skilgannon glanced at him. The events of the morning lay heavy on the Drenai leader. After days of easy traveling they had disembarked on the banks of the Rostrias and headed north for the temple site. The riders had been glad to be free of the boats. As indeed had the Jiamads. The two-day march to the temple mountains had been without incident. Stavut and his pack had also caught and killed eight bighorn sheep, and everyone had tasted fresh meat.

This morning had seen the first tragedy.

They had arrived at the temple mountains, and Skilgannon had seen for himself the enormous crater where the temple had been. It was a disconcerting sight. Although Gamal had said it was gone, Skilgannon had nursed the hope that the man had been mistaken; that he and his companion had traveled to the wrong place.

The riders had reined in on the edge of the crater. Shakul had wandered over the rim, his great head swaying. Then he had stumbled, and almost fallen. Alahir's young aide, Bagalan, had dismounted. When Shakul seemed in trouble, he had run forward. Then he had screamed. Shakul grabbed the rider and lurched back over the rim. Bagalan had writhed in his grasp, blood bursting from his mouth and throat. Shakul lowered him to the ground, and the riders had gathered around. Alahir was the first to the young man's side. Blood was seeping through Bagalan's armor. His body went through a series of violent spasms. Then he died.

Alahir stared down at the boy's twisted armor. His chainmail gorget was mangled and blood covered, his breastplate cracked. Lower down his chain-mail hauberk was embedded in the flesh of his right thigh. It was as if his armor had come alive, and had eaten its way into his body.

Skilgannon stood over the corpse. He did not remind them that he had warned the riders to stay clear of the crater. There was no need. Bagalan's mutilated corpse was enough of a reminder.

"No way for a Drenai warrior to die," said the veteran Gilden. "We cannot even take his armor." Alahir tried to draw the boy's sword from its scabbard, but even this had twisted and melded.

"What kind of magic does this?" asked Alahir, his face ghostly pale.

"I don't know," said Skilgannon.

One of the riders swore—and pointed at the crater. Bagalan's helm was writhing on the dusty ground. It was changing shape—as if a giant, unseen hammer was pounding it. Then, as they watched, the helm rose from the ground, twisting and shimmering in the sunlight. It flew higher, then moved north, like a silver bird. The riders watched it until it disappeared. No one spoke.

"Move back from the rim," said Skilgannon, at last. "Set up camp over there by the stand of rocks."

Moving to his horse, he stepped into the saddle. "Alahir!" he called. "Ride with me. We need to scout for a defensive position."

Alahir backed away from the corpse and mounted his horse. As Skilgannon headed away toward the east, Alahir and Decado joined him.

"I still think she might have been lying," said Alahir.

"It is a possibility, but I don't think so. Therefore, until we know differently, we will assume we are facing a thousand riders and two hundred Jiamads. We cannot take them on open ground. They will flank us."

"I've seen the Eternal Guard in action," said Decado. "They are rather splendid, you know." He looked at Alahir. "No offense to you and your men, but I'd back the Guard to take any force. Would it not be better to stay mobile, rather than pick a battle site?"

"Look around you, Decado," said Skilgannon. "Open land with no cover? A few water holes, and no trees. No hiding places. We cannot run. Our only hope is to locate the temple and end the magic."

"You have not seen the Legend riders fight," Alahir told Decado. "I would wager they will turn back this Guard of yours."

"An interesting idea," said Decado, with a wide smile. "However, if you lose how would you pay the wager?"

"We do not lose," snapped Alahir.

"Let us move on," said Skilgannon.

For two hours they rode over the arid land. Skilgannon stopped often to study the ground. He questioned Alahir about the route the Guard would take. Alahir, who had never been this far north, could offer little constructive advice.

Decado offered his opinion. "They would have taken ships from Draspartha," he said, "and followed the coast. Beyond the mountains ahead of us is the Pelucid Sea. There is only one port on the coast—well, more of a fishing settlement, really—but there is a jetty. I stopped there two years ago after returning from a campaign in Sherak. As I recall there is a mountain road leading to the old silver mines."

"A pass would suit us," said Skilgannon. "Somewhere narrow. That would level the odds."

"You might be expecting too much," said Decado. "In my experience there is rarely only one pass through any mountain range. If we form up in one, what is to stop the Guard from finding another and encircling us?"

"First let us find a pass. Then we'll argue about how to hold it," Skilgannon told him. Angling his horse, he set off toward a tower of red rock that rose like a spear above the surrounding high ground. Dismounting, he walked around the base of the tower, then levered himself up, seeking out hand- and footholds. Decado and Alahir watched him as he climbed ever higher.

Once on the face Skilgannon moved with care. The holds were good, but he was aware that the rock was soft stone, and he tested each hold before applying his full weight.

Several times as he gripped what seemed a solid hold the rock would crumble and fall away. Higher he went, until he was some two hundred feet above the rocks below. He glanced down. Decado and Alahir had dismounted and were watching him keenly.

At last he levered himself over the lip of the peak and sat staring down over the land below. From here he could see the sharp breaks in the mountains signifying passes. Decado had been right. There were several. He could not tell from this vantage point which of them might be blind canyons, but he could see the main pass, and just glimpse the sea in the far distance. He sat for a while, gathering his strength for the return climb, and continued to study the land ahead. When he had finally committed the scene to memory he eased himself back over the edge and climbed carefully down.

Despite his skills he was relieved when his feet touched solid ground.

He told the waiting men what he had seen and sent Alahir back to fetch the rest of the force, directing him to head due east toward the deep V-shaped cut in the mountains. "Decado and I will scout the various passes, and see which offers the best chance of success."

As Alahir rode away, Decado shook his head. "You are the most optimistic man I have ever met, kinsman. Do you really believe these country boys can beat the Guard?"

"It hardly matters what I believe. We cannot run, and we cannot hide. Therefore we fight. And when I fight, Decado, I win. Be it an army or a single man."

"Unlike most people I love arrogance," said Decado, happily. "It is so refreshing. I feel the same way. There's not a man born of woman who could live with me in a duel. And you know what that means, don't you?"

"Tell me."

"One of us is wrong."

"Or both of us," said Skilgannon. "How fortunate we are on the same side."

Decado chuckled. "Fortune is a fickle beast at best," he said.

Skilgannon walked to his horse and mounted. "Tell me all you can of the Guard, their training methods, their tactics, their weapons," he said as Decado moved to his own mount.

Decado swung himself into the saddle. "Mounted or on foot they always attack," he said. "And like you, kinsman, they never lose."

Unwallis had experienced many ambitions in his long life. Most had been fulfilled. One would never be fulfilled. For some reason that he would never understand, none of the many women in his life had ever conceived children by him. It had always been a mild regret. Until now.

He lay in the royal bed, Jianna curled up alongside him, her head on his shoulder, her thigh across his own. She was, at this moment, entirely childlike, and Unwallis felt a strong paternal affection for the sleeping queen. He lay there quietly, stroking her long, dark hair. Intellect told him this feeling was merely an illusion. The women lying in his arms was a ruthless tyrant, with the deaths of nations on her conscience. But in the dark of the tent his intellect faded back, allowing his emotions to roam free.

An hour passed. Unwallis began to doze.

Something caused him to wake suddenly. His eyes flared open.

He found himself looking into the gray face of a Shadow, looming over the bed. A knife blade pricked the skin of his shoulder, and he fell back. The paralysis came swiftly. Two other Shadows moved alongside. He saw Jianna jerk and try to swing her legs from the bed. With a swiftness the eye could not follow they were upon her.

Unwallis, paralyzed, could do nothing to help her. He could not even close his eyes when he saw a cold, gray dagger blade plunge into Jianna's heart. Her body fell back to the bed, her dead eyes staring into Unwallis's frozen orbs. Then the Shadows dragged the queen's corpse from her bed.

Unwallis did not see them take her from the tent. He lay, his unclosed eyes becoming dry and painful, for several agonizing hours. Finally he was lifted up by Agrippon. A surgeon was beside the bed. Together they lifted Unwallis into a sitting position. Slowly the feeling came back to his arms, and with it a terrible pounding pain in his skull.

When at last he could speak he uttered a single word. "Jianna?"

"Shadows struck down the Guard," said Agrippon. "We can find no trace of her."

"She was killed," said Unwallis. "Stabbed through the heart. They took her body away."

*   *   *

Alahir stretched out on the rocky ground at the water's edge and removed his helm and hauberk. The sun was warm, but there was a breeze whispering through the rocks, cooled as it passed over the pool. All around him the Legend riders, save for the men scouting the eastern roads, were relaxing. Beyond them the horses, watered now, were tethered in the shade of the western rock face.

Gilden joined him. The veteran had doffed his armor and was dressed now only in a simple gray, knee-length tunic. He did not look like a soldier now; more a grim-faced teacher. "That tunic has seen better days," observed Alahir.

Gilden glanced down. "It was once green, I think," he said. Then he sat down, reached into the water, and splashed his face. Leaning over, he gazed into the depths. "I wonder how deep it is," he said.

"Amazing that it is here at all," said Alahir. "Is it just trapped rainfall, do you think?"

"Hard to say," Gilden told him. "Desert tanks like these can be connected to artesian wells—even underground lakes. I think that's why the ancients angled the road so close to the cliffs here. It would have made a fine resting place on the journey from the sea to the interior. Merchants could water their horses and rest before the long haul to Gulgothir or Gassima." He glanced across to the other side of the pool, some thirty feet away, where Askari was sitting alongside the brooding Harad. "Beautiful girl. That Stavut is a lucky man."

"I am not sure how lucky any of us are," said Alahir. "We are about to face the Eternal Guard and a few hundred Jems."

Gilden did not reply. He cast his eyes around the area. "Where is Stavut?"

"The pack went off with Skilgannon and Decado. They are scouting the other passes, trying to see whether the Guard can find a way around us."

Gilden laughed. "A part of me hopes they miss us completely."

"I know the feeling," agreed Alahir. "But then what would

we do, my friend? Ride home and die facing yet another regiment—or two, or ten?"

"There is that."

Askari rose and walked over to sit with them. "The water is cool and yet no one is swimming," she said. "Why is that?"

Gilden laughed aloud, and looked at Alahir. "We are not, er, great swimmers," Alahir told her, his face reddening.

Askari glanced at Gilden. "Am I missing something here?"

"Indeed you are, lass."

"Oh shut up, Gil!" snapped Alahir.

"Ours is a society of ancient values, some of which, to be frank, are startlingly stupid," said Gilden, gleefully. "Women come in three groups: angelic maidens, wives, and whores. The first two groups are revered, the third enjoyed. Of course when I say *enjoyed,* it should be understood that this enjoyment comes with a sack of guilt."

"And this has something to do with swimming?" asked Askari.

"At any time the enemy may come in sight. You don't want to be fighting in wet clothes. Therefore we would swim naked. And the Drenai cannot do that while you are here, you angelic maiden you." His laughter boomed out.

"But you do not share this . . . shyness?" she said, sweetly.

"I was part raised in the south, across the Delnoch mountains, so I have greater experience of other cultures."

"Good, then doff that threadbare tunic and show your comrades how well you swim."

Now it was Alahir whose laughter rang out. Gilden reddened. "Ah, well," he temporized, "having said that, I never did quite throw off the shackles of my training."

Askari smiled. "So the Legend riders are really just shy boys, frightened of being seen naked?" She swung to Alahir. "Are you shy, earl of Bronze?"

"Yes," he admitted. "But I would really like to swim." Pushing himself to his feet, he stripped off his shirt and leggings and dived into the water, sending up a mighty splash.

All around the pool the Legend riders hooted and clapped.
Several other men stripped off and joined him.

The water was wonderfully cool, and Alahir swam to the
far side of the pool, resting his elbows on a rock and glancing up at Harad. He was sitting quietly, the great ax in his lap.
"Join us, my friend," said Alahir.

"I cannot swim," said Harad.

"It is easy. Put aside the ax and come in. I will teach you in
a matter of moments."

Harad suddenly grinned. "Aye, that would be good," he
said. Throwing off his clothes, he waded into the water.
"What do I do?" he asked.

"Take a deep breath and lie back. The air in your lungs will
keep you afloat."

Harad leaned back. As his head touched the water he tried
to stand. His foot slipped and he sank beneath the surface,
coming up spluttering. Alahir was beside him in an instant.
"Trust me," said Alahir. "I will support your back. Now
breathe in deeply and we will get you to float."

Askari watched the two men and swung to Gilden. "You
are old to be a soldier," she said.

"Thank you for sharing that observation," he said sourly.

"I meant no disrespect. Far from it. To have survived this
long you must be very skilled."

"Lucky is all."

"You have family? Children?"

He chuckled. "I have these shy boys," he said. "They are
my family. One day they will take my armor and bury me.
Then they will sing songs over my grave. It is enough for me."

"The sky is too blue to be talking about graves and death,"
she pointed out. Rising to her feet, she stripped off her
clothes. "Come, Gilden, swim with me," she said, holding
out her hand. He hesitated for a moment, then sighed and
stood. Pulling his tunic over his head, he displayed a body
with many scars across his chest and shoulders and upper
thighs. Askari held out her hand and drew him into the water.

Just then Skilgannon and Decado rode through the entrance

to the pool and dismounted. Alahir saw them, left Harad happily floating, and waded to the bank. Decado moved away from them, stripping off his clothes and diving into the pool. Skilgannon looked tired. His eyes were red rimmed, his face gaunt. "Perhaps you should get into the pool," offered Alahir.

"We found three other passes that could be used to get behind us," said Skilgannon, "and we don't have enough men to adequately defend them all. There may be even more that I couldn't find. Once down into the low canyons it is like a warren. Stavut is still checking them."

"They will come at us head-on first," said Alahir. "It is the way of the Guard. See the enemy, kill the enemy. They have great belief in their martial supremacy."

"I agree. It matches everything Decado told me."

"Then what is worrying you?"

Skilgannon grinned. "You mean apart from being outnumbered four to one? If we are cut off then I will not be able to reach the temple site, and this whole venture will have been for nothing."

"There is nothing there," Alahir pointed out. "We have seen that for ourselves." His body almost dry in the bright sunshine, he picked up his tunic and slipped it on, and then his leggings. "So let's just finish off this Guard and head back for Siccus."

"The magic is still emanating," said Skilgannon. "It *must* be there."

"I know nothing about magic, Skilgannon, but if the temple is gone, perhaps they took it somewhere else. Another country. Over the sea."

"True," admitted Skilgannon, wearily. "But the prophecy said I would find the answer. And I am here—not across the sea." Taking the reins of the two mounts, he led them to the far side of the pool. Alahir helped him with the unsaddling, and they rubbed the beasts down. Then Skilgannon gestured for Alahir to follow him, and they walked back through the deep cut in the rocks that led out to the trail. It was some thirty feet wide here, dropping steeply away to the north.

Skilgannon walked to the edge. From here they could see the great crater where the temple mountain once stood. Skilgannon stared at the distant ring. Heat waves were shimmering over it. Reluctantly he turned away. "We have an advantage here," he said to Alahir. "The ground dips away to the east, which means the enemy will be coming at us uphill. The cliffs and the precipice mean they cannot flank us." He walked on down the old road; it narrowed to around fifteen feet at the bend, which swung away sharply before continuing down to the canyon below. "They will have no time to form up properly for a charge," continued Skilgannon. "The formation will break at this point, where only five or six riders can stay abreast of one another. Once past this they will be in arrow range. I can't see them risking their horses against trained bowmen on high ground."

"No," agreed Alahir. "They will dismount and come at us fast on foot."

"Or send in their beasts."

"I think they will hold back the beasts at first," said Alahir.

"Why so?"

"I don't wish to sound arrogant, but we are the elite, Skilgannon. The Legend riders have a reputation. I think the Guard will want to test that. Once we bloody their noses *then* they'll send the beasts."

"That sounds right to me," admitted Skilgannon, walking once more to the edge. He gazed down. "It is almost half a mile to the canyon floor, but the enemy, following a winding uphill road, will have to travel four, perhaps five, times that far. I don't know how long they will have been without water, but even with supplies their mounts will be tired, and the warriors will be hot, their mouths dry, their eyes gritty."

They stood in silence. Alahir gazed at the winding road, picturing the Eternal Guard in their black-and-silver armor, their high-plumed helms. Skilgannon was right. The road, some 150 paces from the entrance to the rock pool, was too narrow for them to form up for a charge. They would have to attack in relative disorder, trying to create a strong formation even as they ran toward the bowmen. Moving to the narrow point, he turned and began to run back up the slope, counting as he did so.

"How many?" asked Skilgannon.

"I would be surprised if we couldn't loose six volleys before they hit our front rank."

"Roughly fifteen hundred arrows," estimated Skilgannon. "Against heavily armored men carrying shields. At least half the shafts will be blocked. Half again will strike breastplates or chain mail and do no damage."

"And at least half of the remainder will wound, but not incapacitate," added Alahir.

"That leaves around one hundred and twenty-five taken out of the fight. Leaving eight hundred and seventy-five engaged in hand-to-hand combat with two hundred and fifty. Sheer weight of numbers will drive us back." Skilgannon strolled along the road back to the entrance leading to the rock pool. "It would be natural," he said, "to pull back into here. The entranceway is narrow and could be easily defended. Yet it would be suicidal, for there is no other way out."

He walked on another two hundred paces. Here was the top of the rise. After this the land opened out, as the road meandered down to the desert below. "Once past this point and they will flank us, encircle us, and kill us at their leisure."

"You are beginning to depress me," muttered Alahir.

Skilgannon laughed and clapped the man on the shoulder. "Plan for the worst, expect the best," he quoted. Then he walked back to the main trail and squatted down, studying the land.

"We could send a small group of riders down the trail," offered Alahir, "and hit them as they climbed. That would increase their losses."

"True—but then the Jems would probably come first, chasing our riders. We need the Guard to make the first attack. Then we can strip away their arrogance and leave them terrified of failure and death. The sending of their beasts must be an act of resignation and defeat. Then, when we have turned back the beasts, the day will be ours."

"Ah, this is more to my liking," Alahir told him.

"What is the fewest number of men you need to hold the line there?" asked Skilgannon, pointing to the widest point of the old road.

"A hundred. Perhaps a hundred and fifty."

Skilgannon remained silent, his expression intense. Twice he looked back up the trail, then glanced up at the towering cliffs to his left. Telling Alahir to stand at the widest point, Skilgannon retreated up the slope some fifty paces. After a while he returned. "We need to keep shooting at all times," he said. "When the first attack comes we will meet it here. Once the Guard engage, the rear ranks of our bowmen will move back to the high ground and shoot over our heads into the mass beyond the fighters. They will be crammed together, struggling to get to the action. How many shafts does each man carry?"

"Thirty."

"If we break their first attack we can replenish our supply from the dead. Everything depends on that first charge. We need to hold them until their confidence breaks. Decado and I will be at the center of the first line."

"As will I," said Alahir.

"Indeed. Wear the Armor of Bronze, Alahir. It will lift the men."

"I had that in mind. Where will Harad fight?"

"He is a concern," said Skilgannon. "He is brave and he is powerful, but he is unskilled. Added to which no axman can fight in close quarters, surrounded by comrades. He needs room to swing that weapon. I shall send him with Stavut and the pack to watch the other passes."

"That is a shame," said Alahir. "You are right that the Armor of Bronze will lift my men. So would the thought of Druss's ax being used in the battle."

"It may come to that by the end," Skilgannon told him.

* * *

Harad followed Shakul and Stavut up a long rise and onto a wide plateau overlooking a narrow pass, snaking east through the mountains. Here the rest of the pack were waiting. Harad took a swig from a water canteen loaned to him by a Legend rider. Swishing the water around his mouth, he spat it out, seeking to remove the taste of rock dust. Sweat trickled down his back. He glared balefully at the arid land and found himself longing for the green leaves in the forest back home. This brought an instant image of Charis, smiling as she brought him his food. His mood darkened, a mixture of sorrow and rage swirling through him.

Stavut wandered over. "About two miles ahead the trail you can see merges with the old road. If they split their force, this is the way they will come."

Harad would have preferred to fight alongside the Legend riders, rather than these beasts. He was uneasy around them, though he marveled at the way Stavut wandered among them, clapping some on the shoulder and making jokes Harad was sure the beasts could not understand. The Jiamads stretched out in the sunshine. Many of them began to doze. Stavut yawned and scratched his thickening beard. "Do you know any stories about Druss?" asked Harad.

"A few. Legends probably. His wife was a princess of some kind. She was stolen from the palace by traitors. I think some foreign king had fallen in love with her. Anyway, she was taken across the sea, and Druss went and fetched her back."

"Storytelling is not a strong point of yours, is it?" said Harad.

"I never was much interested in history. I think he fought a demon king as well—but that could have been someone else."

"Why is it that all the heroes married princesses?" asked Harad.

"I guess that's what heroes do." Stavut glanced back down the trail. "I hope they don't come this way," he said.

Shakul suddenly stood and raised his head into the air,

nostrils quivering. The other Jiamads stirred. Stavut swore. Harad took up his ax. "You are as good at hoping as you are at storytelling," said Harad.

Shakul padded back to where the two men waited. "Many Jems. Here soon," he said.

"How many?" asked Stavut.

"Big pack."

"Bigger than us?"

"Many times."

Stavut swore again and drew the cavalry saber Alahir had given him. "I think you should keep back out of the action," observed Harad. "Unless you know how to use that."

"Very droll," muttered Stavut.

Shakul sniffed the air again. "Not all come," he said. Stavut moved forward to where the trail dipped down toward the canyon floor. To the right was a towering cliff; to the left, an awesome drop. The trail was some twenty feet wide. Then he glanced around. There were scores of boulders from previous rockfalls, scattered over the plateau.

"Shak, I want as many of those big rocks pushed to the edge of the plateau as you can."

"Rocks?"

Stavut ran to a huge boulder and placed his hands upon it, pretending to push. "We will roll them down toward the enemy. Come on, lads!" he shouted. Shakul walked to the boulder and heaved his enormous bulk against it. The massive rock did not budge.

"No good," said Shakul.

"Together we can do it. Grava! Ironfist! Blackrock! Over here!" Three more Jiamads joined him. Together they threw their weight against the boulder. Slowly it began to move. "Careful now!" warned Stavut. "We want it right on the edge." Harad moved forward to assist them, and slowly they rolled the giant rock into place. Others followed, until there was a line of colossal rocks perched on the edge of the plateau. Then they waited.

Far below they saw the first of the Jiamads come into

sight. There was an officer with them, on a piebald horse. Stavut ordered his pack to pull back from the crest. He was not quick enough, and the officer saw them. Harad watched as he waved his arm forward. The Jiamads with him began to run up the slope. They were big beasts, all of them as large as Shakul, perhaps larger, and they were carrying long clubs of dark iron. Harad counted them as they came. There were more than forty of them, and they were moving fast. The officer was riding with them. He had drawn his saber, and his black cloak was billowing behind him.

When the beasts were halfway up the slope Stavut bellowed: "Now!"

Shakul and several of the others hurled themselves at the first boulder, tipping it over the edge. Others of the pack pushed another great rock after it. Then a third. The first stopped about ten paces ahead, but the second rolled on, picking up pace. Shakul ran to the first, Grava alongside him. Together they got it moving, then loped back to where Stavut stood with Harad.

Five boulders were now rumbling down the slope. They picked up speed, bouncing off the rock face to the right. One of them rolled over the edge long before it reached the Jiamads. Another hit the cliff face and stopped. The rest thundered on, picking up speed. The charging Jiamads stopped as they realized the danger. They turned and tried to run. The officer's horse reared as he dragged on the reins. Then a boulder struck the piebald, hurtling it over the edge. The officer managed to kick his feet clear of the stirrups just before the boulder struck, and threw himself from the doomed horse.

Harad stared down through the dust cloud the avalanche had caused. At least ten of the Jiamads had been swept to their deaths, or crushed. The others regrouped. The officer, his plumed helmet gone, waved his sword in the air, pointing up the mountainside. And the enemy came on again.

Shakul and the pack waited. Stavut moved up to stand at the center, Harad alongside him.

"I hate fighting," said Stavut.

"Picked the wrong place to be," muttered Harad.

As the enemy neared, Stavut shouted at the top of his voice, "Kill them all!" With a great roar the pack hurled themselves at the enemy. Harad ran with them. A massive beast swung an iron club at his head. Harad ducked and sent Snaga crunching through its ribs. Then he shoulder-charged the dying beast, thrusting it aside as he hurled himself at another. Shakul grabbed a Jiamad by the throat and groin, hoisting it into the air and flinging the hapless beast back into his comrades. Stavut whacked his saber at a charging Jiamad. The blade bounced away, causing no more than a shallow cut. The beast grabbed Stavut by the shirt, dragging him toward its fangs. A mighty blow from Shakul struck the side of its head. Dropping Stavut, it turned toward Shakul. The two beasts roared and hurled themselves at one another.

Stavut pushed himself to his feet and gathered up his fallen saber. The plateau echoed with the sounds of snarls and cries. Shakul tore the throat from his opponent and rushed back into the fray. Harad was attacking with relentless power, blocking and cutting, the great ax cleaving through fur, flesh, and bone. Stavut ran to help him, leaping over fallen beasts and ducking around others who were still fighting. The officer of the Eternal Guard saw him and rushed in. Stavut blocked a fierce thrust, then threw himself back as a second slashed toward his belly. The blade flicked up, tearing his shirt and nicking the skin of his chest. Holding the saber two-handed Stavut slashed and cut, but his attack was easily parried. "You are dead meat!" sneered the officer.

Harad, who was close by, smashed Snaga into the face of an attacking beast, then leapt toward the Guardsman. The soldier saw him coming and swung to meet the new threat. With no concern for fairness Stavut rushed in, plunging his saber through the man's throat. As he did so, he saw that Harad's attempt to save him had put the axman in peril. He had turned his back on the Jiamads coming at him. Stavut tried to call out a warning. A club thundered against Harad's head. The big man staggered. Stavut leapt to his aid. Harad, blood streaming from his temple, clove Snaga through his attacker's chest.

The enemy broke—the survivors running back down the trail.

Stavut, feeling light-headed with relief, sought out Shakul. The big beast was bleeding from several shallow cuts and gashes. "Are you all right?" asked Stavut.

"Strong," answered Shakul. Stavut moved around the killing ground. He found eight of his pack dead, and four others wounded. Then he saw Grava lying close to the precipice. Running to him, he squatted down. "No, no, no!" he pleaded. "Don't you dare be dead!" Cradling the elongated head, he felt for a pulse. He couldn't find one. Shakul leaned over, his snout close to Grava's mouth.

"Breathes," said Shakul. "Not dead."

Stavut stared up at the sky. "Thank you!" he shouted. Grava groaned, his golden eyes opening. He stared at Stavut, then said something unintelligible, his long tongue lolling from his elongated mouth.

"Good to see you, too," said Stavut, happily. Rising, he turned and stared down the slope. "Will they come back?" he asked Shakul.

"Officer dead. They run now. Others come back. Maybe."

"We won, Shak! We beat them!"

Then he saw Harad lying facedown on the ground close by. Stavut ran to him, rolling him to his back. Harad's face was gray. Shakul loomed above him. "No breath," he said. "Friend dead."

Suddenly Harad's body spasmed, and ice-blue eyes flared open. "Dead?" he said. "In your dreams, laddie!"

Skilgannon, dressed now in Alahir's old armor and chain-mail hauberk, knelt at the center of the Drenai defensive line. All around him stood the grim warriors of the Legend riders, arrows nocked to their bows. Beside him knelt Decado, wearing the armor of one of the riders killed in the battle with the lancers. Skilgannon felt uncomfortable in the heavy chain mail, which, while not initially restricting movement, would leach energy from the wearer by its weight alone. Normally Skilgannon preferred speed and freedom of movement, but today the battle would be fought in close confinement, and there was no way he could avoid swords or spears being thrust at him during the initial melee.

Farther down the ancient road the Eternal Guard had drawn up. They could see the Legend riders waiting for them, and Skilgannon watched as their officers gathered together, discussing strategy. He hoped they would take some time, not because he feared the coming battle, but because lengthy discussion among them would show indecision. There was no such delay. Within moments orders were called out, and the Eternal Guard dismounted and put aside their lances. Round infantry shields were unloaded from several wagons at the rear of the column and passed to the warriors. Skilgannon shivered suddenly. The emblem on the shields was the spotted snake—an emblem he had devised for the queen of Naashan's troops so many centuries ago. Back then the men who fought under that emblem had been his; highly trained, superbly disciplined, and wondrously brave.

A quarter mile below, the Eternal Guard formed up smoothly. There was no sense of excitement, no indication of alarm or concern. These were fighting men.

Skilgannon glanced to left and right. He had instructed Alahir to place the burliest and most powerful of his riders at the front of the line, ready to stand their ground against the onslaught. Once the two forces clashed there would be a period of heaving and pushing for ground. It was vital that the line was not forced back in these early moments.

"Fine-looking bunch, aren't they?" observed Decado.

Skilgannon did not reply. The Eternal Guard had begun to march. Beyond them more than a hundred huge Jiamads waited. Alahir had been right. The Guard wanted the honor and the glory of defeating the Drenai.

Shields held high, the Guard came on. There were no battle cries, merely the rhythmic sound of booted feet, marching in step. Alahir eased his way through to the front of the Drenai line. Then he, too, knelt, to give the archers behind him a clear view of the enemy. The Armor of Bronze gleamed in the afternoon sun, glittering on the winged helm and the bright sword in his hand.

As the road narrowed, the Guard came into range. They knew what they were facing, but they did not hesitate. Skilgannon found himself admiring these brave men, and a heaviness settled on his heart. Good, brave men were going to die today, robbing the world of their courage, their spirit, and their passion.

"Now!" yelled Alahir.

Hundreds of barbed shafts tore into the ranks of the marching men. Most thudded into shields or ricocheted from iron armor. Many others sliced into flesh. Soldiers fell—but still the Guard came on. A shouted order came from within their ranks, and they broke into a run. More volleys struck them, thinning the ranks. Then, when they were less than twenty paces from the waiting Legend riders, Alahir raised his sword. The front line of the defenders passed their bows back to the men behind, drew their sabers, and, with Alahir, Skilgannon, and Decado in the lead, charged into the fray.

Skilgannon blocked a wicked thrust, shoulder-charged the soldier, hurling him back. The Swords of Night and Day flashed in the sunshine, cutting left and right. Alongside him Alahir clove into the ranks of the Guard, the golden sword stained now with crimson.

Behind them, higher up the hill, a hundred bowmen continued to rain arrows down on the Guard trying to join the fight. As Skilgannon had predicted, the men were close packed, unable to raise their shields. Sharp arrows ripped into flesh, and the sound of clashing arms was interspersed with the screams of dying warriors. Greater weight of numbers began to force the Drenai line back.

Another fifty archers dropped their bows and rushed forward to reinforce the line. Skilgannon blocked a thrusting sword and sent a lunging riposte through the face of the attacker. The man fell back. Another took his place. Skilgannon was fighting now with a cold, remorseless fury, hacking and cutting, his swords always in motion, glittering and flashing as they clove through armor and bone. Alongside him Decado and Alahir were holding their ground, but on both flanks the Guard were pushing ahead. Soon the three warriors would be surrounded.

Gilden hurled himself forward, seeking to link up with Alahir. A sword blade gouged into his thigh. Another clattered against his helm. Ducking down, he threw himself at the men ahead of him, knocking one man from his feet and forcing another back. Gilden's saber slashed out, and the dagger in his left hand slammed into the unprotected neck of an oncoming Guardsman. Other defenders surged after Gilden, and for a while the line held.

But the Guard did not break. Slowly, inexorably, they were winning.

As with all great war leaders Skilgannon, despite being at the center of the fight, could feel the ebb and flow of the conflict. The Legend riders were battling bravely, but he could sense their growing uncertainty. The Guard were fighting now with more vigor as they caught the scent of victory. A sword hammered into Skilgannon's hauberk. The chain mail stopped the blow from cutting flesh, but the bruising force almost knocked him from his feet. Surging up, he killed the attacker. Then another—creating a brief space around himself. Alahir, his face smeared with blood, was trying to push forward into the enemy ranks, but the shields closed against him, and he, too, was forced back.

Guardsmen surged past Skilgannon on both sides as the Drenai line behind him gave way. There was nothing Skilgannon could do now, save to fight on.

Suddenly the air was filled with snarling screams. The body of a Guardsman came hurtling past Skilgannon. Then Shakul appeared. His huge fist crashed against a wooden shield, splintering it. The great beast grabbed the warrior holding it, hauling him high into the air and flinging him into the ranks of the oncoming Guardsmen.

Another figure loomed. It was Harad.

Skilgannon—for the moment having no foes to face—saw the axman hurl himself into the fight. Snaga rose and fell, cleaving and killing. Skilgannon's eyes narrowed. Harad had always been powerful, but he lacked experience. That deficiency could not be seen now. The axman powered forward in perfect balance, and the Guardsmen were falling back before the ferocity of his assault.

Yet still the Eternal Guard did not break. Skilgannon charged in, Alahir alongside him. The Legend riders surged forward, pushing the Guard back toward the narrowest point of the road. The battle became even more chaotic, the dead and dying trampled underfoot.

A trumpet sounded—and the Guard pulled back. Even in retreat they kept their discipline, the front line steadily backing away.

Some of the Legend riders began to give chase. Alahir called them back. "Re-form!" he shouted. Smoothly they pulled back to their original fighting line. Harad walked back to stand before Skilgannon.

"Is it you?" asked the warrior softly.

"Aye, laddie. I'm back for a time."

Skilgannon wanted to say more, but two men appeared at the narrowest point of the road. Both were slim and young, and they wore no armor. They approached Alahir and bowed. The first, stoop shouldered and balding, spoke. "I am Warna Set, surgeon to the First. This is my assistant, Anatis. By your leave I will attend the Guard wounded. Do you have a surgeon with you?"

"We do not," Alahir told him.

"If it is agreeable to you, my general offers the assistance of Anatis for your own wounded. He also request you allow us to remove the dead from the battlefield." Alahir gazed back along the road at the fallen men, some of them writhing in pain. Then he glanced at Skilgannon.

"How long will this truce last?" Skilgannon inquired.

The sun was already beginning to fall. Warna Set turned to Skilgannon. "The general says that he will hold off the next attack until sunrise."

"You may signal our agreement," Skilgannon told him. The surgeon bowed and returned to the Guard. Anatis remained. He was a small man, sandy haired, with large, brown eyes. His features were soft, almost feminine.

"Might I begin my work, sir?" he asked Skilgannon.

"Of course. We are grateful for your assistance."

Anatis smiled wearily. "My talents would be better used among people who did not seek to cut each other to pieces. Assign me some men, for those wounded who can be moved to a safer place. I understand there is water close by."

"Yes."

"The wounded should be carried there, and those without stomach wounds encouraged to drink." Then he moved back to walk among the wounded. Alahir told Gilden to assist him.

"I don't know who their general is," said Alahir to Skilgannon, "but I must say I warm to him."

"Aye, it is a fine gesture, but it also has strategic merit. His own men know they will receive treatment if wounded, and will not be merely cast aside. Allowing us a surgeon also means we are less likely to butcher wounded Guardsmen. The man is a thinker."

The sound of a horse's hooves upon stone broke through the conversation. Skilgannon swung to see Decado riding out from the entrance to the pool. He strolled back to where the dark-haired young swordsman sat his mount. "Leaving us so soon?" asked Skilgannon.

"I am afraid so, kinsman. This never was my fight. It pleased me to stay while I thought it might be won."

"Well, good luck to you, Decado."

The man smiled. "No pleas for me to stay? No appeal to my loyalty?"

"No. I think you for your help today. You are a fine warrior. Perhaps we will meet again, in happier times."

With that Skilgannon turned away from the man and strolled back to where Druss was standing, apart from the other men. "Not looking good," said the axman.

"No," agreed Skilgannon. "Skills on both sides are even, but their numbers will win the day. I think we can resist two, maybe three attacks."

Druss nodded. Skilgannon saw the blood on the axman's temple, and the huge bruise beneath it. "That looks bad."

"Feels it," admitted Druss. "I think Harad's skull might have been cracked. Damned painful."

The two men stepped aside as Legend riders moved past, carrying wounded men. "I take it you will be staying for a while?" said Skilgannon.

"I think it best," Druss told him. "Harad is a good lad, but this skirmish is going to need a touch more than guts and determination." He glanced across at Alahir and grinned. "Good to see that armor again. And he wears it well."

"He's a good man."

"He is Drenai," said Druss. "Says it all for me."

The sun faded down behind the mountains, and darkness came swiftly. Skilgannon moved away to sit on a rock and clean his swords. As he finished wiping the dried blood from the Sword of Night he lifted the blade to examine it. What he saw caused his breath to catch in his throat.

Reflected in the shimmering steel was the temple mountain, pale and gleaming in the starlight, the Mirror of Heaven bright upon its peak. He turned his head and glanced back down the mountainside. There was no temple, only the huge crater that had killed Bagalan.

Switching his gaze back to the reflection in the sword blade, he wondered if his mind was failing him: Askari wandered over to squat down beside him. "This is no time to be admiring yourself," she said.

"Look in the blade and tell me what you see," he told her, passing her the sword. Askari held it up.

"I have looked better," she said. "There is dirt on my face."

"Move the blade and look down the mountain."

Askari did so. Her expression changed as she saw the reflection of the temple mountain, and she swung around just as Skilgannon had. "What does it mean?" she asked.

"It means it always was some kind of ward spell. It can fool the eye, but not a mirror."

"What will you do?"

Skilgannon sighed. "Everything in me yearns to stand with these men and face the foe. Yet it is not what I came for. I came to end the reign of the Eternal. I cannot do that up here. I must get into the temple."

Twenty

For Stavut there was no sense of even a transient victory. The day had been nightmarish. The first battle, in which Harad had been struck down, was bad enough. Eight of his lads were dead, three others nursing deep wounds that concerned Stavut. Then they had traveled here to find the Legend riders facing massive odds. Shakul, without any order from Stavut, had hurled himself into the fray. He now carried more cuts and a puncture wound to his thigh.

The Jiamad wounded from earlier, who had lagged behind in the march to the high pass, arrived just as night fell. One of them was Ironfist, the scrawny hunchback who had joined them recently. He was being supported by the powerful Blackrock. Ironfist was breathing heavily, and there was blood dripping from his elongated jaw. Stavut ran to him and helped Blackrock lower him to the ground. Ironfist leaned his back against the cliff face. Stavut laid his hand on the beast's shoulder. "How are you feeling, my friend?"

"Much pain. Better when sun shines."

"Sit quietly. I'll fetch a surgeon."

Stavut ran back to the poolside where the seriously injured had been carried from the battle site. He saw the small surgeon, Anatis, kneeling beside a seated rider and inserting stitches in a wound to the man's shoulder. Stavut recognized the burly rider as the man who had screamed at him, and almost caused a war between the Jems and the riders. His name, Stavut had learned later, was Barik. Stavut moved alongside them. "One of my lads is seriously wounded," he said to the surgeon. "Do you know anything about Jems?"

"I don't treat beasts," answered the man, without looking up.

"Then you won't live to treat anyone ever again, you bastard!" shouted Stavut, dragging his saber clear of its scabbard. Terrified, the surgeon flung himself to the ground, rolling behind the wounded Drenai soldier.

"Whoa!" ordered Barik. "Rein in, Stavut! This man came to help us, and I'd as soon you didn't kill him before he's finished sealing this scratch."

"My lads have died in your battle, Drenai! The least you could do is see them tended."

"I agree." Pushing his hand over the still-bleeding wound, he glanced around at the cowering Anatis. "If you wouldn't mind, sir," he said. "I'll sit here while you tend to his friend. Is that all right with you?"

"The man's mad!" said Anatis.

The soldier laughed. "You think sane men would choose to come to this arid place in order to kill each other? Go tend the beast."

Stavut let his saber fall clattering to the ground. "I am sorry, surgeon," he said. "Will you help me?"

Anatis eased himself to his feet and swung his medicine bag over his shoulder. "I do not know how the melding changes the physical structure. But I will do what I can."

Together they walked out into the moonlight. "I should have asked for lanterns," he said. Ironfist was breathing raggedly, his head resting back against the rock face. The surgeon glanced at Stavut. "He's not going to attack me, is he?"

"No." Stavut crouched down on the other side of the beast. "It is me, my friend. I have brought someone to help you. You understand? To mend your wound."

The surgeon took hold of Ironfist's paw, which was resting over an awesome puncture wound in his chest. His fur was covered in blood, some dried, but more flowing from the wound. At the point of entry the blood was coming in small spurts. Ironfist suddenly coughed, and blood sprayed Stavut's face and chest. The surgeon looked across at Stavut. "Now, do not go back for that saber, but there is nothing I can do. All the indications are that the wound is deep and has pierced a lung. It has also severed an artery, which is why it is coming so fast."

"Would you know what to do if he were a man?"

"If he were a man he would be dead already. And before you ask, the answer is no. Even if I got to the man immediately, the way the wound was delivered I could not save him. My best guess is that your . . . friend will not last the night. All you can do is make it comfortable."

"You wouldn't lie to me?"

"No, Drenai, I would not lie about my craft, not even to an enemy. If we had bright light, and perfect surroundings, and the right tools, I could have tried opening the wound farther and attempting to seal the artery. This would cause immense pain to the creature, and would still result in death forty-nine times out of fifty. I do not have the light, or the tools, and this wound has been bleeding too long. Its strength is almost gone. It could not survive surgery. And now, if you will excuse me, I shall finish stitching the soldier's wound."

Stavut said nothing and turned back to Ironfist. "I don't know how much of that you understood, my friend," he said. "So we will just sit together for a while, you and I." Shakul came alongside and peered at Ironfist.

"You die soon," he said.

"Soon," answered Ironfist. Shakul squatted down and laid his huge hand gently on Ironfist's arm. Leaning forward, he touched his finger lightly to the wound, then licked the blood. Pulling back, he made way for Blackrock, who did the same. One by one all the beasts tasted the blood of Ironfist. Stavut had seen this peculiar ritual earlier, but had not asked Shakul about it. By the time Grava came to repeat the maneuver Ironfist was dead. Grava looked inquiringly at Stavut.

"Why do you lick his blood?" Stavut asked. The beast answered in his usual incomprehensible manner. This time, however, Stavut managed to piece together the words.

With a sigh Stavut placed his own finger on the wound, then licked it clean. Then he rose and sought out Alahir.

The rider was talking with Skilgannon and Askari as Stavut approached. Then the group broke up, Skilgannon walking back past the former merchant. He reached out to Askari as she passed. She smiled at him. "I will see you later," she said, then followed Skilgannon.

"Well, we survived the day, Tinker," said Alahir.

"And tomorrow?"

Alahir shrugged. "They are great warriors, and they out-number us. I won't lie to you. Chances are we won't see another sunset."

"I don't want my lads to die here."

"No, nor do I. I don't think the Guard will send their beasts. Though they might, if we hold them long enough. You have done enough, my friend. Take your pack and go."

"No, I will stay. I will send my lads back out over the other pass. I'll need to borrow some armor."

"There is plenty to choose from, Tinker. We lost seventy men today."

"That many? I am sorry, Alahir."

The sound of horses' hooves clattered on the stone. Stavut swung to see Skilgannon and Askari ride from the pass.

"Where are they going?"

"To the temple. Skilgannon thinks he can find a way in. We need to hold the Guard back for another day."

Stavut walked back to where the pack were sitting, by the entrance to the rock pool. He squatted down alongside Shakul. "It is time we had a new leader," he said. Shakul stared at him.

"Bloodshirt leads."

"No. Not anymore. This is Shakul's pack. I want you to trust me, Shak. Tomorrow this battle will be lost, whether you are here or not. The pack has given lives for these men and their war. You have fought well. Tonight I want you to take the pack back through the pass we fought in earlier to-day. From there you can see the green mountains. There will be deer there. You can hunt. You can run free, Shak. You can truly run free."

Shakul's head swayed from side to side. "Hungry," he said.

"Hungry," muttered some of the others.

"Hunt deer," said Shakul. Pushing himself to his feet, he swung to the others. "We go!" he said.

Immediately they rose and padded off.

Stavut stood alone and watched them until they had disappeared over the rim of the road.

"Not a sentimental bunch, were they?" said Gilden, moving alongside him. "No hugs. No long speeches."

Stavut shook his head. "I watched one of them die tonight. Each of the others placed a finger on the wound and licked it. I asked why. Grava told me in three words. *Carry with us.*"
The two men stood in silence for a moment.

"Come on, Stavut," said Gilden, "let's find you some armor. You can be a Drenai warrior for a day."

The moon was bright in a clear sky as Skilgannon rode down the mountainside. The trail was more treacherous here, shifting scree under his horse's hooves, so he rode slowly and with care, constantly glancing back to see how Askari was faring. Once on level ground she drew alongside him, and they moved on in silence for a while.

"You could not have saved them if you stayed," she said.

He glanced at her. "It would not have been to save them. I brought them to this. My head tells me that I must go to the temple, but my heart feels I am deserting them. Stavut is with them. Are you not concerned about his survival?"

"Of course I am. He is a sweet man."

"A sweet man?" he echoed. "Faint praise for a man you love."

She did not reply, and the silence grew. "Have I offended you?" he asked, at last.

"Not at all. I was thinking about what you said."

"About Stavut?"

"No, about love. Do you really believe in it, Skilgannon?"

"What an odd question. It is not about *belief.*"

"Are you sure?"

"Of course I am sure."

"Do you desire me?"

The question shook him. He drew in a deep breath. "Yes," he said, at last. "You are a beautiful woman."

"Is that love?"

"Of a physical kind. Yes. But that is not *just* how I loved Jianna."

"Ah. Two kinds of love then. Did you love your father?"

"Deeply."

"And that is three. Love seems to be a harlot, flitting from object to object. A word with so many uses ultimately becomes meaningless. I have heard Alahir talk of the love of the homeland, and Stavut speak of his love for the beasts. It is all mystifying."

"Yes, it is," he agreed, "but once true love touches your heart you will understand. It has a power beyond any magic in the world. If I walked into a room in which Jianna was sitting, I felt my spirit lift. She was in my thoughts every day for all of my previous life. I would fall asleep thinking of her, and wake thinking of her. The day she died it was as if someone had robbed the world of sunlight."

"And you never felt that way about anyone else?"

"No. There were women I cared for deeply, and others whose company I enjoyed for a time."

"Perhaps it was just because she was the first," offered Askari.

"There is . . . was . . . a belief among the Naashanites that, for every man and woman, there was one great love waiting to be found. Some never found it. Some settled for less. The very lucky would stumble across it. Like finding a diamond in a ditch. Jianna was my diamond. There could never be another."

"Yet you can contemplate destroying her, and sending her soul to the horror of the Void?"

"We all face the horror of the Void," he said. "And, no, I could not kill her. Any more than I could kill myself. What I am attempting to destroy is the *Eternal,* and the magic that has brought this world to vileness and ruin."

"A magic that brought about my own life—and yours," she pointed out.

Drawing rein, he turned toward her. In the moonlight her beauty was startling. It robbed him, for the moment, of speech. She edged her mount alongside his own. His throat was dry, and it seemed as if time ceased flowing. All that existed was this one moment. "What is it?" she asked, softly.

Tearing his gaze from her, he turned his horse. "We must move on," he said, heeling his mount into a run.

Allowing the gelding to have its head, Skilgannon tried to clear his thoughts. The pounding of the hooves, the wind in his face, helped him to focus. Ahead lay the crater. Slowing his mount, Skilgannon rode to the rim and drew the Sword of Night. Staring into the blade, he saw once more the rearing temple mountain and the great golden shield at its peak. More than this he saw, some distance to his left, shimmering blue lights on the desert floor, marking a path to the doors of the temple. He touched heels to the gelding and rode around the rim until he reached the start of the path. Then he dismounted. Askari came alongside. He showed her the reflection.

"How do we know it is a pathway?" she asked.

"My guess is that the priests needed a safe way through the crater in order to bring in supplies. But let us test it."

From around his neck he lifted clear the golden locket, then, holding the Sword of Night high, he tossed the locket over his shoulder to land between two of the shimmering lights. Then he turned to watch what happened. The locket lay on the ground, unmoving. Skilgannon took a deep breath, then stepped out onto the crater to retrieve it. Moving back to

Askari, he said: "I intend to walk the path. It might be safer if you wait here for me."

"I didn't come this far to hold the reins of your horse. I will come with you."

He smiled. "I guessed you would say that." Then it registered that she had not brought her bow with her. Instead she had a scabbarded cavalry saber looped over her shoulder. "The first time I have seen you without the recurve," he said.

"I loaned it to the Legend riders. They are running out of arrows."

Skilgannon drew both swords then, holding one above his head, the other before his eyes. Carefully he adjusted the higher sword until the path could be seen reflected in the blade before his eyes.

Then he walked slowly toward the hidden temple.

"How does anyone find the strength to fight, wearing all this?" complained Stavut as Gilden looped the chain-mail hauberk over his head. The sleeves came down to Stavut's elbows, the hem touching the backs of his calves. It was split, front and back, at the waist, allowing for freedom of movement in the saddle, but the biggest surprise to Stavut was the weight. "I feel like I'm carrying Shakul on my back!"

"The best is yet to come," said Gilden, lifting the chain-mail coif and settling it over Stavut's head. It was lined with soft leather and smelled of rancid goose grease. Lastly came the helm. When Stavut had first tried it, he had laughed aloud. It was way too big and slid around his head comically. Now with the added thickness of the coif the helm fitted perfectly. Gilden tied the bronze cheek guards together.

"How does it feel?" he asked.

"What? I can't hear a thing in here."

Gilden repeated the question. "It feels ludicrous," Stavut told him. "If I fell over I'd never be able to get up."

"If you fall over you won't need to worry about getting

up," observed Gilden. "Walk around for a while. You'll get used to the weight."

The sergeant wandered off and Stavut, feeling foolish, tromped off toward the pool. Most of the warriors had gathered there and were sitting quietly. He noticed that many of them cast furtive glances at Harad, who was standing apart from the men, the ax heads resting on the ground, his huge hands crossed over the pommel on the haft. Stavut found a place to sit close to some of the warriors. Slowly he lowered himself down. The chain mail creaked and groaned as he sat.

"You think it could be true?" he heard a man ask, his voice low.

"It comes from Alahir. He said Skilgannon told him."

"Gods, then we are looking at the Legend!"

"Aye, we are. Did you see him today? I don't know how the Guard felt, but he terrified me."

Stavut had no idea what they were talking about. He felt incredibly tired, and stretched out on the ground. The chain-mail hauberk made him feel as if he were lying on a bed of brambles. With a groan he rolled over and forced himself back into a sitting position. Then he looked around and realized he was the only man in armor. Feeling even more foolish, he undid the chin straps of his helmet and pulled it clear. Then he struggled out of the chain mail. The relief was total.

Gilden wandered back and crouched down beside him. "What happened in the other pass today?" he asked.

"I told you. Enemy Jems attacked and we beat them."

"To Harad, I mean."

"I know. He is speaking most strangely. He seems to be copying Skilgannon's archaic style of speech. He was struck in the head. Ever since he woke he's been . . . been . . ." Stavut struggled for the right description.

"Like someone else?" offered Gilden.

"Yes, that's it exactly. Called me laddie. And those eyes. I've never noticed before how frightening they are."

"Did you see him fight here today?"

"Of course. Completely different. In the pass earlier he was massively powerful, but clumsy and winning through brute strength. On the road he was awesome, balanced and deadly, and terrible to behold."

Gilden sat beside him, then glanced back at Harad. "Skilgannon says he is Harad no longer. He says the ghost of Druss the Legend now inhabits the body."

"I hate to be the man who shoots down someone else's pigeon," said Stavut, "but he got a hefty whack to the head. Could he not have become . . . you know . . ."

"Deranged?"

"I wouldn't go quite that far, but, yes. Not himself."

"Skilgannon told Alahir that Druss had inhabited the body once before, to warn him of the coming battles. He also said that Harad was a Reborn, created from the bones of Druss."

"That cannot be right," said Stavut. "Druss was tall and golden haired. I read that somewhere."

Gilden sighed. "According to our legends he was a silver-bearded giant. But then at the last battle he was very old."

Stavut rose. "Where are you going?" asked Gilden.

"I am going to talk to Harad," he said. "No point sitting here whispering about it. I'll ask him."

Stavut strolled through the ranks of the Drenai and waved as he approached Harad. "How is the head?" he asked.

"Bearable, laddie. Has the word spread to everyone yet?"

"About the Druss . . . er . . . story?"

Harad chuckled and fixed Stavut with a piercing glare. "Aye, the Druss story."

"Yes. Is it true? Do you think you are Druss?"

"What *I* think is unimportant now. It is what *they* think that matters. You know what is going to happen tomorrow, Stavut?"

"We are all going to die."

"And that is the general feeling, is it?"

"I think it is considered to be rather more of a fact," Stavut told him. "We lost seventy today. They lost around twice that. If it is the same tomorrow there will be too few of us to hold the road. And there will still be around seven hundred of them."

"It won't be the same tomorrow, laddie. The wind blows the chaff away first. Good men though they are, it was, in the main, the weakest of them who died today." Stavut was feeling increasingly uncomfortable. It didn't sound like Harad. Many years ago, in Mellicane across the sea, he had attended a theater and watched actors perform. They had been speaking lines written hundreds of years before, and the pitch and style of their speech patterns sounded very similar to Harad now. Was Harad acting? Nothing in his brief experience of the man had given any evidence of a theatrical nature. He looked into those piercing ice-blue eyes. And shivered. If this *was* acting it was of far greater quality than the mummers in Mellicane produced.

The axman hefted Snaga and walked out to stand before the warriors. He said nothing for a moment, his gaze running over the gathered men.

"You can cease your whispering now!" he thundered. Silence fell on the Drenai. Stavut felt goose bumps on his neck. The voice rang with command. The axman pointed at Alahir. "Be so good as to stand, Earl of Bronze," he said. Alahir, still in the golden Armor, rose to his feet. "The last man I saw wearing that was fighting on the ramparts of Dros Delnoch—against an army two hundred times the size of that facing you. The Nadir horde filled the valley. Their spears were a forest. Their arrows darkened the sun, so that we fought in the shade. In the main our army was made up of farmworkers and land laborers. Aye, we had Hogun's legion, but many of the rest had never picked up a sword before enlisting. Yet they fought like heroes. By heaven they *were* heroes. At Skeln we stood against the best warriors I have ever known, Gorben's Immortals. They had never lost before that day." He paused and rested the ax blades on the ground before him, his hands on the haft. "Now I just asked young Stavut what is going to happen tomorrow. He said: *We are all going to die.* He was wrong. Those of you who think the same are wrong. We are going to win. We are going to break their spirit, destroy their morale, and send them running from the road. We are going to hold this position until Skilgannon achieves what he set out to do. Not man or beast will prevent us. Because we are Drenai. The Last of the Drenai. And we will not fail." He fell silent again. Not a sound was heard as his gaze raked the ranks once more. "Skilgannon returned to this world to fulfill a prophecy. The Armor of Bronze reappeared to aid him. I am here for a little while, to stand once more with Drenai warriors in a cause that is just and noble. Now get on your feet. Up! I want to see you standing like men." The Drenai rose and stood before him. Then he raised the ax above his head. "What is this?" he bellowed. A few men called out: "Snaga!"

"Again! Every man!"

"Snaga!" they shouted, the sound echoing around the rocks.

"And who carries Snaga the Sender, the Blades of No Return?"

"Druss the Legend!" came the answering roar.

"Again!"

The men began to chant the name. For Stavut the moment was hypnotic, and he found himself chanting along with the others. "Druss the Legend! Druss the Legend! Druss the Legend!"

The axman let the chanting go on for a short while. Then he lowered his ax and raised his hand for silence. Obedience was instant. "Rest now, Drenai," he said. "Tomorrow we carve a new legend for your children and their children."

With that he turned and walked away, his giant frame passing into the shadows of the entrance and out into the road beyond.

Stavut's heart was beating fast, and his hands were trembling. There was no way that could have been Harad. Deranged or not. Everywhere there was silence. He glanced at Alahir, who was staring in the direction the axman had taken.

Then the earl of Bronze walked away from his men and followed Druss the Legend out onto the road.

*   *   *

Alahir felt unsteady as he followed the Legend out into the night. The speech had been delivered with such power and confidence that he felt his spirits soar. Yet he knew the chances of actually winning were hundreds to one. The Eternal Guard were damned fine fighters, and they weren't likely to break. And if they did there were a hundred Jiamads waiting to tear into the defenders.

He saw Druss ahead. The man had walked to the narrow section of the road and was staring down at the camp of the Guard, a quarter of a mile below.

Alahir was nervous as he approached him. "Am I disturbing you?" he asked.

"No, laddie. I hoped you would come."

"Why are you out here? My men would love to sit around and talk to you about the glory days, and hear firsthand of your exploits."

"I never was much for bragging about the past. However, I can't sit with the men, and joke and laugh. I am the Legend. They need to feel in awe of me. I am not comfortable with that—but it is necessary here and now."

"They were lifted when you said we could win. Did you mean it, or was it just to raise their morale?"

"I never lie, laddie."

"And you never lose."

"Some men are born lucky. A stray arrow could have pierced my eye, or a lancer could have plunged a weapon in my back as I fought someone else. I am not a god, laddie. These Guardsmen are fine fighters, and the odds are all with them. Plus they have made it slightly easier for themselves."

"How so?"

"By sending the surgeon to you."

"That was a noble gesture."

"Perhaps. It was also good strategy. Men fight better when they are full of passion. I do not like hatred, but it is a vital weapon in war. If a leader can convince his men that the enemy they face is evil, and that their own cause is just or holy,

then they will fight harder. If you tell them that the enemy
will plunder their homes and rape their women they will fight
like tigers. You understand, Alahir? While the Guard were
merely tools of the evil Eternal, and the homeland was at
risk, the men were fired up. When the surgeons came your
riders found a new respect for the enemy. The enemy *cares*
about your wounded. Good men. We could all be friends and
brothers, couldn't we? That single gesture, which will not
add one more fighting man to our ranks, leached away the
fire from your warriors' hearts. What do you think will happen if they force a surrender tomorrow?"

Alahir thought about the question. The Guard had fought
many battles, and he had heard stories of their ruthlessness.
Agrias had told him that when Draspartha was besieged
twenty years ago, the Guard had put to death every enemy
soldier, then lined up the civilians of the city and butchered
one in ten of the men.

"Judging from their past victories, they would kill us all."

"And the wounded?"

"Them, too."

"No surgeons then to offer assistance, and stitch wounds?"

"No," said Alahir, his voice hardening.

"No," echoed Druss. "They will come looking to hack us
to death. They are hard, cold murderous men. Even now that
surgeon is in his general's tent, detailing the mood of the
men. This is why I did not give my little talk until he had
gone. He will report that the enemy has been softened and is
ready for the kill. This will be passed to the fighting men.
They will march up here tomorrow with high hopes. What
they will find is men who fight twice as hard as yesterday.
And I'll wager you this, Alahir. When we push them back tomorrow there will be no offer of surgeons."

Alahir sank down to the rock beside the warrior. "If I had
been a better leader I would have seen that ploy. I am a captain, Druss, and not the brightest of our officers. I cannot understand why the Armor came to me."

"Aye, fate does have a sense of humor sometimes. When I

went to Dros Delnoch to train the troops, there was a general in command there named Orrin. A fat little fellow with the fighting instincts of a startled rabbit. Rek, who became the earl of Bronze, was a poser, frightened of the dark, who had only come to the Dros because he was in love with the daughter of the dying earl. There were farm boys with no sword skills. One stabbed himself in the leg when he tried to sheathe his blade. By the end Orrin was a hero, and I was proud to fight alongside him, and Rek held them all together after I died. His was the great victory." Druss suddenly chuckled. "And don't feel too bad about the surgeons. I didn't realize it, either. Skilgannon told me before he left. So don't judge yourself yet. Wait until sunset tomorrow."

Alahir smiled. *"Then* will you sit with my men and tell us stories?"

"We'll see. Now get back to your riders and walk among them. I have put a little passion back, but you need to inspire them."

"Are we not going to discuss strategy?"

Druss laughed. "Strategy, eh? Very well. I shall take up my ax and stand at the center of our line. When the enemy appear I shall wade into them. You and your riders will follow me. Then we keep fighting until the Guard break and run."

"No bowmen?"

"No. That will come later."

"Later?" queried Alahir.

The smile faded from the axman's face, and his eyes grew cold. "When we have broken the Guard they will not regroup for another attack. They will send the beasts. That is when you will need your arrows."

"As good as my riders are, Druss, I have to tell you that one Jiamad can take out three men. They have more than a hundred Jems down there."

"One battle at a time, laddie. First we break the Guard. Then we'll worry about the puppies."

* * *

Even within the pathway of lights Skilgannon could feel the pull of the crater around them. A vague feeling of nausea, accompanied by light-headedness, made balance difficult. His vision swam, and he had to stop several times to adjust his swords and keep the shimmering lights in focus.

Finally they reached the high double doors to the temple. Stepping up to the doors, Skilgannon pressed a handle and pushed. The doors were locked. Sheathing the Sword of Day, he inserted the blade of the Sword of Night into the thin gap between the doors, locating the block of wood that sat in brackets beyond, barring entrance. Holding the sword two-handed, he slid the blade under the block and tried to lift it. It moved an inch or so, then seemed to catch on something. Askari joined him, sliding her saber alongside his own. The block lifted farther—then fell clattering to the floor beyond the entrance. Skilgannon pushed his shoulder against the doors, which swung open.

Inside was the entrance chamber he remembered from his past visit, a deep reception area that branched out left and right into tunnels, leading to a series of stairways. There were chairs here, and long couches, all covered with dust. The sight saddened him. On his last visit this area had been brightly lit, radiating harmony and warmth. It calmed the soul and lifted the spirits. Now it was cold and dead. Askari tapped his arm and pointed to the floor nearby. In several places there were mounds of dried animal droppings.

Skilgannon walked slowly across the reception area, moving toward the right and the tunnel that led to the first of the staircases. As he passed under the entrance arch to the tunnel the lights flickered. Then a voice echoed eerily from the walls.

"Do not enter here," it said. The voice was bizarre, almost metallic. It was accompanied by a sound like wood crackling on a campfire. Skilgannon ignored it and walked on warily, both swords in his hands.

"These tunnels are guarded," said the voice. "It is not my

wish to see anyone suffer harm, but if you do not leave you will die."

Askari moved alongside him. "From the droppings I would say the beasts are large, probably Jiamads." Skilgannon nodded.

Together they advanced down the tunnel. They passed many doors, which had once housed priests of the Resurrection. There were none here now. The floor was dust covered, and there were cobwebs on the occasional chairs and couches placed in the recesses. Once this had been a temple of serenity and beauty. Now it was a shadow-haunted place of death and decay.

Sweat dripped into Skilgannon's eyes. The feeling of nausea had not passed. He glanced at Askari. She, too, was suffering. His fingers began to tingle, and his mouth was dry. The light was poor, but Skilgannon could see the stairwell ahead. He walked on.

Something huge and pale rushed at him from a hidden recess on the left. The Sword of Night slashed out, cleaving into flesh. Then he was thrown from his feet. He struck the tunnel wall hard, then hurled himself to his right as the beast lunged for him. Askari leapt to his defense, the cavalry saber plunging into the beast's back. It gave a shrill cry and spun to meet this new attack. Skilgannon surged to his feet and charged in. The Sword of Day sliced through the creature's neck. Blood sprayed from the wound. The beast staggered. Skilgannon clove the Sword of Night through its heart. As it fell he dragged his blade clear, and the two companions stared down at the dead creature. It was unlike any Jiamad Skilgannon had seen. There were only patches of fur on the pale body, which was covered in huge warts and purple tumors. "It is grotesque," whispered Askari. "Impossible to see with which animal it was melded." The body was lying on its side. Skilgannon knelt to peer at a fist-sized section of skin-covered bone protruding from its back.

"What does that look like to you?" he said. Askari prodded the lump with her saber. The skin around it spasmed—and five bony fingers opened. Askari jumped back. "Sweet heaven!" she said. "It is a hand! A hand in the center of its back!"

"We need to move on," he said, pushing himself to his feet. His stomach suddenly heaved, and he vomited. He stood for a moment, supporting himself on the wall. "We cannot stay here long," he said. "The magic that warps the land outside has somehow seeped into here."

Together they walked on until they reached the first stairway. It was of metal and speckled with rust. "This leads to the main dining and recreation area," said Skilgannon. "There were also libraries and a museum."

He climbed the stairs. The nausea had faded a little, but there was a metallic taste in his mouth, and his teeth began to ache. Behind him Askari staggered and grabbed the stair rail for support.

"I am all right," she assured him. "Go on. I'll follow!"

The top of the stairwell opened out into a vast deserted hall. Tables and chairs had been hurled around the room, as if by a storm. Books and scrolls littered the floors. There were also scattered bones. Moonlight could be seen through the high windows. Skilgannon walked out into the hall. A shadow moved against the far wall. Skilgannon spun. A massive, two-headed hound was padding across the hall toward them. It was the size of a lion. The hound began to run. Skilgannon sheathed the Sword of Night and held the Sword of Day two-handed. "Get behind me!" he ordered Askari.

The hound tore toward them—and sprang. Skilgannon leapt to meet it, the Sword of Day slashing down in an overhead cut that clove between the two heads, plunging down through its chest. The weight of the beast carried it on. It thudded into Skilgannon, hurling him from his feet. The Sword of Day slid clear. The beast rolled over, then came to its feet, both heads snarling. Askari hacked at it with her saber. It leapt for her, then stumbled, blood gouting from the terrible wound in its chest. Askari backed away. Skilgannon moved alongside her. The hound's front legs gave way, and it crashed to the floor. Sunlight suddenly blazed through the windows, columns of golden light illuminating the hall.

Skilgannon watched as the light moved across the bone-littered floor. He blinked, then walked to the window. Askari joined him. Shielding his eyes, Skilgannon watched the sun rise.

"It is too fast," he said. "The sun does not rise that swiftly."

Askari pointed to a flock of birds in the distance. They were speeding across the sky. "Time is flowing faster out there," she said. Skilgannon nodded agreement, and turned away from the sunlight. Taking a deep breath, he walked back past the dead beast and headed across the hall.

"Do you know where you are going?" Askari asked him.

"When I stayed here I was allowed to roam freely—except for the upper levels. So that is where we will make for."

Crossing the hall, Skilgannon glanced at several skeletons. They were twisted and unnatural, some with overly curved spines, others with grossly distended bones. There was a skull with four eye sockets. Skilgannon and Askari traveled on in silence along deserted tunnels and up a second flight of metal steps. The higher they climbed, the better they felt. Skilgannon's nausea passed, as did the tingling in his fingers. Another corridor led them back to a high gallery above the dining hall they had just left. There were creatures moving across it now, some like the giant hound, but other, paler beasts, hulking and brutal. One of them gazed up and saw them. It made no move to follow. Instead it loped to the dead hound and began ripping flesh from it. Other beasts joined in.

From far below they heard a high-pitched scream. Several of the creatures loped off toward the sound.

Skilgannon came to an oval wooden door. It was locked. Stepping back, he took several deep breaths, then hammered his right foot against the lock. The frame shuddered, but the lock did not give. Twice more he struck at the lock. On the third blow the door shuddered, and wood splintered around the frame. A fourth blow snapped the lock, and the door flew open. Skilgannon stepped inside. The room was an antechamber, leading to another door. This was not locked and Skilgannon passed through into a larger room, shelved along the far wall and stacked with books and scrolls. There was an open window with a balcony beyond, and before it stood a wide desk of beautifully fashioned oak. An old man was sitting there. He did not rise in alarm as they entered, merely looked at them with weary eyes. His face was oddly shaped, heavy bone around the brows and cheeks. His mouth was wide, the teeth misshapen.

"What is it you want, Demon Woman?" he asked Askari.

"She is not a demon," Skilgannon told him. "She is a Reborn."

"I know what she is. She is evil. We brought her back. We thought she would tell us the wonders of her age. She told us nothing. Landis begged her, and she laughed. Vestava questioned her, and she said she could not remember. *Give me time,* she asked us. Then she rode out and gathered an army. The days of blood and death began. I know her. I know her too well."

"You are mistaken, priest. This is not the Eternal. She is one of her Reborns, and is, with me, trying to end the Eternal's reign. We need to find the silver eagle and its egg."

The old man laughed. "You cannot find the eagle, warrior. It floats so high that the sky is no longer blue. It moves among the stars."

"But it sends power here," said Skilgannon. "To feed the egg."

The old man lifted a gnarled hand and rubbed at his face. "I am so tired," he said. The hand was webbed, the knuckles grotesquely distorted.

"What is happening here?" asked Skilgannon.

"We made an error—a dreadful error. We tried to move the temple outside of time. Just a few seconds, so that she"—he pointed at Askari—"could not steal more artifacts. We discovered a series of hidden tunnels below the temple. There were artifacts there. Terrible artifacts." His misshapen face turned toward Askari. "She knows this. Weapons that deal death over great distances. There were also scrolls and documents that spoke of even more ghastly devices. Aye, and maps that showed where they were hidden. She wanted them. It was not enough for her that she had corrupted our work. She desired even more power, even greater weapons. We could not allow it. We sought to hide the temple from her. At first we thought we had succeeded." He gave a harsh laugh. "Instead we merely slowed time within these walls. What followed was more horrible than you could imagine. We began to change. Our structures became unstable. Bone continued to grow. Many of the brothers died, others became deformed. It was slow at first, and we did not realize what was happening. Once we did we tried to change the spell. It only made matters worse. The spells around the temple grew in power. After that everything happened so swiftly. There was no time to escape. Some of the brothers managed to reach these higher levels, where the mutations slowed for a while. Gradually they all changed, reverted to beasts, and tore one another apart or fled below to join the packs that roam the lower levels."

"Yet you survived," said Skilgannon.

Lifting his grotesque hand, he pulled clear a golden chain hanging from his neck. Upon it, in a golden clasp, was a black-and-white crescent, part crystal, part stone. "I carry the Abbot's Moon," he said. Idly he stroked the crescent. "Its power is almost gone. Once it shone white and bright. It sustained me."

"It has been five hundred years," said Askari. "How do any creatures still live here?"

"Five hundred years, is it? Not when each day outside passes in under an hour. By my reckoning it is fifteen years since we cast the spell—though my mind is not what it was, and I could be wrong. For a while we could leave and bring in supplies. When more of us became beasts we began to feed on each other." His head drooped. "We believed we were the Keepers of Knowledge, that we could lift the world from its savagery. Instead we became savages. The mutation in our bodies also made us long lived."

"Why did you not just end the magic?" asked Skilgannon. "That would surely have stopped the horror of the Eternal."

The deformed priest looked bemused. "End the magic? How would one accomplish such a feat? We tried to change the spell. We knew it was destroying us. But the more we meddled with it, the worse it became. A few months back we made our last attempt. All we succeeded in doing was accelerating the process. Now there is no food, my people are dead, or changed. They feed on each other."

"Listen to me, old man," Skilgannon urged him. "The eagle feeds the magic. It comes somehow through the Mirror of Heaven. Where does it then go?"

"Magic does not *go,* warrior. Magic *is.* "

"Where is the holiest place here?" asked Askari.

The old priest gave a cackling laugh. "That you of all people should ask that! How amusing. Evil seeks holiness."

"Is there such a place?" Skilgannon pressed him.

"The Crystal Shrine. The great abbot built it, I believe. That is where we used to meet and pray, and heal the sick."

"Is it close, this Shrine?" asked Skilgannon, patiently.

A distant scream sounded. Then another. The old man seemed not to notice. He stared at Askari.

"Where is the Shrine?" asked Skilgannon. The old man did not reply, but his gaze shifted to a far door on the western wall. "Let's go!" said Skilgannon. The priest stumbled toward him.

"No!" he shouted. "She must not go near it. She would defile it!"

"Listen to me!" said Skilgannon, taking the man by the arm. "Try to understand. She is not Jianna! She is Askari, a young woman from the mountain lands south of here."

"She might once have been this Askari you speak of. Not now. I am not fooled. I see beyond the flesh. I see the aura of her soul. She is Jianna. She is the Eternal."

Skilgannon turned slowly toward Askari. She was standing behind him, her saber in her hand.

"The twisted magic here has driven him mad," she said.

"No," said Skilgannon, softly. He sighed. "I knew something was wrong back on the road when I looked at you in the moonlight. My heart almost stopped. I think I knew then. I just didn't want to believe it. How did you do it, Jianna?"

He thought she was going to deny it. Instead she merely smiled. "Decado gave one of Memnon's jewels to the girl. It connected me to her. All I had to do was die. It was most painful. Much like this . . ." As she spoke her saber lunged forward, spearing Skilgannon's chest. He staggered back and tried to draw his own sword. Strength seeped from his body, and he fell heavily. Jianna leaned over him. "Do not fret, my love," she said. "I will have you Reborn. Perhaps by then you will have put aside notions of destroying me. And now I must go. Memnon is waiting for me."

With that she walked past the old priest, and through the far door.

As the sun rose the Drenai warriors filed out onto the road, forming up in ranks twelve men across and seven deep. A little way back a second phalanx formed, ready to rush to the aid of the first when needed. Stavut had been placed at the rear of the second group, along with the less experienced of the Drenai. These were the younger men, new to the front line. Stavut glanced at their faces. Many were nervous, but all stood ready. From this high vantage point Stavut could see the Eternal Guard forming up below. In their black-and-silver armor they looked invincible, and the inspirational speech Druss had given the night before seemed suddenly hollow and unconvincing.

Stavut felt the weight of the chain mail on his shoulders, and sweat was beginning to trickle down his neck. *How odd,* he thought. *Water is running freely from my skin, and yet my mouth is parched and dry.* It was then that he realized his bladder was full. He swore. "What is it?" asked the man beside him. Stavut told him, and the young soldier smiled. "Me, too. It will be the same for every man here."

"Why?" asked Stavut.

"According to Gilden it is the tension and the fear. It tightens the muscles around the bladder. The feeling will go away once the battle starts."

"Oh, I'll look forward to that," muttered Stavut.

The Eternal Guard began to march. Instinctively Stavut reached for his sword hilt. "Not yet," said the soldier. "Your arm will be tired enough by the end. Wait until you actually need to draw it."

Up ahead Stavut saw Druss, dressed now in a long mail hauberk, walking along the front rank, Alahir beside him in the Armor of Bronze. The axman was talking to the soldiers, but his words did not fully carry to the second phalanx. Stavut thought he heard the word *wedge*.

"Can you hear what he's saying?" he asked the soldier beside him.

"Don't need to," said the man. "Alahir told us last night what the plan was. We will hit them when they reach the narrowest point of the road. They will be expecting arrows. Instead they will be met by a charge, in wedge formation. It will hit them like an arrowhead, with Druss at the point."

The Eternal Guard marched on, not swiftly, but steadily, conserving their energies for the battle ahead. Stavut found himself wondering about his lads, and how they were faring in the green hills. He sighed. The sun was bright in a cloudless sky, and he saw several doves flying by. A sense of unreality gripped him. It was hard to believe, standing here in the sunlight, that men were about to die. Then he thought about Askari. She had been acting so strangely these last few days. Ever since the nightmare. She had suddenly awoken beside him with a cry. He had reached over to her, and she had slapped his hand away and looked at him strangely. "It is all right," he said. "You were dreaming. That's all."

"Dreaming?" She relaxed then. "Yes, I was dreaming. Where is Olek?"

"Olek?"

"Skilgannon."

"He is out scouting the passes for sign of the Guard." He had leaned in to her then, and suggested they find a spot away from the others where they could be together.

"Not now, Stavut," she said. It had been odd hearing her use his full name. He had become so used to *Stavi*.

The men around him began to shuffle and swing their arms, loosening the muscles. Stavut saw that the Guard were approaching the narrowest point of the road. They began to shuffle together, raising their long shields to protect themselves from arrows. Without any battle cries the Drenai line surged forward, Druss at the center, ax raised. It was several moments before the marching Guard realized they were under assault. Stavut saw the huge ax splinter a shield and sweep the man beyond from his feet. Then the noise erupted, metal on metal, screeching and clamoring, screams and shouts and death cries. Several of the Guard were pushed over the edge of the precipice, and fell. Stavut watched them, arms flailing as they plummeted toward the rocks far below. Switching his gaze back to the front line he saw the carnage and his stomach knotted. The ax rose and fell, swept and cut, blood spraying from it. It seemed perpetually in motion, as if it were somehow mechanical. There was a gap opening around Druss as men fought to keep back from the slashing blades. Then, with the initial shock of the charge over, the Guard's discipline reasserted itself. They began to push forward. Now Stavut saw Legend riders fall as the black-and-silver ranks hurled themselves at the defenders. Slowly, inexorably, the Drenai were forced back. Druss fought on, and the enemy warriors had almost reached the point of encircling him. Then Alahir threw himself into the attack, battling to reach Druss. Several men, Gilden among them, joined him, and once more the two fighting groups became wedged together, neither giving nor gaining ground.

The battle seemed to go on forever, but Stavut glanced at the sky and saw the sun had barely moved.

Another line of Drenai reserves rushed forward to fill the gaps left by the dead and dying. The soldier beside him had been right, thought Stavut, as he and the men around him shuffled forward. He no longer felt the urge to piss, and his mouth was no longer dry. He saw Alahir go down, and then rise again. The battle looked chaotic now. More men fell screaming from the edge, and the ground was dense with bodies, some still writhing, or trying to drag themselves clear of the fighting. Stavut, though he had no experience of battles, could sense that the tide was beginning to turn. The Drenai had been pushed back from the narrow point. This allowed more Guard to enter the fray. Druss was still holding his ground, but once more the two flanks were pressing inward. A second line of reserves ran in, briefly bolstering the defense. Druss suddenly surged forward into the men trying to join the fighting, cutting left and right with his terrible blades. Stavut shivered as he saw men go down, helms crushed, faces slashed away. This sudden, almost berserk attack opened a gap behind the Guard, and Stavut saw many men in the front ranks glance nervously behind them. Alahir must have seen it too, for he bellowed: "At them Drenai! Kill them all!"

The defenders returned to the attack with renewed vigor, hacking and slashing, hurling themselves at the enemy. The Guardsman at the rear turned and fled from the awesome ax. Then the front line caved. Men spun on their heels and began to run, streaming back down the pass road.

Stavut couldn't believe his luck. He had not been called to battle at all.

Legend riders ran to their fallen comrades, lifting those still breathing from the battle site and carrying them back to the relative safety of the rock pool. Then they began to gather their dead. It seemed to Stavut there were a great many bodies. Swiftly he cast his glance around, estimating the numbers of the survivors. There were considerably less than a hundred men still standing. He saw Druss walk to the narrow point and stare down at the enemy. Then the axman swung back and strode back up the road. Stavut shivered as he saw him. The chain-mail hauberk was splattered with blood, as was his face and beard. There were bleeding cuts on his huge arms, and a long gash on his cheek. A cut above his right eye was seeping blood. "There is a rider coming," the axman told Alahir.

The earl of Bronze and the axman walked back to meet him. Stavut wandered up behind them. The rider was a tall man, hawkeyed and lean. He sat his black horse and stared past the two men, observing the battlefield. Then he turned his dark gaze on Druss.

"You have performed bravely, but you cannot hold out much longer," he said.

"Ah, laddie, that was but a warming-up exercise. Now that we're loose the real fighting can begin."

The man gave a cold smile. "Do I have your permission to remove my wounded and dead?"

"What, no offers of surgeons?" said the axman.

"I fear the amount of damage you have caused necessitates me using both my surgeons," said the officer.

"You can have your wounded," said Druss. "The men you send to carry them better be stripped of all armor and weapons, or I'll roll their heads back to you."

"Your tone is disrespectful, sir," said the officer, tight-lipped.

"I'd have more respect had I seen you among your men, and not watching the battle from afar. Now scuttle back to where you came from. This conversation is over."

Druss turned his back on the man and led Alahir back up the road. Stavut watched the officer wrench his horse around and ride away.

"Why were you so discourteous, Druss?" asked Alahir.

The axman chuckled. "I want him boiling mad. Angry men tend to act rashly."

"I think you achieved that. And you were right about the surgeons."

"As soon as they have collected their dead and wounded, form up the bowmen and prepare for the beasts."

Druss glanced to his right. A wounded Guardsman was desperately trying to unbuckle the breastplate of a fallen comrade. Blood was gushing from beneath the smashed armor.

Druss laid aside his ax and moved alongside the men. Together they wrenched the breastplate clear. The man's right side was drenched with blood. Druss ripped the shirt open to reveal smashed ribs and a huge cut. From the look of the ruined breastplate, and the depth of the wound, Stavut knew it had come from Druss's ax. Druss pulled the shirt back over the wound and told the second man to hold his hand over it. "Press lightly," he said, "for those ribs might be pushed into the lung."

"Where did you come from?" asked the second man.

"From hell, laddie. Let's look at your wound." The soldier had taken a heavy hit on the lower leg, which was broken. "You'll live," said Druss. "Your friend might not. Depends how tough he is." He stared hard at the young soldier with the chest wound. "Are you tough, laddie?"

"Damned right," said the man, gritting his teeth against the pain.

Druss grinned. "I believe you. Normally when I hit a man that hard, the ax cleaves all the way to the backbone. You were lucky. Caught me on a poor day."

Stavut gazed around the battle site. There were hundreds of fallen Guardsmen, and the road was slick with blood.

And noon was still hours away.

Skilgannon struggled to rise. The old priest knelt by his side. "Do not move, my son. Conserve your strength. Hold on to life and I will help you as best I can." Skilgannon felt liquid in his throat choking him. He coughed and sprayed blood to the floor. The priest drew the golden chain from around his neck. Turning Skilgannon onto his back, he placed the black-and-white crystal on the bleeding wound. "Lie still, let its power work."

Breathing was becoming difficult, and Skilgannon's vision swam. His hands and feet grew cold, and he knew death was close. Then a gentle warmth began in his chest and slowly flowed through his body. His palpitating heart grew more rhythmic in its beat.

He lay there, staring up at the ceiling, and cursed himself for a fool. Askari never traveled without her bow, and the few arrows in her quiver would have meant nothing to the Legend riders. Feeling stronger, he placed his hand over the crystal and sat up. His shirt was ripped, and he pulled it open. Smearing away the blood, he found no wound below it. He turned to the priest. "My thanks to you . . . ," he began. Then he stopped. The old man was sitting down with his back against the desk. His face was waxen, his breathing ragged. Skilgannon moved to his side, holding out the crystal. Then he saw that it no longer glittered, and was instead merely a lump of black stone.

"The Moon has been growing weaker," said the old priest, his voice a dry whisper. "It is because I have not taken it to the Shrine to pray. It always gleamed when I did that."

"You allowed me to take all its power," said Skilgannon. "Why?"

"To pay a debt. I am the oldest of the brethren, Skilgannon. The last of them. You look at me now and you see a twisted ancient. I looked different when you rescued me from the Nadir. I was young then, and full of idealism. Did you keep in touch with little Dayan?"

"No."

"A sweet girl. She wed a young man and went to live in Virinis. I visited her there several times. She had seven children. Her life was happy, and she gave joy to all who knew her. She was over eighty when she died. A full life, I think."

"That is good to know."

"Do not let the evil one desecrate the Shrine."

"Her evil will end today. I promise you that."

Skilgannon rose, drew the Swords of Night and Day, and walked from the room.

Outside the sun was beginning to set.

Twenty-one

It took several hours for columns of unarmed men to climb the high road and carry away the Guard dead and wounded. Stavut walked back to the poolside, where a number of the veterans were trying to stanch the wounds of the Drenai injured. Many of the older riders carried needle and thread, but so great were the numbers of wounded that many were unattended. Stavut removed his hauberk and helm, casting aside his saber. He moved to a young man who was trying vainly to stitch a wound in his own side. The cut extended over his hip and around to his back. Stavut ordered the man to lie down, then took the needle from his hand. "The chain mail parted," said the soldier.

"Lie still."

"It was made for my great-grandfather. Some of the rings were badly worn."

"There'll be plenty of mail to choose from after today," Stavut told him, glancing across to the pile of hauberks that had been removed from the dead and stacked against the cliff wall. Stavut drew the last flaps of flesh together, drawing the thread tight and then knotting it. Taking the man's knife from his belt, he cut the excess thread clear. The rider's face was pale, and a sheen of sweat covered his face.

"My thanks to you, Stavut," he said, pushing himself to his feet with a grunt of pain.

"Where are you going?"

"To find a new hauberk." The man staggered off. Stavut saw him sifting through the discarded armor.

Stavut moved on to the next wounded man, only to find that he had bled to death. A number of the injured had broken arms or legs. Several Drenai soldiers brought enemy shields back to the poolside and began breaking them up to make splints. Even as he stitched wounds and offered comfort to the bleeding men, Stavut found himself wondering why. The beasts were coming, and there was no way they could be turned back. All this effort was a waste of energy. Every man here would be killed when the end came. Yet around him he could hear wounded men making jokes and chatting to one another.

He worked on. Druss came by to talk to the wounded, then stripped off his armor and waded into the pool, washing the blood from his face and body.

Druss.

Stavut no longer thought of him as Harad. How could he? What he had seen today had been awesome. The axman had stood like a great rock against an onrushing sea. The immovable against the unstoppable. Druss emerged from the pool and sat in the sunshine for a while. Then, once dry, pulled on his clothing and hauberk. There was still blood upon his face. The water had washed away the forming scabs. Stavut walked over to him. "I'll stitch those cuts," he said.

"Just the one above the eye," said Druss. "It was damned annoying trying to fight and blink away the blood."

"What will happen to Harad?" asked Stavut.

"Do not fret, laddie. When this day is done he will return. I am not a thief."

"I didn't think you were. Not for a heartbeat," said Stavut with a smile.

"He didn't have the experience to survive this—especially not with a cracked skull."

Stavut suddenly laughed. "You really still think we are going to win?"

Druss looked at him. "Winning is not everything, Stavut. Men like to think it is. Sometimes it is more important to stand against evil than to worry about beating it. When I was a young man, serving with Gorben's Immortals, we took a city. The ruler there was a vile man. I heard a story there. His soldiers had rounded up a group of Source priests, and they decided to burn them all. One citizen stepped out from the crowd and spoke against the deed. He told them that what they were doing was evil, and that they should be ashamed of themselves."

"And did he save the priests?"

"No. And they killed him, too. But that's what I am saying, laddie. I remembered that man's deed, and it inspired me. Others who saw it would have been inspired. Evil will always have the worst weapons. Evil will gather the greatest armies. They will burn, and plunder, and kill. But that's not the worst of it. They will try to make us believe that the only way to destroy them is by becoming like them. That is the true vileness of evil. It is contagious. That one man reminded me of that, and helped me keep to the code."

Stavut inserted the needle into the split flesh above Druss's eye and carefully sealed the cut. "You believe that you can defeat evil with an ax? Is that not a contradiction in terms?"

"Of course it is, laddie. That's always the danger. However, in this instance I am merely standing my ground. If they come at me I will cut them down. I am not invading their land, or burning their cities, or ravaging their women. I am not trying to force them to bend the knee, or accept my philosophy or religion. Do I think we can win today? I think we have already won. I have seen it in the eyes of the Guard. Will we die? Probably."

Stavut tied the knot in the stitch, then cut the thread.

"Almost time," said Druss, glancing at the sky. "Best get your armor on."

"I don't think so, Druss. I shall help the wounded. I'll stand my ground without a sword in my hand."

"Good for you, laddie," said the axman.

Taking up his ax, he strode away toward the road.

*   *   *

Alahir stood and watched as the last of the bodies was carried down the hill road. The battleground was clear again, and if Druss was right, the Jiamads would come next. There were less than a hundred Drenai warriors to face them, and many of those were carrying wounds. Even those who had escaped injury were exhausted. Had the troop been at full strength it was unlikely they would be able to defeat a hundred Jiamads. Alahir's heart grew heavy. He had learned so much in these last few days, about leadership, and courage, and the nobility of spirit that so often characterized fighting men. He had also learned what separated the ordinary warrior from legends like Druss. Earlier today he had been knocked from his feet, and a warrior had loomed over him, ready for the death blow. In that moment Alahir saw Druss glance in his direction. But the axman did not come to his aid. Instead it had been Gilden who flung himself at the attacker, blocking the blow and killing the Guardsman. After the battle Alahir had replayed the scene in his mind. Druss was holding his ground. To turn away and aid Alahir would have meant showing his back to the enemy. He had made an instant judgment. Alahir's death, while hopefully regrettable, was less important than containing the Guard. Such intensity of focus was beyond Alahir. *In fact it is beyond most men,* he thought. Druss in combat was a killing machine of relentless power and determination. He radiated a kind of invincibility that cowed those facing him. Alahir hoped he would have the same effect on the Jiamads.

Even as the thought came to him, he glanced down the long road. The Jiamads were forming up. Many of them carried huge swords, others clubs. Swinging around, Alahir called out: "Form ranks!"

Drenai soldiers gathered up their bows and ran along the road. Druss approached, walking past Alahir and scanning the advancing beasts. "We need to hit them from here, then fall back, line by line, to the poolside," said Druss. "The entrance is narrow. Easier to defend." Alahir agreed, and issued orders to his riders. Forty men gathered, nocking shafts to the string. Twenty paces behind them fifteen more bowmen stood in line. Alahir organized three other ranks of fifteen, spaced all the way back to the pool entrance. Then he walked back to stand with the first group, leaving Druss standing by the entrance.

The Jiamads were halfway up the slope when the Drenai sent the first volley sailing through the air. The arrows rose and curved, then flew down into the Jiamad ranks. The range was long, and only two Jiamads fell, and one of those rose again. Others ignored the arrows jutting from their flesh, or ripped them clear. Then they began to run. Another volley hit them. This time three went down and did not rise.

They were closer now, and their roaring echoed through the mountains. As they neared the defenders, the arrows struck them harder, and with more penetrating force. Alahir counted at least ten dead.

Not enough, he thought.

One last volley struck them. They were only twenty paces away when the shafts struck.

"Back!" bellowed Alahir.

The archers spun on their heels and sprinted up the road, moving between the next rank, who loosed another volley before themselves turning and running.

The beasts charged, their speed incredible. They overran the fourth rank of bowmen, smashing through them. One archer was dragged from his feet and hurled out over the precipice. Others were ripped or hacked to pieces. Throwing aside their bows, the Drenai who had made it to the pool entrance drew their sabers. Druss hefted Snaga. The first of the beasts rushed at the waiting men. Druss leapt to meet it, Snaga crunching through its skull. As it fell Druss wrenched the ax clear, sweeping it out in a murderous cut that clove through the rib cage of a second beast. Alahir surged foward to support the axman, spearing his golden blade through the heart of a huge creature bearing a massive sword. In its death throes the beast hammered his weapon against the bronze breastplate. Alahir was lifted from his feet and thrown against the cliff wall. Around him the soldiers were fighting courageously, but the dead were mounting. The beasts were just too large and powerful. Only Druss was able to hold his ground. Two of the creatures burst through the Drenai lines and, maddened by the smell of blood from the wounded, raced into the pool area. Several of the wounded, armed with bows, shot them down.

Alahir struggled to regain his feet. Someone reached down and hauled him up. It was Stavut. The merchant was not wearing armor, but had a saber in his hand. There was no time to speak. Alahir pushed forward, hacking and stabbing. Instinctively he knew it was to no avail. They had but moments left before the line broke and the beasts swept through.

Then he saw the giant form of Shakul appear behind the Jiamad lines. An enemy beast was hurled from its feet, a second lifted high and pitched from the precipice. Others of Stavut's pack appeared. They tore into the enemy ranks, forcing back the Jiamads. "Now!" yelled Druss. "Attack!"

It was a pivotal moment. Alahir knew it, and Druss had voiced it. Raising the golden sword, Alahir bellowed: "On Drenai! Victory!" The surviving defenders surged out of the entrance. Ahead Alahir saw the mighty Shakul, his body pierced by two huge spears, still fighting. A sword smashed into his side, bringing a roar of pain. Druss, coming alongside, killed the wielder. Stavut ran past Alahir, heading for the stricken Shakul. Alahir tried to call him back, but the merchant was not listening.

"Shak!" he cried out. "Shak! I am with you!"

As he tried to reach the beast a Jiamad thrust a spear into his back. Stavut staggered and fell. Shakul leapt upon the spear wielder, flinging him aside. Another spear plunged into him. This time even Shakul's mighty strength gave out. Falling first to his knees, he pitched sideways to the ground. Alahir and several Legend riders charged into the beasts around him.

And the remaining Jiamads broke and ran.

Members of Stavut's pack gave chase. Alahir swung

around to see Stavut crawling to Shakul's side, leaving a trail
of blood as he moved. Alahir ran to him. Stavut reached
Shakul and struggled to his knees. The great beast rolled to
his back, two spears embedded in his chest. "Oh Shakul,"
said Stavut, "why did you come back? I wanted you to run
free." Blood was flowing fast from the death wound in
Stavut's back and the exit wound in his belly. As his strength
failed, he sagged across Shakul's chest. Alahir was joined by
Gilden and some of the other riders, and they stood staring
down at the dead man and the dying Jiamad. Shakul's arm
came up around Stavut. "Run free . . . now," he said.

Alahir knelt beside Shakul. "I thank you, my friend," he
said. "We all thank you."

Gilden came alongside. Reaching out, he touched his finger to one of the wounds in Shakul's chest. Then he lifted it
to his mouth. "Carry with us," said Gilden. Shakul's golden
eyes stared at the man. Then they closed. Others of Stavut's
pack gathered around. One by one they each took blood from
the wound. Alahir rose.

"Good-bye, Tinker," he said. "I shall miss you." A stoop-
shouldered Jiamad approached Alahir. It spoke, and Alahir
struggled to understand it. Slowly the beast repeated the
words.

"Go now. Hunt deer."

With that he led the fifteen surviving members of the pack
away. As they left Alahir saw Druss waving to him from the
narrow point in the road. Alahir walked down to him. The
axman pointed down to the Guard's camp. Their Jiamads had
fled, and there was no indication of another attack.

"I think we won, laddie," said Druss.

"Aye, we did, but what a cost. I feel a great sense of
shame, Druss. All our lives we have been taught Drenai legends. Nobility, bravery, truth. Part of that truth was that Jiamads were soulless beasts, devils in flesh. Yet they came
back and died for us." He looked at Druss and asked: "Were
there animals in the Void?"

"No. Just human souls."

"Then they have nowhere to go when they die."

"I didn't say that," Druss told him. "I don't know the answer, but my heart tells me that there is a place for them. A place for all living things. Nothing truly dies, Alahir."

Gilden called out from above them, and pointed down into the valley below.

Alahir and Druss walked to the edge.

Where the crater had been now stood a mountain. Shining bright upon its peak was a dazzling shield of gold.

Jianna walked out of the room, leaving Skilgannon dying on the floor. Stabbing him had been instinctive rather than planned, and as she walked on the full horror of it seeped through the centuries of emotional barriers she had constructed in her mind.

She felt a tightness in her stomach and a lump in her throat. Tears welled. In truth Jianna had known she would have to kill him. Olek would never have compromised. This realization clashed with her promise to bring him back. Another twenty years in the Void, while a new Reborn was cast from his bones, would do nothing to change who he was, what he believed in.

You just killed the man you loved.

The thought was sickening. One by one the barriers crumbled. The first to fall was Justification. She had always told herself that she never set out to become the Eternal. Her first actions had been to save the temple. Everything after that had become self-perpetuating. She saw now that it was untrue. She had gloried in her new life, building armies and conquering cities. She had adored the near worship she inspired in her followers. In the beginning she had convinced herself she would build a new world, perfect and peaceful, and she would one day bring Skilgannon back to rule by her side. They would be happy. They would have the life she always believed she had dreamed of.

Another lie.

Jianna stood head bowed at the foot of a high circular stairwell.

Back in Naashan, in those early days, when she first met Olek, she had also been full of dreams. She remembered them talking in the gardens of Olek's house, about the need for hospitals and schools, and clean water for the center of the city, where disease was rife. About building a better Naashan, where the people would be happy and content, secure in the knowledge that their leader cared for them. The naive dreams of the young, she had told herself later. Dreams that were crushed by the harsh reality of betrayal, and the unbridled ambition of those who sought to usurp her. A ruler needed to be cool and detached, ever alert to treachery. The people needed to respect that ruler, and respect was bought by fear.

Now, in the aftermath of the killing, she knew that this was also largely a lie.

Alahir and his men had ridden into peril for Skilgannon, not because they feared him, but because they were inspired by him. The beasts had followed Stavut not because he would kill them if they didn't, but because he loved them.

Jianna let out a long breath and wiped away the tears. The crowning achievement of her five hundred years of power was the murder of the one man she had truly loved.

Her thoughts somber, she climbed the stairwell, the rusting metal steps groaning under her tread. At the top she came to another doorway. This was unlocked, and she stepped into the Crystal Shrine. The room was vast and circular, the walls decorated with bright metal, full of flickering lights, displaying arcane symbols in reds and greens. At the center, on a raised dais, circled with a silver railing, was a golden column, rising up through the vaulted ceiling. As she walked in Jianna became aware of a tingling in her skin and a faint vibration from the floor beneath her. Drawn to the dais, she climbed the ten steps that led to it and gazed at the base of the golden column. Brightly colored swirls of smoke writhed within a three-foot-high transparent tube. At the center of the tube a massive white crystal was slowly spinning, light reflecting from its facets and casting rainbow colors across the high, vaulted ceiling.

The Eagle's Egg! The source of all magic. It was beautiful, and as she came close to it Jianna felt all weariness leave her body.

The voice of Memnon whispered into her mind.

We are close, Highness. Is Skilgannon with you?

"I killed him," she said, aloud. Again her stomach knotted.

Excellent.

A door opened on the far side of the chamber, and she saw Decado step through, the Swords of Blood and Fire in his hands. Blood dripped from the blades.

He looked up and saw her, but did not smile. Behind him came Memnon. He was not wearing his familiar robes, but dressed in riding clothes, a dark blue tunic, purple leggings, and exquisitely designed boots of lizard skin. He advanced into the room and did not bow.

For all her grief and self-absorption Jianna had not lost her intellect, nor her blade-sharp sense of danger.

"Do I catch the scent of treachery here, my dear?" she asked, moving to the silver railing and gazing down on the two men.

"Treachery, Highness?" responded Memnon. "Let us pause for a moment and examine the question. Would you say that I have served you loyally, and with devotion? Can you offer a single shred of evidence that I have ever conspired to cause you harm?"

"Not until now," she said.

"Ah, but I did not know then what I know now. All these years you have been murdering my children, preventing me from acquiring the benefits of true longevity. In these last moments of your immortal life perhaps you would tell me why?"

Jianna laughed. "You already know why. As a mortal you served me. As an Immortal you would have been a threat to me. As with so much else, Memnon, it all comes down to self-survival. I take it you have already killed my other Reborns?"

"The last one died an hour ago. Your reign ends here, Highness. An apt place, don't you think?"

Transferring her gaze to Decado, she smiled. "And it will be you, sweet lover, who delivers the death blow?"

"Is it a difficult choice for me?" asked Decado. "On the one hand there is the treacherous bitch who ordered me murdered. On the other . . . oh wait . . . it's still the treacherous bitch who sanctioned my death. No, I can honestly say I am quite looking forward to it."

Jianna drew her saber. Decado laughed aloud. "We have fenced before, you and I. In happier times. Fighting me will buy you no more than a few heartbeats of life. However, I am in a charitable mood today. So let us even the odds a little." Sliding the Sword of Fire back into its scabbard, he raised the Sword of Blood. "I shall fight you left-handed. I am marginally less skilled with my left."

"That is true," said a voice. "Like watching a child swatting bees with a stick."

Jianna spun to see Skilgannon standing in the far doorway, the Swords of Night and Day in his hands.

"Oh now my joy is complete," said Decado, happily. "I get to kill the great hero."

Despite his lightness of tone Decado was troubled. It was not fear that concerned him. Decado feared no living man, and was utterly sure he could kill Skilgannon. It was more the coalescing of doubts that had been growing ever since Memnon's spirit contacted him, after the first fight with the Shadows.

He had ridden away from Skilgannon and the others, heading up into the hills, to think and to plan. Later that night, in a shallow cave, Memnon had appeared to him. Decado had seen this magical trick before, and, after the initial shock as the swirling image materialized, he merely added another stick to his fire. "Send as many Shadows as you have," he said. "I will kill them all."

"Oh be calm, my boy," chided Memnon. "You know how

anger brings on your headaches. I sought you because I was concerned for you."

"You showed your concern so well last night. They almost had me."

"I sent the oldest and slowest. It was all that I could do. The Eternal ordered your death. I have always been your friend, Decado. You know this to be true."

"Aye," he admitted, "you have always been most kind to me, Memnon. When I come for the bitch I will not kill you."

"She has become an evil creature," agreed Memnon. "Her turning on you has stretched my loyalty to the breaking point. Together we could bring her down. You and I need to meet. Will you trust me and stay where you are until I reach you?"

"Trust the man who tried to kill me? I think not, Memnon."

"Think on this: I have located you. Had I wished I could merely have sent more Shadows to kill you while you slept. Not so?"

"That is true. Very well. I will wait."

It was almost a full day before Memnon rode up the hillside to the cave. "How is your head?" Memnon had asked even as he dismounted.

"It has been good."

"Excellent. I have brought some narcotic to aid you, should it return."

Once inside the cave Memnon had given him the jeweled necklet and instructed him to pass it to the mountain girl, Askari.

"What will it do?"

"When the time is right I shall—through the magic in the jewel—assist the Eternal to possess Askari's body. This will place Jianna at the heart of our enemies. It will also separate her from her Guard. You will join with Skilgannon and assist him in every way."

"Why?"

"Because he just may find a way to bring back the temple. There is so much there that we could use, Decado. Greater artifacts, with incredible power. I will continue to commune with you, and we will make our plans, depending on how the situation changes. And now I must return." Memnon rose. Decado stared up at him.

"Before you go, Memnon, tell me honestly: Was it just her treatment of me that led you to this course?"

Memnon dropped to one knee and laid his hand on Decado's shoulder. "Yes, my boy. It hurt me greatly when you were sentenced. I look upon you as a son."

The sincerity in his voice had touched Decado.

He had suffered no problem of morality when he joined Skilgannon. There was no sense of disloyalty. Yet while traveling with the man he had grown to like him, and he felt a kinship with the riders of the Drenai. Even the merchant, Stavut. They were men on a mission, and it had nothing to do with material wealth, or revenge, or glory. They merely wanted to protect their world from a powerful evil, and were willing to die for it. Decado had found a sense of camaraderie among them, and an emotional warmth he had never before experienced.

Fighting alongside Skilgannon, in a just cause, had been the greatest moment of his life, and he had felt torn when Memnon's voice whispered in his mind following the battle. "Leave them now, my boy. I have traversed a pass beyond the battle road, and am waiting close to the temple site. Skilgannon will come soon. Jianna will be with him. Victory is within our grasp."

They had hidden among the rocks close to the crater, and Decado had felt a sinking of the heart when Skilgannon and Jianna rode to the rim. He truly did not want to kill this man, and in that moment he wished he had ignored Memnon and had waited with the Drenai for the last battle. None of this had felt like treachery until then. The queen had betrayed him and sought his death. His hunting down of her was merely revenge. But now Skilgannon was walking into danger, not knowing that the woman beside him was intent on his death and that two more enemies were close behind.

He had remembered then his last conversation with his kinsman.

"Well, good luck to you, Decado."

"No pleas for me to stay? No appeal to my loyalty?"

"No. I thank you for your help today. You are a fine warrior. Perhaps we will meet again, in happier times."

Happier times?

He and Memnon had watched Skilgannon and Jianna make their way across the rim—and then disappear. Decado had run down to the crater, drawn his own swords, and seen the hidden pathway. Using the same method as Skilgannon he had—with Memnon behind him—made it to the open doorway and entered the temple. Once inside Memnon had crouched down, closed his eyes, and gone into a trance. It had lasted some time. While Decado waited, swords in hand, he heard the screams of beasts and a wailing death cry. Memnon had stood. "Lead the way," he said. "I will direct you. We need to get to the uppermost levels. Walk warily. There are beasts everywhere."

They had been attacked three times. The first was a huge, deformed hound. Decado had slain it with ease. The second had proved more durable. It was a hideous creature with two heads and four arms. One of the heads was gray and decomposing; the other constantly shrieked. The beast had charged at Decado, arms flailing. In one of its hands it held a jagged length of twisted metal. The flailing arms, and the club, made it difficult for the swordsman to deliver a death blow. Also, the space in the corridor was narrow. He had fought the beast off with slashing cuts that tore through its flesh, and had then used a trick he had practiced many times back in Diranan. Stepping back, he held out his sword, the blade pointing upward—and released it. As the sword dropped he lifted his foot, catching the hilt on the toe of his boot. Then his leg lashed out. The sword flew like a spear into the creature's pale chest. As it staggered back, its limbs no longer flailing, Decado ran in and cut the living head from its shoulders.

The third attack had been—potentially—the most deadly.

Scores of the beasts had gathered. Decado and Memnon had run to a narrow winding stair, made of metal, and climbed swiftly. The beasts had gathered around the base. Not following them at first, Decado had glanced back. Several hound creatures began bounding up after them.

At the top was a doorway. Memnon opened it and stepped through. He and Decado pushed it shut. There was a wooden lock bar set against the wall. Together they heaved it into the brackets. Even as they did so the door juddered, dust spraying out from the frame.

"I don't know how long that will hold," said Decado.

"Then we should press on," said Memnon.

They had climbed two further flights of stairs, emerging at last into this chamber with its golden column and flashing lights.

Here Decado's heart had sunk farther. He heard Memnon talk of the murders of *my children* and realized his mentor had not betrayed the queen for him. He was merely a tool for Memnon's revenge.

Then Skilgannon had come, and Decado's emotional misery deepened. He heard himself say: "Oh now my joy is complete. I get to kill the great hero."

Regret washed over him like a dark river.

Jianna watched as the two swordsmen circled one another. Olek was holding his blades in the Naashanite manner, right-hand sword trailing, left-hand blade held across the chest. As Decado sought an opening Olek suddenly switched the blades, the left snapping down and out, the right moving to the chest defense. It was a technique Malanek had taught centuries ago in his training school. The trailing blade was used for the riposte. Fully ambidextrous fighters like Olek could switch back and forth, keeping the opponent confused as to where the attack was to originate. Decado leapt in, the Sword of Blood lancing toward Olek's chest. Olek parried it easily and swept out a riposte that Decado blocked with the Sword of Fire. The flickering blades then came together, the blows, lunges, and blocks coming faster and faster. The song of the swords echoed in the chamber. Jianna was mesmerized by the speed and skill of the two men. She had seen Olek in action before, but never against a man with Decado's speed and talent. They were moving now like dancers, as if every strike and counterstrike were elaborately and carefully choreographed. The glittering blades sometimes moved so fast that Jianna could not follow the action. It was only when fresh blood appeared on Decado's upper arm that she even realized he had been cut. The frantic pace could not last, and the two swordsmen moved back and began to circle again. Now Jianna saw that Olek was also cut, at the base of the neck and across the chest, where his shirt had been sliced. The neck cut had missed his jugular by a hairbreadth. Now Skilgannon moved from defense to attack, surging forward, both blades flashing. Decado blocked desperately and backed away. His footwork was incredible, and not once did he lose his perfection of balance. Blocking an overhead cut, he tried a riposte, which Skilgannon blocked. As the two men came closer together Skilgannon suddenly head-butted Decado, sending him staggering back, blood spurting from a cut above his right eyebrow.

"Not a move they taught us in training school," said Decado. "I must remember it."

"You won't have to remember it long, boy," Skilgannon told him.

Decado laughed. "Nice try, kinsman," he said, circling again, "but, as you know, anger is the third enemy in any duel."

With lightning speed he launched a counterattack. Now it was Skilgannon's footwork that kept him alive, as he backed away, defending desperately. Decado's sword lanced out, slicing through Skilgannon's long coat. Jianna thought it was a death blow—and gasped. The Sword of Night swept up. Decado blocked it. Skilgannon hooked his foot around Decado's and shoulder-charged him. Decado fell, but rolled to his feet as Skilgannon moved in for the kill.

They circled again.

Just then the door behind Memnon crashed open, the top hinges parting, the frame splintering. A massive form, blocking the light from beyond the door, ducked its head and lurched into the chamber. It was grotesquely malformed, with three arms, one growing from its chest. The head was elongated, the mouth lipless and wide, showing two rows of sharp fangs. As it entered other beasts poured in through the shattered doorway. Two huge hounds, larger than lions, surged at Memnon. The Shadowlord ran for the dais and leapt. Instinctively Jianna threw out her arm, grabbing his wrist and hauling him over the railing.

"Thank you, Highness," he said—ramming his dagger into her side. Jianna cried out and fell back. As she did so a huge hound leapt the dais. Jianna saw its great jaws close on Memnon's head, and heard the crunching of bone. Blood and brains sprayed from the beast's mouth. Ignoring Jianna it lifted the dead Memnon in its mouth and strutted from the dais.

Jianna stared down at the dagger hilt jutting from her body. Judging by the angle of entry the blade was close to her heart. Her rib cage was burning, her head spinning. *I ought to be dead,* she thought. Then she looked at the beautiful crystal, slowly spinning within the swirling smoke. *It is keeping me alive,* she realized. Grabbing the dais rail, she hauled herself to her feet. Decado and Skilgannon, no longer fighting each other, were battling against the beasts back to back. Decado's tunic was blood drenched, and she could see he was growing weaker. They could not survive for long.

Swinging back, she looked again at the crystal. Skilgannon and the Legend riders had risked all to destroy this marvel. She stared at it. Rainbow lights flickered around her. Pain lanced through her. She knew then that the power of the crystal was trying to heal her body, the flesh forming around the dagger blade in her chest. Gripping the hilt she prepared to pull it clear. Then she paused and glanced back at Skilgannon. He was fighting desperately. Decado half fell. Skilgannon leapt in front of him, plunging his sword into the chest of a towering Jiamad.

While this crystal survived Jianna would always be the Eternal, and men like Skilgannon would fight and die to bring her down.

Gasping for breath Jianna took up her saber and hammered it against the glass cylinder protecting the crystal. The blade bounced clear. Twice more she struck it. To no effect.

Her strength failing she turned toward Skilgannon.

"Olek!" she shouted. "I cannot destroy it! Throw me a sword!"

A three-armed creature lunged at Skilgannon. Ducking under a murderous punch, he clove the Sword of Day into the creature's heart. Even as the beast fell Skilgannon dragged the blade clear, spun away from another attack, then threw the Sword of Night toward Jianna. The razor-sharp blade spun through the air. Jianna judged the flight—then her arm swept out, her fingers closing around the ivory hilt.

Darkness was closing in on her and she fought it back.

The Sword of Night hammered against the glass. A small crack appeared in the cylinder. Then another. With the third stroke the cylinder disintegrated. Colored smoke billowed from it, flowing out into the room. The floating crystal dropped to the base of the golden column with a dull thud. With the last of her strength Jianna raised the Sword of Night and hammered it down on the crystal. The massive gem shattered in a blinding blaze of multicolored light.

As the shards of crystal exploded outward all the lights in the Shrine dimmed, and the floor ceased to hum and vibrate. All was silence. Around the room the beasts were standing very still. Then, one by one, they toppled to the floor. Some writhed for a while. Then there was no movement.

It grew darker. Soon the only light in the Shrine came from moonlight shining through a high window. Jianna dropped the Sword of Night and looked around for Skilgannon. He was kneeling beside the fallen Decado. Jianna staggered from the dais and made her way to the two men.

Decado was conscious. Moonlight glistened on the length of blood-smeared metal jutting from his belly. "There's no pain," said Decado. "Which I must say is a novel experience for me. And I can't feel my legs. I take it that is *not* a good sign?"

"No," said Skilgannon. "Tell me why you didn't kill me."

"You were too good, kinsman."

"I know how good I am," said Skilgannon. "But, as my old tutor once taught me, there is always someone better. You were that man. Three times you had me. Three times you ignored the death blow. Why?"

Suddenly more figures entered the room. Skilgannon surged to his feet, his sword held high.

"Whoa there, laddie," said Druss. Beyond him came Alahir and several Legend riders. Skilgannon knelt again by Decado's side. "Tell me," he said. "I need to know."

But Decado was dead.

He glanced at Jianna. "Do you know why?"

He saw that her face was unnaturally pale. She swayed and sagged forward into his arms. His hand touched the dagger. Gazing down, he saw the black hilt, the blade buried deep in her chest. Jianna's face settled against his shoulder. "I . . . thought I had . . . killed you," she whispered.

"The abbot had a shard of—" In that moment he thought of the shattered crystal. Heaving her into his arms he ran for the dais. Jianna cried out.

"The pain! Put me down, Olek. Please!"

"In a moment, my love. Hold on!" He carried her back up to the dais and laid her on the ground, then searched among the shattered glass. Finding a large shard of crystal, he returned to her side. Skilgannon raised the crystal shard—then stopped. Realization struck him, and he groaned aloud.

"I can't," he said. "I cannot save you. I would give my life to have Jianna by my side. But I can't allow the Eternal to return."

"It is all right, Olek," she whispered. "The Eternal's time is over. I'm glad we . . . met . . . again. I missed you . . . so much."

Her eyes closed, and her head sagged. Skilgannon leaned down and kissed her lips. Then he sat alongside her, head bowed. Her body spasmed. A single word escaped her lips.

"Stavi!"

Skilgannon spun around. Grasping the dagger hilt, he pulled it from her. She cried out. Instantly he took the crystal shard and held it to her wound. "Lie still, Askari," he ordered her. "Just lie still until the strength returns."

He saw the color begin to return, and her eyes opened. "Where is Stavi?" she asked.

"I don't know."

"Where am I?"

"Lie still. I will explain all when you are well again."

Her eyes closed. Alahir came alongside and touched Skilgannon on the shoulder. Leaning in close, he whispered: "Stavut is dead."

"Sit with her for a while," Skilgannon told him. "Hold this crystal to the wound."

He rose and walked across to Druss. "I'm ready to return to the Void. How do I do that, Druss? How do I give that young man his body back?"

"You can't, laddie," said Druss. "I took Charis to the Golden Valley. The lad chose to cross with her."

The shock was intense. "I don't want it! The only person I ever loved has just gone to the Void! I should be there!"

"You will be. But not now," said Druss. "If I see her there, I'll help her as best I can."

"You are going back?"

"Aye, laddie. My time here is done. I'm going home to Rowena. It was good to breathe the mountain air, but I am done with death and slaughter. I'll not return."

Skilgannon sighed, then reached out and shook Druss by the hand. "One day, perhaps, I'll make it through that Golden Valley."

"You could have done it anytime, laddie."

"No. I remember I was scaled, like the other demons."

"There never was anything stopping you—save your own conscience. You believed you needed punishing—so you punished yourself. Now you have a life again. Live it well. There is a world full of evil out there, and a lot of defenseless people who will need your strength. Give it freely. *Then* when you go to the Void, walk straight toward the light. I'll see you there."

Druss walked to the wall beneath the window and lay down. "Harad will be here soon. Tell him I was proud of the way he stood his ground against the beasts."

"I'll do that. You be careful in the Void, Druss. Wouldn't like to think of a demon stopping you getting home."

The axman laughed. "In your dreams, laddie!" he said. Lying back, he closed his eyes.

Skilgannon walked back to the dais and retrieved the Sword of Night. Askari was sitting with Alahir. He had his arm around her shoulder.

Sheathing his swords, Skilgannon began to fill his pockets with more shards of crystal. Then he returned to the abbot's chamber.

The old man was still alive, but he looked different now, his hair white and thin, his face heavily wrinkled. His breathing was ragged. Skilgannon knelt beside him, opening the man's deformed hand and pressing a shard of crystal into it.

The abbot sighed, and his eyes opened. "Thank you," he said. "It will not be enough to save me." Skilgannon reached into his pocket for more shards. "No!" said the abbot, placing his hand over Skilgannon's arm. "Save them for those who will need them more."

"What is happening to you?" asked the swordsman.

"Time is . . . catching up on me. Those five hundred years you spoke of were not cheated. They were merely waiting to claim us all." He fell silent for a moment. "You destroyed the crystal?"

"Yes."

The man looked desolate. "No golden age to discover now," he whispered. "No end to disease and starvation. No bright, sparkling cities reaching the clouds."

A slow rumbling sound came to Skilgannon, and the walls began to vibrate. "What is happening?" he asked the abbot.

"The Mirror is closing, drawing itself back." Tears fell from his eyes. "All I have lived for is gone now. I am so tired."

"Then think on this, priest: You stopped the Eternal from finding greater weapons. Your actions here have led to her death. The world is free again."

"Free? Of one tyrant perhaps. You think there will be no others?"

"No, I do not. But I know there will always be men to stand against them. You grieve because of a pure magic lost. That magic was corrupted by evil. This is how evil thrives. We find an herb that cures disease, and someone will make a poison from it. We forge iron to make a better plow, and someone will make a sharper sword. There can be no power that evil will not corrupt. There may be no golden age to come now, but equally there will be no more Joinings, no more twisted, malformed beasts. No more wizards casting dark spells."

The old man's fingers opened, and a black shard of stone fell from them. "The Eternal is no more?" he said, his voice barely audible.

"She is gone from the world."

"Then . . . some small good came from . . . my actions."

"Aye, it did."

His eyes closed, his head sagged back. Skilgannon sat by the body for a few moments. The decay continued rapidly, the hair growing, the skin drawing tight over the skull. Then it split and peeled away, falling in dust to the floor. Skilgannon rose.

Then he walked from the temple, and out into the desert night.

Epilogue

The next few days were spent by the rock pool. Skilgannon used the crystal shards to heal the worst of the wounded, but the power was soon used up, the shards turning black. Of the two hundred fifty men who had set out with Alahir, less than sixty survived to make the return trip.

Every day more bodies of the dead were transported down into the valley, where deep graves were dug. Alahir presided over all the funerals, speaking movingly about each man. Harad helped with the digging, and not once did Skilgannon see him holding the ax of Druss the Legend.

On the third morning Skilgannon saw Harad sitting by the pool with Askari. He joined them. "How are you feeling, my friend?" he asked.

"I am alive. I would not have been had Druss not returned. I heard what he did—and how he turned back the enemy."

"It makes you sad?" asked Skilgannon.

"No. It makes me proud. He is a part of me. It shows me what I may become."

"That gladdens my heart, Harad. Where will you go now?"

"Back to Petar, I think. It is my home. I am sorry about Stavut," he said to Askari. "I liked him greatly."

"He was a good man," she said. "Alahir says he will miss him." She looked at Skilgannon.

"You think his beasts survived the ending of the magic?"

"I hope so. We three survived, and we were created by the same magic."

"And where will you go, Skilgannon?" she asked.

"I am leaving today. I will cross the sea, to the ancient kingdom of Naashan. I loved that land, but most of my life was spent away from it. I will ride the valleys and the plains, and see what is left that I still recognize. But first I will collect the white horse."

"I think that merchant is not trustworthy," said Harad. "He may not want to keep his promise to you."

"One way or another he will keep it," said Skilgannon.

"He had a lot of men," Harad pointed out. "I wouldn't like to think of you dying over a horse."

Skilgannon laughed, then leaned in and clapped Harad on the shoulder. "In your dreams, laddie!" he said.

Harad looked bemused. "What does that mean?"

"I haven't the faintest idea. It just seemed the right thing to say." Skilgannon rose and turned to Askari.

"I hope you find happiness," he said. Rising smoothly to her feet, she stepped into his embrace. Leaning down, he kissed her cheek. "It was a privilege to have known you."

"We may meet again," she said.

"That would please me," he told her.

Moving to the rear of the pool, Skilgannon saddled his horse and prepared to leave.

Alahir found him there and urged him to ride with them to Siccus. "Harad is coming with us. We're going to put Druss's ax in the Great Museum. It would be an honor for us if you were there, too."

Skilgannon shook his head.

"I am going back for the white stallion," he said, "then I'll make my way southeast to Dros Purdol. I want to go home, Alahir. I want to see Naashan again. I want to look upon the mountains of my childhood."

Alahir was disappointed. Then he brightened. "When you have done that, you might want to come and see us. There'll be a place of honor for you at my table."

The two men shook hands, in the warrior's grip, wrist to wrist. "I may just do that," said Skilgannon, stepping into the saddle. With one last look around the battle site he rode away.

Soon afterward Askari saddled her own mount. "Are you leaving us, too?" asked Alahir.

"I think I'll travel with him," she said. "Good-bye, Alahir." Then she smiled. "Or should I say Earl of Bronze?"

"Alahir is just fine."

Vaulting to the saddle, she swung her horse and began to ride away.

"Wait!" called Alahir. "You have forgotten your bow."

She drew rein and glanced back at him. "Of course I have. How foolish of me." Alahir fetched it, and she looped the weapon over her shoulder.

"I hope we meet again," he said.

"You should always be careful of what you hope for," she told him.

Then she heeled her horse and rode after Skilgannon.

And now a sneak preview from the launch of David Gemmell's ambitious new trilogy, set in the time of Troy. This is a tale of kings and queens, of legendary heroes and epic combat. The action begins with Book One,

LORD OF THE SILVER BOW

From Del Rey Books, available wherever books are sold

The Golden Ship

The storms of the past two days had faded into the west, and the sky was clear and blue, the sea calm, as Spyros rowed his passenger toward the great ship. After a morning of ferrying crewmen out to the *Xanthos*, Spyros was tired. He liked to tell people that at eighty years of age he was as strong as ever, but it was not true. His arms and shoulders were aching and his heart was thumping as he leaned back into the oars.

A man was not old until he could no longer work. This simple philosophy kept Spyros active, and every morning, as he woke, he would greet the new day with a smile. He would walk out and draw water from the well, gaze at his reflection in the surface, and say "Good to see you, Spyros."

He looked at the young man sitting quietly at the stern. His hair was long and dark, held back from his face by a strip of leather. Bare chested, he was wearing a simple kilt and sandals. His body was lean and hard muscled, his eyes the brilliant blue of a summer sky. Spyros had not seen the man before and guessed him to be a foreigner, probably a rogue islander or a Kretan.

"New oarsman, are you?" Spyros asked him. The passenger did not answer, but he smiled. "Been ferrying men like you in all week. Locals won't sail on the Death Ship. That's what we call the *Xanthos*. Only idiots and foreigners. No offense meant."

The passenger's voice was deep, his accent proving Spyros's theory. "She is beautiful," he said amiably. "And the shipwright says she is sound."

"Aye, I'll grant she's good to look upon," said Spyros. "Mighty pleasing on the eye." Then he chuckled. "However I wouldn't trust the word of the Madman from Miletos. My nephew worked on the ship, you know. He said Khalkeus wandered about talking to himself. Sometimes he'd even slap himself on the head."

"I have seen him do that," the man concurred.

Spyros fell silent, a feeling of mild irritation flowering. The man was young and obviously did not appreciate that the gods of the sea hated large ships. Twenty years earlier he had watched just such a ship sail from the bay. It had made two voyages without incident, then had vanished in a storm. One man had survived. He had been washed ashore on the eastern mainland. His story was told by mariners for some years. The keel had snapped, the ship breaking up in a few heartbeats. Spyros considered telling this story to the young oarsman but decided against it. What would be the point? The man had to earn his twenty copper rings and was not going to turn back now.

Spyros rowed on, the burning in his lower back increasing. This was his twentieth trip out to the *Xanthos* since dawn.

There were small boats all around the galley, stacked with cargo. Men were shouting and vying for position. Boats thumped into one another, causing curses and threats to be bellowed out. Ropes were lowered, and items slowly hauled aboard. Tempers were short among both the crew on the deck and the men waiting to unload their cargo boats. It was a scene of milling chaos.

"Been like this all morning," Spyros said, easing back on the oars. "Don't think they'll sail today. It's one of the problems with a ship that size, getting cargo up on that high deck. Didn't think of that, did he—the Madman, I mean?"

"The owner is to blame," said the passenger. "He wanted the largest ship ever built. He concentrated on its seaworthiness and the quality of its construction. He didn't give enough thought to loading or unloading it."

Spyros shipped his oars. "Listen, lad, you obviously don't know who you are sailing with. Best not say anything like that close to the Golden One. Helikaon may be young, but he is a killer, you know. He cut off Alektruon's head and ripped out his eyes. It's said he ate them. Not someone you want to offend, if you take my meaning?"

"Ate his eyes? I have not heard *that* story."

"Oh, there's plenty of stories about him." Spyros stared at the bustle around the galley. "No point trying to push my way through to the stern. We'll need to wait awhile until some of those cargo boats have moved off."

A huge bald man, his black beard greased and twisted into two braids, appeared on the port deck, his voice booming out, ordering some of the cargo boats to stand clear and allow those closest to clear their cargo.

"The bald man there is Zidantas," said Spyros. "They call him Ox. I had another nephew sailed with him once. Ox is a Hittite. Good man, though. My nephew broke his arm on the *Ithaka* a few years back and couldn't work the whole voyage. Still got his twenty copper rings, though. Zidantas saw to that." He turned his face toward the south. "Breeze is starting to shift. Going to be a southerly. Unusual for this time of the year. That'll help you make the crossing, I suppose. If it does get underway today."

"She'll sail," said the man.

"You are probably right, young fellow. The Golden One is

blessed by luck. Not one of his ships has sunk. Did you know that? Pirates avoid him—well, they would, wouldn't they? You don't cross a man who eats your eyes." Reaching down he lifted a waterskin from below his seat. He drank deeply and then offered it to his passenger, who accepted gratefully.

A glint of bronze showed from the deck, and two warriors came into sight, both wearing breastplates and carrying helms crested with white horsehair plumes.

"I offered to ferry them out earlier," Spyros muttered. "They didn't like my boat. Too small for them, I don't doubt. Ah well, a pox on all Mykene anyway. Heard them talking, though. They're not friends of the Golden One, that's for sure."

"What did they say?"

"Well, it was more the older one. He said it turned his stomach to be sailing on the same ship as Helikaon. Can't blame him, I suppose. That Alektruon—the one who lost his eyes—was a Mykene, too. Helikaon has killed a lot of Mykene."

"As you say, not a man to offend."

"I wonder why he does it."

"What? Kill Mykene?"

"No, sail his ships all over the Great Green. They say he has a palace in Troy and land in Dardania and somewhere else way north. Don't remember where. Anyhow, he is already rich and powerful. So why risk himself on the sea, fighting pirates and the like?"

The young man shrugged. "All is never as it seems. Who knows? Maybe he is a man with a dream. I heard that he wants to sail one day beyond the Great Green, to the distant seas."

"That's what I mean," said Spyros. "The edge of the world is there, with a waterfall that goes down forever into darkness. What kind of idiot would want to sail off into the black abyss of the world?"

"That is a good question, boatman. A man who is not content, perhaps. A man looking for something he cannot find on the Great Green."

"There you go! There's nothing of worth that a man cannot find in his own village, let alone on the great sea. That's the problem with these rich princes and kings. They don't understand what real treasure is. They see it in gold and copper and tin. They see it in herds of horses and cattle. They gather treasures to themselves, building great storehouses, which they guard ferociously. Then they die. What good is it then?"

"And you know what real treasure is?" asked the young man.

"Of course. Most ordinary men do. I've been up in the hills these last few days. A young woman almost died. Babe breeched in the womb. I got there in time, though. Poor girl. Ripped bad, she was. She'll be fine, and the boy is healthy and strong. I watched that woman hold the babe in her arms and gaze down on it. She was so weak, she might have died at any moment. But in her eyes you could see she knew what she was holding. It was something worth more than gold. And the father was more proud and happy than any conquering king with a vault of treasure."

"The child is lucky to have such loving parents. Not all children do."

"And those that don't get heart-scarred. You don't see the wounds, but they never heal."

"What is your name, boatman?"

"Spyros."

"How is it you are a rower and a midwife, Spyros? It is an unusual pairing of talents."

The old man chuckled. "Brought a few children into the world during my eighty years. Developed a knack for delivering healthy babies. It began more than fifty years ago. A young shepherd's wife had a difficult birth, and the babe was born dead. I was there and picked up the poor little mite, to carry it away. As I lifted him he suddenly spewed blood, then started to cry. That began it, you know, the story of my skill with babies. My wife . . . sweet girl . . . had six children. So I knew more than a little about the difficulties of childbirth. Over the years I was asked to attend other births. You know how it is. Word gets around. Any girl within fifty miles gets pregnant and they send for old Spyros, come the time. It is strange, you know. The older I grow, the more pleasure I get bringing new life into the world."

"You are a good man," said the passenger, "and I am gladdened to have met you. Now take up your oars and force your way through. It is time for me to board."

The old man dipped his oars and rowed in between two long boats. Two sailors above saw the boat and lowered a rope between the bank of oars. Then the passenger stood and from a pouch at his side pulled out a thick ring and handed it to Spyros.

It glinted in his palm. "Wait!" shouted Spyros. "This ring is gold!"

"I liked your stories," the man said with a smile, "so I will not eat your eyes."